As always, Dave

Jack Weyland

Salt Lake City, Utah

To all the amazing young single adults
we met during our service in the
New York New York South Mission

This is a work of fiction. Characters and events in this book are products of the author's imagination or are represented fictitiously.

Visit us at DeseretBook.com

Library of Congress Cataloging-in-Publication Data

(CIP on file)

ISBN 978-1-59038-849-5

Printed in the United States of America
Malloy Lithographing Incorporated, Ann Arbor, MI

10 9 8 7 6 5 4 3 2 1

CHAPTER ONE

My newest best friend was Helen Gabriella Sanchez, an editorial assistant for *The New York Times*. She and I had sat next to each other on our flight from Salt Lake City. We'd just landed at New York's JFK Airport a little before five-thirty in the afternoon and were standing outside the terminal. It was the second Friday in June, just ten days after being released from my mission.

"Dave, it's been such a pleasure meeting you," she said. "I guess this is where we part company, though. You see where all those people are?" She pointed to a place in front of the terminal. "That's where you need to be standing when your friend comes to pick you up."

"Thanks." I shook her hand. "I really enjoyed talking to you. Here, let me give you this." I handed her a pass-along card. "If you ever get curious about what we believe, just call this toll-free number, and they'll send you a free DVD."

"Thank you," she said, putting it in her purse.

"How are you getting home?" I asked.

"Oh, I'll just grab a train into the City and then take a subway to my neighborhood. I'll end up less than a block from my apartment."

"Where do you live?"

"About a block from Central Park."

"How far away is that?"

"About twenty miles."

"Twenty miles? Is that all? I'm sure Abbie won't mind giving you a ride."

"Oh, no, I couldn't let you do that. Subways, trains, and taxis are how most people get around in the City. In fact, I don't even own a car."

"I'm sure Abbie wouldn't mind. She's a really nice girl."

"Tell me about her."

"Her family moved next door to us the summer before she and I started kindergarten. Even then, I thought she was a real beauty. Long, naturally curly hair the color of a field of ripe barley. Whenever things got bad, I'd look forward to when we'd be together again, and somehow that made it all worthwhile."

"Sounds like this could turn into a serious relationship."

"I hope so. I'm hoping we'll get married and have a nice, big family. We both love kids."

"I'm happy for you both. I would never think of letting you go out of your way to give me a ride, but I would like to at least see this girl who's captured your heart. That's so rare these days."

Eventually we pushed our way through the crowd to the curb where cars were pulling up to pick up passengers.

I was halfway through explaining the plan of happiness when Abbie pulled in, driving a late-model, gray Mitsubishi.

"Oh, wait, there is she now! I'll go ask if she wouldn't mind us giving you a ride. She always likes to help out, so I'm sure it'll be okay with her, especially if it's only twenty miles from here. I'll go talk to her about it."

"It's not the miles, it's the traffic!" Gabriella called out as I headed to see Abbie.

The first thing I noticed when I got to the driver's side was that Abbie had cut her hair. That was a big disappointment. Also, the color of her hair was no longer that of a field of ripe barley. It was in streaks of color, some of it her natural color and the rest the color of, well, a school bus—kind of bleached and yellowy.

"Abbie?" I asked, stunned at the way she looked.

"Throw your things in the trunk and let's get out of here," she yelled.

"I met a woman on the plane. She works for *The New York Times.* I was wondering if we could give her a ride home. It's only twenty miles from here."

"Where does she live?"

"Across from Central Park."

Abbie banged the steering wheel with her hand. "Are you out of your mind? You want me to drive into the City this time of day?"

"But I gave her a pass-along card."

"I'm not giving anyone a ride into the City during rush hour! There's a forty-minute wait on the tunnels. The BQE is stacked up. The Queensborough Bridge has a jackknifed semi blocking two lanes of traffic. The Van Wyck is bumper-to-bumper. You think I want to drive into that mess?"

I glanced at Helen Gabriella Sanchez. She'd seen enough. She waved and slipped back into the crowd.

I wasn't ready to give up. "But she seems really receptive. I think if we give her a ride home she'll call for the free DVD."

Abbie pointed an accusing finger at me. "I don't have time for this! Throw your carry-on in the trunk and get in!" I didn't remember her talking so loud or being in so much of a hurry before my mission.

I did as she directed and got into the car. "It is so great to see you, Abbie!"

"Yeah, right," she grumbled, "welcome to rush hour." She also seemed more sarcastic.

She was wearing an oversized New York Yankees T-shirt, ragged jeans with a hole in one knee, and a beat-up pair of red Converse shoes. It seemed to me she could've dressed up more for someone she'd been waiting for—for two years.

She glanced in her side mirror, looking for a chance to pull into traffic.

"Wow, look at you!" I said. "You look . . . well . . . good, I guess you could say. You did something to your hair, right?"

"It's *my* hair. I can do what I want with it. You got a problem with that?"

"No, it's good. Really. It's just . . . well . . . different, that's all. Are you thinking of changing it back anytime soon?"

No answer.

"And it's shorter too. A lot shorter."

"That's what happens when you cut your hair. It gets shorter."

"And it's so . . . well . . . multi-colored. It's like looking at a school bus parked next to a field of ripe barely. Didn't you have enough color solution to do it all?"

"You know what? It's *my* hair. End of discussion."

She was just about to pull into traffic when a white limousine pulled up alongside us and stopped and people started getting out. "What are these clowns doing?" Abbie said.

She honked a couple of times, then rolled down her window. "Hey, you're in the wrong place! This isn't where you drop people off!"

The chauffeur, wearing a suit and a black turban on his head, smiled as though he had no idea what she'd said. He opened the right rear door of his car, a late-model Cadillac. A man and woman wearing elegant East Indian clothes got out of the back seat.

We were boxed in, and Abbie stepped out of the car. "Hey, you're blocking my way! I'd like to get out of here sometime this year!"

The chauffeur came over and began speaking in what may have been English, but the madder Abbie got, the faster he spoke, and the faster he spoke the less we could understand.

"Move your car so I can get out of here!"

The chauffeur nodded politely and then hurried back to the Cadillac. He opened the trunk and set the bags on the curb.

This was a time for hugs. Not for Abbie and me, of course. Oh, no. I'm gone two years and I don't even get a hug. The man hugged the chauffeur, the woman hugged the chauffeur. All the time they were saying something that sounded like a chant.

"Hey, enough with the good-byes already!" Abbie shouted. "I don't have all day!"

The three of them came over and began to apologize. But Abbie, fearing for her safety, jumped into the car, rolled up the window, and locked her door.

"Let me handle this," I said confidently. I got out of the car and hurried over to them. "Hi, there, where you folks going?" I asked.

"India."

"India? Whoa! That's a ways from here, isn't it? That's great! Good for you! Look, I know you're in a hurry, but let me give you this card." I handed them a pass-along card. "There's a toll-free number on the back. If you call it, you can get a free DVD!"

"Very thanks!" the chauffeur said enthusiastically, taking one of the cards.

"Hey, you know what? I have another card for each of you also. For this one you get a free book."

As I was handing out the cards, Abbie got out of the car, slammed the door, and marched over to me. "What do you think you're doing here?"

"I'm giving these good people some pass-along cards."

She threw up her hands and started to walk away. "I'm leaving now! You coming or not?"

She got in her car and tried to back up far enough so she could get around the Cadillac, but it was no use. She wasn't going anywhere.

The chauffeur and I shook hands. And then I shook hands with the man and then with the woman, and then with the driver again.

They asked me to take their picture, which I was more than happy to do.

They even took one picture with me in it.

"Dave!" Abbie called from the car.

"Yes?"

"Your mission's over! You had your chance, now get back in the car!"

"Yeah, sure, I'm coming."

As I returned to the car, I called back to my new friends, "It's a toll-free number, even from India!"

I got into the car. Abbie was angrily drumming her fingers on the steering wheel.

"They're such friendly people," I said. "I hope they call for the free DVD. Whoa, I just thought of something! I wonder if it really is toll-free from India."

She turned on me. "Don't you ever hold me up in rush hour traffic again!"

The chauffeur waved one last time to his departing passengers, got in the Cadillac, and pulled out without looking. A hotel courtesy van had to slam on his brakes to avoid him.

But at least now we had a way out. "Finally," Abbie raged, quickly pulling out into a very slow-moving line of cars.

I looked around at the maze of cars all trying to leave. "So this is New York City, huh? The Big Apple! Home of the New York Yankees and the New York Mets! America's City . . ."

"Yeah, yeah, I got it," she grumbled.

"Lots of traffic, huh?"

"Yeah, Dave, just like it always is this time of day. That's why I begged you to come late at night. But, no, you had to pick rush hour."

"If I'd come later, then I wouldn't have as much time with you. I mean all we've got is this weekend. I fly out Monday."

"At this rate we'll still be here on Monday when it's time for you to leave."

I studied her profile. "Even with your hair that way, you're still cute."

"I hate it when people say I'm cute."

"But, face it, that's what you are. Even in kindergarten, you were the cutest girl in our class. I can picture it now in my mind. I remember thinking then that you were as cute as my cocker spaniel puppy Diamond, and that's going some because, my gosh, that dog was something else. You remember Diamond, don't you?"

She stared at me in disbelief. "You want to know why I tried to discourage you from coming out here? It wasn't just because of how much it was going to cost you. It's because I was afraid you'd go back really disappointed."

"You don't have to worry about me. I've been on a mission. I am very familiar with disappointment. The way I see it, every day is a new day."

She was looking over her shoulder, impatient to change lanes. "Why exactly did you come out here?" she asked.

"Because you weren't around when I got home from my mission."

"I told you why I couldn't leave. I've got a five-year-old boy and a three-year-old girl who depend on me. I can't just pick up and leave anytime I want."

"What are their names?"

"Andrew and Olivia."

"I bet they're cute. I love kids. But you know what, they're not actually your kids. You're just the nanny. It's a job. The family you work for had a nanny before you came and they'll have one after you leave. You can quit anytime you want. Like, for example, when a guy you've been waiting for comes home from his mission. I think you should quit and come back home with me so we can see how we feel about each other now."

"Go back to Ririe, Idaho? I don't think so. I'm not sure I can ever live there again."

"Everyone asked about you on Sunday."

"I'm sure they did," she muttered.

"We had a little get-together at our place after church. Great food. Oh, and your folks came over for a while, so I got to talk to them. Mostly your mom, of course. We must have talked for an hour."

"Did she tell you how bummed-out she is about me wanting to stay another year?"

"Yeah, she did bring that up."

"Was it her idea for you come out here?" she asked.

"She might have mentioned it, but I was the one who decided to come."

"Who paid for the tickets?" she asked.

"I did . . . mostly."

"You just got back from a mission. You don't have any money."

"Well . . . I will pay for it . . . once I start working."

"How much did my mom put in?"

"Well, actually, half, and my folks did the other half, but I'm going to pay everyone back."

"So basically my mom paid you to come out here and talk me into going home. Right?"

"She didn't pay me to do anything. I wanted to see you. I've been thinking about you my whole mission . . . even after you quit writing."

"I didn't quit." She paused. "I just didn't write as often as I did when you first left."

"Three months ago you sent me a postcard that said, 'Wish you were . . . ' You left out *here*. Must have been in a hurry, right? You didn't even sign your name. That was the last time I heard from you."

"I've been busy."

"I came out here to find out about us."

"Us? What are you talking about?"

"Well, before I left, you and I talked about, well, some day . . . you know . . ."

"No, I don't know. You're going to have to tell me."

"We talked about getting married," I said, wondering why she couldn't remember what had seemed so important to both of us at the time.

"Dave, I was eighteen years old! You were the only guy I'd ever gone out with. All my friends were waiting for missionaries. It seemed like the thing to do. Besides, all my mom could talk about was us getting married after you got back. She loved the idea of me marrying the boy next door. That was two years ago. A lot can happen in two years. I'm not the same person I was then."

"It's been two years for me, too, you know. I'm not the same either."

"You look the same, you talk the same, you sound the same. So how are you different?"

"I'm more independent."

"Really? Tell me, where are you going to live now that you're home from your mission?"

"I'll be living at home," I said.

"What a surprise. And where are you going to be working?"

"I'll be working for my dad," I said.

"Oh, you mean like you have since ninth grade? Oh, sure, I can see how much more independent you are now. Tell me, is the plan still that you're going to take over your dad's hardware store some day?"

"Yeah, when he and my mom go on a mission. They're almost ready to go."

"And will you live in their home while they're gone?" she asked.

"Yeah, so?"

"And after your folks come back from their mission, when you're married and running your dad's store, where will you live?"

"Well, in Ririe."

"So if you and I got married, we'd be living just a few blocks away from both our parents, right?"

"Yeah, so?" I asked.

"You know what? It just takes my breath away, seeing how independent you are now."

I couldn't believe the traffic. Cars were stacked up in the lanes on either side of us, and a lot of drivers were honking their horns.

"Well, I can tell you one thing. Living there is a lot better than living here."

"You've been here ten minutes and already you're an authority on life in the New York Metro area?"

"Your mom told me what it was like for you out here."

"And did she also mention she'd be delighted if you and I got married so we could start producing grandbabies for her?"

"No, she didn't, but even if she had, what would be so awful about us getting married and having kids?"

"My gosh, I have two kids now and they take up all my time. I don't want any more."

"But they're not yours."

"That's right, which means I can walk away, which is not an option I'd have if they were my own. I never knew how much work it is to raise a family. Also, Duane and Addison have shown me what a nightmare a marriage can be."

"Who are Duane and Addison?"

"The so-called parents. They yell at each other all the time. They must have loved each other when they got married, right? But something happened. So if it happened to them, why couldn't it happen to me and my husband? Talking to me about getting married and having kids is not going to get you very far."

"If it's so awful where you work, why do you want to stay another year?"

She sighed. "All right, that's a fair question. It's because . . . well . . . I like living out here."

"Why?"

"I'm an hour by train from the City. I can go in there on my days off. It's such an exciting place. Pick any category—museums, entertainment, restaurants, the arts, whatever. The best in the world live and work in the Metro area."

"The best potato farmers in the world come from southeastern Idaho."

"I know this will be a big shock to you, but potato farmers are not big celebrities out here."

"I still love you, Abbie. Doesn't that count for anything with you?"

"You don't even know me now. I've changed."

"I've changed, too. That's why we need to spend time together. That's why I'm here."

She shook her head. "Look, I hate to burst your bubble. But the bottom line is I'm not moving back to Idaho. I'm not about to marry you or anyone else anytime soon. I am going to stay here another year. And there's nothing you can do to change that."

"You've still got your dimple. That is so cool."

"I give up." She pulled the brim of her Yankees cap down so I wouldn't find something else to admire.

Her cell phone played a loud and annoying musical segment. She put on her ear piece. "Yeah, what are you doing? . . . Oh, not much . . . We're just leaving Kennedy. It's bumper to bumper just like I said it would be . . . No, I've got time . . ."

I looked at the people in the car next to us. An entire family. I wondered if the Church made pass-along posters.

"Who are you talking to?" I asked.

"Megan," she said. "She's a new nanny."

Abbie listened until she was so frustrated she had to interrupt. "Megan, you can't let them do that! You're not their slave. You have to establish how many hours a day you're going to work. This is insane . . . You've got to talk to them . . . No, you can't just let it go. If you do, they'll walk all over you. Look, do you have a contract? . . . Well, why not? . . . You should have a contract . . . I'm sure they didn't want to give you one."

I found myself staring at the hole in the knee of Abbie's ragged jeans. In high school I remember her having a pair with a hole in the knee. Were these the same jeans? Were things that hard for her here in New York?

A minute later, Abbie unloaded again on Megan. "Look, you go to them and you say, 'When I applied for the job, you told me I'd only be working until six. You told me I'd have a car to drive. You told me I'd only have to take care of the kids . . . Now you want me to work from seven in the morning until nine at night. And you have no car for me to drive. And in addition to watching the kids, you're saying I need to do the laundry, cook dinner, buy groceries, and make you and your husband lunches . . . and take care of the kitty litter . . . and tend your rose garden? Well, you know what? That's not what I agreed to do when I came here. You totally misled me when I talked to you about the job. So if we can't work out something here, then I quit. I'll give you two weeks to find someone else, but if you give me any hassle, I'm walking out right now. So what's it going to be, folks? Do I start packing and call a taxi, or not?' That's what you got to tell 'em. You want to practice it with me?"

Abbie scowled at Megan's answer.

"What do you mean you could never talk to them like that? Listen to me. You've got to stand up for yourself or they'll just keep piling on extra jobs . . . Don't cry, Megan! . . . Well, I'm sorry if I made you feel bad, but I'm just trying to look out for you . . . I know you love Klarissa and Thomas . . . So what if they run past their mom to you for a hug when they've hurt themselves? She's the mom . . . I know they'd miss you if you quit. But you've got to stand up for yourself because nobody else is going to do it for you."

When we were on the Van Wyck Expressway, it was bumper-to-bumper traffic, so Abbie had no choice but to follow the car in front of her. But once we entered the Belt Parkway, traffic thinned out enough that there were a few small openings in the traffic that would appear occasionally.

Still talking on her cell phone, Abbie began switching lanes to find open spots. Everyone else was going about sixty miles an hour but we were going at least seventy-five, and we changed lanes every few seconds.

I was scared for my life. "You want me to drive?" I asked.

"What for?"

"So you can talk on your cell."

"I'm okay."

"You're driving recklessly. Pull over and let me drive."

"I'm not letting you drive. You'd get us both killed. Driving here isn't like driving in Idaho. You've got to be aggressive. You should see how people drive in the City. It's crazy. A friend told me how to drive in the City. He says, 'Drive like you're going to hit the pedestrians . . . but don't!'" She laughed.

I didn't like Abbie's laugh now. It was like a witch's cackle.

"If everyone drove like you, what would happen?" I asked.

"We'd be in the City!"

I sighed and wished I could have my sweet Abbie back again.

"Megan, hold on, I've got another call." She looked at the number on her cell. "Oh, no!"

"What?" I asked.

She ignored me and talked to Megan. "It's the so-called mom. I'll call you back, okay?"

She took the new call. "Yeah, Addison, what is it? . . . No, Olivia was fine all day . . . No, I don't know how she got a sore throat . . . No, she didn't get chilled. We did go into the wading pool, but it was two in the afternoon and it was eighty degrees outside. . . . How is Andrew doing? . . . Good . . . Well, actually I won't be able to come back and take care of Olivia . . . You remember me telling you I have a friend from Idaho visiting me this weekend, and he'll only be here three days? I promised him we'd do something together tonight . . . Well, I'm sorry Olivia is crying for me but, with all due respect, Addison, you *are* the mom . . . Look, we've gone over this before. My workday ends at 6 P.M. After that, you're the mom and Duane is the dad, and it's you guys' responsibility to take care of your own kids . . . No, I don't want you to put Olivia on the phone so she can cry her heart out for me to come back. Actually, I can hear her now. Look, just get her favorite blanket and sit down and hold her."

I looked over at Abbie. She wasn't the same girl I'd left two years ago. If I were seeing her for the first time, I wasn't sure I'd even want to talk to her.

"Don't say that, Addison. I have the greatest confidence that you *can* be a mother figure in Olivia's life . . . I know they didn't train you for this at Harvard, but it's not that hard. Just be her mom . . . No, I really don't think that I need to talk to Duane. . . . Oh, hello, Duane . . . Yes, I heard . . . Actually, I *am* sorry Olivia has a sore throat . . . No, I didn't do anything to cause her to get a sore throat. Kids get sore throats . . . Well, I'm not there because at four I took the rest of the day off to pick up a friend at Kennedy . . . I did discuss it with Addison yesterday. She warned me that leaving two hours early would ruin her career, but after a while she said it was okay . . . Well, actually you already owe me an extra day off because I worked an extra day last week . . . Duane, it's in my contract . . . Well, just because you haven't read my contract doesn't mean it doesn't apply . . . Yes, Duane, I realize you're an attorney . . . No, I wasn't trying to talk down to you . . . Well, because I have a guy friend from home visiting me this weekend . . . No, he won't be staying in my room . . ."

She raised her eyebrows, looked over at me, shook her head, and smiled.

"Well, that's very generous of you, Duane, but, the truth is, we'd rather not go that route just yet . . . Yes, that is part of my religion, too. We call it chastity . . . I can't help it if you've never heard of it . . . I'm sorry they didn't discuss it at Harvard. They probably should have . . . Two hundred dollars? Are you serious? Just for coming home now and working until Olivia goes to sleep? . . . Hold on, okay?"

She turned to me. "Olivia is sick. They want me to take care of her tonight, just until she falls asleep."

"Yeah, sure, no problem, go ahead."

She nodded. "Duane, okay. I'll drop my friend off at where he'll be staying and then head home. I should be back within an hour. Oh, that extra two hundred dollars. When will I be getting that? . . . Well, I'd rather have it tonight . . . in cash if possible. The reason I say that is because the last time you promised me extra money, I never saw it . . . Yes, I'm sure you don't remember it, but I keep a journal, so I'll just show you the journal entry and maybe tonight you can pay me for that time, too . . . That amount is one hundred dollars. So if we're in agreement you'll be giving me an extra three hundred dollars tonight . . . Yes, Duane, I can see how you might think I'm nickel-and-dime-ing you to death, but actually you're the one who makes these extravagant offers, not me. I just want to make sure you meet your obligations. As an attorney, I'm sure you can understand that. So, will that extra three hundred dollars be given to me tonight? . . . What time tomorrow morning? Well, okay, I'll agree to that. . . . All right, a check will be fine . . . Duane, do you know what will happen if I don't get the money? . . . Well, my contract expires in two weeks, so unless I sign another contract, I'm out of here. I hope you don't do anything between now and then that would make me decide to leave, like not pay me that extra three hundred dollars. . . . I'm glad we understand each other. So, summing up, I expect to receive from you three hundred dollars extra, let's say, by nine-thirty tomorrow morning. I'm so glad we have such a good working arrangement . . . Yes, I will see you in about an hour."

She set her cell phone down and glanced over at me. "What?"

"That poor little girl. I'll bet she's in a lot of pain."

"That poor little girl is a hypochondriac. The only time she gets any attention is when she says she's sick. The moment I walk in, Duane and Addison will be out the door, on their way out for an evening of drinking with their friends."

"You weave in and out of traffic a lot, don't you?"

"So?"

"That's kind of dangerous, isn't it?"

"It would be if you did it, but it's not when I do it."

It took me a minute or two to work up the courage to ask my next question.

"Did you miss me while I was gone?"

"The first three months I did, but then I got used to it. To be truthful, the last six months I hardly even thought about you."

"That's good, I guess."

She glanced over at me. "Don't give me that sad puppy-dog look, Dave. You didn't think about me much either after the first few months, did you?"

"Well, maybe not. But I was on a mission."

"We're different people now. There's no reason we should have expectations about any kind of a future together, is there?"

"Well . . . maybe not."

"Good, I'm glad we've got that resolved. You put on a little weight on your mission, didn't you?"

"A little."

"And your hair is a little thinner now than before you left . . . mainly in the back."

My face turned red. "I guess so."

"Before long, you'll look like your dad."

"That's what time does. It changes people. Time changed you and it changed me. It's nobody's fault."

Her cell phone rang. It was Megan again.

Thirty minutes later, we pulled into a driveway and stopped.

"Megan, I've got to go now. Remember to stand up for yourself."

We were in a tree-lined neighborhood of old houses with lawns and screened-in porches. The houses were nothing special, like what you'd find in the old part of Rexburg, except here almost every house had some kind of flowering bush that had amazing pink blossoms. Abbie told me they were azaleas.

I followed her around to the back of the house.

"You'll be staying here with Nathan," she said. "He's just finished med school and is doing his residency now. You'll like him, but he's not around much. Have him take you to our singles branch's sports activity tonight."

We came to a separate entrance. She used a key on her key ring to let me in.

"You have a key to his apartment?" I asked.

"Sometimes we have family home evening here, even when he's not around."

She let me in and showed me around the place. "Okay, you'll be sleeping on the couch. It pulls out into a bed. Nathan says there's some frozen pizza in the freezer you're welcome to have. Also, he has cable. I see he's set out some towels for you and a pillow and a blanket. So I think you're set. I might catch up with you at the church later after I've got Olivia and Andrew to sleep and Addison and Duane are home." She took a deep breath. "There is just one other thing. Let's sit down for this, okay?"

We sat together on the couch. "What?" I asked.

She gave a big sigh. "I just recently started dating a guy. His name is Eldon. He's just here for the summer. He sells home security systems. We're not serious or anything yet, but it does have possibilities. So anyway, when you called two nights ago and said you were coming out, I was with Eldon when I took your call. So afterwards, he asked about you, and, well, I sort of panicked . . . and . . . well, actually, I told him you were my cousin."

My mouth dropped open. "Your cousin?"

"Yeah. So now everyone in the singles branch thinks my cousin is coming to visit me, and, well, I was wondering if you could just go along with it. I mean, it's only until you leave on Monday."

I got up and started pacing back and forth. "I can't believe you'd do this to me! Do you have any idea how much I paid to come out here?"

She stood in my path so I'd quit pacing. "Did I even ask you to come out here? No, I did not. In fact, I did everything I could to talk you out of it."

"Well maybe if you'd told me about this guy, that might have done it for me."

She said in a little quieter voice, "Well, the thing is, I don't want my mom to know about Eldon."

"Why not?"

"Because she'd fly out here to meet him, and, let's face it, my mom scares off most guys. The first question she'd ask is how many children he'd like to have. My mom is crazy when it comes to wanting grandchildren. Just like your mom actually."

"So you want me to pretend I'm your cousin while I'm here?"

"Yeah, if you wouldn't mind. It might even make your trip more interesting. Some of the girls in the branch definitely want to meet you."

"And it doesn't bother you that you're lying to your friends?"

"It's not totally a lie. There were times when you were more like a cousin to me than anything else."

"When was that?"

"All the time we were in grade school, maybe until the middle of ninth grade. Even part of our sophomore year . . . and then we started kissing and it wasn't as much like being cousins."

"I am really disappointed in you, Abbie. I expected more from you than this. I've never known you to lie."

"I admit I'm not proud of it, but what's done is done. I'd be so grateful if you'd just go along with it." She gave me one of those smiles I always loved and touched me on the arm. "Please, Dave. Eldon just might be the guy I end up marrying, and I don't want to confuse him . . . with you."

A part of me wanted to punish her for doing this to me, but on the other hand it seemed like anything we'd had before my mission was now gone, so what harm would it do to go along with this for the next four days?

I took a deep breath. "Okay, I'll be your cousin."

She came over to me and gave me a hug. "Thanks, Dave, you're a great friend. Well, I've got to go. I'll see you tonight. Oh, and tomorrow we'll do something fun. I owe you that. See you later."

At first I wasn't going to eat because of the emotional pain of being rejected by Abbie. That lasted about five minutes and then I went to the freezer and got out the pizza and looked at the box. It was advertised as a Classic New York Pizza.

When I opened the box, I was disappointed. All there was on the pizza crust was cheese.

A few minutes later I was eating my pizza. *So this is a Classic New York pizza?* I thought *Well, they're welcome to it. In Idaho we'd call this toast with melted cheese on it.*

I turned on the TV to a baseball game. Even though I hated the Yankees and loved when they lost, I wasn't awake enough to watch the game. I'd gotten up at five in the morning to drive from Ririe to Salt Lake City to catch my flight, and I'd stayed up late the night before.

I pulled out the couch into a bed and laid down on it. Just before falling asleep, I remember wishing I'd never made the trip.

CHAPTER TWO

When I woke up, the pizza was cold, the game was over and, to make matters worse, the Yankees had won.

I felt like a fool for wasting so much money to fly to New York to see Abbie. And for what? So she could tell me she had no interest in me anymore? She could have told me that over the phone.

Okay, to be fair, she probably did try to tell me, but I didn't want to hear it. Who can ever understand a girl anyway? If she'd just come out and said it, instead of trying not to hurt my feelings, it would've been better.

All I'd ever wanted from life was to marry Abbie, take over my dad's hardware store, have a few kids, and live out my life in Ririe, Idaho.

The plane ticket had cost seven hundred dollars. Seven hundred dollars, and for what? To have Abbie talk me into pretending she's my cousin?

Did she ask me anything about my mission? No. Has she any idea how hard I worked as a missionary? Does she even care?

If she'd just give me a little time, then she'd know how much my mission had changed me. But how was that going to happen before I left on Monday?

Seven hundred dollars to have the girl I'd planned on marrying tell me I've put on weight and my hair is thinning in the back. Well, I wasn't going to take this sitting down. Over the next hour, while I watched another game, I did two hundred sit-ups and a hundred push-ups. And then I ran in place for twenty minutes.

By then I was sweating so much I had to take a shower. Drying off, I couldn't see that the sit-ups had done me much good. In fact the muscles I'd exercised doing sit-ups seemed to be pushing my stomach out even more than before. Oh, and also, it hurt to take a deep breath.

Nathan didn't have any sausage in his fridge, but he did have bacon, so I fried up a bunch, broke it into little pieces, scattered it on the pizza, then put it back in the microwave to heat it up.

About that time Nathan walked in. He was taller than me with a full head of curly brown hair and a great smile. Because of the way I felt about myself at that moment, I hated him.

He smelled the bacon, saw me taking the pizza out of the microwave, and laughed, "Looks like I don't have to tell you to make yourself at home, do I?"

"Not really. You want any of this?"

"Yeah, sure, in a few minutes. So you're Abbie's cousin?"

"Yeah, something like that."

He headed toward his room. "I've got to take a shower. I've been either working or on call for the last thirty-six hours."

"Sounds rough."

"At ER it's not the hours, it's the pressure to perform. We had five accident victims, two shootings, and a burn victim."

"So are you a doctor?"

"Not yet, but almost. Look, we'll talk later. Put a couple of slices of the pizza on a plate. I'll eat it in the car on the way over to the church."

Half an hour later we were in his car, heading for the church in Meadowview. He drove a ten-year-old Honda Civic.

"How long have you known Abbie?" I asked.

"Since she came here. She's changed a lot in that time."

"For the better?"

"That's hard to say. She stands up for herself more now than she used to. You ever wonder why families hire Mormon girls from Utah and Idaho to be their nannies? There's lots of local girls who could do that, so why fly in someone from Utah?"

"Why?"

"Because LDS girls are so nice. They want to be liked, they want to do a good job, they want to reduce tension, so they let the parents walk all over them. And that's what happens a lot of the time . . . until the girl quits or starts being assertive back."

"Do you tell the new girls they have to stand up for themselves?"

He finished a big bite of pizza. "Not really. I just listen to them. More than anything they just need a listening ear. I can give them that. Take it from me, if you want to make a lot of friends tonight, just listen."

"Sounds easy."

"It's harder than you might think. Most guys, when they talk to a girl who has a problem, want to tell her what to do. But don't do it. Just listen. That's what I've learned being in the singles branch."

"Okay. Thanks."

"How long you staying?" he asked.

"Just until Monday."

"Then what?"

"I'll go back home. My dad wants me to take over his hardware store while he and my mom serve a mission."

"That okay with you?"

"Yeah, it is, actually. We're from a small town in Idaho. We know everybody in town. It's a good life."

"Sounds good. All this time I've been in this apartment, I still don't know the people next door."

A few minutes later we pulled into the church parking lot. The Meadowview building is as large as any stake center back in Idaho. Nathan told me it had been constructed from the columns used in the Church's World Trade Fair exhibit in New York City in the sixties.

"Give me a minute," he said, pulling out some three-by-five cards and glancing momentarily at each one.

"What are you doing?"

"Going over my notes of the things that girls in the branch told me the last time I saw them."

"Why?"

He smiled. "It makes me seem like a warm, caring human being. This is something I picked up in med school. You know—'bedside manner.'"

We entered the cultural hall where the young single adults were playing volleyball. About twelve girls and six guys. A good ratio if you're a guy.

The game stopped when the girls spotted us and many of them came over to say hello. Nathan of course was the main attraction, but they were friendly to me, too.

I could see that Nathan had a routine. When talking to a girl, he'd ask a question based on his last conversation with her. "Kaitlyn, is your brother still in the MTC? How's he doing?"

This guy is good, I thought.

While I was watching Nathan be charming, a girl with a great smile, blue eyes, and long blonde hair came up to me. "You must be Abbie's cousin Dave, right?"

"Yeah."

"Good to meet you. I'm Megan." She reminded me of Goldilocks from *Goldilocks and the Three Bears,* a video I used to watch when I was little. Except then I was rooting for the bears.

"You were the one talking to Abbie on our way back from the airport, right?" I asked.

"Yeah, that was me. Trying to learn how to keep my family from turning me into their slave. All the new nannies ask Abbie for advice. She's terrific, isn't she?"

"Yeah, sure."

Megan took me to meet everyone, telling them I was Abbie's cousin and that I had just gotten home from my mission.

After that, she grabbed my arm and said, "Please be on our team. We need all the help we can get."

"I'll do my best."

"Actually I don't care if we win or not, I just want you close by me."

I was confused. "Why?"

"Abbie said you've just had the girl you left on your mission break up with you, and you're taking it kind of hard. She told me to latch onto you because if I didn't, you'd go off by yourself and sulk."

Abbie knew me pretty well.

We played one more game and then stopped for refreshments.

Megan and I sat on the stage and ate. Carrots and celery and chocolate chip cookies. And water to drink.

Megan sat close to me and would occasionally touch my arm or lean into me. At first it was almost too much after two years of being at arms' length. But I was able to adapt quickly.

Because she had a great laugh, I tried to be witty and charming and funny. If I made her laugh especially hard, she would sometimes lean into me and I'd feel her hair on my face and neck.

She had a great nose too. Not too big. Not too small. Just right. It even looked great from the side.

At one point, I got three lean-ins within like two minutes. Then I heard someone clear her throat. I looked over to my left and saw Abbie standing off stage. I felt guilty and wondered how long she'd been watching us.

She sat down next to Megan. "Well, it looks like you two are getting along."

"Dave is so funny!" Megan said.

"Really? Dave, I don't remember you being all that funny before your mission."

"It helps to have someone with a great sense of humor. Besides that, Megan has gone out of her way to make me feel welcome."

"Yes, I can see that," Abbie said with a big grin.

"How are the kids?" I asked.

"Good. Olivia fell asleep in my arms not long after I got there. Andrew stayed awake until after I gave him his snack and told him a story. Duane and Addison left to have a few drinks with friends. But now they're home and happy. So they let me leave."

"Where's Eldon?" I asked.

"He's on his way. I just talked to him. He had a great night. He made three sales. He gets a hundred dollars for each one so he'll be stoked when he gets here. Nothing like money, right?"

"I'm in the wrong business," I said.

"We all are." She stood up. "Dave, come out in the hall. We need to talk."

She led me far as she could get from the cultural hall. We ended up in an empty hall outside the family history center.

"You're mad at me, aren't you?" she asked.

"No, it's just that—"

"It's okay to say you're mad at me. You don't have to be nice all the time. If there's anything I've learned out here, it's to say what's on my mind. So if you're mad at me, say it."

"All right, I'm mad at you."

"Why?"

"You don't know why?"

"I want you to say it. Tell me why you're mad at me."

"Well for starters, you told everyone I was your cousin."

She nodded. "You have a right to be mad at me for that. What else?"

I sighed. "I want it to be the way it was before my mission."

"That would be nice, wouldn't it? We were really close. You were the first boy I was ever in love with." She touched my arm.

"Me, too."

"But, you know what? Two years is too long. I can never be like I was and neither can you. The sooner you realize that, the better off we'll both be."

"I still love you."

"You love the girl I used to be. She's not around anymore. Sorry."

"We could get it back if we had some time together."

"Maybe that's true. I don't know. But I do know I'm not going back to Idaho anytime soon."

"Maybe I could stay here a little longer."

"Your folks need you home to help them get ready for their mission."

"Yeah." Long pause. "So that's it?"

"That's the way it looks to me." She took my hand. "Dave, I do care about you. You're the best guy friend I've ever had."

I looked into her eyes. For just a second she looked like the girl I'd been in love with.

"You're thinking about kissing me, aren't you?" she asked.

"No, of course not. I just got back from a mission."

"You liar. You are. I can tell. I've seen that look before."

"Maybe."

She smiled. "Go ahead, Dave. Live dangerously."

I took her in my arms and kissed her. She relaxed and for a minute it was just like old times. It felt so good.

But then she pulled away with a grin on her face. "You thought that's all it would take, right? One kiss from you and I'd change my mind and go back to Idaho with you. That *is* what you thought, isn't it?"

"No."

"You're lying. Guys have such inflated egos about things like that. Okay, it was nice. I'll give you that. But it doesn't change anything. I know you thought it would. Sorry."

"I won't make that mistake again."

"No, you won't. From now on we're just friends."

"Have you made a study of how to destroy a guy's self-esteem or does it just come naturally to you?"

"It's called honesty. It's what we do out here. We say what's on our mind. If you got a problem with that, then go back to Idaho."

Her attitude was getting to me. I hesitated for a moment, then said, "You want honesty? I'll give you honesty. I don't like your train-wreck hair style. I don't like the way you drive. I don't like the way you talked to Duane and Addison when little Olivia was sick."

"The trip hasn't been a complete waste then, has it? I'm glad I've burst all your bubbles. Now you can get on with your boring, predictable life in Idaho."

"You make me so mad, Abbie. Nobody can make me as mad as you can."

"Okay, look, I'm sorry about the kissing part. It was a really bad idea for me to encourage you to kiss me. But the other part, about wanting to be your friend, that was for real. Oh, one more thing, if you want to do anything with me tomorrow, I'll be free most of the day."

"Why would I spend more time with you? To let you mock me some more?"

"No, I'm done with that. Let me take you to Jones Beach."

"Forget it. I've had it with you."

"What are you going to do all day tomorrow? Nathan will be gone. You don't have a car. C'mon, let me take you to the beach. I make a very good friend. And I can be very respectful and pleasant."

"Not interested."

She put her hand on my arm. "We used to be friends, you know, before the other took over."

"Did we? I can't remember."

"When we were in grade school we used to go sledding together. In seventh grade you had your piano lesson just before mine. Sometimes you'd wait and we'd walk home together. Remember?"

"Until I told my mom I didn't want to take any more lessons."

"In eighth grade, we used to do our homework together. You helped me get through math."

"Your mom always had cookies," I said.

"In ninth grade, I helped you when you ran for student council."

"I lost."

"That's not my fault. I made you excellent posters. I even kept one of them. It's still in my closet. Remember when you broke your arm? I came over and brought you some homemade ice cream. You told me how bad you felt that you wouldn't be able to help your grandfather on the farm. You cried a little."

"I didn't cry."

"You did cry, Dave, just a little. But it's okay. I was flattered you'd feel comfortable doing that in front of me. I told you I felt real bad for you, and that, if I could, I'd take the broken arm from you instead of you having it. That made you cry too."

"All I remember is the ice cream."

"You don't remember what I told you?" she asked.

"It was fresh peach ice cream."

"You don't remember me telling you I would have been willing to have broken my arm if it would mean you'd be okay?"

"No, sorry. There were big chunks of peach in the ice cream."

"Boys are dumb," she said.

"That's what you always used to say to me."

"And it's still true. Boys are still dumb, even when they're in their twenties."

I sighed. "Friends, then?"

"Yeah, that's what I'm suggesting. Tomorrow is Saturday. It's going to be miserably hot and humid, and the beach will be crawling with people. Traffic will be backed up for miles. It'll be a nightmare just getting a place to park. Once we get to the beach, we'll be lucky to even find a place to put down our towels. On top of that we'll probably get sunburned. Come and enjoy all that with me."

"It won't get in the way of you and Eldon?"

"No, he'll be working all day. Please, let me do something for you. I'll feel better sending you back to Idaho if we've had at least one good day together."

"I didn't bring a suit."

"Nathan has three or four. He won't mind letting you use one of them. How about if I pick you up at ten?"

"I'll think about it."

As we reached the foyer outside the chapel on our way back to the cultural hall, we saw a guy sitting on the couch eating a small pizza. He hadn't been there before. He was barrel-chested, like one of those wrestlers you see on TV, and he had a head of thick, dark brown hair.

We weren't sure how long he'd been there and if he'd heard us talking.

"Antonio, have you met my cousin Dave yet?" Abbie asked.

He shook his head. "Is he the guy you were making out with a few minutes ago?" Antonio asked, standing up. He had a very loud voice. Abbie quickly looked around to see if anyone had overheard him, but the hallway was empty.

"Let's go down the hall and talk," Abbie said.

When we reached the end of the hall we'd just left, Abbie turned to Antonio. Her face was a bright red. "I need to make a clarification. Dave and I weren't making out. Okay, we did kiss one time, but that's all."

Antonio laughed. "Are you two really cousins, 'cause if you are, I'm never sending my kids to Idaho for school."

Abbie took a deep breath. "Okay . . . we aren't actually cousins. We dated in high school. I told Dave I'd wait for him on his mission. But then I came out here and everything changed." She paused. "I didn't want people here thinking we were serious . . . so I told everyone that he's my cousin."

Antonio was continuing to chew his pizza as he asked, "So if he's not in your life anymore, why were you kissing him?"

"Well . . . actually . . . it was . . . a *farewell* kiss," she stammered.

He puckered up his lips. They were greasy from the pizza. "You suppose I could have one of them farewell kisses, too?"

"Antonio, please, don't tell anyone about this. Let me be the one to tell Eldon, okay?"

He thought about it for a moment, then said, "Let me talk to Dave here."

She left us.

"Friend, it looks to me like you got blind-sided," Antonio said.

"Yeah." I paused. "She says she just wants to be friends."

Antonio laughed. "That's girl talk for 'Don't ever call me again.'"

"She offered to take me to Jones Beach tomorrow."

"Fuhgetabout it! You're not that desperate!" At first he laughed, but then studied my expression. "Oh, sorry. Are you that desperate?"

"Maybe. I don't know."

"You want to go to a Yankees game with me tomorrow? I got tickets."

I shrugged. "Probably not."

"No problem. I'll take my dad."

He reached for a donations slip from the supply on the wall and wrote down his cell phone number and gave it to me. "If you change your mind, give me a call later tonight."

"Thanks." I paused. "What can you tell me about Eldon?"

He laughed. "You mean Security Boy? That's what some people call him. What can I say? He's an impressive guy. Almost too impressive if you ask me, like he practices in front of a mirror. You know the type, right? But what can I say? Chicks dig him."

When we got back to the cultural hall, Antonio was content to watch the game, but that wasn't my style. I chose not to be on the same team with Abbie, though. I was mad enough that I thought about spiking the ball at her but of course would never have actually done it. She might have been ready to write me off, but I still felt the way I always had about her—in spite of her new attitude.

After the game we all went into the kitchen to have salsa and chips. There were about twenty of us packed in there.

"Abbie, why don't you tell us some stories of when you and Cousin Dave here were growing up," Antonio teased.

"What kind of stories?" she asked.

"Oh, I don't know. Like what was Dave like when he was growing up?"

"Well, he was smaller then. I was too, I guess."

"Wow, that is so fascinating! Anything else?" Antonio asked. He was having such a good time with this.

"He didn't talk much," she said.

"Kind of a cowboy type, right? Yeah, that fits."

"I talked growing up," I said.

"You never talk much, Dave. I talk way more than you do."

"That's true," Antonio said to Abbie. "You talk a lot. Maybe too much sometimes. C'mon, Abbie, throw us a bone here. Tell us about you and Cousin Dave. You must have been real close, seeing that he flew all the way out here just to see you. Tell us all about it."

Abbie looked as though she wanted to choke Antonio, but she tried to sound natural as she said, "I don't know, Tony. I never invited him. Why don't you ask Dave that question?" She sounded mad.

"Dave, why did you come out here to see your cousin Abbie?" Antonio asked.

Abbie glared at me.

"Well . . . I . . ."

Time seemed to come to a complete stop, and everybody was listening to the conversation.

"Actually, I guess I can answer that," Abbie said, her face a bright red.

"You can?" I asked.

"Yes." She took a deep breath. "The truth is that Dave and I aren't really cousins. We dated in high school. We even talked about getting married after he got back from his mission, but I've changed and don't feel the same way I did about him."

"So if he's not your cousin, but you told everyone he was, does that mean you lied to all of us?" Antonio asked, sounding hurt and disappointed.

"It wasn't exactly a lie."

"Let's see. You said he was your cousin, but he's not. Gosh, you know what, I don't have my *Webster's* unabridged right here in front of me, but I'm pretty sure that would fall under the category of a lie."

"Leave it alone, Tony, for crying out loud!" Abbie blurted.

Antonio put on a hurt look. "Please, show a little respect. My name is Antonio now," he said.

"Hey, Italian Pride Week is over, okay? Why don't you go back to the way you used to be? Tony isn't good enough for you now? I don't see that you have any room to be critical of me."

"Just admit you lied," Antonio said.

"All right, I lied! Are you happy now?"

Antonio smiled at her. "You know what? I'm always happy when the truth finally comes out."

Just then, a tall, heroic-looking guy stepped into the kitchen. He was wearing a police-like uniform with the name of an alarm system company embroidered over the pocket.

"My gosh, can my eyes be deceiving me?" Antonio asked. "Is that Security Boy? We are totally honored, Security Boy, to be in your presence this night."

Security Boy, a.k.a. Eldon, apparently didn't catch the sarcasm in Antonio's voice. He smiled warmly at all of us as a group, making no eye contact with any of us.

"Have you met Abbie's cousin Dave?" Antonio asked.

Security Boy shook my hand. He had a firm handshake. "Welcome aboard!"

Yes, he actually said, "Welcome aboard."

"It's okay that people call you Security Boy?" I asked.

"Not really. It doesn't really capture what we're doing out here."

"How about Captain Security?" Antonio teased. "Darth Security?"

Security Boy ignored Antonio. "I'm Eldon. And you're Dave, right? Abbie told me you were coming."

"Abbie and Dave are cousins," Antonio said with a grin in Abbie's direction.

"I know. She told me," Eldon said.

Everyone stared at Abbie, waiting to see what she'd do.

Abbie took a deep breath. "Actually, Eldon, Dave isn't really my cousin. We went out in high school. When he left on his mission, I told him I'd wait for him." She paused. "But, obviously, I didn't."

"So why did you tell me he was your cousin?" Eldon asked.

"Great question!" Antonio called out.

"Because I didn't want to discourage you," Abbie said.

Eldon smiled. "It would take more than that to discourage me. I thrive on competition. Ask anyone on the Summit Security Team. This week, for the fifth week in a row, I am leading in sales for the entire East Coast." He had a radio announcer voice that was really annoying.

I decided to find out how serious Security Boy was about Abbie. "Eldon, I just want you to know that Abbie is *so* into you! That's all she talks about. I might be wrong about this, but I really think we'll be hearing wedding bells in the very near future. Maybe even by the end of the summer! Congratulations! You know what? I can tell you're going to be a great dad. Did Abbie tell you she wants at least ten kids? By this time next year you'll probably be a dad!" I punched him playfully on the shoulder.

"I do not want ten kids!" Abbie objected.

"You two can work out those details in September after the honeymoon," I said.

Antonio caught my eye and grinned. We were now partners.

At first, Security Boy had a deer-in-the-headlights look, but almost immediately he replaced it with a forced grin. "Well, isn't that . . . interesting?"

"Oh, one other thing you ought to know," Antonio said. "Abbie here was making out with Dave in the hall a few minutes ago. But don't worry. It doesn't mean anything. You see, Abbie has this series of nineteen ceremonial farewell kisses she likes to give a guy when she breaks up with him." He smiled smugly at Abbie.

"We only kissed once, Antonio, and you know it!"

"Sorry, but I don't know that. For all I know I might have come in at the end. Well, Security Guy, I think that about covers the situation at the present time. And let me say to you, on behalf of all of us here, welcome aboard!"

"Oh yeah!" I said to Antonio. We high-fived each other.

"We need to talk," Abbie said and hustled Eldon out of the kitchen.

"Well, that worked out great, didn't it?" Antonio said with a laugh.

"Yeah, we're a great team," I said.

"You're part Italian, right?" he asked.

"Oh, yeah, sure," I lied.

A few minutes later Nathan told me he had to go home and get some sleep.

As we were leaving the building, Eldon and Abbie were sitting together on the front steps of the building.

"Dave, you still want to go with me to Jones Beach in the morning?" Abbie asked. "I talked to Eldon about it and he's okay with it."

"No thanks."

"Hey, you really should go to Jones Beach while you're here," Security Boy said. "Please go and have a good time."

I sighed. What else did I have going for me? "Okay."

"I'll pick you up about ten. Nathan, can he borrow a swimming suit?"

"Sure. No problem."

"Great. It's settled then."

On the way home, Nathan had me drive while he made notes on what each girl he'd talked to had said.

At one point he looked up for a minute, and then said, "You're going too slow."

"I'm going the speed limit."

"This is New York. Nobody goes the speed limit."

I sighed and sped up. I could hardly wait to get back home to Idaho.

CHAPTER THREE

The next morning around eleven, Abbie and I started our trek from her car to the beach. We were in Parking Lot 4 at Jones Beach. There were acres and acres of parked cars in just that one parking lot, and Abbie told me there were five other parking lots just like it.

Abbie had me dragging a cart containing a cooler, beach towels, and a blanket, with a beach umbrella tied onto the back. She was a trooper too, of course; she carried her cell phone and a bottle of water.

"Don't worry about me. I'll be okay," I complained, trying to keep up.

She didn't even bother to look back. "I never worry about you."

"Why are there so many people at the beach today?"

"I've seen it worse."

We were both wearing baggy T-shirts over our swimsuits. For me it was because of the little pouch of flab I'd gained on my mission, and also because compared to all the regulars at the beach my body was a pale white. Abbie said I looked like I'd just been released from a long stay in a mental hospital.

"Why does it have to be a mental hospital?" I asked.

"If you have to ask why, that's your answer."

After twenty minutes of trying to keep the beach umbrella from falling off the cart as we walked down the path, we finally got to the boardwalk. But we still had a quarter of a mile to the beach.

On that day, unusually hot for June, Jones Beach was crammed with people.

"There's no room for us," I complained.

"Hey, we're New Yorkers. There's always room for another million or so."

We slowly made our way closer to the water, stepping over and around hundreds of sunbathers who had each staked out their claim to a few square feet of sand with their beach blankets, towels, coolers, and beach umbrellas. Many of the girls and women were wearing bikinis.

We finally found a tiny open spot where we could set up. "Quit gawking at the girls, and put up the beach umbrella," Abbie teased.

"I wasn't gawking at the girls."

"You're such a liar."

"What am I supposed to do? Everywhere I look there're people."

"This is probably more skin than you've seen your entire life, isn't it?"

I was having a little trouble shoving the beach umbrella into the sand but was determined not to ask for help. "In terms of total square inches, you're probably right."

"What are you talking about?" she asked.

"How many people do you suppose are here?"

"I don't know. On like the Fourth of July they get 250,000 here. So maybe today there's half of that."

"Let's say there's one hundred thousand people. How many square feet of skin does a typical person have?"

"I have no idea."

"Let's just make a rough estimate. Five feet by one foot, both front and back. That's ten square feet. So you take one hundred thousand people times ten square feet. That's roughly one million square feet of exposed skin. I wonder how many gallons of sunblock it'd take to cover that much skin."

"Why do you do that?" she asked.

"Do what?"

"What you just did. With the numbers."

"It's from working for my dad. Customers come into our store. They're about to paint a room. They want to know how much paint to get. We ask them how big the room is and estimate how many square feet and then tell them how much paint they need."

"Look, the point I was trying to make is that there are a lot of beautiful girls who aren't wearing much of anything," she said.

"There are also families here. I prefer to look at the families."

She was standing by me as I wrestled with the beach umbrella, and she ruffled my hair. "Yeah, right, Dave, you're such a saint."

Finally I got the umbrella in position. I stood up. "Let's go in the water."

"Not yet. I have to put you through an orientation first."

"I'm very familiar with water, Abbie. Let's just go." I grabbed her wrist and began pulling her toward the water.

She held back. "Not yet, we need to talk first."

"What have they done to you out here? Come on, I'll show you how it's done." My plan was to boldly run into the water to impress her, but once we got closer, I was surprised how big the waves were.

I stopped in my tracks.

"You're afraid, aren't you?" she teased.

"No, not at all."

"Don't give me that! You're totally petrified! Does Little Davey want his mommy? This is so unlike anything you've ever seen before, isn't it? You're totally unprepared for this, aren't you?"

"It's just water."

She made an expansive motion with her hand toward the water. "Standing before you, my timid Idaho friend, is the mighty Atlantic Ocean! Not some dinky irrigation canal like back home. Let me tell you something, my boy. You do not mess with the Atlantic Ocean! It has the power to crush you like a bug. Here, take my hand and I will show you how we do it out here on Long Island."

Male pride was at stake here. "I don't need your help." I boldly started charging into the water.

The first wave hit me at my chest, but I managed to stay upright. I turned around to gloat. "See? No problem! That's what I think of your mighty Atlantic Ocean!"

Abbie had a strange expression on her face. It was a combination of concern and amusement.

"What?" I asked.

"Dave," she said with a silly grin. "Perhaps you should turn around."

I turned around just as a huge wave crashed down on top of me. I ended up being scraped along the hard sand as it washed me past her onto the beach.

She was laughing when she caught up with me. "You okay?"

"I was in total control the whole way."

"No, you weren't! You got hammered!" She laughed way too much, so I splashed her. She screamed and told me I was in big trouble. And then she splashed me. And then I chased her down the beach. I was surprised how fast she could run barefoot in the sand.

When I caught up with her, I wrapped my arms around her waist from behind and pulled her back until we were deep enough for me to pull her down into the water with me.

We played in the water for a while and then got out and watched the other swimmers, then we went back to our blanket and umbrella and had sandwiches and fruit and bottled water from the cooler.

"This tastes great!" I said, polishing off my second sandwich. "Thanks for fixing this up for us."

"It's self-preservation. They charge a fortune for even a burger here."

I looked around at the ocean and the people. "I'm glad you talked me into coming here with you."

"I'm happy you're having a good time. I love Jones Beach. Look around. There's like every nation in the world represented here."

I did look around.

"You are just looking at the families, right?" she teased.

"Yes, I am."

"Let me ask you a question. How do I compare with the other girls here?"

"You're way more modest than any of them."

"That's not what I mean. Do you think I'm . . . well . . . sexy?"

I started laughing.

"What?"

"Abbie, c'mon, you're from Idaho, for crying out loud."

She slugged me in the arm. "Thanks a lot."

"It's just that I don't think of you that way. When you've known a girl since kindergarten, it's hard to think of her as sexy."

She pretended to be insulted. "Are you saying I have the same basic shape I had in kindergarten?"

"No of course not. You're . . . well . . ." I grinned. " . . . taller."

She turned her back to me. "Go away! I don't want to talk to you anymore."

"I'm not saying you haven't changed, but I don't think of you that way. You're the complete package, Abbie. You've got everything. Personality, looks. You're fun to be with, but there's a spiritual side to you too. You're everything I ever wanted in a girl."

She turned to face me. "You mean as a friend," she said softly.

I paused. "That's right, as a friend."

She nodded. "Can I tell you something, as a friend?"

"Yeah, sure."

"I forgot how much fun we have when we're together. But . . ." She paused. "I also feel sorry for you just a little."

"Why?"

"You're a good person, Dave. You always have been. You always did what you thought was the right thing. And that's good. But now, you're going to go back home, look around for a girl to marry, find one, and get married so your folks can go on their mission. You'll spend the rest of your life in Ririe."

"Is there something wrong with that?"

"Listen to me. Have you ever stood in Times Square on New Year's Eve? Have you ever gone to a Yankees or a Mets game? Have you ever come here during a nor'easter and had the wind almost knock you over and watch twenty-foot waves crash onto the beach?"

"Can't say I have."

"And you never will. You'll end up a dull man in a tiny boring town."

"And what are you going to do? Spend the rest of your life watching waves crash onto a beach?"

"I'll go back west sometime, when I've had enough excitement to last me a while. Let me ask you something. What do *you* want out of life? Do you even know? I don't think you've ever had a selfish thought in your life. I'm just saying you need to do things just for you because you're important too."

"Okay, I got it."

"When you first left on your mission, you used to close your letters with, *All my love, Dave.* But after about a year, you closed with *As always, Dave.* But that's not just how you end your letters. It is the way you are. Always the same. Never changing. I'm just saying maybe there's a few things you could change and it'd be all right. Like sometime, maybe even just once in our life, doing the unexpected. Other than that, you're just about perfect."

"You want unexpected? Sure, why not? Abbie, will you marry me?"

She shook her head. "No. Nice try, though. Besides, you asking me to marry you isn't unexpected."

"If I were to end up marrying your sister Courtney, would that fit into the unexpected category for you?"

She threw a wet towel at me.

"I'm serious," I said. "Has she graduated from high school yet?"

"Dave, you're making me crazy here!"

"I know that. And I'm enjoying it very much. Do you have Courtney's number? Maybe I'll call her now and see if she'll go out with me when I get home on Monday. Could I borrow your cell?"

"If you end up being my brother in law, I will boycott all family reunions."

"You're probably right. Courtney is too mature for me."

"Actually, that's true. She's way more mature than I am, even now."

We stayed under the umbrella to protect ourselves from the sun. We talked and made each other laugh. She filled me in on what had happened to all our high school friends. And we made fun of some of the teachers we'd had in school. Once in a while, when we got too hot, we'd go in the water to cool off.

At one point when we were in the sun I happened to notice that, although Abbie was wearing a T-shirt over her suit, it seemed to me that she might be getting a sunburn on her back.

"You want me to put some sunblock on your back?" I asked.

"What for? That's why I'm wearing a T-shirt."

"I know, but I think you're still getting a sunburn through it. If you take off your T-shirt for a minute, I'll put some sunblock on your back."

That broke Abbie up.

"What?" I asked.

"How long have you been off your mission?"

I was blushing. "A little less than two weeks."

"So in that time you go from just a handshake to asking a girl if you can put sunblock on her back? That's quite a leap, wouldn't you say?"

"You know what? I withdraw the offer. Don't blame me if you get a sunburn, though."

A few minutes later we returned back to the shade of our umbrella. She checked her cell phone. "You want to leave?" she asked. "We've been here a long time."

"No, not really. I like it here . . . with you."

"It has been good. But you know what? I need to get back. Eldon said he might quit early tonight."

We packed up and started on our way back to the car.

"Thanks for a great day," I said.

"I had a good time too. I forgot how much fun you can be."

"Just like it used to be at Ririe Reservoir, right?"

"I guess so." She paused. "Don't take this wrong, but I would have had a good time with anybody from the singles branch. That's the way it is here. We're all very close."

"Why are you telling me this?"

"This time in your life will never come back. So enjoy it. Go back home and get in a campus ward at BYU—Idaho. You don't have to hurry up and get married, do you?"

"No, I guess not. I wish I could marry you though."

"I understand that, but it's not going to happen. We're just friends now."

"Okay, I got the picture."

"Good. Just don't go back home and get married right away, okay?" she said. "As a friend, I'm asking you to take some time. Don't go marrying the first girl you see, okay?"

"I won't."

"I still like you, Dave. Very much. I always will. I hope we'll always be friends."

"Yeah, me too."

Forty-five minutes later she dropped me off at Nathan's place. He wasn't home and there was nothing on TV I was interested in, so after taking a shower and changing clothes, I decided to take a walk.

Where I come from, if you want to know what direction you're walking, you just look at the mountains, and they'll give you a bearing; but on Long Island, there aren't any mountains.

An hour later I found myself standing outside a hardware store in a mini-mall.

I've always loved hardware stores. Entering one for me is like being a kid and waking up on Christmas morning and going downstairs to see all the presents Santa brought.

So I went in to look around. I liked the place the minute I walked in. It was well-stocked and there were signs hanging down from the ceiling that told you where everything was.

I slowly went from aisle to aisle.

"Can I help you?" a girl my age asked. She was wearing a red Ace Hardware vest. She had long dark brown hair and an olive complexion. She was about three inches shorter than Abbie.

"No, just looking. Thanks."

"If you tell me what you're looking for, I'll find it for you," she said. I'd never known anyone to chew gum with so much energy.

"I'm just looking around."

"Hey, don't do me any favors, okay?" She walked away like she was mad.

Down another aisle I came across a man who looked puzzled. As I walked past him, he turned to me. "Do you know anything about doorbells?"

"Well, yeah, a little."

"Our doorbell doesn't work. My wife has been on me for weeks to get it fixed. I replaced the bell, and it still doesn't work. So what else could it be?"

"I don't actually work here, but are you sure you hooked it up right?"

"I had my brother-in-law check what I'd done. He said it looked okay to him."

"It could be your transformer."

"What transformer?"

"These things have to have a transformer to knock down the voltage. When they built the house, they may have slapped the transformer on some two-by-four before they put up the Sheetrock."

"So how do I find it?"

"That could be a problem."

"Look, my wife's folks are coming to visit on Monday. If the bell isn't working by then, my wife will be mad at me, and my mother-in-law will never let it go." He imitated his mother-in-law. "'What kind of a man can't fix a doorbell?'"

"Well, I can tell you what I'd do."

I had just started my explanation of what he needed to do when another employee came up to us. He was a large man with a barrel chest and thick gray hair. He looked like the kind of man that no matter where he is, he always figures he's in charge. "I'm the manager here. What do you think you're doing?"

"He asked me a question," I said.

"So what is this, Amateur Hour? What happens if you give him bad advice and he goes home and burns down his house? He'll come back here and you'll be gone. But I'll be the one he sues."

"Let him finish," the customer said. "I want to know what he has to say."

"All right, Smart Guy, say what you were going to say. I'll decide if you know anything."

I explained to the manager the customer's problem and then added, "If it were me, I'd buy a doorbell that only requires batteries. The batteries last about a year and then you replace 'em. You can have the doorbell installed in like fifteen minutes. Here's one I'd recommend."

The customer picked up the doorbell I'd pointed to. "I can do that. Thanks." He walked away with the new doorbell package.

"So what makes you think you're qualified to hand out advice to my customers?" the manager asked. He spoke louder than anyone I'd ever known.

"My dad owns a hardware store. I've worked there since ninth grade."

"A real hardware store? I mean one with nuts and bolts in bins so people can buy 'em one at a time?"

"That's right."

"Where is this store?"

"Idaho."

"So what are you doing here?"

"Visiting a friend."

"You any good?"

"My dad is thinking of letting me take over the store when he retires."

"Your dad is either an idiot . . . or . . ."

"Or I'm as good as I say I am."

"I suppose that is a possibility. You looking for a job?"

"Not really."

"I'm desperate to find someone. When could you start?"

"Monday, but I didn't come out here to get a job."

He shrugged. "So? You change your plans."

"You probably wouldn't pay me as much as my dad does."

"How much does he pay you?"

I told him the amount.

"I'll double that plus you'll be full-time so you'll have health insurance. I'm not saying it's good insurance, but it's not too bad."

"I don't work Sundays."

"What do you mean, you don't work Sundays? This is New York. Everybody works Sundays."

"Not me."

"How about one Sunday a month?"

"No."

"Even if I pay you double-time?" he asked.

"No, sorry."

"One Sunday every two months?"

"No."

"One Sunday every six months?"

"No."

He put his large hand on my shoulder. "Son, let me give you a little advice. You'll never get a job on Long Island if you won't work Sundays."

"I'm not looking for a job."

"So what are you saying? You expect everyone else to work Sundays just so you get it off? What makes you so special?"

"If you don't like it, don't hire me."

He rubbed the stubble on his chin. "You drive a hard bargain. Okay, as a special favor to you, you won't have to work Sundays. Sure, you go have your special day! Don't worry about us. I'll give you a few minutes to decide."

"I didn't say I even wanted a job, did I?"

He put up his hand and brushed me off as he was walking away.

A minute later the girl who had talked to me when I first came in approached me. "I'm Hannah. So, are you the new guy?"

"I'm not the new guy."

The manager called out from the next aisle. "He could be the new guy if I could talk him into working an occasional Sunday. But he's giving me a hard time."

"Is this a chu'ch thing with you?" she asked in her New York accent.

"Yeah, it is."

The manager poked his head back into our aisle. "Hannah, you come in Sundays so he can go to mass."

"What, are you crazy? You want me to work so this schmuck can have a religious experience? What if some day I want a religious experience?"

"Go to Thursday night Bingo!"

"What's the matter wit' you? I've worked my tail off here for three years! And some stranger walks in looking for a job and you're willing to make me work Sundays so he can go to chu'ch? How fair is that?"

They were yelling at each other in front of me.

"Look, I'm in charge here. If you don't like what I do, why don't you just quit?"

"You know what? I've had it with you!" She ripped off her Ace Hardware vest, threw it on the counter, and walked out of the store.

I was stunned.

The manager shrugged his shoulders. "I'm going to miss her. She was a good worker, too. But what are you going to do, you know what I'm saying?"

"Do you want me to catch up with her and try to talk her into coming back?"

"Naw, let her go. She's history." He sighed. "There's just one thing."

"What?"

"Now that she's quit, I'm kind of shorthanded. I was wondering if you'd be willing to work Sundays until I get someone to replace her."

I noticed he was having a hard time keeping a straight face.

"Excuse me. I'll be right back," I said. I went outside and read the store hours posted on the front door.

And then I came back inside. "You're not even open on Sundays."

"Oh, yeah, that's right. I forgot. Okay, so take the day off."

Hannah came back into the store. She and the manager couldn't stop laughing.

As soon as they got over the joke they had played on me, we introduced ourselves. He was Murray Gianopoulas, and she was Hannah Rinaldi.

I've got to admit that the way Hannah looked interested me. Her hair had a part down the middle of her head. Her long, straight dark brown hair sort of cascaded down her face on either side. Her face was long and angular, and she had a low voice for a girl.

"I've got to go now," I said.

"Look, if you take the job I'll throw in a pickup," Murray said. "I might need you to get something from our wholesalers once in a while, but other than that you can use it for your personal use as long as you put in the gas you use."

"You're giving him the pickup? The one I use to get prescriptions for Grammy?" Hannah complained.

"I guess if Grammy needs a prescription filled on a Sunday and the new guy has the pickup and he's in church, she's a goner."

They started laughing again.

Murray turned to her. "Talk to him. I'll leave the final decision with you whether or not we hire him." He left us.

She was smiling again. "What's you' name, again?"

"Dave. And you're Hannah?"

"Yeah. Where you from?"

"Idaho."

"You mean Iowa, right?"

"No, Idaho."

"Never heard of it. Is it close to Iowa?" she asked.

"No."

She tossed her head. "Looks like Murray wants to hire you."

"I didn't come in here looking for a job."

"And then you met us. And how could you resist? Okay, let me be serious, okay? Murray's a great guy to work for. We get the job done, but we have fun doing it. Oh, and he was serious about the pickup. So if it's something you think you'd like doing, I think you'd enjoy working here. I love it."

"I'll think about it."

"So when are you going to decide?"

"By Monday."

"We'll be waiting with bated breath." She started laughing and walked away.

"What do you think?" Murray asked her privately, but he had such a loud voice everybody in the store could hear him.

"He's from Iowa, right? So why does he keep calling it Idaho?"

"It's the accent," Murray said.

"Weird accent. He says he'll let us know Monday if he wants the job."

"What's there not to like about working here with us?"

Walking back to Nathan's place, I had a lot to think about.

CHAPTER FOUR

Church began at one o'clock, but since Nathan was the branch clerk, we got there early.

By quarter to one I found a seat near the middle of the chapel. I was the first one there, and it was interesting to watch as the chapel filled up. A few girls sat together, but almost none of the guys. Instead, they sat by themselves in back.

Five minutes before church started, Abbie came in, and walked over to say hello. "You want to know if my back got sunburned yesterday?" she asked with a mocking grin on her face.

"Not really."

She laughed. "It didn't. Nice try though."

"I was only thinking of the well-being of your skin."

She started laughing but then suddenly stopped when she saw the chapel door open. She wouldn't want Security Boy to see her talking to me.

It was a girl who entered the chapel. She walked to the organ and began playing prelude music.

"Well, I'd better grab my seat. Eldon and I usually sit on the third row."

She went up to the third row and sat down.

A few minutes later Megan came in. I stood up and motioned to her.

She came over to see me. *She might sit with me!* I thought. *That would be so great. I don't want to sit all alone watching Abbie and Security Boy together.*

"Will you sit with me?" I asked.

"Of course. Who else would I sit with?"

We sat down, and she scooted close to me. "Did you talk to Abbie when she came in?" she asked.

"We said hi."

"Good. She'll probably sit with Eldon," she said.

"I know. Does he ever put his arm around her during church?"

"No. Look, are you going to be okay?" she asked.

"Yeah, sure."

"Good. So you and Abbie had a good time at the beach?"

"Yeah, we did."

"She called me after she got back and told me all about it. We laughed so hard when she told me about you asking her to take off her T-shirt so you could put sunblock on her back."

"I didn't want her to get a sunburn."

Megan laughed. "That's what she told me! That is so funny."

I was blushing. "What else did she tell you?"

"Everything. Even about you two in high school." She paused. "Guys never have friends they can talk with like that, do they?"

"No."

"That's too bad."

"If you and I were married, would I be your best friend or would it still be Abbie?" I asked

"Dave, this is so sudden," she teased.

"You know what I mean."

"I'm not sure. If we were married, you'd be right up there near the top of the list, but I think Abbie and I will always be best friends."

"Why's that?"

"Because we can talk."

"You and I are talking now."

"Yeah, I guess we are. It's just different, that's all."

The branch president, President Alexander, came into the chapel and went around shaking people's hands. He was taller than me and wore glasses. He reminded me of my high school principal, a warm and respected leader.

He shook my hand. "Let's see, you're Abbie's cousin, right?"

I didn't want to go into a long explanation. "Yeah, more or less. I'm Dave. It's a pleasure to meet you."

"How long will you be with us?"

"I leave tomorrow," I said, watching as Security Boy came in and sat down next to Abbie.

"Well, we're glad to have you with us today." He turned to Megan and shook her hand. "Megan, how are you doing?"

"Better than last Sunday," she said with a smile. "Thanks for helping me get over feeling sorry for myself."

He smiled and said, "Come see me anytime."

"I will. Thanks."

"You have my card, don't you?" he asked her.

"I do. You gave it to me last week."

He moved on to talk to a few others.

"Isn't President Alexander great?" Megan said. "Everybody loves him."

"I can see why."

When President Alexander made it to where Abbie and Security Boy were sitting, he spoke to each of them briefly, then, glancing at the clock, made his way to the stand and sat down.

When the meeting began there were only about twenty people in the chapel. Ten minutes later the number had doubled, and just after the sacrament, there were about seventy in the chapel.

President Alexander was the first speaker. His topic was chastity.

During his talk, Megan fell asleep and rested her head on my shoulder. I didn't feel all that comfortable with her so close especially during a chastity talk and also because I'd just met her.

At one point in her sleep, she lurched forward a little so her head landed on my chest instead of my shoulder, and I had to prop her up a little to get her back where she belonged. To make sure she didn't move again I put my arm around her shoulder, to more or less stabilize her.

With her sleeping, it gave me a good opportunity to look at her face. I wondered if she had any idea how beautiful she was. She didn't act like she did. She was just out of high school and yet one of the most beautiful girls I'd ever met.

And it wasn't just her looks. Friday night I found what a reward it was to make her laugh. When she laughed, it spilled out in waves, and it made everyone around her happy.

As President Alexander talked about the evils of immorality, I started to feel a little guilty, seeing we were the only couple in the chapel draped over each other. I started to blush, which made me feel even more self-conscious. I wondered if anyone was thinking my face was red because Megan and I had done some of the things President Alexander was warning us against.

I turned around to see if anyone was watching. Antonio had a big grin on his face and gave me a thumbs up. I knew he'd tease us after church.

Mercifully, the next speaker, a member of the high council, talked about building Zion. I was much more relaxed about this topic since it really had nothing to do with me and certainly didn't make me feel guilty.

Maybe I was a little too relaxed about the subject of building Zion because eventually I fell asleep too.

I woke up during the closing hymn. But at least I woke up before Megan.

"I'm so sorry I fell asleep," she said on the second verse.

"Hey, don't worry about it."

"What did the last speaker talk about?" she asked.

"Building Zion. It was an excellent talk."

"What did he say?"

"He said, well, that we should build Zion."

"Oh."

After the closing prayer, Antonio sauntered over to us. "I just want you both to know I admire a couple who feels liberated enough to make out during their branch president's chastity talk."

"We weren't making out," Megan said. "I just fell asleep, that's all."

"You were both zonked out."

"You were sleeping, too?" Megan asked me.

"Well, maybe, for a minute or two."

"So, did you two have a late night?" Antonio asked, grinning.

"No."

"That's what they all say," he teased. "But, no matter. I'll sit between you two in Sunday School and try to keep you awake and respectable."

Our Sunday School teacher was Security Boy. It was a little depressing to me to see how at ease he was in front of people. Where I would have been all nervous, he seemed to come alive.

It was also evident that the guy was made for public speaking. He had a very prominent jaw combined with a long narrow face. In some ways it looked like a face that only a cartoonist could imagine. But he had a way of responding to questions that made him seem really confident, and his vocabulary and gospel knowledge were very impressive. In spite of how I felt about him as a rival, I couldn't help admiring his ability as a teacher.

During the lesson, he related an experience he'd had on his mission. He'd been serving as a zone leader, and he was able to help a new missionary who was struggling. He told the class the experience had helped him realize how important it is to be a leader others can look up to.

I wondered if the only reason he had told the story was to make himself look good. What depressed me even more was that it succeeded, especially with Abbie.

I looked over at her during the lesson and realized she probably didn't even know I was there. Well, you know what, I'd had experiences on my mission too. I raised my hand.

Security Boy didn't call on me. I kept my hand up but after a short time I began to have second thoughts that I was going to share this experience just to make myself look good to Abbie. A worthy goal, of course, but maybe not in a Sunday School class. Besides, somehow I knew I'd never outdo Security Boy.

I finally decided that trying to impress somebody wasn't a good enough reason to share a mission experience that to me was sacred. To tell it for the wrong reason would be like violating a confidence between me and the Spirit. I lowered my hand and gave up any hope of impressing Abbie.

Security Boy finally called on me. "Dave, did you have something you wanted to add?"

"No, you've already covered what I was going to say." Very impressive, right?

After class, Security Boy graciously accepted Abbie's congratulations for doing such a good job. The best I could do was, "Yeah, it was real good."

He excused himself because he'd been asked at the last minute to teach priesthood and needed to get some materials in the library.

"What do you think of Eldon?" Abbie asked.

"He's a very impressive guy."

"Yeah, he is," she said.

She could have thrown in something like, "But so are you." But she didn't.

"What time does your plane leave in the morning?" she asked.

"Ten twenty-seven."

"That means you'll need to be at the airport by eight-thirty. So you'll have to leave here a little after seven. I'll be working in the morning, but I talked to Eldon, and he said he'd be glad to take you."

"I can take a taxi. If he drives me, it will take up his whole morning."

"He's happy to do it for you. He doesn't usually start going door to door until about four in the afternoon anyway. He insists."

"Well, okay."

Abbie and I were alone in the hall. Most everyone else was in priesthood or Relief Society.

"So, is this good-bye?" I asked.

"We'll see each other after class."

"Look, let's just do it now. I don't want Antonio standing next to us doing a comedy routine when we say good-bye."

"Okay, then."

"It was good to see you, Abbie. Thanks for taking me to Jones Beach. It was the most fun I've had in a long time."

"It was fun for me, too."

I hesitated to say it but then blurted, "I still love you."

"I know. She reached for my hand. "And you'll always be very special to me."

"Look, I can see why you like Eldon so much. It kills me to say it, but he's a great guy. Let me know how you're doing from time to time, okay?"

"I will. I'll also let you know how things go with Eldon and me."

"Please do. Well, I'd better get to priesthood."

We hugged each other for longer than either one of us might have predicted, and then we went our separate ways.

During Eldon's lesson I decided that out of respect for Abbie I should quit thinking of him as Security Boy. Besides, he was going out of his way to give me a ride to the airport in the morning.

I assume Eldon did a good job teaching priesthood, but to tell the truth I didn't pay much attention. All I could think about was how much I was going to miss Abbie.

* * *

The next morning Eldon picked me up at seven. He was driving a sporty red Toyota with a sunroof.

"Is this your car?" I asked.

"No, but if I keep my sales up, it will be by the end of the summer."

"It's sweet."

"Thanks. Oh, I got us each a breakfast from McDonald's," he said, handing me a sack.

"Wow, thanks. You didn't have to go to so much trouble."

"A guy's got to eat, right? And the food in airports is always so expensive."

I had just taken a big bite of my breakfast burrito when he said, "You want to say a prayer on the food?"

I felt guilty. "Oh, yeah, let me finish this bite first."

"Sure. If it's okay, I won't close my eyes."

I looked over to check if he was serious or not. I could tell by a slight smile that it was a joke.

I was actually surprised that I enjoyed talking with him. It turned out that on his mission he'd served with a friend of mine from Ririe. And on my mission I knew an elder from his home ward in California.

I'd have been happy to continue talking about our missions, but after we'd both finished eating, he changed topics. "I've enjoyed getting to know Abbie," he said. "She's really something, isn't she?"

"Yeah, she is. Always has been," I said.

"I could see us getting serious, but . . ."

"What?"

"Well, before my mission, I met a girl at BYU. Her name is Elizabeth. She was in one of my classes. She was a sophomore. I'd taken so many A.P. classes in high school, I was able to start taking upper level classes."

"Yeah, sure." I tried to make it sound like something I'd done too, but the truth was I'd worked for my dad full-time after high school to earn money for my mission and had never taken even one college class.

Eldon continued. "Elizabeth and I started seeing each other every day. And, well, after a while we even talked about getting married after I returned from my mission. But after I'd been out a while, she decided to go on a mission too, so we'd have that experience in common. I'll be flying back to Utah to hear her talk in sacrament meeting on the twenty-sixth. I'm not really sure how that's going to play out."

"Have you told Abbie about Elizabeth?"

"Not yet. Actually, I thought that Abbie and I were just friends, but then when I found out that she'd told me you were her cousin so I wouldn't get jealous, I realized she thinks this is way more serious than I thought it was." He sighed. "Is that how it looks to you?"

"Yeah. She told me that you two might get married some day."

"I suppose that could happen if things don't work out with Elizabeth and me. Let me ask you a question. How do you feel about Abbie?"

"I went on my mission thinking we'd get married when I got back," I said.

"That's tough, isn't it, to come back and find out that it might not happen?"

"Yeah, it is. When are you going to tell Abbie about Elizabeth?"

"Now that I know how she feels about me, I'd better tell her real soon."

Maybe he'll go out to Utah and come back engaged to Elizabeth, I thought. *Then maybe I'd have a chance with Abbie.*

But even if Abbie and I didn't have a future together, she'd still been my best friend all through high school. She was so into Eldon, but obviously he didn't feel the same way. Chances were that she was going to get hurt.

You can't walk away from your best friend in a time of crisis. Especially if you might be able to eventually talk her into marrying you.

It was a long shot, but that was the little bit of hope I needed to make a decision. "You know what?" I said. "I've changed my mind. I'm not going back to Idaho. Take me back to Nathan's place. I'm staying here for the rest of the summer." Eldon gave me a strange look but didn't ask why I'd changed my mind.

On the way back I called Nathan and asked if I could room with him if I paid half the rent. He was more than agreeable since he only spent two or three days a week in his apartment. He told me there was a key under a rock by the front door.

Eldon dropped me off at Nathan's place. Before he drove off, he asked me to keep confidential what he'd said to me about Elizabeth, until he had a chance to tell Abbie himself.

I said I would. We said good-bye, and I found the key and let myself into what was now my place too.

As I entered the apartment, I wondered if Eldon had insisted on giving me a ride to the airport just to find out how Abbie felt about him. I couldn't tell then if he was a nice guy who liked to help out or just someone who was very good at getting what he wanted.

I couldn't understand how he could be with Abbie and not be totally in love with her—like I'd been since high school.

I had one big obstacle still in front of me, and that was to tell my folks about my decision to stay. I called my dad first because I had always been able to talk to him. I waited until ten o'clock New York time, then called him at the hardware store.

"Dad, hi, it's Dave. I need to ask you a question."

"Okay, shoot."

"Uh, well, the reason I came out here was to try to see if I could talk Abbie into quitting her job as a nanny and going back with me to Idaho."

"And how's that going?"

"Not too good. She wants to stay here for another year."

"Well, that's her choice, isn't it?"

"Yeah, I guess so. She's acting like she's outgrown Idaho . . . well, I wouldn't care about that, but she's seeing another guy."

"Sorry to hear that. I always liked Abbie . . . always hoped she'd be my daughter-in-law some day."

"Yeah, I know. Dad, the thing is, I still care about her."

"So what are you going to do?"

"I was thinking of staying back here for a while, maybe until September. That would give me a little more time with her. The guy she's seeing has a girl coming home from a mission in a couple of weeks. So there's a chance things might work out for Abbie and me after all."

"Well, that sounds worth pursuing. How would you support yourself back there?"

"On Saturday I dropped by a hardware store, just to look around, and, well, they're actually looking for someone to work for them, so I applied, and they offered me the job. I told them I'd let them know today. It would pay my expenses while I'm here, and then after two or three months I'll come back home. Also, they'll even let me use their store pickup after work at no cost except for gas. If I decide to stay here, would that work out for you?"

"I don't see a problem with that, if that's what you want."

"I know you and Mom want to serve a mission."

"We probably won't be going until February. We want to get organized before we leave. It's surprising how much clutter accumulates over the years. It'll take some time to do that."

"Are you sure it'd be okay for me to stay out here for a little longer?"

"We got by without you for two years. I don't think another two months would do us in." He paused. "Of course, you'd better run it by your mother."

"I'll call her now."

"Let me know what you decide."

"Thanks, Dad. Talk to you later."

"'Bye, Son."

That's the way my dad has always been, easygoing and easy to talk to.

I dreaded talking to my mom, though. In high school no matter what good thing I might have done she could always find some small detail I'd overlooked. I guess she was just trying to help me be better, but sometimes I held back telling her everything.

At my new apartment, I had something to eat, watched TV for a while, and then finally got up the courage to make the call.

"Hi, Mom. What are you doing?"

Somehow Mom had never been told that the correct answer to that question is "Not much." She gave a detailed description of what she was doing and then asked, "Where are you? Are you calling from the airport?"

"Not exactly."

"What time is your flight?" she asked.

"Ten twenty-seven, but—"

"Isn't New York two hours later than Idaho? Is your watch still on Mountain Time?"

"No."

"Well, it's almost eleven there, isn't it?"

"That's what I wanted to talk to you about."

"You missed your flight? I knew I should have called this morning to make sure you were up, but your father said you'd served a mission and didn't need me checking on you every second. What ever are you going to do now?"

When my mom asked a question like that, it always made me feel bad. "That's what I called about."

"It's going to cost a fortune to rebook your flight. Do you still have the credit card your dad gave you?"

"Mom, stop, okay? I've decided to stay here for the rest of the summer."

After a painful silence, my mom said, "Why on earth would you do that when we need you here to help us get ready for our mission?"

"Abbie isn't sure about us now, and she definitely doesn't want to come home, so I thought that if I stayed out here for a while, she might change her mind."

"What do you mean, she isn't sure about you now? You two grew up together. She knows you better than any other boy she'll ever meet."

"Mom, the thing is, I've decided to stay back here until fall, and then I'll come home. I talked to Dad about it, and he's okay with it. I've got a job at a hardware store, and they're going to let me use their pickup after work, and I've got a place to stay."

After a long pause, with a tremor in her voice, she asked, "You're not coming home?"

"No."

She didn't say anything for a long time. "But you've been gone for two years already. Isn't that enough time to be away from your family?"

It hadn't occurred to me that my mom would be upset I wasn't coming home. She'd seemed happy enough to send me on a mission. I guess this was different. I wondered if I'd made a big mistake.

"I'm thinking that if I can stay back here, Abbie and I will have some time to spend together, and maybe that will be all she'll need so we can get married."

"What if it isn't?"

"Then I'll know within a month, and I'll come home."

"We'll have so little time with you before we leave on our mission," she said. "I thought you'd be home until then."

"Yeah, I know. Me, too. Sorry. I thought you'd want me to see if I can get Abbie to agree to marry me."

"Maybe you should just forget about her. Three girls in our stake have asked about when you're coming home. I think at least one of them would probably like to get married soon."

I remembered that Abbie had warned me about getting married too soon. "Mom, I'm thinking I might not get married for a while."

"It would be hard for your dad and me if you got married while we're on our mission . . . and we end up missing the whole thing." She sighed. "Maybe we should wait for a year or two before we go."

"No, Mom, please don't wait. They really need senior couples in the mission field. Please, just go. It will all work out. I'm sorry if I've disappointed you."

By the time I ended our conversation, I felt awful. I wondered if my mom was right and that I should just give up on Abbie and go home. What made me think that Abbie would change her mind if I stayed here?

After thinking about it for a while I decided to stay at least a month before returning to Idaho. I called my dad and told him my final decision and asked him to tell Mom.

An hour later, when I entered the hardware store, Murray, the manager, saw me. "Hannah?" he called out.

"I'm busy," she called out from one of the aisles.

"Remember that guy from Iowa? Well, he just walked in."

"You mean the one who refuses to work Sundays? The one you offered your pickup to?"

"Yeah, that one. Come here. He's standing right here."

"I'll be there in a minute."

"If the job's still open, I'd like to take it," I told Murray.

"He's taking the job!" Murray called out.

Hannah called out from one of the aisles. "Our prayers are answered!"

Murray told me again how much I'd be getting and what my

hours would be and that part of my job would be to run errands and make deliveries using the store pickup.

Near the end of our discussion, Hannah came over to us.

"Show him around, Hannah. Get him a vest," Murray said.

"Follow me, Rookie."

As we walked to the back of the store, she talked nonstop. I wasn't sure if she thought what she was saying would be helpful to me, or if she was teasing me.

"This is the tool section. Hammers, screw drivers, pliers, and so on."

"I can see the sign. You don't have to tell me."

"And this is plumbing."

"I know."

"Some things will be hard for you to pick up. But don't worry. If you can't find something, just tell the customer you're new and totally hopeless, and then go find me. I'll bail you out." She snickered.

We stopped in front of plumbing supplies. "Some things are self-explanatory. Like this o-ring." She picked it up and shoved it in my face. "This is used in plumbing. You can remember its name because, see, it looks like an O. I'm pretty sure that's why they call it an o-ring."

We continued on. She stopped to pick up a c-clamp. "This is called a c-clamp. Notice that it looks like the letter C."

She looked back at me and gave me a mischievous grin. "You getting all this down, Rookie? You want to take notes?"

"No. Are you having fun?"

"Yes, I am, Rookie. I want you to think of me as being the assistant manager."

"Are you the assistant manager?" I asked.

"Yes, I am." She paused. "At least to you I am. I'll always be your superior in the Ace Hardware corporate structure."

We ended up in a storage room at the back of the store. It was full of new merchandise still in boxes that needed to be opened and cataloged, and there were a workbench, a microwave, a small refrigerator, and a coat rack.

From the coat rack, she grabbed a red vest with the Ace Hardware logo on the front. "You want the official ceremony where we sing the store song and read in unison our mission statement and motto?"

"Not really."

"Fine, then, be that way." She handed me the vest. "Put it on. This has got to be a proud moment in your life, right? You're now a part of the Ace Hardware family. You want me to take a picture so you can send it to your family?"

"Look, like I said before, my dad owns a hardware store and I've worked in it since ninth grade."

"Oh, yeah. In Iowa, right?"

"Idaho."

"Whatever. So what are you saying? You don't want my ten-hour training complete with DVD lesson manual?"

"No."

"Then let's cover where you're really lacking, and that's in the way you talk."

"What's wrong with the way I talk?"

"Well, one thing for sure, you talk weird. Look, if you want to get along, learn to talk like us. When a customer comes in and needs help, you walk up and say, 'Ow ya duen?' Now you try it."

"How are you doing?"

She slugged me on the shoulder. "Listen to me, Knucklehead. Ow ya duen. Ow not How, ya not you, duen not doing. And on the duen stick your lips out. Try it again."

"How ya doing?"

She shook her head. "You know what? I personally never would've hired you. Nobody will be able to understand you. Try it again."

"Ow ya duen."

She smiled. "Not bad. We'll keep working on it. What is this place?"

"A hardware store."

She shook her head. "No, no, no. it's a adwa sto-ah. Say this for me, 'I'm goen to the sto-ah.'"

"I'm going to the store–ah."

"It's hopeless. Sto—ah. Drop the r. Two syllables."

"Sto—ah."

"So much to do, so little time to do it. And me with a hangover." She gingerly put her hand to her forehead. "I had a party last night with some of my friends. I drank a little too much. So I'm a little hung over today. What do you take for that?'

"Nothing."

"Yeah, that's me, too."

"What I mean is, I never get a hangover."

"I've heard of people like that. They say if you drink every night, after a while you don't get hangovers."

"I never drink."

"What else is there to do?"

"Go to church."

"Yeah, right! That's a good one." She walked away, chuckling to herself.

"What do you want me to do now?"

She turned to face me. "Wait on the customers, Rookie. What do you think we're paying you for? And when there's no customers, come back here and open up new shipments. Save the packing slips and give them to me."

So I went to work. A few times I had to ask Hannah where something was, but other than that, it went okay.

Around four o'clock a man entered the store. He looked to be in his mid-sixties, and even though it was summer, he wore a windbreaker and a baseball cap.

He said something to Hannah, who turned and pointed in my direction.

"See that guy? He'll be able to help you. Oh, yeah. In fact, that's his specialty."

The man came up to me.

"Ow ya duen? Welcome to ah sto-ah," I said for Hannah's benefit. "Can I help you?"

He thrust his cell phone in my face. "See this phone. It's brand new. It works fine, but after I hang up, it calls me back."

"What calls you back?"

"The phone."

"What does the phone say?"

"It says the number you called is not in service at this time. So then I hang up."

"Does it call you back a second time?"

"You're not listening to me. No, just the one time." He handed me the phone. "So, fix it, Mister Smart Guy, the Phone Expert of the Century."

"Did you buy the phone here?"

"What difference does that make? Either you can fix it or you can't. So what's it going to be?"

I handed him the phone. "I can't fix it."

"That's it? I walk three blocks in the heat of the day to have you tell me you can't fix it? You call this a full-service hardware store? Believe me, this is not full-service! This is no service whatsoever!"

"Sorry. I suggest you contact the place where you got the phone."

"What, are you crazy? I got it at Wal Mart. You think any of them people know anything? They're as bad as you. Where's the manager? I need to complain to him about you."

I pointed to Murray. "He's over there."

He talked with his hands. "You think I don't know who the manager is? Is that what you think? I've been coming here for thirty years! I know who the manager is. And let me tell you something, in thirty years this is the first time I've been treated so shabbily."

"He's the one to talk to, then. Have a nice day." I started to walk away.

He followed me. "You think you can get rid of me that fast?"

I turned around. "Is there anything else I can do for you?"

He threw his hands in the air. "Anything else? You haven't done anything for me. Zip! Squat! Nada! I oughta give you a piece of my mind!"

"Excuse me, I need to go help some other customers."

"Wait a minute. There's something very important I need to tell you. It's actually the reason I came in here. Do you know Lenny?"

"Not really."

"He's a little man. He carries a little white sack around with him. You want to know what's in that sack?"

"What?"

"Pens he stole from this store. Every time he comes in here he takes a pen."

"Where does he get them?"

"At the register. They're free. Anyone can take 'em. But who knew he'd take so many. You watch him like a hawk the next time he comes in. If your profits are down, he's the reason. Lenny, the pen thief."

"Okay, well, thank you. I've got to go in the back and take care of some new merchandise we received today."

"What? You're too busy for an old man? Is that what's going on here? I wasn't treated like this twenty years ago when I added a garage. No, then it was, 'Thank you, Mr. Denuchy. We appreciate your business, Mr. Denuchy.' Now it's different, let me tell you."

"If you need any help finding something, I'd be glad to help you. If not, then please excuse me."

He jabbed his finger into my chest. "That's what I'm talking about! Right there. What's your name? I'm going to report you."

"Dave."

"Dave what?"

"We've only got one Dave working here."

"Oh, I get it! Mister CIA, is that it? You can't reveal your name because of national security? Well, let me tell you something. We don't have any national security anymore! And that's the truth! This country is going to ruin in a handbasket."

Hannah, overhearing this, came up to us. "Mr. Denuchy, ow ya duen? Did Dave here help you?"

"No, he did not. He was no help to me at all. Plus he insulted me."

"What did he say?"

"I can't repeat what he said, but, believe me, it was bad. Why did you ever hire him? Between Lenny stealing pens and this guy incapable of helping customers, this place is on the road to bankruptcy. Mark my words."

"I'm so sorry you feel that way, Mr. Denuchy."

He looked over at me. "You see how she's treating me? That's called respect. I suggest you learn to speak with respect to your customers like she does."

"I'll do that, Mr. Denuchy," I said.

"And I'll make sure he does, Mr. Denuchy," Hannah said.

He pointed his finger at me. "I'll be back and when I do I'm coming to you for help. Don't fail me next time."

Hannah punched me lightly on the shoulder as he left. "Mr. Denuchy comes in every week, complains a lot, and never buys anything. I'm so glad you'll be serving him from now on."

I worked until seven when the store closed, then stayed another hour while Hannah showed me how to close and make the deposit.

And then I drove the store pickup to my new apartment. I expected to have some time to myself, but when I walked in there were about a dozen people from the singles branch having family home evening.

Abbie didn't seem particularly happy to see me.

Megan was, though. "Dave, wow, you really didn't go. Eldon told Abbie you've decided to stay all summer! Is that true?"

"Yeah, it is."

Megan gave me a big hug. "I'm so glad to hear you're staying. We're going to have so much fun together!" She looked around at everyone who was watching us. "What I mean is that all of us in the singles branch will have a great summer. That's what I meant. Come sit with me."

"Sure. Hi, Abbie."

"Hi, Dave," she said with little enthusiasm.

After the lesson, Abbie said she wanted to talk to me, and we went outside.

"You like my pickup?" I asked. "I get to drive it all the time I'm here."

She was not in the mood to admire pickups. "Why did you decide to stay here all summer?" she demanded. "I made it clear how I feel about you now, didn't I?"

"You did. We're just friends now."

"So why did you decide to stay?"

"All your talk about not being in too much of a hurry to go back to my life in Idaho made sense. I can always go back to Idaho."

She wasn't buying that. "Did my mom call and talk you into staying?"

"Nobody called. In fact my mom is not very happy with my decision to stay."

"Then what made the difference? Eldon says you changed your mind on the way to JFK."

"Yeah."

"What did he tell you in the car that would make you change your mind?"

I waited too long to answer. "Nothing."

"I can always tell when you're lying. What did he tell you?"

"If you want to know what he told me, I suggest you ask him," I said.

"Please tell me what he said. Is there another girl in his life?"

I didn't answer, but she knew me too well, and my silence told her everything.

She turned her back to me. I saw her touch her eye with her hand like she was getting rid of a tear.

"You okay?" I asked.

She turned to face me. "What's her name?"

"Abbie, he's going to tell you everything, maybe even tonight."

"I won't tell him you told me first. Please, Dave. What's her name?"

"I promised him I wouldn't say anything."

"I don't want him to see me getting emotional, so please tell me now so I'll be prepared for it."

I'd never been able to hold back anything when it came to Abbie. "Her name is Elizabeth. He met her at BYU before his mission. Now she's serving a mission. She gets back in a couple of weeks. He's flying out to see her."

"That's why you decided to stay here, isn't it? Because you think you might have a chance with me."

"It's not only that. We've been friends for a long time. Whatever happens, Abbie, I'll be here for you." I paused. "In fact, if the position of cousin is still open, I'd like to apply for it."

She dabbed at her cheek again with her finger. "Dave?"

"Yes."

"I could use a friend right now. Will you please hold me?"

"Yeah, sure." I held her in my arms as she fought to control her emotions. "I'm sorry things aren't going as well as you'd like with Eldon," I said.

"Thank you for saying that," she said softly.

A minute later Antonio pulled into the driveway. He must have seen us in his headlights.

"Dave, is that you?" he asked as he stepped out of his car.

"Yeah."

"Abbie, you giving Dave another one of them farewell kisses?"

"No, we're just talking."

"Yeah, right. Dave, tell me, what's your secret?"

"He cares about his friends," Abbie said. "Maybe you should try it sometime."

"You sound like my mother." Antonio went inside.

Abbie sighed and pulled away. "Right now, Antonio's in there blabbing about us. So we might as well go in and defend ourselves."

We started back. "Eldon likes you, Abbie. He just wants to see how things are between him and Elizabeth after she gets home from her mission. He'll finish out the summer here. So, with you two together, time is on your side."

She looked at me. "You're hoping it's on your side, too, aren't you?"

"Maybe, but even if that doesn't happen, I'll still be your friend."

"Lucky me. Let's go in."

As we started around the side of the house to the door to the apartment, she turned to me. "Oh, one thing."

"What?"

"Megan thinks the reason you decided to stay is because of her."

"That's not true."

"I know that, but would it kill you to be her friend? She's having a tough time as a new nanny. Besides, what have you got to lose? I hope to be spending all my free time with Eldon."

Inside, when I sat down next to Megan, she asked if she could talk with me after home evening.

Eldon called Abbie and told her he was hung up in traffic in Connecticut and would be late. She told everyone she had a headache and left.

A few minutes later, Megan and I went out to sit in my pickup to talk.

Antonio, now on his way home, banged the side of the pickup with his fist on his way to his car. "So, Dave, do you have each girl take a number?"

"Something like that."

He was laughing as he got in his car and drove off.

"How did your day go?" I asked Megan.

"It was pretty bad. Today when I was about to leave for home evening, Estelle got real mad at me. She said she needed me to do the dishes and start the laundry."

"Who's Estelle?"

"The mom."

"What did you do?"

"I told her I'd do the dishes after I got home. And I'd do the laundry in the morning. She got mad at me and threw a pan on the floor."

"That's crazy."

Nathan had told me not to give any advice but just let the nannies talk. It sounds easy but I found it just about impossible to do. I'm a hardware guy.

Like, do you walk up to a clerk at a hardware store and tell him what's wrong with your toilet so that he can say, "Oh, my gosh, that must be so frustrating not to have your toilet working. I really feel for you."

No, you help fix the problem. So listening was very difficult for me.

But finally I discovered the secret of listening the way Nathan told me to. I found out that if I didn't pay too much attention to what she was saying that it was easier not to give solutions. To let her think I was paying attention, though, I would occasionally repeat a phrase or two from what she had just said.

" . . . told me it was my duty now to make lunches for both of them the night before."

"Make lunches for them the night before? No way!" I said.

"Exactly. Well . . ."

Twenty minutes later she was still going on, but I'd lost track of what she was talking about.

And then she gave me a hug. "Thanks so much for listening to me. I feel a lot better."

"You do?"

We said good night and she got in her car and drove away.

I felt like I'd cheated her. In the time we'd talked I'd had at least ten solutions come to mind, but I hadn't told her any of them.

She hadn't gotten her money's worth, but she was happy with me anyway.

Go figure.

By then everyone else had left, and I went inside and got ready for bed.

I felt guilty and at first I wasn't sure why. But then it came to me while I was brushing my teeth. I hadn't really cared about what was bothering Megan.

I can do better than that, I thought. *From now on, even if I don't give solutions, I'll at least try to care more what people are going through.*

Just before I was about to crawl into bed, I got a call. I answered it.

"Ow ya duen?" Hannah said.

"Good. Ow *ya* duen?"

"Sorry to bother you."

"No problem. What's up?"

"I've had a little too much to drink."

"Okay."

"Don't worry. I'm not drunk. And I won't be driving tonight. I always have a beer or two after work. But tonight I had a lot more than just a few."

"Okay."

"Because there's nothing else to do. You want to know what's worse? I drink alone in my boat tied up to the dock. In the dark. There's got to be something wrong with that, right? Today I told you

I was drinking last night with my friends. Well, that was a lie. I have no friends. I drink by myself. Pathetic, right?"

"It's hard to believe you don't have any friends."

"I agree. I'm messed up. You seem happy, though. Are you?"

"Yeah, I guess so."

"So what's your secret?"

I wanted to tell her, but she'd been drinking, and I knew it probably wouldn't do any good. "I can't tell you now, Hannah. It's late. We both need to get some sleep. Ask me some other time and I'll tell you."

"This is my some other time, Dave. I'm hurting here and I need answers."

"You're not going to like my answer."

"Try me."

"Jesus Christ is the answer."

That set her off. "Look, just forget it, okay? I don't want religion. I just want to be happy."

"Those two things go together; at least they do for me."

She swore at me and hung up.

Suddenly there were so many girls in my life. Abbie, the one I always thought I'd marry, but who now only wanted me as a friend. Megan, just out of high school, one of the most beautiful girls I'd ever known. She needed a friend to help her get through the trials of being a nanny. And then there was Hannah. She needed the gospel to make her happy but didn't want it.

I said my prayers and got into bed and after a little tossing and turning I finally fell asleep.

CHAPTER FIVE

The next day at work Hannah didn't say much to me at first. But later, when I was in the back unpacking boxes, she came to see me. "Ow ya duen?" she said.

"Good. Ow *ya* duen?"

"Can't complain." She cleared her throat. "Sorry about calling you last night. It won't happen again."

"It's okay."

"No, it's not. I'm sorry if I freaked you out."

"It's okay, really."

We could hear Murray calling out for us. Hannah grabbed one of the boxes and opened it up and called out. "We're in the back . . . working."

He came in. "Working? I don't think so. No matter. I need you both to do me a favor not related to the store. My wife bought an antique dining room table and chairs from a woman who's moving to a retirement community. I need you both to go get everything and haul it back here." He handed Hannah a piece of paper. "Here's the address."

"Now?" Hannah asked.

"Yes. Please. I know this isn't hardware business, but I can't handle it myself. I've got a bad back."

"You want us to take the furniture to your house?" I asked.

"You don't need to. Just bring it all back here. I'll take the truck home after work. My next door neighbor and his boys will help move it inside."

"I'll drive," Hannah said as we walked out to the big Ace Hardware truck in the back parking lot of the mall.

"I can drive."

"No, that's just it. You can't drive, at least not out here. This is not Iowa, Davey Boy."

"I'm from Idaho."

"Yeah, right, like there really is an Idaho."

"Also, I'm a guy. I have to drive. My self-esteem is on the line."

She laughed and then suddenly started running toward the truck.

"What are you doing?" I called out.

"We're having a race to decide who gets to drive." She slapped the side of the truck with her hand. "I won."

"I'll race you but only if it's fair."

"Why would I want it to be fair?"

"You're afraid of losing, aren't you?" I asked.

"Afraid? I'm not afraid of man or beast, but with you I can't figure out what category you are. Are you a beast pretending to be a nice guy? That's what I'm thinking."

"Nah. I'm pretty much a nice guy."

"Impossible. A truly nice guy is like the Loch Ness monster—people talk about it, but nobody's actually seen one."

I tossed her the keys to the truck. "I guess I'll be your first then."

"You wish." She smiled. "Tell me, would I be your first?"

I paused. "What do you mean?"

She gave me a knowing grin. "You know what I mean."

"It's true that I don't have experience in all areas of life." I was blushing as I said it.

She laughed. "Do you have to always dance around an issue?"

"Let's change the subject, okay?"

A few minutes later she pulled into an apartment parking lot. "See that door with the *Beware of Dog* sign? That's where I live."

"Do you have a dog?"

"No, just a sign. You want to come in for a while?"

"Why?"

She laughed. "What a dumb question. It *will* be your first time, won't it? Whataya say? Want to go in with me?"

I couldn't believe what she was asking. "No."

"You're not that into me, right?"

"That's not it. I've made a promise to God."

"What kind of a promise?"

"Not to have sex with anyone except my wife."

"But you're not married."

"That's right."

"So if you're not married, how exactly does that work?"

"It means nothing happens until I get married."

"Nothing?"

"Yeah."

"Nothing at all?"

"That's right."

"Not even a little something?"

"No."

"You're saying nothing?"

"That's right."

She shook her head. "That would be like . . . well . . . impossible."

"Not really."

"Without going into any details, would you say that you are . . . I really don't know how to say this. . . . biologically normal?"

I laughed. "Yeah."

"Then I don't understand what you're telling me."

"I have a book I want you to read."

"Is it a book about not having sex?" she joked. "Let me guess what's in it. Page one: 'Don't even think about it.' Page two: 'I said no, didn't I?' Page three: 'Run two miles and then take a cold shower.' Page four. 'What did I tell you on page one? Fuhgetabout it!' And so on through the rest of the book."

"No. It's a book of scripture like the Bible. It's called the Book of Mormon."

"So it's about being a Mormon, right?"

"Not exactly, but you're close."

"The way I see it, religion is like a winter coat. When you need it, you wear it. Otherwise you put it in the closet and forget about it."

"That's not the way it is with me. Oh, by the way, the real name of the church is The Church of Jesus Christ of Latter-day Saints."

She laughed. "No wonder you're so good. It takes so much time telling people what church you belong to, you don't have time to get into trouble."

"I just got back from a mission for my church. For the last two years I went around telling people about the Church."

"It's just a church, like all the others, so what's there to say?"

"A lot. Would you like me to tell you about what we believe?"

"Not really. I'm Catholic."

"Do you go to church every Sunday?"

"No, but I go with my family every Christmas and Easter. Not only that, but I've got an uncle who's a priest, so we've pretty much got it covered. But I guess it's a compliment you'd ask me, right?"

"Yeah."

We were driving again and she went through a yellow light. I was getting used to it. For her, yellow just meant "Keep going." But at a light she actually stopped for, she turned to me. "Look, about what I said, you know, about inviting you to my apartment. I had no intention of us doing anything. Okay? I wasn't even going to get out of the truck. I just wanted to prove to myself that you're like all the other guys I've ever known. I thought you were just more subtle than most." She sighed. "I was wrong. I'm sorry for freaking you out."

"It's okay. Don't worry about it."

"I don't think I've ever been more embarrassed than I am now," she said.

"Let's just forget it happened, okay?"

"You know what? I could've been like you if it hadn't been for a senior who cornered me at a party when I was in ninth grade. He didn't ask. He just took what he wanted. I never even knew his name. So that was my introduction to guys."

"I'm sorry."

"Yeah, me, too." She sighed. "But I don't think about it much. What's done is done, right?"

"I guess so."

"Let's talk about something else, okay?" she asked.

"Tell me about your boat."

Her face lit up. "Oh, that's easy. My boat is the best thing that ever happened to me. I call her *Blue Skies.* Isn't that a great name for a boat?"

After that I couldn't get her to shut up about her boat.

A few minutes later we arrived at the address Murray had given us. There was a car in the driveway and cars parked on either side of the street in front of the house. Hannah just stopped in the middle of the street with the hazard lights on. "Let's go."

"You can't leave the truck here, in the middle of the street."

"Sure I can. Besides, we'll just be a minute. It'll be okay."

We rang the doorbell, and an old woman with frizzy hair came to the door. She was wearing a ratty-looking purple housecoat with sequins.

"Murray sent us to pick up a dining room table and chairs," Hannah told her.

"Oh, yes, come this way."

She walked slowly in front of us, which meant we walked slowly, too.

"This is Sweetheart," she said, pointing to a cat that was on the table lapping milk from a saucer.

"Is this the table that goes?" I asked.

"Yes, it is."

"Does the cat go with the table?" Hannah joked.

"No, my, no. Sweetheart has been my cat for eight years. I remember the first time I saw her. It was in a pet store in Flushing."

I laughed. "Like there could be a town called Flushing. I mean, what's the name of their high school football team? The Constipated Conquerors?"

They both stared at me as if I was out of my mind.

"Actually, Dave, there is a town in Queens called Flushing," Hannah said softly.

I felt my face turning red. "Oh."

The woman talked and talked and talked about her cat.

We heard a car honking. I went to the window and looked out. There was an angry driver in a car behind the truck wanting to get past us.

"We should move the truck," I said to Hannah.

"I'll take care of it, okay?"

I followed her outside.

"Hey, you got a problem?" she yelled at the irritated driver.

"You're blockin' the street!"

"Go around on the other side!"

"There's a car parked on the other side!"

She walked into the street to look at the parked car, then self-righteously announced, "Sir, that is not my car!"

The man went ballistic.

Hannah held up two fingers. "Two minutes! We'll be done in two minutes!"

We both hustled back inside the house. "We'd love to hear more about your cat, but right now we've got to get our truck out of the way," I said.

The man continued to honk. We picked up the table and walked it outside and loaded it into the back of the truck.

Hannah called out to the driver. "We've got six chairs to move also and then we'll be done. Thank you for your patience."

That made him even madder. He started swearing at us.

"That's it!" Hannah said to me as we walked back inside. "He's crossed the line."

"So?" I asked.

"We take our own sweet time."

We made a couple of trips back into the house and finally had the chairs loaded into the back of the truck. Then we got into the cab of the truck and moved slowly down the street. The man followed about six inches behind us, honking his horn, revving his engine, and swerving to the right and then to the left, looking for an opening where he could pass us, but the street was too narrow.

Finally we came to a light. When we turned right, the driver behind us laid rubber as he screeched away.

"That's how we do it out here," Hannah said to me with a big grin.

The closer we got to the store, the more worried Hannah looked. "So, we both learned something today. You learned how to be self-assertive and not let people push you around. And I learned that you're unlike any guy I've ever known. Sorry for freaking you out. I wasn't serious about the offer, okay? Do you believe me?"

"I believe you."

"Good. So who are you going to tell about this? I mean if someone asks you how work went today, what are you going to tell 'em?"

"Nothing about that."

"Promise?"

"I promise."

She gave a sigh of relief. "Good. Thanks. Because I'm not like that, okay? I don't want people thinking I am. You won't tell Murray either, right?"

"No."

"What about the people in your church?"

"No."

"Thank you. I'm really sorry. It just never occurred to me that a guy would turn down sex because of some promise he'd made to God. I've never heard of a guy doing that. This book, the one you told me about, what's the name of it again?"

"The Book of Mormon."

"It must be some book to cause a twenty-something guy to live without any action."

"It's an awesome book. I can get you a copy if you want."

"Maybe sometime. I'm not saying I'll read it though, but it might be okay to have on my bookshelf."

"Okay."

"One more thing," she said.

"Yes?"

"I know I've pretty much botched things up, but you think it's possible we could be friends? Like we could go out on my boat sometime? I could teach you how to sail."

"I'd like that."

"I'm just going to take a wild guess at this, but Sundays are probably out for you to go sailing, right?"

"That's right."

"Maybe sometime after work then."

"Yeah, sure. I'd like that."

"To have a friend who's actually a nice guy, that would be a first for me."

"You deserve that."

"That's what I've always thought too."

We pulled into the parking stall behind the store. "So, we're friends now?" she asked.

"You bet."

I got off work at seven, grabbed a sandwich, and hurried over to church for institute class. The class was taught by Elder and Sister Scott, a senior missionary couple from Utah.

Because I got there before anyone else, I had a chance to talk with the Scotts.

Three round tables were set up in the Relief Society room. When Megan came, she sat with me. Elder and Sister Scott went into the kitchen to cut up a pineapple for treats after the class.

"How did your day go?" I asked Megan.

"The housekeeper is turning the kids against me. She told them they don't have to do anything I say."

"That's awful."

"And then she told me I couldn't do a wash because it was her day, but she only had one load, and she kept saying she was going to run it, but she never did, so then when Estelle got home, she was all mad at me because I hadn't done the wash, and she told me I had to stay there tonight and do the wash."

"Oh, no. What did you do?"

Megan went on for another five minutes and then Sabra, another nanny, came and sat down and complained about her day.

Before long we had six girls at our table. And me.

When Antonio came in and saw me sitting with six girls, he couldn't let it pass. "So what's the deal here, Dave? One guy and six girls?"

"Be my guest."

He sat down and listened for as long as he could stand it, then blurted out, "Look, if you don't like your job, just quit! Nobody's making you stay there."

"You never listen to us, Antonio."

"I'm listening to you now."

Antonio sat around for a while, but it was very frustrating for him to just listen without giving solutions, like I was doing, so he moved to another table.

I was amazed how well listening works. I felt like I'd cracked a secret code and that it would be very useful to me my whole life. It still worked even if I couldn't really relate to the problems these girls were having with the dysfunctional parents they worked for.

But then something unexpected happened. It wasn't just a technique I'd learned that helped me talk with girls. Suddenly I wanted to be like a big brother they could come to when they needed to talk.

When Abbie showed up, she came over to me and said, "Can I talk to you?"

"Of course."

We walked outside to a far corner of the church parking lot.

"I need some advice."

"Okay."

"Late last night Eldon came by and we went to a diner. I gave him every chance, but he still didn't tell me about Elizabeth. I don't know what to do. Should I bring it up to him?"

"Give him a little more time. He's a good guy. He'll get around to it. Maybe even tonight."

"Something else. Last night he kissed me for the first time."

The thought of her kissing him gave me a weird feeling, but I managed to say, "That's good, actually."

"But then later he apologized. He said he shouldn't have done it. What does that mean?"

"It means he feels guilty he hasn't told you about Elizabeth."

"I let him kiss me. Do you know why?"

"No."

"Because I was hoping it would make him forget about Elizabeth. Do you think that might happen?"

"Probably not."

"What am I going to do, Dave?"

"I don't know. The guy's an idiot."

I held her in my arms while she complained about Eldon. Talk about mixed messages. Even though on the surface I wanted her to be happy, in some perverse way I hoped she'd continue to be disappointed by Eldon because it would mean she'd come to me for support.

And talk about bad timing. When Eldon showed up, we were in his headlights as he pulled in.

He got out of his car.

Abbie walked toward him. "We were just talking."

As I walked toward Eldon on my way to the church, he seemed almost cheerful to have caught us together. It gave him the perfect reason to distance himself from Abbie.

"She knows," I said softly as I passed by him.

He nodded. "Okay. Thanks for telling me."

I went inside and stood in the doorway and watched Abbie and Eldon. A few minutes later they got into Eldon's car and drove away.

I wondered if Abbie would need me later that night. I knew it would be hard for her to hear about Elizabeth.

And then I went to institute class.

After class Megan asked to speak to me.

We went across the street to the park and sat on a bench. "Dave, I hate to see you get hurt. You're wasting your time on Abbie. She likes you as a friend, but that's all."

"That could change, though."

"No, that's just it. It won't change. She tells me that every time I talk to her."

We took a walk. I talked about Abbie. Megan was a good listener.

Somewhere on that walk, she gave me a hug to help me get over Abbie. I misinterpreted it somehow, or maybe because I was feeling such a sense of loss with Abbie. Whatever the reason was, I kissed her.

Twice, actually.

After our second kiss, she said, "Dave?"

I wasn't exactly sure what "Dave?" meant. Surprise, shock, or disappointment? Either way I felt bad. *Why did I do that?* I thought.

"We'd better go back," she said.

"Yeah, we'd better. Sorry, about, you know, what happened."

"That's okay. I just wasn't expecting it, that's all."

I knew I was in trouble. Megan would tell Abbie.

Sure enough. About eleven that night, after I'd gone to bed, Abbie called me. "So what's going on between you and Megan?" she asked.

"Nothing."

"Nothing? Really? Then why were you making out with her tonight?"

I had no idea what the acceptable answer to that question was. I needed to stall for time. "We were *not* making out. Okay, I might have kissed her, but it was no big deal."

"It was to her. She told me she thinks you're falling for her. Are you?"

"No, of course not. I love you."

"We're not talking about me! We're talking about Megan. Good grief, Dave, what were you thinking?"

"I don't know. It just happened."

"Things like that don't 'just happen.' Do you have any idea how old she is?"

"No."

"She's eighteen. You remember when you and I used to babysit my sister. Well, Megan and Courtney are the same age."

"Wow, that is young."

"So when are you going to talk to her?" Abbie asked.

"Why do I have to talk to her?"

"Because she thinks you like her. She's talking about going to BYU—Idaho in the fall so you two can continue to see each other."

"Nothing wrong with that. Lots of people go there to school."

"Dave, wake up! I just got off the phone with her. She actually used the M word."

I panicked. "M . . . m . . . m . . . marriage?"

"Yes. What did you expect?"

"It was, like, one kiss."

"Two, actually. She kept count."

"Okay, it was two kisses, but the first one was just a test kiss."

"A *test* kiss? What are you talking about?"

"You know, like before a concert when the sound man checks the mikes. 'Testing, testing, testing.' That's what I was doing at first. So only the second one counts."

"You're out of your mind. I'm serious. This is not like you. I am so disappointed in you."

"Yeah, I know. Me, too. I don't know what happened. I'll talk to her. What should I say?"

"Tell her the truth."

"You mean tell her the only reason I kissed her is because I'm so bummed out about you?"

"Don't bring me into this! I didn't tell you to kiss her!"

"Okay then. Give me a reason why I kissed her because I can't think of a single one."

"Maybe it's because you have no moral character and, if you could, you'd go around kissing every girl you met."

I had to think about that one for a while. "No, that's not it."

"You've known Megan less than a week. And you just got off your mission. What is wrong with you, anyway? It's like you're falling apart."

Because Abbie was making me mad, I sort of lost control. "I know what I'll tell Megan. How about if I tell her I'm waiting for a girl on a mission? But to be fair to this other girl, I need to wait until she gets back before I'll really know what to do. How about if I tell her that? You think she'd be dumb enough to buy that?"

After a long silence, she said, "I didn't think you could be so cruel. Good-bye." She hung up.

I've really done it this time, I thought. *What do I do now?*

I called back, but she wouldn't answer. Abbie and Megan were probably talking to each other. They would come to an agreement on how they were going to treat me from then on, and there probably was nothing I could do to change that.

There was a good chance I'd just lost two friends.

Abbie had made me even more ashamed of myself for kissing Megan. From past times when I'd messed up, I knew I'd be beating myself up all night about it. And I wouldn't get any sleep.

There was nobody I could talk to about this. That's the trouble with being a guy.

I'd messed up once again. And just like all the previous times when I'd done something I wasn't proud of, it brought me to my knees.

I told Heavenly Father what I'd done, and why it was a mistake, and that I felt bad for not being a better example to Megan of someone who has served a mission. I asked him to forgive me and to help me do better in the future. I asked him to help me have the courage to talk to Megan and apologize.

In the middle of my prayer, Nathan showed up. I heard the door being unlocked and stood up so he wouldn't know I'd been praying.

He looked exhausted.

"I was wondering if you were locked up in the hospital," I said.

"I was wondering that, too."

He went to the fridge and began to pull out some sandwich makings.

"How long have you been in the singles branch?" I asked.

"Seven years."

"Any advice you can give me about, well, kissing girls in the branch?"

"Oh, yeah. Never kiss any of them."

Talk about an answer to my prayers. "Why not?"

"In this branch, anytime you kiss a girl, everyone will know about it the next day. They'll all have you married off in their minds. And if you want to see someone else, they'll think you're a player. So don't kiss. It's too risky."

"But there are times when it's okay to kiss a girl, right?"

"Yeah, sure. The day you call your folks to tell them you've been dating this girl and you really like her and you think you two might get married, then you can kiss the girl. It's a simple rule, but it will save you a lot of grief."

"Are you speaking from experience?"

Nathan smiled. "Afraid so. At first I'd date a girl for a few weeks and then break up with her. That made everyone mad at me. The nice thing about being here is that people move in and out all the time. It's like a giant conveyor belt. I quit dating and just began hanging out with everyone at branch activities. After a few months my bad reputation vanished. And now I make friends but don't hurt anyone's feelings. It works for me. I'm not ready to get married, but I do like being around girls. And it's a bonus that new ones keep coming."

"Thanks. I'll try that."

"It's the best way. Don't get me wrong. I'll get married some day, but first I have my residency, and then maybe a couple of years at a research hospital associated with a university. It seems that the best time to get married is always about two years away. That's the way it was when I was just off my mission, and seven years later it's still about two years away. But I'm in no hurry. Once you're married, it's forever; so the way I look at it, take your time. Once kids start coming, you lose a lot of options about what kind of a car you're going to drive, what places you're going to go on a vacation, and how you're going to spend your money. I'm not ready to own an SUV."

"Yeah, I see what you mean."

I decided to take Abbie's advice and apologize to Megan. So I called her.

She picked up. "Dave?"

"Yeah. Are you up? I was wondering if I could talk to you tonight? Give me directions and I'll come to where you are."

Forty-five minutes later I pulled into the driveway of the home where she was a nanny. It was a large house built on stilts in Westhampton Beach, with the Atlantic Ocean in the back and Moriches Bay a hundred yards away in front. It was built alongside a road lined with huge mansions.

As soon as I pulled up in front, she came out to the curb.

When I got out of the pickup, she said, "You want to take a walk along the beach?"

"Yeah, sure."

I wasn't in the mood for a long walk in the moonlight along the beach. After walking a couple of minutes, I stopped. "There's something I need to say."

"Okay."

"I apologize for kissing you tonight."

She nodded. "It *was* too soon, wasn't it?"

"Yeah, *way* too soon. I've decided that from now on I'm not going to kiss a girl unless I've decided I want to marry her."

"That sounds like a good rule."

"Nathan told me about it. It's what he does."

"So it's the Nathan Rule then, right?" she asked.

"I guess so."

"Can I ask you a question? Why did you kiss me?"

"You're so beautiful."

"So?"

Because of the way she said it, I was pretty sure Abbie had coached her.

"You're right. That's no excuse."

"The way I see it, Dave, time is on my side."

What does she mean by that? I thought.

"My mom got married just after she turned twenty."

I gasped. My first instinct was to run away and never come back. But I didn't. "We'd better go back. It's getting late."

"Of course."

On the way back, mainly because of bad lighting, our hands brushed each other, and the next thing I knew we were holding hands.

Let go of her stupid hand! I thought.

No, you'll hurt her feelings!

Forget about her feelings. She's going to call Abbie and tell her about this.

That was enough for me. I let go.

We made it back to her driveway.

"Thank you for coming to see me," she said. "I'm glad we had a chance to talk about what happened."

"Yeah, me, too. Oh, one more thing. About us holding hands. That was just a safety precaution . . . because it was so dark out."

Megan started laughing. "Safety precaution? You mean like when you wanted to put sunblock on Abbie's back. Was that a safety precaution, too?"

She laughed all the way into the house. And it sounded a little like Abbie's witch laugh. Where else could sweet Megan have learned to laugh like that?

Abbie was poisoning this poor girl's mind.

On my way home, I complained to myself that it wasn't fair. I had done everything I could think of to get the guilt to go away. I'd prayed, I'd talked to Nathan, and I'd adopted his rule. I'd driven out to see Megan, and I'd apologized. But so what? I was still not going to be able to sleep because Abbie was going to find out I'd held Megan's hand. She'd be all over me for that, too.

To avoid Abbie's disapproval, I called her. It was one o'clock in the morning.

"Yeah?" she said sleepily.

"I apologized to Megan."

"Oh."

"I went to where she lives. We walked along the beach. On the way back, it was very dark, I was afraid she'd fall, so I held her hand as a safety precaution. But it was only for a short time and then I let go."

"Oh."

"You were sleeping, right?" I asked.

"Yeah."

"Okay, well, I'm pretty much caught up in the apology department then."

"Okay."

"See you later."

"Good-bye."

That went well, I thought. I should talk to her more often when she's asleep.

* * *

The next day Hannah asked if I wanted to go sailing with her after work.

"Oh, yes! Thank you! Thank you! Please, please take me sailing!"

I was desperate to get away from the drama of the singles branch.

CHAPTER SIX

After work the next day I took a shower, shaved, got dressed, and then drove to Port Washington to the dock where Hannah kept her boat.

She'd given me directions to where it was docked, but as I approached the end of the dock, the only boat I could see was a huge yacht. But once I passed the yacht, I saw a small sailboat.

Hannah was topside firing up her grill. She looked up at me and smiled. "You're just in time. Welcome aboard *Blue Skies.*"

Hannah had done something with her hair and eyes since I'd seen her at the hardware store. It was also only the second time I'd seen her out of the Ace Hardware vest she always wore at work. I thought about telling her she looked good but then decided against it. To tell a girl you like the way she looks is like walking into a minefield. It's best never to bring up the subject.

"How do you like your hamburger?" she asked.

"Well done. For me that means not even a hint of red on the inside. I like everything to be dark brown. It's the way we eat 'em in Idaho."

"You mean Iowa, right?" she joked, still refusing to admit there was a state named Idaho. She took her hamburger off the grill and put it on her plate.

After waiting another minute, she asked, "How about now?"

"No, it's got to be really cooked."

She turned her head away in disgust and handed me the turner. "Do what you want, just don't make me look on. I'll be in the cabin. Bring your burnt offering with you when you've finished."

She went down the steps into the cabin.

"Nice boat!" I called after her.

I could hear her moving around down there as she answered. "It was my grandfather's. He used to take me out in it all the time. My dad was a long-haul trucker driver. He died in a wreck when I was only ten, and Grandpa sort of filled in. We were very close, and after he died, I found out he'd put me in his will to have the boat. It's the best gift I've ever received. Every time I come here, it reminds me of him. I guess he knew that would happen. Everyone else in my family told me to sell the boat to get some money for college. But you know what? I didn't care about the money. Besides, it's not that expensive of a boat. He bought it second-hand as it was. And he had it for as long as I can remember, so you know, like twenty years. But he kept it up good, and I'm trying to do the same thing."

She came back on deck.

"I can see why you come here after work."

"Yeah. Even if I don't take it out, it's great just being here. Also, it's been a great experience learning to sail. At first I had trouble getting back to the dock, but now I can . . . usually."

"Just as long as we don't have to sail clear around the world to get back."

"Actually, that is how I get back. We'll be gone about a year. After we run out of food, we'll catch what we eat. You did bring a change of clothes, right? And a journal. So when they find our dead, bloated bodies they'll know how we spent our last days at sea."

I slid my burger off the grill and onto my bun, doused it with ketchup, and we went down a couple of stairs to enter the cabin.

We sat across from each other at a small table. She looked at my burger and scowled. "I've had that ketchup bottle for a year, and you've pretty much used it up with one hamburger."

"So?"

"Ketchup is a condiment."

"What exactly does that mean?" I asked.

She cuffed me on my shoulder. "It means it's not the main course, Moron! There is a hamburger somewhere in that pile of ketchup, right? Don't they teach you people anything in Iowa?"

"Idaho." I took a big bite. "Oh, that's so good! Let me fix you one."

"Fuhgetabout it!"

I looked over at her and smiled.

"What?"

"Thanks for inviting me here. So far I'm having a very good time."

"Really? I just called you a moron."

"I know, but you didn't mean it."

"You're right. I didn't."

"So you come out here a lot?" I asked.

"Almost every day after work. I usually stay until a little after ten."

"Why ten?"

"I have a roommate, and she has this guy she's seeing, and he comes over a lot. He works days at a parts store and nights as a security guard. He goes to work at ten every night, and it's better for me not to be in my apartment when they're together, if you know what I mean."

"Oh."

"So I hole up here and wait for him to clear out."

"You could tell them to get their own place."

"Yeah, I could." She cleared her throat. "Except she's my sister."

"Why don't they get married?"

"Their families would never accept that. He's Jewish, and we're Catholic."

"So the families would rather have them living together than be married?"

"Both families pretend that nothing's going on. But those two are living like they're married. Except he only stays a few hours every day. That's why I come here after work."

We were both about finished with our burgers. "You want another one?" she asked.

"No, thanks."

"Because I could burn one for you. Of course, I'd first have to alert the Coast Guard so they wouldn't freak out about all the smoke pouring from my boat, but, hey, I'm willing to do that, just so you can have the kind of burnt-to-the-crisp burgers you grew up on in Iowa."

"Idaho. You're very considerate."

"Well, then, you ready to go to work, Sailor?"

"Aye, aye, Captain."

She laughed. "Oh, I love that: 'Captain'!" You suppose you could do that at work?"

"No."

She got up. "Let's take this thing out and see what she can do."

We went topside. Hannah made her way to the back of the boat and bent over a small outboard motor. "Untie the mooring ropes while I see if I can get this thing started."

She pulled the starting rope a couple of times, and the little motor sputtered to life. Then she maneuvered us away from the dock.

A few minutes later we were free and clear in the bay. She killed the motor, showed me how to unfurl the sails, and we slowly began to glide through the water. The only sound was the hiss of the hull cutting through the water and the waves slapping against the sides of the boat.

I'd been in small boats before on Idaho lakes, but with them there were always the fumes and noise of the motor to remind you that you were an intruder.

But this was different. It was like we were a part of nature—that we were like the fish and the seagulls and the ocean breeze. That we belonged there.

"This is so great!" I said, keeping my voice down so as not to disturb the solitude.

"You want to take the helm?" she asked.

"What does that mean?"

"It means do you want to steer the boat?"

"Oh, yeah, sure. Is there anything I need to know?"

"Just keep us going the same direction."

"Sure, I can do that."

"I'm going down to the cabin."

I panicked. "You are? Why?"

"So you'll know what it's like to be out here all by yourself."

"What if a huge ship comes along and we're heading right for it?"

"Turn," she said, brushing past me on the way back to the cabin.

"I'm not qualified to do this," I called out.

No answer.

I couldn't see any collision coming up. So I relaxed.

Ten minutes later I was hooked on sailing.

Hannah came topside carrying two small plates of dessert.

"So where are we now?"

"Just off the coast of China," I said.

"Sounds about right. Ow ya duen? You duen okay?"

"I'm having a great time!"

She handed me a plate. "Want some New York cheesecake?"

I looked at it and scowled. "No thanks."

"You got a problem with cheesecake? What's the matta wit' chew?"

"I had New York pizza when I first got here. All it had on it was cheese. The way I see it, people here don't know what tastes good."

"Hey, eat the cheesecake! I made it for you."

"You made this?"

"Didn't I just say that? You going to eat it or not?"

"Yeah, sure, you want to steer?" I asked.

"Steer? Say, 'Take the helm.'"

I shrugged. "Same thing."

"It's not the same thing. Say it."

"Do you want to take the helm?"

"Yeah, now shut up and eat your cheesecake."

I took a bite. It was a little more cheesy than what I was used to, and not as sweet, but other than that, it was good.

"I like it."

"Of course you do. It's from New York."

After another half hour, she said we needed to head back while we still had some light.

She let me take the helm until we entered the harbor and then she took over.

We passed a large docked yacht.

"See that boat? It belongs to Everett Brown. He and I graduated from high school together. He married a friend of mine. Her name is Catherine. I used to call her Cat. His dad paid his way through college. He was a very good student. And then he got married. Now he works for his dad's investment firm. He and Cat have one kid. Sometimes when I come out here, I see them on their boat. They always look so happy and rich. Not a bad combination, right? Sometimes I think I should drop by and talk to them, but I never do."

"Why not?"

"Because I haven't got a degree and I work in a hardware store and I'm not even seeing anyone. At night I sit huddled in my little boat eating tuna out of a can and waiting for ten o'clock so I can go home and open the windows and get the smell of my sister's loverboy out of the apartment." She shook her head. "Somehow I don't think Everett and Cat would be overly impressed with the way my life is going right now."

"It doesn't matter what they think. It matters what you think. Would you say you're happy?"

"I don't know. Sometimes maybe. At other times, I would definitely say no. It's like my whole life is on-hold. Ten years from now am I still going to be doing the same thing? Maybe so. That really depresses me."

"Do you want to be like Everett and Cat?"

"Not really." She sighed. "I'm not sure what I want. I just seem to be in some kind of limbo. Sometimes I'm ashamed of the way I'm living. Does that mean I'm unhappy? I'm not sure."

A few minutes later we docked the boat. While she washed and dried and stowed the dinnerware, I told her I'd be right back. I ran to my truck, grabbed a copy of the Book of Mormon, and hurried back to the dock.

She saw the book in my hand. "What's going on here?"

"Before we leave, there's something I want you to read. It will only take five minutes."

"I guess I could give you five more minutes of my precious time."

We went down into the cabin. She lit a kerosene lantern and placed it on the table. And then she saw the title of the book. "Dave, c'mon, don't do this to me."

"Hold on. This'll just take a minute." I read the title page to her, then turned to the Introduction. "How about we each read a paragraph? I'll read the first, okay?"

"Five minutes you said, right?"

"Maybe ten."

She sighed. "All right, go."

After three minutes, she stopped me. "Why are we doing this?"

"Because you're not happy."

"I didn't say I wasn't happy. I said I wasn't sure how to answer the question. Sometimes I'm happy. Besides, what has this book got to do with being happy?"

"Give it some time and you'll see."

We got all the way through to where the only thing left to do was to start chapter 1 of First Nephi.

I shut the book and handed it to her. "Keep reading. After you've read some more, we'll talk. Now there's just one more thing. We need to pray and ask God if it's true."

"Why?"

"So he can answer your prayer."

"What makes you think he'll do that?"

I read verses 4 and 5 from chapter 10 of Moroni, then asked, "Will you offer the prayer?"

She snorted. "Fughetabout it. I don't know how to pray."

I explained the steps of prayer and bowed my head, waiting for her to pray.

There were a few moments of silence, then she begain, "God . . . I mean . . ." She touched my hand. "What'd you call him?"

"Father in Heaven."

"Father in Heaven, ow ya duen? Dave here says you'll tell me if this book is true, whatever that means. So here's the deal. I'm not a big reader, so if I actually go to a lot of work to read this, you'd better give me an answer, that's all I got to say." She stopped. "I'm done," she said.

"You didn't actually ask."

"I asked."

"No, you demanded."

She shook her head and closed her eyes. "God, please tell me if it's true, if it is, although I don't personally believe books are true. I mean they're just books, right? I mean there's no way, right? Angels, plates, who makes this stuff up, anyway?"

We both opened our eyes and looked at each other.

And smiled.

"Okay, okay, I get it." She closed her eyes again. "Look, if this book is true, let me know. Is that asking too much? I mean, it's not like I've been bothering you much lately, right? Anyway, that's my prayer. Take it or leave it because I'm not doing this again. By the way, you need to do something about Dave here. He's so pushy about his religion. That's all I got to say. Amen."

"In the name of Jesus Christ, Amen," I corrected her.

"Yeah, what he said." She stood up. "This is beyond creepy. I feel like I've been to a revival. Let's pass the collection plate and then get out of here."

She locked up the boat, and I walked her to her car.

"So, what do you think?" I asked.

"About what? New York cheesecake? I like it very much. And you would too, if you had any taste buds."

"No. About what we read."

"I don't know. If this really happened, how come I never heard about it?"

"Did missionaries ever come to your door?"

"I don't know. Maybe . . . once when I was like six or seven. When they were knocking on our door, my mom looked out the window and saw them and told me not to open the door."

"That's how we tell the world."

"Going door to door? No wonder nobody's ever heard of it."

"It's not the best way. The best way is for members to tell their friends about what we believe."

"So that's what you did tonight? Why?"

"Because you're my friend . . . and because this is the most important thing in my life . . . and because it makes me happy . . . and because it will make you happy, too."

"Yeah, whatever." We were in the parking lot. "Well, see you tomorrow."

"Yeah. Thanks for taking me on *Blue Skies*."

"Did you really have a good time?" she asked.

"Yeah, I did. I had a great time."

"Did you have to pray about whether or not you had a good time?" she asked.

"No."

"See, that's the difference between what you love and what I love."

"Maybe so. Good night."

"Whatever."

I was happy all the way back to my apartment. Just before going to bed, I knelt down by the couch I slept on and said a prayer for Hannah.

The next morning, when Hannah showed up for work, she walked up to me with a silly grin on her face. "Guess how much I've read?"

"I don't know."

"I'm on page forty-one."

"You are? I can't believe you read that much!"

"It wasn't too bad. My favorite part was where Nephi found that guy passed out drunk and then whacked him with his own sword and then stole the plates. Just one question though, Nephi's the good guy, right?" She pronounced his name "Neh-fee."

"It's 'Nee-fi,'" I corrected her. "He didn't want to kill him. The angel told him to do it."

"Isn't that what every psycho killer says? God made me do it." She gave me a big smile. She was obviously having a good time at my expense.

"You read enough to know what kind of person Nephi is."

"Yeah, he does seem like a good guy later on. It just seems like a really strange way to start a book, that's all."

"If would be if Joseph Smith had written it."

"You probably think you've made a really good point, don't you?" she asked with a grin.

"Yeah, I do."

"We're going to have fun with this, aren't we? Me shooting down the book, and you defending it."

"Are you praying about this?"

"I don't see that's any of your business. If I pray, it's between me and God. He and I don't need you prying into our private business."

I took that as a yes.

"You want to go sailing tonight?" she asked.

"Yeah, I would. Maybe we can read a little more together."

She shrugged. "Maybe so. It's not that bad. I also liked the part where Nephi stretched forth his hand and shocked his brothers. Now that's my kind of religion. Can you shock people like that?"

"No."

"That's a relief. I'll keep giving you a hard time then."

It was a good day at work. Hannah and I kept running into each other in the aisles, and every time we did, we gave each other a big smile. It wasn't flirting though. It was something else.

Around two o'clock we had kind of a slack period where there were no customers in the store. Hannah and Murray and I were standing up front by the cash register machine.

"So how's the new kid working out?" Murray asked Hannah.

"With my expert coaching, he might work out, but just barely."

"What are you talking about? I'm way better than you are now," I said.

"No way! I am the Picasso of Plumbing! The Rembrandt of Repair! The Einstein of Electricity! People come from miles around for my advice on their home projects."

"Maybe so, but that's only because they don't know about me," I said.

"Let's see how good you are, Rookie."

"Any time."

Hannah turned to Murray. "You be a customer with a problem. You tell us what part you need and we'll see who can find it the fastest."

Murray looked over at me and smiled. "We'll need a stop watch."

I ran down one of the aisles and a short time later brought back a stop watch. "Dave one, Hannah zero."

"Wait just a minute!" Hannah complained. "That doesn't count. We hadn't started."

"You snooze, you lose," I said.

"It doesn't matter. I'll give you one point. It's the only one you're going to get. Go ahead, Murray."

"I need a 3/32-inch, flathead Phillips machine screw, one-inch long."

We both ran down the same aisle. I got there first, but as I pulled out the drawer, Hannah shoved me away, grabbed the screw, and started running back to the cash register. I tried to catch up with her, but she was too fast for me.

"I am the champion!" she shouted.

"You pushed me."

"Did little Davey get his feelings hurt by the mean girl?"

"I'm just saying if this is only about who can shove the most, then it's not fair."

"Why's that?"

"Because I'm not going to shove you around."

"Why not?"

"Because you're a girl."

She slugged me on the arm and began to dance around me with her fists up. "Maybe so, but I'm a mean girl from New York."

But then a customer came into the store and we had to stop.

After work we stopped by a grocery store and bought salmon fillets and a package of frozen fried potatoes and then drove out to her boat.

It was overcast and looked like it might rain, but we were not about to let that stop us.

After we got out a ways she let me take the helm, so she could grill our salmon.

"I've been really happy today," she said. "What about you?"

"Yeah, I have."

"Also, I decided something."

"What?"

"I can't stay with my sister anymore. If it was totally her apartment, I wouldn't care what she did, but it's my apartment, too. The way it is now I should be paying a lot less than I am because I can only be there half the time."

"Yeah, you're right."

"But that's not the only reason. It's depressing to me to come home after he's been there. Why do you suppose that is?"

"I'm not sure. Why do you think it's depressing?" I asked.

"She thinks he'll eventually marry her, but I'm pretty sure that's the last thing on his mind."

"You're right. It's not fair to her."

"No, it isn't. It's better the way your church teaches. Nothing before and then marriage and then, it's like, 'Let the loving begin!'"

"Yeah, it is better."

"You want your fish burnt to a crisp?" she asked.

"Yeah, pretty much."

"You are so weird."

"Probably so."

"It's a nice kind of weird though."

When she brought me my plate, we looked into each other's eyes and I thought *What is happening here?*

But only for a moment and then I remembered how much hassle it was to get involved with a girl. You kiss a girl and then you spend hours trying to explain why you did it. And if you answer the girl's questions truthfully you end up in more trouble.

Add to this that because we worked together we'd see each other after we broke up.

I'd learned my lesson. From now on I was going to do what

Nathan suggested and only kiss a girl after I'd called my folks and told them this was the girl I intended to marry some day.

But in the back of my mind I started to wonder what it would be like if Hannah joined the Church and we got married and moved back to live in Idaho while my folks went on a mission. We could both work at my dad's store. I'd never known a girl who loved hardware as much as I did. I knew my dad would love her. I wasn't sure about my mom, though, but I figured if we had enough kids, she'd be okay with the mom of her grandchildren.

It's funny how thoughts like that go through your mind so soon after meeting someone. Or at least through my mind.

"You want to go to church with me Sunday?" I asked while we were eating.

"Yeah, sure. Why not? Where is your church?"

"Well, you've got a choice. The closest place to here is probably the Little Neck Ward. It starts at nine and gets out at noon."

"Three hours of church?"

"About an hour of church and then an hour of a Sunday School class, and then an hour where the men go one place for instruction. We call that priesthood. The women get together for a lesson, too. We call that Relief Society."

"And you do this every week?"

"Yeah."

"And you enjoy it?"

"Most of the time."

"Okay, I'll try it. Is Little Neck where you go to church?"

"No. The church at Little Neck is more of a normal ward, you know with families, usually lots of little kids. I've been going to a young single adult branch in Meadowview. They're all single and somewhere in age between eighteen and thirty."

She thought about if for a long time and then said, "I like kids."

"Me, too."

I was relieved she didn't want to go to the singles branch. I'd had it with the saga of Abbie and Eldon, and I didn't want to see Megan looking hurt because I was with another girl, or asking why I hadn't called her lately, or having to deal with Antonio's sarcasm.

I needed a break.

We ate and talked, sailed for an hour, and then came back and docked. And then we went below for scripture study.

"You want to pray first?" she asked.

"Yeah. This is your place. You're in charge. Who do you want to say the prayer?"

"I want you to pray," she said.

"Can we kneel down?"

"Will that help?"

"It helps."

"Okay, whatever you say."

We knelt down. All I intended was a simple little prayer, you know, we thank thee, we ask thee, and the closing.

I did pretty good on the thanking part, but when I started on the asking, I got a little carried away. "Please bless Hannah as she reads the Book of Mormon to know by the influence of the Holy Ghost that it is true, that Jesus Christ is our Savior and Redeemer, and that Joseph Smith was a prophet. Bless her to find peace and joy in her life."

I suddenly realized that Heavenly Father loved Hannah. For some reason, I'd never thought of that before. I'm not the kind of person who likes to show emotion in front of others. I'm like my dad that way. But this time I just couldn't help it.

I didn't want to totally lose it in front of her, so I ended the prayer.

"That was good," she said softly, as we got up from our knees and sat down at the table.

We read to the end of First Nephi. When we finished, I looked at my watch. It was ten-thirty. "It's late. We'd better stop for now."

We stood up and looked at each other.

"This has been good," she said. "Can we do it again tomorrow night?"

"Yeah, sure. Let me bring some Idaho potatoes. Idaho has the best spuds on earth."

She laughed. "Are we gonna eat 'em or salute 'em?"

"Both."

"You people in Iowa have so little to brag about, don't you? You knew you had to pick something, so you chose, of all things, potatoes? That is so sad."

We had arrived at the parking area.

But we didn't know what to do. I thought about giving her a hug but didn't know if I should or not.

"Dave?"

"Yeah."

"Thank you for being so nice to me. I've never known a guy like you before. Well, let me just say I'm very . . . well . . . grateful." She shook her head and said, "I don't think I've ever used that word before."

"Thanks. You know, this reminds me of what I loved about teaching the gospel on my mission."

She glanced at her watch. "Well . . . it's late."

"Yeah."

I unlocked the pickup and opened the door. "See you at work?"

"Yeah. See you."

I followed her to her apartment, waited for her to unlock the door, then flashed my headlights and drove off.

At a stoplight, I looked at my cell phone. I'd left it in the pickup because I didn't want to be taking calls while I was with Hannah.

There was a voice mail from Abbie and another one from Megan.

Abbie said she needed to talk to me tonight and for me to call her no matter how late it was.

She picked up on the first ring. "Dave?"

"You called?"

"I did. Can we talk? It's real important."

"You mean on the phone?"

"No, can I meet you somewhere?" she asked.

"It's kind of late."

"I know. Where have you been all night?"

"I went sailing with someone from work."

"What's his name?"

"Actually, it's a she, and her name is Hannah."

I could almost hear Abbie thinking before she said, "So you were sailing clear to eleven o'clock. How could you see where you were going?"

"We were reading in the Book of Mormon. She's going to go to church with me Sunday."

"Oh, well, I want to meet her."

"We're not going to the singles branch."

"Why not?"

"She wants to go to a family ward, and, besides, it's closer."

"So when am I going to meet her?"

"When did you suddenly become my mother?" I asked.

"Like I do for all my friends, I care about what happens to you."

"Why do you need to talk to me?"

"It's about Eldon. I need your advice."

"Can't you just ask your question over the phone?" I asked.

"No, I can't. C'mon, Dave, help me out here. I'm really confused. You're the only guy I can trust."

"Then why won't you marry me?"

There was silence on the line.

I felt guilty for bringing it up again. "I'm sorry. That was dumb of me to say. Look, I'll meet you wherever you want."

"You know that diner on the corner in Meadowview? Can you meet me there?"

"Give me fifteen minutes."

"All right. Thanks."

On my way there I called Megan.

It took her three rings to answer. "Hello . . ." she said sleepily.

"This is Dave. You called and left a message."

"Oh, yeah. I just wanted you to know I finished my application for BYU—Idaho and submitted it online. You will be going there in the fall, right?"

"Uh . . . sure."

"Have you applied?"

"I'll probably work for my dad in the fall and just take one or two classes."

"That's okay. As long as you're there. Where were you tonight?"

"I went sailing with a girl I work with at the store."

"Oh." She sounded disappointed.

"She's just a friend. I'm trying to get her to listen to the missionaries."

"Is that all there is between you and her?"

"Yeah."

"Good. Oh, I told my folks about you. They want to meet you."

I felt sick. "Really?" Now more than ever I regretted having kissed her.

"Oh, I called up and talked to one of my favorite teachers from last year. I told her about you too."

"You talked to one of your teachers from high school?"

"Yes, of course, silly. What other teachers have I ever had?"

That depressed me even more. When I was with Megan, it was easy to forget she'd just graduated from high school. But this made it very clear how young she was.

"Well, it's late. I'd better let you go," I finally said. The only person I knew who told people she'd better let them go was my mom. It depressed me that I was beginning to sound like her.

But it did the trick. And a short time later I got off the phone with her.

This wasn't all Megan's fault, though. It was mine, too. When I was with her, I got distracted by how gorgeous she was. And when that happened, my mind left me. I wasn't proud of that, but it was what had happened.

A few minutes later I pulled into the diner. Abbie's car was already there.

She wasn't in her car so I went inside and found her sitting in a booth in the corner of the place.

"You come here often, Stranger?" she asked with a slight smile.

"Not often enough if you're here all the time," I said. She looked good. To be with her was like being home, where everything is comfortable and safe and good and predictable.

"Can I buy you a drink?" she asked, pointing to the drinks already on the table.

"Thanks. I need a drink," I said, sitting down across the table from her.

"Why?"

"I just talked to Megan. She told her folks about me, and one of the teachers she had in high school." I shook my head. "It's hard to believe that a few weeks ago she was still in high school."

Abbie laughed. "Is that a look of panic I see on your face?"

"Yes, it is."

"That's what you get for robbing the cradle."

"You're the one who told me to spend time with her."

"As a friend. Why is the concept of being a friend to a girl so foreign to you? Why do you think you have to kiss every girl you're with?"

"I don't think that."

"How many girls have you kissed in your life?"

I thought about it. "Three."

"Three? Wait a minute? The answer is supposed to be two. Me and Megan. So who's the third girl?"

"It was in ninth grade, and it was only one time."

"You kissed somebody in ninth grade? Who?"

"Let it go, Abbie."

"No, who was it?"

"Emily Randsburger."

"You kissed Emily Randsburger?"

"We were in a play. It was in the script."

"You were never in a play."

"She wrote the play. We read it one day in her backyard."

"Oh, I see. That brazen hussy."

"She's on a mission now."

"That brazen, although somewhat religious, hussy."

"Look, it's getting late. Why did you want to talk to me?"

She sighed. "Okay, here's the deal. Tonight I asked Eldon how long he thought it would take after Elizabeth got home before he'd be able to say for sure which one of us he wanted to marry."

"That's kind of a bold question, Abbie."

She smiled. "It's my New York upbringing. If you're thinking something, say it. Not like back home where a guy and a girl can dance around this for months. I need to know. I haven't signed my new contract yet. Do I sign up for another year or six months or three months, or do I just quit and go home and start preparing for a wedding?"

"So you asked. Very practical. What did he say?"

"That's why I need you to translate. He goes, 'Well, I'm not exactly sure.'"

"Okay."

"What does that mean?" she asked.

"Well, this is just a guess, of course, but it might mean he's not exactly sure."

She pointed to my drink. "I'm paying a dollar twenty-five for that, so if you can't do any better than that, I want my money back."

I laughed. "You are so abrasive these days."

"So? You got a problem with that?"

"Not really. I like it."

"C'mon, Dave, talk to me, earn your drink."

"What Eldon said probably means that he's suddenly realized that if he gives you and Elizabeth a timeline, then he's pretty much committed himself to getting married to one of you within that time."

"So?"

"Most of the time when an LDS, temple-worthy guy first talks about marriage, he's only thinking of one thing."

"And that is?"

"His honeymoon."

She threw up her hands. "Oh, good grief, why do I even talk with you?"

"For a guy a honeymoon is like having been on a strict diet all his life and suddenly after a little ceremony being told he can have all the dessert he wants."

She scowled. "Not all guys are like you, Dave."

"No, they are. Trust me."

She rolled her eyes.

"I'm serious," I said.

"Okay then, Einstein, if that's the way Eldon is thinking then why should he feel threatened at the thought he might be getting married soon, when of course he would have a honeymoon."

"Because, Sweet Girl, the more planning a girl makes about the wedding, the less he thinks about the honeymoon, and the more he feels threatened. You want to know what's the biggest fear an LDS guy has when it looks like he is actually going to get married?"

"I'm afraid to ask."

"Instead of that BMW he's always dreamed of, he suddenly realizes he'll be driving an SUV filled with screaming kids for the next twenty years. It's like his worst nightmare."

"I'm not trying to trap Eldon."

"This is not about you, okay? This is about what guys are like. When they're about to get married, they have to come face to face with their worst fear, which is that they're going to end up exactly like their dad. There will be lawns to mow, gardens to tend, leaks to fix, kids to be responsible for. For a guy it's the end of his time to be selfish and self-centered. It's a sad day when that happens."

"Hey, I'm just as selfish as most guys, so I'd be giving up a lot too."

"I know you would, but I think it's more traumatic for a guy. Take Eldon, for example. Most likely when he graduated from high school he didn't buy a motorcycle or a dirt bike. Instead he saved up for a mission. He had friends with tricked-out cars, but he drove either the family car or else a junker. But that doesn't mean he didn't have dreams. He dreamt of fast cars and dune buggies and snow machines and adventure vacations to Australia or Alaska. But he gave it up to serve a mission. And when he gets home from his mission, his non-member buddies from high school are driving Corvettes and bragging about climbing Mount Everest. Some of them are sleeping around with girls with smoking hot bodies." I took a sip of my Sprite.

She shook her head. "I can't believe you just said 'smoking hot body.' I will never understand how your mind works. But go ahead."

"So for one brief moment of time, he thinks that maybe with a little luck he'll earn enough to afford at least a used Honda Civic with a sunroof. And if that was all there was to it, he'd postpone marriage and go ahead and buy all the toys he's always wanted. But that's not good either because there is something else that's a great motivator to an LDS guy."

"What?"

"Well to put it bluntly, he's in his twenties, and he's never known a girl . . . in the *biblical* sense of the word."

"Girls think about that, too. Probably not in the same way, though."

"Some day I'll have you tell me about girls, but right now I just want to earn my drink and go home and go to bed."

"Don't let me stop you."

"So there're two opposing forces. For a temple worthy returned missionary the only honorable way for him to experience guilt-free intimacy with a girl is to marry her, but if he does that, there goes his dream of a flashy new car. That's some of what's going through Eldon's mind right now. My advice is give him some slack and let him work it out. If you try to rush him, I'm guessing he'll break up with you."

She thought about it. "Thanks."

"Glad to help out."

"That was so valuable I probably owe you another drink."

"No, this is enough for me."

"What about you, Dave? What dreams did you bring from high school?"

I shook my head.

"What?"

"You're my only dream from high school, Abbie."

She reached for my hand. "Sorry."

"It's okay. Water under the bridge, as they say."

"Next Friday Eldon is flying to Utah to be with Elizabeth. She's speaking in her home ward's sacrament meeting on that Sunday."

"How do you feel about him going to see her?" I asked.

"To tell you the truth, it scares me, but I'll be glad to have it over. I can't stand the way things are now. I want it over, one way or the other." She stood up. "Let's go. We both need to get some sleep."

After she paid for the drinks, I walked her to her car.

"You know what?" she said. "I'm glad you're here this summer."

"Yeah, me, too. Don't worry, though, I don't have any hopes for you and me anymore. I know where I stand with you. You know, the just-friends thing we've got going for us these days."

"Good." She gave me a hug. "Thanks for talking to me tonight."

"Anytime."

She opened her car door. "See you around, okay?"

"Yeah."

After getting into the car, she ran the window down. "Dave, you do realize that Megan is falling in love with you, right?"

"Why?"

She shrugged. "It doesn't make any sense to me, either. Maybe it's because you're a returned missionary and she's so young."

"It will pass, though, right?"

"I hope so. I'm trying to discourage her about you, but so far it doesn't seem to be doing any good. Maybe I'll tell her about that book you still haven't returned to the high school library. That's the only bad thing I know about you."

"First thing I'm going to do when I get back home is look for it."

"You want to tell me about the girl you went sailing with tonight? Are you hiding her from us? Is that why you're going to the family ward with her on Sunday?"

"It was her choice. She likes kids."

Abbie smiled. "That's got to send warning signals to you, right?"

"Not really. I like kids, too."

"Whatever. I'd like to meet her. Hannah's her name, right?"

"Yeah. Why do you want to meet her?"

"Because at some point she'll need someone other than a guy to be her friend."

"I'll bring her to the singles branch some time."

"Hannah is a lucky girl to have you for a friend. I wish every girl could have a friend like you."

"Thanks."

"Well, I've got to go," she said.

"I know. Me, too."

She started the engine and drove away.

I couldn't get Abbie out of my mind even after I went to bed. It finally occurred to me it was because I loved her more now than I had before my mission.

Go figure.

CHAPTER SEVEN

Saturday is always a busy day at a hardware store. By closing time, Hannah and I were wiped out. We picked up a pizza and drove to her boat. Fifteen minutes later we were sailing in the bay. In just a few minutes the sun, blue sky, and gentle breeze refreshed us.

"This is great. Thanks for letting me come here with you," I said.

"Yeah, sure, no problem. I was always going to get a dog—you know . . . for company. My landlord goes 'no way,' but you pretty much provide the same service, and I don't have to worry about fleas and licensing. So it's all good."

"Except I don't catch Frisbees in my mouth."

She patted me on the head. "Not to worry. We're going to work on that tonight," she said.

"Hey, one thing, you are going to go to church with me tomorrow, right?"

"Yeah. It'll be a little tricky, what with my sister and me rooming together." She paused. "I know what I'll do. I'll tell her I'm going sailing and then I'll take a dress with me and change in the boat, and you can pick me up there. That'll work."

"Why can't you let her know you're going to church?"

"Because our family has been Catholic since, like, Peter, you know what I'm saying? We're Catholic to the bone and always will be. My Uncle Victor is even a priest. I just don't want to get into a big argument with my family. I'll change into church clothes on *Blue Skies*. And then everyone will be happy."

"Whatever works. Church starts at nine. I'll come by about eight-thirty."

We sailed less and read more that night. We got through about half of Second Nephi, although I did summarize the Isaiah chapters for her.

We prayed together again. That was good.

On my way home, I got a call. It was Abbie. "Megan and I are all alone tonight. Meet us at the diner. We'll treat."

"Where's Eldon?"

"He had some regional sales meeting he had to go to."

"All right. I'm on my way."

I found Abbie and Megan in a corner booth in the back of the diner. There were some strange-looking fries on the plate.

"What were these fried in? Carrot juice?" I asked.

"Have one," Abbie said with a sly grin in Megan's direction.

"Why?"

"They're a special kind."

I put a couple of fries in my mouth. "Wow, these are good! What are they?"

"Sweet potato fries."

"Where are they grown?"

"The waitress said she thought they came from North Carolina."

"They're okay," I said, pushing the plate away from me.

"Have some more," Abbie said.

"No, that's okay."

Abbie, with a silly grin on her face, turned to Megan. "Dave feels guilty for eating sweet potato fries because they weren't grown in Idaho."

"That's not true," I said.

Abbie slid the plate toward me. "Have some more, then."

"No, what I had was plenty."

"You know you want it," Abbie teased.

"No, thanks."

"Everybody else is eating sweet potato fries," Abbie said.

"Not me, though."

"I like 'em. Megan likes 'em. Everybody likes 'em."

Megan handed me a single fry. "Just have one more. For me."

"No, thanks."

"You think you're better than us?" Megan asked, and then she and Abbie began laughing.

Finally I understood the game. They were running through all the reasons used to get a member of the Church to stray.

"Nobody will know if you have a few sweet potato fries," Abbie said. "I won't tell anyone."

"I'd know though."

"If you won't do this, we won't be your friends anymore," Megan said.

"If that's all our friendship means to you, it's not much of a loss."

Abbie turned to Megan. "He's good, huh?"

"Very good."

"Okay, Dave, we give up."

"Do you have greater respect for me now?" I asked Abbie.

I meant it as a joke, but that's not how she took it. "I've always had great respect for you." Abbie said it with all seriousness, which was unusual for her when it came to me.

Abbie began to tell Megan about me. "Dave isn't a flashy dresser, and if there's more than one fork at a place setting, he won't know which one to start with. At a classical music concert he'll make a check on the program with a pencil as each piece is performed so he'll know how much longer it will be until it's over. In a romantic situation, if you ask him what he's thinking about, he'll tell you something about overhead cam engines. In high school he was never a student body officer. He wasn't a big football star although he was on the team his sophomore year. He didn't win any scholarships when he graduated from high school. He can't play a single musical instrument. When he dances, you have to show him the steps every time. His favorite food is steak and potatoes. He speaks no foreign language. His mission was in Minnesota, where he worked in little farming towns, talking to farmers."

She placed her hand on mine. "Dave is going to be just like his dad, and there's no better person in our town. It has been a great honor to be Dave's best friend all these years, and I know I'm going to miss him tremendously when we . . . go our separate ways."

She leaned over and kissed me on the cheek. "That is what is so good about my friend Dave." She looked as though she might be going to cry. "Excuse me. I'll be right back."

Abbie left.

"She's right about you," Megan said.

"Is she? I can't say. I'm just me."

"Abbie says you were an assistant to the mission president on your mission."

"Not exactly. I worked in the mission office, but my job was to be in charge of all the mission cars."

"That's a big responsibility."

"Yes, but not always very spiritual."

"She has nothing but good to say about you."

"Then she's forgotten a lot."

"She says you always treated her with respect."

I nodded. "Well, yeah, I did do that."

"I hope we get to spend time together when I'm at BYU—Idaho."

"Me too, Megan. That'd be great."

"Maybe I should just check on Abbie and see if she's okay."

"Yeah, sure."

Megan left.

Suddenly I was alone, facing a plate of sweet potato fries. Who would miss it if I ate just one?

I looked around and made sure Abbie and Megan weren't coming and snuck a sweet potato fry.

Oh, my gosh, these are so good! I thought.

I tried in vain to remember all the hard-working potato farmers in Ririe who came into our store for parts. Facing nearly impossible odds every year—low prices or bad weather or a late frost or a foot of snow in the fields before they've harvested the potatoes. Those men deserved my loyalty.

None of that worked.

I had a couple more sweet potato fries. *These don't even need ketchup,* I thought. *They're good just the way they are.*

Five minutes later I'd eaten all the sweet potato fries on the plate. I panicked. Abbie would never let it go if she found out I'd given into temptation and eaten all the sweet potato fries. I desperately looked for a way to cover up what I'd done.

Next to me there was an empty table with some uneaten sweet potato fries on two of the plates. I got up and grabbed a bunch of fries from the other table.

I was dumping them onto the plate at our table when Abbie and Megan came around the corner from the restroom and saw me. I sat down.

"What did you just do?" Abbie asked.

"Nothing. Just got up to stretch."

"How come there are more fries on the plate now than when we left?"

I cleared my throat. "Maybe they swell up after they've been left out for a while."

She looked at the table next to ours. "Did you eat all our sweet potato fries and then take the leftover fries from another table so we wouldn't notice? Is that what's going on here?" Abbie asked.

"Why would you think that?"

She slugged me on the arm. "Don't even think about lying to me, Dave. I always know when you're lying."

I had no defense. "Okay, you're right. I did eat all the ones on our plate, but then I felt guilty and tried to cover it up."

Abbie and Megan sat down and laughed.

And laughed.

And laughed.

When someone at a nearby table asked them what was so funny, they told them.

And they laughed.

And laughed.

And when we paid our bill, and the cashier asked why they'd been laughing so hard, they told him.

And he laughed.

And laughed.

As I walked them out to Abbie's car, Abbie told me it was too bad I wasn't going to the singles branch the next day because she was going to have so much fun telling everyone the story of how I'd given into the temptation of non-Idaho sweet potato fries.

Abbie and Megan were still laughing as they drove away.

As I drove home, I told myself that my eating so many sweet potato fries in no way changed my primary allegiance to fries made from Idaho potatoes. I was just going through a stage of experimentation, that's all. And when it came time to go back to Idaho fries, it would be an easy thing to do.

* * *

Sunday morning at eight-thirty, I picked Hannah up at her boat. She looked great, but she also looked very Catholic with the small gold cross necklace she was wearing.

Without makeup Hannah looks good. But with makeup it's like a sign that says, "Stop whatever you're doing and take a look at this girl!"

Her high cheekbones became more prominent with makeup. And her eyes just drew me in. In the sunlight, her long dark brown hair showed some copper highlights. Because of her dark hair and complexion, she looked like someone you'd want to play Mary in a church movie.

When we first entered the meetinghouse, a woman came up to us. She was Hispanic, probably in her mid-thirties. "Good morning, are you new here?"

"Yes. I usually attend the singles branch in Meadowview, but my friend here is not yet a member and wanted to attend a family ward."

The sister shook my hand but leaned over and embraced Hannah and kissed her on the cheek. Giving Hannah a kiss seemed a little strange to me, but I later discovered that was just the way that the Hispanic sisters greeted each other. "We are so glad to have you here with us today," she said.

"Thank you. My name is Hannah and this is my friend Dave."

"I'm Sister Castro. Come and let me introduce you to the missionaries."

Two elders stood just outside the chapel in front of a table that had about forty headsets sitting on it.

"Elders, this is Dave and Hannah. This is Hannah's first time to church so please explain to her what we do here." She turned to us. "I need to go to the library and check out some things for my class, but we'll talk later." She left us.

Elder Hawkins and Elder Smith introduced themselves and gave us each a headset. "This is a bilingual branch so when someone who speaks Spanish gives a talk, if you put these on, one of us will translate and you'll be able to understand what they're saying."

At first I wasn't sure if I hadn't made a mistake taking Hannah to this ward where half of the members were Spanish-speaking. Most all the members in my ward in Idaho were white, and all of them spoke English.

At first I was a little critical. The meeting started late, the pianist only played the melody with one hand, and more than half the people came late.

During the sacrament hymn I whispered to Hannah that she could either take the sacrament or not, whatever she wanted to do.

"I want to take it," she said.

"Okay."

Even though the boys passing the sacrament didn't look like they came from well-to-do families, they all were dressed in white shirts, and they all showed respect for what they were doing.

The first sacrament prayer was given in English, the second in Spanish.

After the sacrament, the first speaker was a girl maybe twelve or thirteen.

She spoke at first in English and then did her own translation in Spanish. She spoke about how her family came to join the Church when she was nine years old, and what a blessing that had been to her family, and how proud she was to have a brother on a mission, and how much their family had been blessed financially so they could pay for his mission.

"This is good," Hannah whispered in my ear.

"Yeah, it is."

The second speaker was Sister Castro, the woman we'd met when we first came into the building. She told everyone she was going to speak in Spanish, so we put on our headsets.

Elder Hawkins did a simultaneous translation as she talked about the importance of family prayer and family home evening. When I glanced at Hannah, I was surprised to see tears in her eyes.

The last speaker was a member of the stake high council. His name was Brother Gallardo. He spoke in English, but sometimes he'd forget and start speaking Spanish.

He spoke about the importance of keeping the Sabbath day holy and told us that he used to work for a company that required him to work Sundays. At any moment he could be called out of his meetings to go to work. But then one Sunday, after missing all his meetings, he said to his wife, "No more. I will not work Sundays anymore."

And something that seemed as though it would lead to financial disaster turned into an opportunity for another job that paid more money but did not require him to work on Sunday.

"We just have to have faith that if we do what Heavenly Father asks us, He will bless us."

He quoted Nephi's famous statement: "I will go and do the things which the Lord . . ." And then he bore his testimony and sat down.

After the meeting, I turned to Hannah. "What did you think? Do you have any questions?"

"No. It was good. What's next?"

"Sunday School."

The elders invited us to attend Gospel Essentials class, and we went with them downstairs to a classroom.

Our instructor was Brother Chirinos from Peru. He spoke English well and was warm and friendly.

In his lesson, by using the scriptures, he carefully laid out the entire plan of salvation.

At the end of the lesson, Hannah told Brother Chirinos, "Thank you so much. Nobody has ever told me any of this before."

"We are the only church who can tell you."

"Why's that?"

"Because God has revealed these things to a prophet by the name of Joseph Smith, who lived upstate near Rochester. This is a New York church. We can all be proud of that."

As we left the Sunday School class, Sister Castro found Hannah and took her to Relief Society.

In elders quorum, I was struck by the diversity in the group. There were five Hispanics, two of them recent converts, two Blacks, two from the Philippines, and five Gringos like me. And yet we were a quorum.

After priesthood I waited outside the Relief Society room for Hannah. She was talking to Sister Castro. As they parted, Sister Castro again gave Hannah a hug and another kiss on the cheek. It was such a contrast from going to church in Idaho, where none of the sisters kissed each other on the cheek.

As we walked down the hall on our way out, I asked her how Relief Society was. She just smiled, and said, "It was awesome."

The elders caught up to us on our way out to our car.

Elder Smith had a habit of ending every sentence as if it were a question. "We're so happy you came to church?"

Hannah glanced at me and smiled. "We had a great time."

"We would like to teach you?"

"Okay. How would that work?"

"We'll come to your house."

Hannah thought for a moment. "How about doing it on my boat? Say tomorrow night at eight o'clock."

"We can't go boating?" Elder Smith said.

"It's docked. It's like an apartment."

"But it's a boat. We're not supposed to be on a boat?"

Elder Hawkins took over. "It'll be okay," he said to his companion.

"Let me give you directions," Hannah said.

Half an hour later we were back on her boat.

"I could change into something else or I could stay the way I am?" she said, mimicking Elder Smith.

"It doesn't matter to me."

"Then I'll change?" She turned it into a question the way Elder Smith did.

She did it a couple more times, and then asked, "How come you're not laughing?"

"The elders are doing the best they can."

"Was that what it was like for you on your mission?"

"Yeah, like that. I'm sure there were people who made fun of the way I talked."

"Sorry. I wasn't trying to be mean."

"It's okay. Don't worry about it. There's something you don't know yet about the missionaries."

"What?"

"I'll tell you later."

"No, tell me now."

I took a deep breath. "They are God's messengers. He loves and sustains them. So it doesn't matter how they talk. If you listen to them and pray about their message, God will bless you to know that the message they have is true."

"Okay, I won't make fun of them anymore. Thanks for telling me. I'll go change now."

She went below to change. While she was doing that, she called out to me, "I've got a question. When I was with the women, one of them read something from a book called Doctrines and Covenants. What's that?"

"It's *Doctrine* and Covenants. It's another book of scripture."

"Another book? How many books do you people have?"

"The Bible, the Book of Mormon, the Doctrine and Covenants, and the Pearl of Great Price."

"I want to look at the Doctrine and Covenants just to see what it's like," she said.

I opened my triple and turned to Section 1 of the Doctrine and Covenants.

When she returned, wearing jeans and a sweatshirt, I handed her the open book and said, "Start reading."

In the next few minutes, as we read, I sensed a change in her attitude from a healthy skepticism to a growing awareness of the significance of what this might mean in her life.

And then she read, "'What I the Lord have spoken, I have spoken, and I excuse not myself; and though the heavens and the earth pass away, my word shall not pass away, but shall all be fulfilled, whether by mine own voice, or by the voice of my servants, it is the same.'"

She stopped reading and looked up from the page, and I could see she had tears in her eyes.

"What?" I asked.

"This is true, isn't it?" she said softly.

"Yeah."

She paused. "How amazing that this should come to me."

"Why do you say that?"

"Because I'm like nothing."

"Not to God you aren't."

"What do I need to do?"

"Let the elders teach you."

"Let's not wait for tomorrow. Let's call and see if they can come now."

Hannah called them. "I want to know more. Can you come by today?"

They said they'd be there in an hour.

"There're some things you need to know about the Church." I paused. "Things that might be hard for you to live."

"Like what?"

"The Word of Wisdom."

"What's that?"

"The elders will teach you about it."

"What's the bottom line? What restrictions are there on Mormons?"

"No drinking. No smoking. No coffee or tea."

"You gotta be kidding!"

"I'm serious."

"No drinking? You mean like even beer?"

"Yeah. And wine, whiskey, and anything else that has alcohol in it."

"I always have a can of beer after work."

"Yeah, sure, lots of people do."

"Coffee, too?"

"Yeah."

"That's how I get going in the morning."

"I understand."

She sat thinking for a few moments. "I don't know if I can do this."

"I understand."

"How come you can live this way?"

"I was raised in the Church, so that helps."

"The one thing that's kept my family together is our traditions. Going to mass on Christmas and Easter. Family dinners—my gosh! We always drink wine. This feels like your church expects me to give up my family. It's all I've got now. All my friends from high school are gone. I don't have much left except my family." She shook her head. "I don't think I can do this. It's asking way too much."

"It's up to you. At least listen to the missionaries, okay?"

"Yeah, okay."

An hour later, Elder Hawkins, the senior companion, came on board, but Elder Smith hesitated. "Can we just teach on the dock?" Elder Smith asked.

"Why would you want to do that?" I asked.

"We're not supposed to be on a boat?"

"We're docked," Hannah said. "The boat can't go anywhere. Some people here totally live on their boats, so this is more like an apartment."

"But . . . still . . . it is a boat?"

"It'll be okay," Elder Hawkins said. "If you want, after we finish we'll call the president and tell him what we did and ask him if that was okay."

Elder Smith checked the mooring ropes and then cautiously boarded the boat.

"I think I'll go down and change," Hannah said, leaving us.

"What's she doing?" Elder Smith asked.

"She went down to change back into her Sunday clothes. Is that okay?"

"She's just down those stairs?"

"Yes."

"There's not even a door. Just a curtain. I'm not sure we should be here while she's changing?" Elder Smith said to his companion.

"Elders, think of this as her apartment, and down those stairs is her room."

"At the MTC, they never said it would be like this, where a boat is an apartment and down two stairs is a room, and a curtain is a door. I don't care what you say. This is definitely a boat, and she's like only ten feet away from us changing her clothes? If the wind blows hard, we'd see her. That's not right."

"The wind's not blowing that much," I said.

"I take full responsibility," Elder Hawkins said.

"Well, okay, but I still say it's not right?"

"Elder Smith, can I make one suggestion?" I asked.

"Yes?"

"You have a habit of ending almost every sentence like it was a question. That's okay, of course, but it does detract a little from your message, so if you could work on that I think it would help you in your teaching."

He closed his eyes and shook his head.

"You okay?" Elder Hawkins asked.

"Yeah, I'm okay. It's just that . . . this is so hard. I'm always slower than everybody else. Learning to speak Spanish . . . then trying to learn the lessons in both English and Spanish . . . I keep wondering when I'll actually pull my weight."

"That's the way I felt on my mission," I said. "All the time . . . until my last few months, and then it all came together. You've got to just keep working and don't give up. You're doing great, really. Just that one thing."

Apparently Hannah had heard me railing on Elder Smith because when she came up to join us, she said, "Okay, I'm ready. Teach me. Elder Smith I want you to know what a good example you are to me."

He got a big smile on his face. "I am?"

"Absolutely. I just want you to know I've been listening in while I was changing and I've been inspired by you."

"In what way?"

"You never give up no matter how hard things are for you."

He gulped. "Thanks."

We began. Elder Hawkins was the senior missionary, but maybe because of what Hannah had said, he let Elder Smith take the lead.

At first when Elder Smith said something, it would come out as a question, but then he'd say it again, and his voice wouldn't go up at the end of the sentence.

After a while, though, it didn't matter. The message was infinitely more important than the way it was delivered. We felt the Spirit.

And then Elder Smith asked a real question. "When you come to know these things are true, will you follow the Savior's example and be baptized?"

Hannah sighed. "I guess I already do," she said.

"Already do what?" Elder Smith asked.

"Know these things are true."

"Then will you be baptized?"

She sighed. "Wow, you guys don't waste time, do you?"

"If you know it's true, what other choice do you have?"

She thought about it for a while and then nodded her head and softly said, "Okay, I'll be baptized."

Elder Smith looked as though he couldn't quite believe it, but he pressed on anyway. "How about this Saturday?"

She thought about it for a long time, and then said, "Okay."

Elder Hawkins's eyebrows raised. I couldn't believe it either. On my entire mission I had never met anyone who so suddenly accepted the gospel. What had happened to the fears she'd expressed just a few minutes earlier?

"Can we teach you three or four times this week so you'll know about the covenant you'll be making when you're baptized?" Elder Hawkins asked.

"Yeah, sure, every night if you want. What's a covenant?"

"It's a promise you make to Father in Heaven. And He makes a promise to you."

Even though I was happy she wanted to be baptized, I had some reservations about whether she'd be ready or not. "Hannah, are you sure about this?"

"I don't know. This is a difficult decision. Elder Smith, can you teach me about the not drinking policy of the Church? I think I'm okay with the no sex part. Dave explained that to me already."

Elder Smith blushed.

They taught her from the Doctrine and Covenants and the Bible. In addition to the Word of Wisdom, they also taught her about tithing.

She turned to me. "So basically all I got to do is live like you do, right?"

I felt uneasy. "I'm not perfect, far from it." I sighed. "But I do live the Word of Wisdom, and I do pay tithing from each paycheck. And that has been a blessing to me. I'm sure that will be the case with you."

She nodded, went below deck, and returned a minute later with a six-pack of beer, a large can of coffee, and a half-empty bottle of wine. She handed them to the elders. "There, that's it. Take these with you and get rid of them for me."

"We'll be happy to do that."

"Can you really make so many changes in less than a week?" I asked.

"It's hard for Elder Smith to be a missionary. But he's doing it. Maybe I can do the same as him."

"We'll be here to help you," Elder Smith said.

After Hannah offered a prayer, the elders left.

"I need to go tell my family about what I'm going to do," Hannah said.

"You want me to come with you?" I asked.

"Would you? I might need somebody to explain to them better than I can the beliefs of the Church."

She drove us to her parents' home.

We pulled into the driveway but didn't go in right away.

She shook her head. "Oh, no, this is not good," she said.

"What?"

"That's my Uncle Victor's car . . . he's the one who's a priest."

"Oh."

"We can come back later," she said.

"No. Let's go in. We've got the truth on our side."

She shook her head. "You don't know my family."

"Are you sure you want to do this?" I asked.

"I'm sure."

"Okay, then, let's go."

We walked in and all eyes turned to me.

I stood facing a family of giants. And except for Hannah, a family of overweight giants with booming voices. A family with dark, almost black hair, and thick eyebrows and deep-set eyes. The smell of garlic filled the house.

"This is my friend Dave. We have an announcement to make," Hannah said.

I had never seen so many people so suddenly happy.

"Welcome to the family, my boy!" her Uncle Victor, the priest called out.

"Wait!" Hannah said. "It's not that kind of an announcement!"

"Come in, come in!" a large woman said to me. "We are about

to have some of the baklava Hannah's grandmother made for us. Sit down, make yourself comfortable. Oh, I'm Hannah's mom, and this is Hannah's grandmother."

"Hello."

"Come here, my boy." Grandmother grabbed me and pulled me in tight for a hug. "We are so glad you're going to marry our sweet Hannah." She was a large woman and I felt that she could easily crush me. Also, she had a mustache. Not intentionally of course.

"Nana, that's not what this is about. I'm not getting married," Hannah said.

Grandmother released her death grip. "Maybe not yet, but soon, you think?"

"I don't know, Nana. Right now Dave and I are just friends."

Hannah's mom took me around to introduce me to the rest of the family.

"This is Hannah's Uncle Victor. He's a priest."

"He could marry you two," Grandmother called out. "He's a very important person. He even gets letters from the Pope. He showed me one."

Victor and I shook hands. He was a tall, handsome man in his mid-fifties with a head of thick, gray hair. "Welcome to the family. Oh, by the way, stay for the baklava. It's worth the wait."

We moved on. "And this is Hannah's sister, Marjorie. She was named after her grandmother."

"You can call me Madge," she said, smiling and pumping my hand.

Madge was taller than Hannah. She was a large woman, wearing a low-cut dress that revealed way more than I was comfortable with. I was relieved that she didn't try to hug me.

"And this is Sully. He and Madge have been seeing each other since high school. Some day we hope they will get married."

"I've heard a lot about you," I said to Sully.

"What have you heard?" he asked. He sounded a little hostile.

"Oh . . . well . . . lots of things."

"If it came from Hannah, I'd lay odds it wasn't very good. I'm not as bad as she says. If you ask me, she's the one who's messed up."

"Dave, come sit here with me," Hannah said. We sat down together on a couch.

"Sully is going to be a doctor some day," Madge said proudly.

"Are you in med school now?" I asked.

"No, not yet."

"You still working on your GED?" Hannah asked.

"Hey, what can I say? I work sixty hours a week."

"What do you do?" I asked.

"I work for a car parts place. I haul parts to shops. People always want their parts right away, you know what I'm saying? But I'm not Superman. I got to put 'em in the truck and drive to their shop. And at night I work the graveyard shift as a security guard."

"When do you sleep?"

"I can sleep a little on my second job."

With a great deal of effort, Hannah's grandmother struggled to stand up. "I'm going in the kitchen to dish out the baklava. Who wants some?"

"Everyone wants some, Mom," Hannah's mother said. "You know how we all love your baklava."

Grandmother smiled, then hobbled into the kitchen.

"You need any help?" Hannah's mom called out.

"You think I can't do this myself?" she called from the kitchen.

"No, Mom, I just wanted to know if you need any help."

"I can do it. I can do plenty. I can do way more than you think I can. I pruned a tree last week. I was up on the ladder. There was no problem except I couldn't move the ladder back to the garage. It's still there."

"Mom, how many times do I have to tell you if you need things done around the place, call me and we'll send someone over," Hannah's mom said.

"Who will you send?"

"I'll do it," Victor said.

"What, leave God's work for an apple tree? I would never let you do that."

"Sully can help you," Madge said.

"Last time I checked, Sully was not part of this family."

"If he's willing to help, let him help," Madge said.

Hannah leaned over and said confidentially, "Don't worry about Nana. She's always talking about how she just pruned a tree, but the truth is I took the ladder from her garage a year ago so she couldn't use it."

"There's something I need to tell everyone, too," Madge said quietly. "I'm pregnant."

"Where did you move the small plates?" Grandmother called from the kitchen.

"Excuse me. What did you just say?" Hannah's mom asked Madge.

"I said, 'where did you move the small plates?'" Grandmother replied. "They're not where they usually are. They've always been in the cupboard to the left of the stove, but now I look and they're not there."

"They're on the counter, Mom. I put them out for you."

Madge stared at the floor and talked fast. "Well, it turns out that I'm a tiny bit pregnant, but it's okay really because Sully and I are going to get married."

"How soon?" Hannah's mom asked.

"Before the baby's born, for sure," Sully said. "I'm expecting a raise. Once that comes through, I'll be able to afford a better place than the one I'm in."

"You're living with your mom now for free, Sully," Hannah said.

"So? We'll need more room, and like I said, I'm expecting a raise."

"I found the small plates!" Grandmother called out. "They were on the counter! Where are the forks?"

"They're on the counter next to the plates, Mom!"

Taking courage from Madge, Hannah took a deep breath and said, "I have an announcement, too. Dave here is a Mormon. I've been learning about his church from the missionaries. And I've decided to get baptized next Saturday. You're all welcome to come."

"I'm making the pieces small!" Grandmother called out. "I didn't know there were going to be so many people."

"What? Are you out of your mind? What's the matter with you anyway? I can't believe this!" Victor, said, practically shouting. "This family has been Catholic for hundreds of years. Why would you give all that up now?"

"Is something wrong?" Grandmother called out from the kitchen.

"Hannah says she's joining another church," Madge replied, happy to have the diversion from her announcement.

Hannah's grandmother staggered back into the living room and sank down into her chair. "Oh, no! Say it isn't so."

She grabbed her chest. "Please," she gasped. "Someone get my medication."

Hannah's mom ran into the kitchen and came out a minute later with a tiny pill and a glass of water.

"Now look at what you've done," Hannah's mom said, glaring at her.

Hannah's grandmother looked as though someone had just slapped her in the face. "Hannah, how could you even think of going against family tradition and joining another church? Your grandfather must be turning over in his grave right now. And to think you were his favorite. He loved you so much. That's why he gave you his boat."

"I love him, too. I think he actually approves of me doing this."

"Why would you think that?"

"Because after he died, he was taught the same things I just learned."

"And how do you know that? Did he send you a letter from heaven?"

Sully laughed. "And how much postage did he pay, huh?" Unfortunately, Sully was the only one who laughed.

"If we want anything from you, Sully, we'll ask you," Hannah's mom said.

Grandmother turned to Victor. "Can we take the boat away from her? She doesn't deserve it if she goes ahead with this foolish notion of hers."

"Actually, Grandfather's giving her the boat was in his will," Victor said.

"What are you saying?" Grandmother asked.

"That it's a done deal. He gave her the boat. It's part of a legal document. What can you do?"

"She doesn't deserve the boat anymore. There's got to be a way. Maybe we can declare her insane and have her committed."

"That seems a little over the top," Victor said.

"Talk some sense into her, then," Grandmother said. "I'm not having my granddaughter walk out on the religion that was good enough for our family for hundreds of years."

"Do you want me to serve the baklava now?" Hannah's mom asked Grandmother.

"How can you think of baklava at a time like this?" Grandmother asked.

"It's getting late. People have to go. They can't wait around for the perfect moment," Hannah's mom said.

"All right then, but this is not the happy occasion that I thought it would be." Grandmother pointed an accusing finger at Hannah and me. "No baklava for these two!"

She then turned to Victor. "Victor, you're a priest, for crying out loud. Talk some sense into the girl."

Victor gave it a try. "Hannah, maybe you should spend time studying your own church instead of running off and joining another. I'm sure we have many of the same things you have found in Dave's church."

"Do you have several hundred additional pages of scripture?"

"If we did, would you even know about it? You hardly ever show up for mass. Look, I'm pretty sure the Mormon Church is a cult."

"In what way?" Hannah asked.

Victor sighed. "I'm not exactly sure. We don't deal much with Mormons out here. But I remember we studied them in school. I'd really have to do some more reading. Could I meet with you two tomorrow night after you're done with work?"

"Okay."

"Where do you want to meet?" he asked.

"My boat."

That set Grandmother off. "Your boat! I don't think so, Missy! Not any more. We'll find a way to take it away from you, won't we, Victor?"

"I'm not sure we can, Nana."

"If we can't, then just torch it! You do it, Victor. You're a priest. Nobody would ever suspect you."

"That's arson, Nana. I'm not going to do that," Victor said.

"In my day we had loyalty to the family. Now look at what we've become." She looked heavenward. "Take me now. I'm ready to go."

"Okay, here's the baklava," Hannah's mom announced.

"Where is the boat now?" Grandmother asked.

"It's docked," Hannah said.

"And who pays the monthly fee to keep it there?"

"I do," Hannah said.

Grandmother seemed disappointed. "Oh."

Madge and Sully stood up. "We need to be going now."

"Before you've had your baklava?" Grandmother snapped.

"Can we have ours on a paper plate?" Madge said.

"Take all you want," Grandmother said, casting a sneering glance in our direction. "Give an extra large piece to Sully. He'll soon be a part of the family."

Sully looked a little depressed at the thought.

Nana made sure Sully and Madge got double servings of baklava. On their way out, Madge leaned over and said quietly to Hannah, "You've really done it this time, haven't you?"

"At least I'm not pregnant."

The two sisters glared at each other, and then Madge and Sully left.

"Why can't you be more like your sister?" Grandmother asked Hannah.

"What are you saying? It's okay with you that she's been sleeping with Sully for over a year?"

"At least she doesn't betray her family's beliefs. And they are going to get married. The way I see it, 'All's well that ends well.'"

Hannah had had it. "That's it! Let's go, Dave." She stood up.

"I'll call Herman Weissman!" Grandmother said. "He'll find a way to take your boat away."

"Who's he?" I asked.

"My grandfather's attorney," Hannah said.

"He'll find something wrong with the will. We'll have it nullified."

"But Mr. Weissman was the lawyer who helped Grandfather prepare the will," Victor said.

"Who better to tell us what's wrong with it! I'm not sure how he'll do it, but he'll find a way. And then with your boat parked in my driveway we'll see how much you want to go against your own family! And another thing, no baklava for you! Ever again! You hear me?"

"Oh, yeah, well, you know what? I don't even like baklava!" Hannah shot back.

"You see what this new religion of yours has done to you? Teaching you not to like baklava! The very idea! You know what?

Victor's right! They are a cult! Hannah, you are a disgrace to this family! Just wait until Herman Weissman gets done with you!"

"I've got to get out of here," Hannah said privately to me, moving toward the door.

I followed her. "Bye, everybody, so nice to visit with you all."

She asked me to drive. On our way back, she kept her face turned away from me, but I could tell that she was crying.

I parked in the marina parking lot.

We just sat there. Hannah kept dabbing at her tears as though if she could only get them to stop, all her problems would be solved.

After a minute or two, I asked, "Ow ya duen?"

She glared at me. "What do you think?" she snorted.

"Yeah, that was rough."

"What will I do if I have to choose between having my boat or being baptized?" she asked.

"That'd be a tough decision for you, wouldn't it?"

"It's not just the boat. My family is important to me, too. I know they're all crazy. But even so, they are my family."

"Of course."

"My sister announces she's pregnant, and everyone tosses it off like it's no big deal, but I tell 'em I want to become more religious, and they act like I'm the worst person in the world. Go figure."

"Right."

"What do you think I should do?" she said.

"I think you'd better pray about it."

"I don't want to pray. I'm afraid of the answer. God doesn't know or care how much I love going out in my boat after work."

"He knows you love it. And He loves you."

"How can you say that?"

"I'm just sure He does."

"You want to pray with me?" she asked.

"This might be a good time for you to pray by yourself. It's your decision, not mine."

She nodded. "All right, I'll do it. So . . . I'll see you at work in the morning."

"Yeah."

"Thanks for going with me to meet my family."

We got out of her car. Just before I got into my pickup, she said, "Oh, one thing."

"Okay."

"My grandmother's baklava really is good. Sorry you didn't make the cut."

"Maybe next time."

She shook her head. "I'm not sure they'll ever want to see you again. They hold grudges for years. Anyway, see you tomorrow."

I made sure she made it to her boat safely and then left.

When I entered my apartment, I looked around to make sure Nathan wasn't around, and then I knelt down to pray.

"Heavenly Father . . ." I began.

CHAPTER EIGHT

On Monday when I first saw Hannah at work I could tell she'd had a hard night. "Ow ya duen?" I asked.

"Not good. Let's go in the back and talk," she said.

There wasn't much work to do there, so we just had to face the fact that if Murray came in we wouldn't have an excuse for not being on the job.

"What am I going to do if my grandmother finds a way to take away my boat? *Blue Skies* is my life. Without it, I don't know what I'd do."

"I know. It would be a great loss for you."

"Sometimes when I'm sailing, it's like my grandfather is still alive, like maybe he's down in the cabin taking a nap, letting me do things on my own, like he used to do. But if I ever get into any trouble, he'll come up and help me. At least that's the way I feel sometimes. But if my grandmother takes *Blue Skies* away, I'll lose the closeness I feel with him every time I'm sailing."

"Maybe you should explain that to her."

"Maybe so." She sighed. "Oh, by the way, are you ready to face Uncle Victor after work in the religious debate of the century?"

"I've prayed about it and I've thought about what I'd like to say, but other than that, I don't know what else to do."

"Uncle Victor is very persuasive. He used to have a program on TV where he talked about Catholic theology. So he knows his stuff."

I sighed. "Great."

"What if he finds a fatal flaw in your church's doctrine and the whole thing falls apart? What will you do then?"

"That won't happen."

"How do you know that?"

"Because it's true."

"So you're not worried?"

"Of course I'm worried. I'm an average guy from a small town with only a high school education. I'm about to face a priest who's spent his life studying religion. Let's face it. If Heavenly Father doesn't help me, I'm toast."

She smiled at me. "He'll help you. Do you know why? Because you're a nice guy. Actually, the only one I've ever known. I think God must be very happy with you."

"Thanks, Hannah."

We could hear someone coming down the hall. Most likely Murray. There was only one small box that had come in with the morning delivery. We both put our hands on the box as if we were about to open it.

Murray came into the back room, looked at us and then at the box. "What's going on here?"

"We're just taking care of the shipment," Hannah said.

"It takes two people to open one box?"

"It's being real stubborn," she explained.

"I need you both out front. We've got customers. You remember customers, right? It's why your paychecks don't bounce."

"Maybe we can work on the box later," I said to Hannah.

"Yeah, when we have more time."

Murray threw up his hands. "Sometimes I wonder why I put up with you two," he said.

We knew he wasn't serious, but the trouble with Murray was that most of the time he didn't let his face know that he was joking.

From then on we were busy until quitting time. That was good in a way because we didn't have time to worry about our meeting with Uncle Victor.

After we closed the store, Hannah and I went to her boat and ate some beans, rice, and chicken we'd picked up at a fast food place that sold Central American dishes. The man who ran it spoke very little English, but the food was great.

As we were eating, Hannah set her fork down and looked around. She shook her head. "I really like coming here every day. I'll miss it if this is taken away from me."

"I guess you have a choice. If you don't get baptized, you can keep the boat."

She nodded. "I've thought about that."

"And?"

"There used to be only one thing in my life that gave me joy, and that was *Blue Skies*. Now I've found another. But I might have to give up one for the other. I'm not sure what to do."

We finished eating, then cleaned up and waited for her uncle to show.

When Hannah had talked to Uncle Victor earlier in the day, he'd said he'd be there at eight o'clock. He was actually a couple of minutes early.

He knocked on the side of the boat. "Permission to come aboard!" he called out cheerily.

"Permission granted," Hannah said, sticking her head up out of the galley. I followed her up the stairs to the deck.

"Here, give me a hand." Uncle Victor had a box of books that he handed to me before boarding the boat. The box was heavy.

After stepping onboard, he shook my hand and gave Hannah a big hug.

"Let me catch my breath. That's quite a walk from the parking lot." He was wearing a black suit with his priest's collar and was fanning himself with his hand.

"You brought us some books?" Hannah asked.

"Yes. About Joseph Smith. You probably haven't had a chance to read them. I thought you might as well see things from an objective perspective before you consider becoming a Mormon. I've got them checked out for two weeks from the parish library, but if you need more time, I can renew them."

Hannah gave him a weak smile. "That's a lot of reading."

"Yes, it is, but I think you ought to take some time before rushing into a decision like this."

He turned to me. "Dave, that's your name, right?"

"Yes."

"Dave, you seem like a very good person, and I don't want to get into a big debate about doctrine, so why don't we just let Hannah read this material. Then, if she still wants to become a Mormon, I won't stand in her way. How does that sound to you?"

Whenever I didn't know what to do on my mission, I prayed, and that seemed like a good idea now. "Would you mind if we said a prayer?" I asked him.

He hesitated a moment, then said, "No, of course not."

"Hannah, would you offer our prayer?" I asked.

I could tell from the look on her face that she wasn't comfortable, but she bowed her head and began.

"Father in Heaven, I have always looked up to Uncle Victor. When I was young, he was always the one who tried to teach me about God and Jesus. He is the one in our family we all look up to. We are so proud of him and the good work he does as a priest. I've always loved him because of the good example he has been to me."

After a pause, she continued, "After that time when that boy did bad things to me, I went to my Uncle Victor. He helped me so much. I don't know what I would have done without him. He will always be someone I look up to. How can I ever go against what he wants me to do?"

This was getting to Uncle Victor. I could hear him clearing his throat.

"So, Father in Heaven, here's what we got here. Me thinking that You want me to get baptized into Dave's church, and Uncle Victor telling me that would be a big mistake. It seems like there's no way this can be resolved. So any help You can give us would be greatly appreciated." She paused. "That's it. Amen."

I touched her hand to remind her.

"In the name of Jesus Christ. Amen," she added.

After the prayer, they both looked at me. But I wasn't at a loss anymore. I knew what to do.

"What I thought we might do for a few minutes is read a few pages from the Book of Mormon just so you can understand why the book is so important. How about if we each read three verses?"

To set the stage, I explained to Uncle Victor that shortly after the Savior was resurrected in the Old World, He appeared in the New World. He descended from heaven and taught the people.

I asked them to turn to chapter 15 of Third Nephi, where the Savior explains that when He said other sheep would hear His voice, He was referring to the people of the Book of Mormon.

And then we skipped over to chapter 17. I read the first three verses, Hannah read the next three.

And then Uncle Victor read this:

"Have ye any that are sick among you? Bring them hither. Have ye any that are lame, or blind, or halt, or maimed, or leprous, or that are withered, or that are deaf, or that are afflicted in any manner? Bring them hither and I will heal them, for I have compassion upon you; my bowels are filled with mercy.

"For I perceive that ye desire that I should show unto you what I have done unto your brethren at Jerusalem, for I see that your faith is sufficient that I should heal you.

"And it came to pass that when he had thus spoken, all the multitude, with one accord, did go forth with their sick and their afflicted, and their lame, and with their blind, and with their dumb, and with all them that were afflicted in any manner; and he did heal them every one as they were brought forth unto him."

When he first started reading, Uncle Victor's voice was flat, and he sounded bored, but as he continued, his tone changed and he became more animated.

When he reached the end of chapter 17, he stopped, and I said, "We can go on or else stop and talk about what we've read. What would you prefer?"

Uncle Victor was staring at the floor, deep in thought. For a long time he didn't say anything.

"Uncle Victor, do you want us to keep reading?" Hannah asked.

He silently read some of the verses again and then shook his head and handed back the book.

"You okay?" Hannah asked.

"I'm okay." He looked at his watch. "Well, look at the time. I'd better be going. I need to meet with some parishioners tonight."

He stood up and grabbed the box of books he'd brought for Hannah to read.

"Do you want to leave those?" she asked.

He pursed his lips. "No."

He turned to leave.

"Do you want to keep a copy of the Book of Mormon?" I asked.

Instead of answering, he said, "Hannah, I'll talk to your grandmother and suggest she let you keep your boat, even if you are baptized."

"Thank you."

"I'm not sure it will do any good, though. As you know, she's a very headstrong woman." He smiled thinly. "Like you are, actually."

And then he left.

Hannah and I were in shock. "What just happened?" she asked.

"I don't know."

"He felt something, didn't he?" she asked.

"I think maybe he did."

"If he did, why didn't he take the Book of Mormon with him? Why doesn't he want to know more?"

"His ministry is his whole life. It would be a difficult thing for him to throw it away."

"Will it be hard for me to be a Mormon?" she asked.

"Yeah, sometimes. Like now. You might lose your boat if you get baptized."

I read her the parable of the pearl of great price in the New Testament.

"That's my story," she said. "Giving up all I treasure for a new faith in God."

"Yeah. But there are other things you might lose by being baptized."

"Like what?"

"Some of your friends."

"So, what you're saying is, this is a big deal."

"Yeah, it is."

"I can always get other friends, but I can't get another family. That's what worries me. If my grandmother turns against me over this, it'll be like I am disowned. I don't know what I would do if I was never invited to get-togethers at her house. Those family gatherings have been the center of my life."

"So what are you going to do?"

She sighed and looked away. After a long moment, she quietly said, "How can I turn my back on the truth? I'm going to be baptized."

I was so excited that I called Abbie that night and told her about Hannah's decision.

The next morning I woke up energized by the help Hannah and I had received from Father in Heaven in talking with her uncle.

I made a pledge to Him that I would try to be a better person. *Complete integrity,* I thought. *That's the way it's going to be for me from now on.*

A little after six P.M., my resolve to be honest with everyone was tested when Megan and Abbie entered the store.

If they hadn't seen me I'd have hurried to the storeroom until they left.

Hannah was at the cash register, so there was little hope of protecting her from them.

"Dave, how's it going?" Abbie asked with an evil grin. "Bet you never expected to see us here, did you?"

"We thought we'd come and check up on you," Megan added.

"Where's Hannah?" Abbie asked.

"I'm Hannah."

They walked over to her. "Hi, we're friends of Dave and we've heard so much about you we thought we'd come meet you. I'm Abbie and this is Megan."

"Hi. I'm glad to meet you."

Abbie turned to me. "Don't you have something to do, Dave?"

I had the feeling that my whole world was about to unravel.

"Dave, why don't you go in the back room and pretend you're working?" Hannah suggested.

"Yeah, we don't need you here," Abbie said with a big grin.

I made my way to the back room and stared at empty boxes that needed to be thrown out, but I was too worried about what Abbie and Megan were up to. How could Abbie do this to me? Wasn't it enough she didn't want to marry me? Did she need to ruin the rest of my life, too?

After a few minutes of fuming I decided I needed to find out what half-truths Abbie and Megan were telling Hannah about me.

As I approached the three girls, each had a big smile on her face.

"Dave, we have a question for you," Abbie asked innocently. "Which of us do you like the best?"

That was a loaded question, and I knew I had to be careful. "I like you all the same, but in a different way."

That broke them up. "What did I tell you?" Abbie said.

"How did you know he'd say that?" Megan asked.

"You have to remember, we've known each other practically all our lives," Abbie said.

"He's a great guy to have as a friend," Hannah said.

"Yeah, he is, that's for sure. But look, guys come, and guys go, but Megan and me, we'll always be here for you. We're so happy you're going to be baptized, Hannah. It'll be the best decision you'll ever make. We want to be there. Are you okay with that?"

"Sure."

"Oh, and after you get baptized and confirmed why don't you start coming to the singles branch? Then you can meet some other guys. We wouldn't want you thinking Dave is the only game in town."

"Wait just a minute," I interrupted, pretending to be insulted. "Are you saying I'm *not* the only game in town?"

"Sorry, Dave. Your game got called because of rain," Abbie teased.

"Oh, yeah? Well, I ought to give you a piece of my mind," I said, trying to sound angry and echoing the phrase I'd first heard from Mr. Denuchy.

"You sure you want to do that? You don't have that much to spare!" Abbie said.

The three of them couldn't stop laughing.

"Go ahead, make fun of me," I said.

"Thanks, we will," Abbie replied.

For the next few minutes, the girls were on a roll, laughing at my expense.

I acted like I was mad, but I really wasn't. I was glad Hannah seemed so comfortable with Abbie and Megan. With church friends like them, I was pretty sure Hannah was going to be all right.

"Sometime I'd like to take you both sailing on my boat," Hannah said. "I usually take Dave. Once I told him he was a better companion than a dog because I didn't have to get him a flea collar."

Abbie laughed. "I'd get him one just in case. Well, our work here is done. Nice to see you, Dave. As always." She gave her witch laugh and then she and Megan left.

"I like your friends, Dave."

"What did Abbie say about me while I was in the back room?"

"Lots of things. Mostly hilarious."

"Look, if she said anything about the library fine from high school, I'm going to take care of it, okay? As soon as I find the book."

"She didn't bring that up. But she did say she's never met a guy who tries as hard to be a good Mormon and that there's no guy her age she trusts more than you. So the three of us agreed that you're a good guy."

I was a little surprised. "Oh."

"There's something I need to tell you, though."

"Okay."

She sighed. "I want to go sailing after work tonight."

That didn't seem like news to me. We always went sailing after work. "Yeah, sure."

"But . . . actually . . . this time I want to go alone."

"Whatever you say."

"I don't know how many more times I'll be able to sail. I want to be by myself . . . and maybe even with my grandfather."

"Okay."

After work, as we both headed out the store to the parking lot, she asked, "Do you wish you were going with me?"

"Yeah, I do."

"We'll go again, just not tonight. I need some time by myself."

I watched her drive off and then suddenly had an idea. I went back into the store and made a few purchases of my own.

Thirty minutes later I knocked on Hannah's grandmother's door.

She didn't recognize me. "What do you want?"

"I'm Dave. I'm one of Hannah's friends."

"What do you want?"

"I came to prune your tree."

"Who sent you?"

"Nobody."

"I can't pay you."

"I don't want to get paid."

"We need a ladder. Mine got stolen."

"I have a ladder. It's in my pickup. And I brought a saw, too."

"Who are you again?"

"I'm the guy who got Hannah interested in the Mormon Church."

"Oh, so you're the one! You think I want a Mormon pruning my tree? Well, I most certainly do not."

"You'll never get a better offer."

"What if you fall down and kill yourself?"

"If I do, you can have the ladder and the saw."

She laughed.

"What do you say? I've been doing things around the house all my life. I'm pretty sure I can do this."

"All right, I'll show you what I want you to do. The tree is in the backyard. I'll meet you out there."

It took her forever to come out. I wondered if she'd forgotten I was there. While I was waiting, I pulled some weeds in her flower garden.

The reason she took so long was because she had changed into her gardening clothes—white coveralls, a long-sleeved shirt, and a big sun hat.

"See all the dead branches? We need to get rid of them."

At first all I could see were dead branches. I started up the ladder I'd leaned against the tree.

"Don't lop that branch off where the ladder is now. Move the ladder around over there and then saw it off."

"Does it really matter where I'm standing as long as I get rid of the branch?"

"Are you going to do this my way or not?" she asked.

I obediently moved the ladder to where she said and made the cut.

It seemed like for every branch she wanted the ladder in a different place. But I kept my mouth shut and followed her instructions.

After an hour, she said, "It's looking a lot better now, isn't it?"

"Yes, it is."

"It will grow now. I think the dead branches were stopping it from growing," she said.

"Could be."

"I think we're done."

"Is there anything else you'd like me to do?" I asked.

"Well, I was thinking my flower garden needed weeding, but looking at it now, it doesn't look very bad."

"I weeded it while I was waiting for you."

"That's why it looks so nice. You're a good boy. Thank you."

"You're welcome."

"Would you like some lemonade?"

"Yeah, sure. Let me clean up first. I'll cut up the branches so they're small enough to get in garbage bags. Do you want me to put them out on the street?"

"Yes, please, that would be wonderful."

It took me half an hour to bundle everything up and get the bags out onto the curb, and then I knocked on her front door.

"Come in, come in." She looked past me to the curb. "Oh, look at all those branches bundled up so nice, and the rest in bags. You've done so much today. It would have taken me a year to do what you did in such a short time."

"I can come back every week if you want."

"Well, I wouldn't want to impose on your valuable time."

"Actually, my time is not all that valuable," I said.

We sat at her dining room table. She'd set out two glasses and a pitcher of iced lemonade and some cookies.

She told me how her husband had liked to spend time working in their yard during the summer and how much better the place had looked then.

And then she changed gears. "So you're a Mormon, are you?"

"Yes."

"Have you always been one?"

"Yes. I have ancestors who joined the Church in England and came over here. They walked across the plains to Utah. They pulled handcarts."

"I can't imagine that."

"I know. Me either."

"Why would they do that?"

"They believed that God had called a modern-day prophet, and they were trying to escape persecution and find a safe place to live."

"You mean like Moses and the burning bush that talked?"

"Something like that. Actually it wasn't the bush that talked. It was God."

She laughed. "Yes, exactly. So who is this modern-time prophet, and where did he come from?" she asked.

"His name was Joseph Smith, and he was living in upstate New York when God called him to be a prophet. He was fourteen years old when he went out into a grove of trees near his family's farm and knelt down and prayed to know which church to join."

"It's hard to believe anything good could ever come from upstate New York."

"Why's that?"

"Our state capital is upstate in Albany, and they never do anything right. What proof do you have that he was a prophet of God?"

"He translated a book that is an ancient record made in the Americas. It tells us that after Christ was resurrected, he appeared in the New World and taught the people here. The book records what he taught."

"What does your church teach about Mary?"

"Let me run out to my pickup and get a book so I can read it to you."

"Can't you just tell me?"

"I'd rather read it to you."

"Very well, then."

A minute later I began reading from 1 Nephi 11:13: "In the city of Nazareth I beheld a virgin, and she was exceedingly fair and white. And it came to pass that I saw the heavens open; and an angel came down and stood before me; and he said unto me: Nephi, what beholdest thou?

"And I said unto him: A virgin, most beautiful and fair above all other virgins. And he said unto me: Knowest thou the condescension of God? And I said unto him: I know that he loveth his children; nevertheless, I do not know the meaning of all things. And he said unto me: Behold, the virgin whom thou seest is the mother of the Son of God, after the manner of the flesh. And it came to pass that I beheld that she was carried away in the Spirit; and after she had been carried away in the Spirit for the space of a time the angel spake unto me, saying: Look!

"And I looked and beheld the virgin again, bearing a child in her arms. And the angel said unto me: Behold the Lamb of God, yea, even the Son of the Eternal Father!"

I stopped. Hannah's grandmother sighed. "That was nice."

"Yeah, it is."

"You revere Mary, then, as the Mother of God?"

"Yes, of course."

"Do you pray to her?"

"No."

"Well, I think you should."

"Why's that?" I asked.

"When I go to the doctor, which I do quite often, sometimes the doctor is so busy he can't see me, but he has me see William. William is a physician's assistant. He can help me for most of my aches and pains. If he ever has any questions, he can go to the doctor for advice. I think Mary is like that. She takes the load off of God. He's got to be busy, right? So that's why we pray to Mary. Of course, I'm not saying that's Catholic doctrine. It's just the way I think of it."

"Apparently God can take the traffic of all of our prayers."

"How do you know that?"

"He never told the prophet Joseph Smith any different."

"Well, perhaps you're right. But what does it matter? You didn't come here to convert me to Mormonism." She paused. "Or did you?"

"No, I came to prune your tree."

"And what a grand job you did of it, too." She reached over and patted my hand.

"Thanks."

"I'm sure people couldn't understand why I wanted it done. It's because every morning when I get up I look out at the backyard. I've done that all the time I've lived here. When my husband was alive, I could look back there and see the results of all his work in the garden. He wasn't one to express his feelings to me much, but I could look and there would be the flower garden and the tomatoes growing and the lawn trimmed, and I would know that I was loved. But now he's gone, and I have precious little proof around me that he ever lived. A few pictures, of course, but when we were young and first married we never took pictures of ourselves, and he was always the one who took the pictures, so I don't even have many pictures of him. And almost none of us together. It's sad. I still miss him a great deal."

"You can be with him after you die."

"I've always known that."

"And your marriage can continue on even after you're both dead."

"I believe that, too."

"Does your church teach that?" I asked.

She shrugged. "I don't know. What does it matter what my church teaches as long as I believe it?"

"I could read something to you about that."

"No, please. If you read any more I *will* suspect you want to convert me."

I smiled. "I'm willing if you are."

"Well, the truth is, I'm not willing. I like my church. I was born a Catholic. I'll die a Catholic, and that's just the way it is." She paused. "Oh, Victor called today and told me about his visit with you and Hannah."

"What did he say?"

"Not much. He just said he didn't think it would do any harm if Hannah became a Mormon. Isn't that a strange thing for a priest to say? I know the Catholic Church has become more liberal recently, but I never thought it would go this far."

"Are you going to try to take Hannah's boat away from her?"

"Is that why you came?"

"Hannah is my friend. I care what happens to her. But that's not why I came. I came because you said you had a tree that needed pruning, and I wasn't doing anything after work."

"Are you falling in love with Hannah?"

"It's too early to tell. I thought I was going to marry another girl, but she's found another guy she likes better."

"Let me talk some sense into this other girl's head."

"I think it's too late for that."

"Well, her loss. You and Hannah seem good together."

"We are. Time will tell, I guess."

"I would love to have you in our family. If you marry her, I'll make you your own baklava."

"Everyone raves about your baklava."

"Yes, they do." She sighed. "I have a confession to make. I don't make it anymore. It's such a pain to make. Layers and layers of the thin phyllo soaked in butter. It takes hours. And then chopping the nuts just right, and then working with honey. You spill one drop of honey on the floor and you're mopping the floor for days to get rid of the sticky mess. I made it for every holiday for twenty years and then one day I realized my family wasn't savoring it. They were wolfing it down. And nobody has ever asked me to show them how I make it. It's a family tradition that nobody cares about. Except me. So I thought, *Why am I knocking myself out for this?*"

"Good for you."

"So now I order it at the deli. I pick it up and take it out of the box and put it in a pan and scatter some flour and a few chopped nuts on the counter and I'm done." She winked at me. "But you must never reveal this secret to anyone."

"I won't. I promise."

"You're a good boy. Tell me, is Hannah still going to be become a Mormon?"

"Yeah, she is."

"When?"

"She's going to be baptized on Saturday."

"Is the phrase 'over my dead body' used much these days?"

"Not too much, but I know what it means."

"My father used it on me once when I was about Hannah's age."

"What did you want to do?"

"Go to California with a friend of mine to see if we could become movie stars." She smiled. "On the back of his motorcycle."

"Did you go anyway?"

"No, I didn't. We were more respectful in those days. Now, of course, I can see that my father was correct to forbid me to go." She sighed. "Just as Hannah will eventually see that I'm right about this."

"What if the things she's been taught by the missionaries are true?" I asked.

She shook her head. "Oh, to be young and worry about such things as truth. Don't you see? I just want to preserve the way things are."

"You won't be able to do that. Hannah will join the Church with your permission or without."

"How do you know that?"

"Because she's as stubborn as you are."

At first she glared at me as if I had insulted her, but then her lips turned up in what slowly developed into a weak smile. "I suppose you're right, but I am not a big supporter of how independent youth are these days."

I said to her, "This isn't about riding on the back of a motorcycle to California to try to get into the movies. Even I don't think that was a good idea. But this is different. It's about her own spiritual journey. You can create a barrier between Hannah and you, but I'm not sure you can stop her."

With some difficulty she walked to the window and looked out. And then she turned to me and said, "For years I could hardly stand to be in the same room with my father because I was so angry with him for standing in my way. Eventually I realized he was right. I don't want Hannah to feel that way about me . . . because . . . well, to be quite frank, I don't have that many years left. I don't want to go to my grave with her still angry with me."

"It's actually a pretty good church," I said.

She gave a troubled sigh. "All right, I won't stand in her way."

"That's great. Would you like to come to the baptism just to see what it's like?"

"No, I will never set foot in that church."

"After the baptism we'll have refreshments."

She glared at me. "Why are you telling me that?"

"I've never had any of your baklava. And it would let Hannah know you still love her."

"You never give up, do you? Well, because you were such a help to me in the backyard, I will break down and actually make some baklava for the occasion."

"Thank you. I'm sure we'll love it. Hannah has told me how good it is."

"Let me call Hannah and tell her my decision," she said. "I'm also going to tell her about your visit. Can't hurt, right?"

"Thanks. I'll be going now."

She came with me to the door, and we said our good-byes. On my way to the pickup, she called out, "You're a good boy."

I hadn't eaten yet, so I went back to my apartment and nuked a frozen pizza. I was working on the last piece when there was a knock on the door. It was Hannah.

"Hi," she said.

"Hi."

"Can I come in?"

"Sure."

We walked into the living room. "You want to sit down?" I asked.

She sat but didn't say anything.

"What's up?" I asked.

Hannah cleared her throat, then said, "My grandmother called me. She told me what you did for her after work."

"Okay."

"Why did you do it?" she asked.

"If a woman like your grandmother wants her tree pruned, then somebody ought to do it for her."

"Why? She's not your grandmother."

I shrugged. "I didn't have anything else to do."

"She also told me you persuaded her to give permission for me to be baptized."

"We talked about it. But she came to the decision on her own."

Hannah had tears in her eyes, and she stood up. "Can I give you a hug?" she asked.

"Are you kidding? You can hug me anytime."

She gave me a hug and then stepped back and said, "I will always be grateful for what you've done for me."

"I didn't do that much."

"Can you be the one to baptize me on Saturday? I mean, you're not still on your mission, but can you do it?"

"I can, and I'd be honored."

"Good. It will mean more to my grandmother if I tell her you're going to do it."

She hesitated for a moment, then said, "Well, I guess I'd better go."

I walked her to the front door and watched her walk away. When she was halfway to her car, I called after her, "Hannah?"

When she turned to look at me, I said, "I like you . . . a lot."

She gave me a little half smile. "I like you, too, Dave. Very much."

* * *

On Wednesday night the elders met us at Hannah's boat and taught her another lesson. They also told her that she would need to visit with President Alexander prior to her baptism.

"What for?" she asked.

"So you'll already know him when you start coming to the branch," Elder Hawkins explained.

Hannah shrugged. "Okay."

I was amazed by how fast she was soaking up the principles of the gospel and how easily she was fitting in.

Then, on Thursday at work, Uncle Victor called her and asked if she would meet him in his office at the rectory that night.

"Why?"

She told me later that he was practically shouting as he said, "I'm not going to take this lying down!"

"Can I bring Dave?"

"No. This is a family matter, and he's not family."

"He's my friend, though. My best friend, and I want to bring him."

Uncle Victor paused. "All right. He can come, but only if he stays out of our discussion."

"We can be there by seven-thirty."

"Fine. I'll be waiting for you."

It didn't look good.

At seven-twenty we knocked on Uncle Victor's office at the rectory. Here, though, he wasn't Uncle Victor. He was Father Victor Serino.

He opened the door, and gave Hannah a hug and me a not-too friendly nod. He had us sit at the two chairs in front of his desk, while he sat behind the desk.

He folded his large hands and rested them on the desk in front of him, then took a deep breath and said to Hannah, "It would be a terrible mistake to join the Mormon Church."

"Why?"

"Did you know they practiced plural marriage?"

"No."

"We don't practice it anymore," I said.

"Did I ask your opinion?" he challenged.

"That's not an opinion. That's a fact," I shot back.

"This is between my niece and me. If you can't keep out of this, then I suggest you leave." He then continued with Hannah. "Did you know they used to deny people of color the priesthood?"

Hannah looked over at me, then turned to him. "When did they change that?" she asked.

"That's not the point," Uncle Victor said.

"What is the point?" she asked.

"If they're led by a prophet, why did they institute a policy that was clearly racist?"

"I don't know."

"I'm afraid there's a lot you don't know about the Mormon Church."

"That could be said of you, too, couldn't it?" Hannah said.

"Don't be impertinent." He stood up. "Follow me."

He led us to the cathedral. It was half a city block long, with high ceilings and ornate stained-glass windows depicting various scenes, had a huge crucifix at the front, and an imposing raised podium from which the priest could speak.

He had us sit in one of the pews while he climbed up into the pulpit. Even though there were a few worshippers scattered in the huge chapel, he turned on the sound system, then said into the microphone, "This cathedral holds two thousand people." His voice reverberated through the vast chapel. He went on, "We have four masses every Sunday. Every seat is filled. That's eight thousand people. Are you going to say that these eight thousand people are wrong? That they are deceived? That they are ignorant? That they get nothing of value from participating each week? Are you prepared to say that I have wasted my life tending to their needs? Every week I visit the sick, give hope to the downtrodden, pray with sinners, meet with inmates in our jails, give communion to the bed-ridden. Does all that count for nothing with God? Because that is what Mormons would have you believe."

"Everything you do is for God, Uncle Victor. I've known that all my life." Hannah's voice sounded weak and puny compared to Uncle Victor's amplified questions.

"Then why would you even think of walking away from a church that has been such a blessing to your family?"

Hannah looked over at me. I knew I wasn't going to be much help. This was between the two of them.

He came down from the pulpit and sat on the pew in front of us.

He turned to look at Hannah and said, "You don't know the history of the Mormons. You don't know what religious leaders of all faiths say about their flawed doctrines. How can you even think about abandoning the faith that has given succor to your ancestors for hundreds of years? You will break your grandmother's heart. You will bring discord into our family. So why would you even consider this?"

She took a deep breath, sighed, and softly said, "Uncle Victor, I can't answer all your questions. I only know how I feel when I read the Book of Mormon and when the missionaries are teaching me. For the first time in my life, I've had a religious experience. How do you explain that?"

"Don't do this, Hannah! I'm your uncle, and I love you. I've always loved you. I've always known you were someone very special in God's eyes."

"You're the reason I'm where I am today—because you gave me the example of someone who devotes time and energy to God's work. I want to be like you. But I can't do it here. I believe that what I am learning from the Bible and The Book of Mormon are God's word. So maybe now in time I can be an example to you. I think you can come to know that it is true, too. I love you, Uncle Victor, and I always will." She turned to me. "Let's go, Dave."

We were halfway down the long cathedral aisle when he called out. "Hannah!"

She stopped and turned around. "Yes?"

He cleared his throat, paused, and then said softly, "Godspeed."

She ran back to him and threw her arms around him and sobbed. "I'm so sorry," she said to him.

"I know."

"I love you, Uncle Victor."

"I love you, too, Hannah."

She kissed him on the cheek, stepped back, and walked quickly to where I was waiting.

"Let's go," she sniffled.

I was so proud of her—for the way she handled herself. I mean, she had essentially borne her testimony to a Catholic priest. And even though Uncle Victor wasn't able to accept the teachings of the Church, one thing I was sure of—he was a man of God.

* * *

On Friday night after work Hannah invited Abbie, Megan, and me to go sailing with her.

But when I called Abbie after work, she said she wasn't going.

"Why not? You've got to go."

"Eldon left this morning for Utah." She sighed. "To see Elizabeth. I'm not handling this very well. I just want to stay in my room."

"You can't do that. I'm coming over to pick you up."

"Don't. I wouldn't be any good for you or Hannah or Megan tonight."

"If you won't come out, I'll stand outside your window and sing Boy Scout camp songs to you through the window."

I could hear her laugh.

"Come on," I said. "It'll be fun. And it will take your mind off old what's-his-face."

She finally agreed, and a half an hour later, when I picked her up, she looked okay, except she was wearing sunglasses.

"Don't ask. My eyes are a mess. I've been crying a lot today."

"Sorry."

"Can you give me a priesthood blessing sometime tonight?"

"Yeah, sure."

"Thanks."

By the time we'd parked and were within a few feet of Hannah's boat, Abbie seemed to be back to normal. "So Hannah's the captain, right? I think you should show her the respect she deserves. Let me hear you say, 'Aye, aye, Captain!'"

"Fuhgetabout it."

Hannah came up out of the galley to meet us.

"Seaman third class Dave here is reporting for duty," Abbie said. "You got any decks that need swabbing?"

"No, but Dave's been a big help to me sailing. And in other things."

"Really? What other things?" Abbie said, always looking for something to tease me about.

Hannah told them about me pruning her grandmother's tree.

"I'm not surprised. Dave's an Eagle Scout. I even went to his court of honor. Dave, why don't you tell Hannah about each of your thousand merit badges?"

Hannah scowled at Abbie.

We waited another half an hour for Megan to find us. She had gotten lost, but she called on her cell phone and we talked her in.

Megan had a million questions about the boat. She followed Hannah as she went to start the outboard motor.

I showed Abbie how to untie the knot holding the boat to the dock and cast off the line.

"She doesn't like me teasing you, does she?" Abbie asked.

"No."

"I wonder why. Don't you?"

"Yeah, a little."

"I think she's so into you."

"I hope you're right."

"I'm always right."

Once we were sailing in the bay, all skepticism, jibes, and sarcasm fell away. It was incredible being on the water, where we were face-to-face with beauty and grace.

While Hannah grilled some hamburgers, she let each of us take a turn at the helm. Whoever was at the helm was my favorite for that moment—the sea breeze in her hair and a big grin of pure delight on her face.

Abbie noticed what I was doing. "You having a good time scoping us out, Dave?"

"Yeah, I am."

"We're all babes, right?"

I laughed. "Yeah, I guess."

"So, if you could marry any of us, which one would it be?" Abbie asked.

"That's not a fair question."

"When have I ever been fair?"

"Let's just enjoy this experience," I said.

"No, tell us, Dave," Megan said.

"I'd be your first choice, wouldn't I?" Abbie said.

"No, I'm so over you."

"After I'm married to Eldon, will you ever think about me?"

"I never think about you now."

"You will. I know you will."

"Don't flatter yourself," I said.

"I'll probably think about you, too. Whenever I go to a hardware store, I'll go, 'What was the name of that guy I went with in high school? His dad had a hardware store. I wonder what ever happened to him.'"

"Great. I'm so glad you won't forget me."

She sighed. "Actually, I'll remember you as the best friend I ever had in high school. But not my best friend *ever* because that will be Eldon. Hands down. I'm not just getting married, I'm getting a friend for life . . . no, actually, for eternity."

"We're all so happy for you, Abbie," I said with little enthusiasm.

"So anyway, I'm taken. So let's move on. Who's next on your list?"

"I don't know. Hannah maybe."

Hannah looked surprised. "We're more friends than anything else." She smiled. "Fast becoming good friends though."

"What about Megan?" Abbie said.

"Megan, you'd be great," I said. "You're drop-dead gorgeous. I could spend a lifetime just admiring you."

She blushed.

"Don't take it to heart, Megan. Dave's basically a voyeur," Abbie said.

"And Abbie's basically a liar," I added.

"Actually, I'm very impressed, Dave," Abbie said. "You started at the oldest and worked your way down. How Old Testament of you. Way to be."

"Yeah, that's me, all right."

We were out for a couple of hours, and when it started to get dark, Hannah took over and we made our way to port and docked.

"Dave and I usually read a few pages from the Book of Mormon on the boat," she said. "Do you guys want to do that too?"

They agreed, and we went down into the cabin and turned on a light and read for about half an hour and then we knelt down and had a prayer. With the four of us in that small area, it was cramped, but praying together felt good.

As we were about to leave, Hannah asked, "Are you guys being nice to me just because I'm about to be baptized?"

"No, girl, you've got us for life," Abbie said.

"I've never had friends like you guys. And I've never had a guy friend like Dave."

As we were about to separate, Abbie couldn't part on a somber note.

"Dave, say that thing to them you always wrote in your letters to me," Abbie said.

"You mean, 'Why haven't you written me back?'"

"No, the other, at the end of each letter."

"I love you."

"No, no, the other." For Megan and Hannah's sake, she said, "He always used to write 'As always' at the end of his letters. So I start thinking, what does that mean? That sometimes he isn't Dave? I mean, what's that all about? Does he have a multiple personality disorder? 'As always'? What were you thinking?"

"Dave is always a good guy," Hannah said. "That's what it means."

"Maybe so. Well, good night, you guys."

I still hadn't given Abbie a priesthood blessing. As we left, I asked if she'd mind if we did it at Nathan's place. She asked why. I said because I wanted to change into a white shirt and tie. She said I didn't need to go to all that trouble. But I told her it was what my dad had taught me about exercising the priesthood, and then added, "I don't have anything to give by myself. Everything I do with the priesthood, I need Heavenly Father's help for."

"Okay."

I had hoped Nathan would be home so he could assist me, but he wasn't.

While Abbie waited in the living room, I changed in the bathroom because I didn't have a bedroom. I was still sleeping on the couch.

I was having a difficult time with this. I wondered if I was too close to this to be able to do much good, giving her a priesthood blessing. The truth was I hoped Eldon would come back engaged to Elizabeth, so I'd still have a chance with Abbie.

After I finished tying my tie, I said a silent prayer for help.

In the living room, I asked Abbie to say a prayer first, and then I gave her a blessing.

It went okay, I guess. I felt the Spirit as I gave her the blessing.

She gave me a hug afterwards and thanked me. And then I took her home.

After I got home, Megan called me. At first I thought she'd called because she was mad I'd put her as number three on my list of who I might marry, but that wasn't it at all.

"Dave, I need to talk to you about something. Do you have time now?"

"I guess so."

"There's this guy I knew when I was growing up. His name is Sterling."

"Sterling? What kind of a name is that?"

"I know. Anyway, he's about two years older than me. He and his dad were our home teachers. They took a real interest in us. When I got to high school, Sterling always looked out for me and made sure everything was going all right."

I looked at my clock. It was getting late, and I wanted to get some sleep. "Yeah, so?"

"Uh, well, nothing, really. Sterling is just a very sincere guy who's always been very kind to me. He's back from his mission now. And he called me a couple of nights ago. He's working for his dad, building houses in St. George."

I slipped under the covers hoping I could carry on the conversation in my sleep. "So?"

"He said he and his dad are building a house for me . . . and for him."

"I don't understand."

"He wants me to marry him."

"Why? So they'll continue to get a hundred percent on their home teaching?"

"No. He says he fell in love with me the first time he and his dad came home teaching. That was when I was thirteen and he was sixteen."

"And he just got around to telling you now?"

"Well, he couldn't really make it a part of the monthly lesson, right?"

"What did you tell him?"

"I told him I couldn't make a decision like that over the phone. We haven't even been on a date together."

"Good. Keep it that way."

"He said he understood, but he was wondering while they were building the house if I'd mind giving him some preferences about various things in the house that I'd like if it ever turned out to be our home together."

"But why would he care what you think if you're not going to marry him?"

"That's what I asked. He said for me not to worry. He told me to just think of it as being a home decoration consultant."

I sat up in bed. "Why doesn't he do this like all the rest of us? You ask girls out, eventually they tell you they just want to be friends, and then you move on to someone else."

"He's kind of shy."

"Either this guy is good at manipulation or else he's a social washout."

"He asked if I wanted multiple shower heads in the master bathroom."

"Are you out of your mind?"

"Really? I think multiple shower heads would be nice. That way I wouldn't have to turn around to get the other half of my body wet."

"My point is you shouldn't even give him an answer to a question like that."

"Why not?"

"Because . . . because it means you're buying into the whole idea."

"The shower decision is water under the bridge, so to speak. Next week he wants me to say if I want marble counters in the kitchen. What do you think?"

I got up and started pacing back and forth. "You absolutely can't play this game. If you do, he'll think you're going to marry him. That would be a huge mistake."

"You don't have to yell at me."

"Sorry." I sat down again. "Please, Megan, just tell him to quit calling you. If he wants to marry you, then tell him to come out here and get a dead-end job like me and take his chances like everybody else. Besides, what about us going to BYU—Idaho together in the fall? Remember?"

"You think there's hope for you and me, Dave?"

"Yeah, sure. Why not?"

"Me, too."

So finally we were done with Sterling's con job. Or so I thought.

"Some countertops look like granite but they're a lot cheaper," she said.

I sighed and told Megan I had to get some sleep, said good night, turned my cell off, and got back in bed. Mercifully, the day was finally over.

CHAPTER NINE

On Saturday night, at about seven-thirty, I stepped into the baptismal font. The water was a little cool but not too bad. Hannah, wearing a white jumpsuit, came down the opposite stairs and into the font. She looked at me and smiled.

We looked into each other's eyes. She looked radiant, like how we picture angels.

Then I baptized her.

When she came out of the water, she gave me a hug, then started back up the steps, where Abbie and Megan waited to assist her.

Fifteen minutes later, after changing our clothes, Hannah and I returned to the Relief Society room. Megan and Hannah and Abbie sang "How Gentle God's Commands." It was Megan's idea, something she'd thought of that morning. Even with her damp hair, Hannah looked great—totally happy, and the three of them sang well together.

President Hinckley had said that every convert needed a friend. Hannah had three friends, so I was pretty sure things would go okay for her because she had Abbie, Megan, and me.

After the closing prayer, we had refreshments. Besides the mandatory chocolate chip cookies, Hannah's grandmother had sent baklava.

The baklava was so outstanding that I tried to make it possible for me to take more home.

"What are you doing, Dave?" Abbie asked.

"Just cutting these pieces in half. These portions are way too big, don't you think?"

"No, I don't." She took one of the big pieces.

I glared at her. "Hey, save some for somebody else."

"There's plenty left." She grabbed another big piece and put it on a napkin for later.

"Okay, but that's all you get."

"You're trying to hog it all for yourself, aren't you?"

"No, no, I'm just being considerate of others."

"Really? Well, let me help you do that," she said, picking up the pan and going out and talking everyone into having another piece.

It should have made me mad but it didn't. In fact, I started laughing.

She turned around, gave me a big smile, and winked.

When she returned, there was only one piece left. She said she was going to save it for Eldon when he returned from Utah on Sunday night.

"Okay."

"Thanks. I've got to go now. Duane and Addison have an office party they want to go to. Since Eldon is gone this weekend, I said I'd watch the kids."

"Let me walk you to your car."

"You like Hannah, don't you?" she asked once we were outside.

"Yeah."

"I could tell. Sometimes you look at her the way you look at me."

"You mean the way I *used* to look at you."

"No, you still do. That's why you and I argue. It keeps us from having to face the fact we still have feelings for each other."

"You do, too?"

"Yeah, crazy, isn't it? It's probably because Eldon is gone so much."

"Tell him to work harder."

She smiled. "Yeah, right. Are you coming to the singles branch tomorrow?"

"No. Hannah is being confirmed in her home ward."

"Okay, well, maybe I'll see you Monday night for family home evening."

"Maybe so. I'll bring Hannah."

She paused. "Dave?"

"Yeah."

"You've turned out real well. Don't get me wrong. You were a good guy in high school, but your mission has made a big difference. I was thinking that as I watched you baptize Hannah. You've come a long way, Hardware Boy."

"Thanks."

"I'm proud of the person you've become. I'm the only one here who knows how much you've grown. That's it. That's my feel-good talk for you today."

On Sunday I confirmed Hannah a member of the Church in the sacrament meeting of the Little Neck Ward. After the meeting, many of the sisters she'd met the previous Sunday came up and gave her a kiss on the cheek and a hug. It made me feel grateful for these good women who showed her such great support. I decided I liked bilingual wards.

That night I called my folks. It wasn't something I ever did lightly. I could always talk to my dad but not as much with my mom because she had a way of turning everything into a crisis. Whenever I'd give her one bit of information about my life, she'd always see it as something she needed to worry about.

My dad was on the living room phone, my mom on the phone in their bedroom. "Mom, Dad, I met this girl at work. Her name is Hannah."

"A New York girl?" my mom asked.

"Yeah. I baptized her last night, and today she was confirmed."

"That's great!" my dad said.

"How do you feel about this girl?" my mom asked.

"Well, I'm thinking she might be *the one.*"

"What about Abbie?" Mom asked.

"Abbie is taken."

"Are you still planning on moving back here and running the store while we're on our mission?" my mom asked.

"Yeah, sure."

"If you marry this girl, what if she wants to stay in New York?"

I hadn't thought about that yet.

"It will all work out," my dad said.

I was glad I'd called. Mainly because I'd done my part. I'd told my parents about Hannah. So now, according to the Nathan Rule, it would be okay to kiss her.

I planned for our first kiss to be after branch home evening on Monday. I wanted it to be just right, so I called her and asked if I could pick her up. She couldn't understand why I'd want to do that but finally she agreed.

I was stoked. Monday night would be the night I would have my first kiss with the girl who might some day become my wife.

Monday during work I was a little nervous around Hannah. I think we both felt that something was going to happen. Once when she came into the storeroom to get a special order insect bomb, she brushed past me. "Sorry," she said.

We turned and faced each other and looked into each other's eyes.

The customer called out from just outside the back room. "Hey, is it in there or not? If it isn't, I want an explanation!"

That broke the spell. "Yeah, here it is." Hannah said, picking up the box and leaving the back room.

It was a close call. In a way I was glad we hadn't kissed. It would be embarrassing if our kids asked us when we first kissed, and we had to tell them it was over an insect bomb in the back room of a hardware store.

I was excited that night when Hannah and I entered the Relief Society room of the Meadowview building for family home evening.

Abbie and Megan took Hannah around and introduced her to everyone. It made me happy to see how warmly everyone welcomed her.

When she was on the other side of the room, Antonio entered. He took two steps, stopped, and walked over to Hannah. "Ow ya duen?"

Hannah's eyes opened wide. She broke into a big grin. "Not bad. Ow ya duen?"

"Not bad. What's ya name?"

"Hannah. What's yous?"

"Antonio. You Italian?"

"Yeah, I am. Three-fourths Italian, one-fourth Greek."

"That's good enough for me. We don't get many Italians in the chuch."

"Ya got one now. Good to meet yous, Antonio."

"What ya ea faw?"

"Family home . . . family home . . . Eden . . . even . . ."

"Got it. How come I nevuh saw you 'ear befau?"

"This is my fist time. I was baptized Sat-a-day. Dave baptized me."

"How do you know Dave?"

"We wuk in the same stoa."

"So, you two eve' get togeter afta wuk?"

"Yeah, once in a while, I take 'im sailing in my boat."

"Get out of 'ere! Yous got a boat? I used to 'ave a boat!"

"Get out of 'ere!"

"I swea'."

They continued to talk with their New York accent, but after a while I could translate what they were saying into actual English.

"What kind of boat did you have?" Hannah asked.

"Twenty-five footer."

"You know how to sail?" Hannah asked.

"Hey, one time I sailed from here to North Carolina."

"No way!"

"Way!"

"I've always wanted to do that! I never get out of sight of land."

"It's not ha'd with a good GPS system."

"Take me with you some time," she said.

"I wish I could. I had to sell my boat. Maybe we could go in yours."

"Yeah, sure, but let's take some smaller trips first, okay?"

"Yeah. Could I see your boat?"

"Yeah, sure, anytime," she said.

"How about now?" Antonio asked.

"Now?"

"Yeah. Why not? We can have family home evening by ourselves, you know what I'm saying? In my car I got my own personal copy of the *Ensign*."

"You got a flag in your ca'?"

"The *Ensign* is a church magazine. I'll read it to you while you show me your boat and that'll be our family home evening."

Hannah came over to me. "Antonio and I are going to go look at my boat."

"Okay."

"You okay with that?"

"Oh, yeah, sure, whatever."

"Great. See you at work in the morning."

Just after they left, I noticed Abbie staring at me. I gave her a faint smile.

She came over. "You okay?"

"I'm always okay. You know that."

"You want to talk?"

I shook my head. "They're just going to look at her boat. It doesn't mean anything."

"I know. They both like to sail. It's no big deal. Let's take a walk," she suggested.

We walked out onto the grounds of the church.

"Is Eldon coming tonight?" I asked.

She looked at her watch. "Yeah, in about forty-five minutes."

"Have you talked to him since he got back from Utah?"

"Just on the phone."

"Did he say much?"

"Not too much." She paused. "He called me from the airport in Utah and told me that whatever he had with Elizabeth is now pretty much over."

"That must be a relief. So, is it all right if Eldon finds out you and I took a walk?"

"Hmmm, good point. How about if I get Megan to take a walk with you?"

"You're assigning me to her as a service project? Am I that pathetic?"

"Megan likes you a lot, Dave."

"She's too young."

"She's getting older by the day. As are you. I'll be right back."

Abbie went back into the building, and a few minutes later the two of them came back. Abbie waved good-bye and left.

"You okay?" Megan asked.

"Yeah, I'm fine."

"Abbie told me about Hannah and Antonio."

"It's no big deal."

"I guess Abbie and Eldon are back together, stronger than ever."

"Yep, it's my week, right?"

"So, do you want to take a walk?"

Even though I knew Abbie had put her up to it, I actually did want to get away from everyone else. "Okay."

We went across the street and walked in the park. Megan was a good listener, and I ended up telling her about calling my folks and telling them that Hannah might be the girl for me, and even how I had been planning on kissing Hannah for the first time that night. But then she and Antonio left together. And now it looks like Abbie and Eldon might get married. And how nothing ever works out for me with girls.

She told me she was sorry it hadn't worked out.

And then we hugged, and I told her she was the most beautiful girl I'd ever known. I almost made the mistake of kissing her again, but I didn't.

This was getting confusing.

You know how people are always talking about true love? With me the whole thing seemed to be about ranking. Like with baseball teams.

So here was the current ranking. If Abbie would ever agree to it, I'd marry her. If that didn't pan out, then Hannah would be my next choice. And if neither of those worked out, then Megan would naturally take over the number-one position. For a guy like me, courtship is a lot like running a baseball team. Sometimes you have to move the players around in the lineup.

For family home evening we all played a stupid game that had no purpose and then we had cookies left over from Sunday's munch-and-mingle.

It was a rotten day. Not even the cookies were good.

Tuesday morning at work things were awkward between Hannah and me. At first we stayed away from each other. But then later on she wanted to talk. So I took her to lunch at a deli a couple of doors down.

They didn't have any tables, and we stood in the aisle and ate our food. People kept having to get around us, so we went to the back aisle and ate.

"So, uh, did Antonio like your boat?" I asked.

"Yeah, he did. He showed me some things about it I'd never seen. Like he found a secret cupboard with maps I didn't even know about. He wants to take me sailing to North Carolina sometime this summer. It's all very exciting."

"Great, good, that's really good. I'm happy for you and *Blue Skies*. Looks like it might finally leave the bay."

"Yeah, that's true. Spread your wings, little boat, and be free." She paused. "Oh, Abbie called me last night after I got home."

"Really? How come?"

"Oh, you know, just to talk. She told me you were really bummed out when I left with Antonio."

I figured I might as well confess since Abbie had let the cat out of the bag. "Yeah, I was."

"Why?"

"I called my folks last week and told them about you being baptized. They were really happy to hear about that. I also told them that I thought that you and I might have a future together."

Her eyes opened wide. "How come I didn't know about this?"

"It's a little hard to explain."

"Is this about the Nathan Rule?"

"How do you know about that?"

"Abbie told me. She said you kissed Megan right after you met her, but then you made a rule that before you kissed a girl again you'd call your folks and tell them you were serious about her. We both laughed about that. You know, you having to call Mommy and Daddy for permission."

I threw up my hands. "I can't win with Abbie around, can I? No matter what I do, it's wrong."

"It's not wrong, just a little unusual." She paused. "So you were thinking about kissing me last night?"

"Yeah."

"I'm not sure I'd have been ready for that. I thought we were just friends."

"We are. That's all I am to anyone. Just a friend. But I need more than that."

"Why?"

"My mom is hoping I'll get married before they leave on their mission. And they're planning on leaving in February."

She began laughing.

"What?" I asked.

"Does love have anything to do with this, or are you just going to get married to the first girl who says yes?"

"Look, just forget it, okay? Let's talk about something else."

We stood without talking, then she said, "I have some news."

I groaned. "You kissed Antonio last night, didn't you?"

"What, are you crazy? My news is that Antonio and I are going sailing every night after work this week. We've got to get ready for when we sail to North Carolina."

"Yeah, sure. So when will I see you?"

"We'll see each other at work."

"I mean when will I see you after work?"

"Abbie says we're all going into the City on the Fourth of July. We all want you to come with us, Dave. We want to show you the City."

I didn't know what to do with myself after work now that going sailing with Hannah wasn't possible. So I stayed and cleaned up the store and made some preliminary orders for Halloween and Christmas. And then about nine-thirty I went to the diner for sweet potato fries. While I was there, I got a call. It was Abbie.

"What are you doing?" she asked.

"Nothing."

"Where are you?"

I didn't want to talk to her. "I'm at the store working late."

She gave me her wicked-witch laugh and then hung up.

A few seconds later Abbie and Megan entered the diner. They had called me from the diner parking lot after seeing my pickup and knowing I was there.

"Working hard at the store, Dave? What a trooper!" Abbie said, grabbing a handful of my fries. "Are these sweet potato fries, Dave? Idaho is going to revoke your citizenship."

They each slid into my booth across from me, and I scowled at both of them. "Go away. I don't want to talk to either one of you."

"Why's that?" Abbie asked.

"Because you two are ruining my chances with Hannah."

"How do you figure that? I told her you were disappointed she left with Antonio. How did that ruin your chances with her? Besides, I really think she likes Antonio now."

"Yeah, sure, why not? They're both from New York and they're both Italian, so they've got a lot in common." I said all this with my teeth clenched.

"I suppose. Don't you have something to say to Megan?" Abbie said.

"Hi, Megan. How's it going?"

Abbie reached across and bopped me on the forehead. "That's not what I had in mind."

"What?"

"Megan is the only good thing you've got going for you now. You ought to treat her better than you do."

Megan shrugged. "It's okay. I know he's not that into me."

"I'm not sure that's true," Abbie said. "With guys their hearts and their minds are totally separate. It's like one doesn't talk to the other. It could be that Dave is in love with you but hasn't told his mind yet. I mean, Dave isn't a player. He never was in high school, and I don't think he is now. He's only kissed three girls his whole life. You and me and one other girl who conned him into kissing her once when they were in ninth grade."

I was tired of being made fun of. "I want to know about Eldon's trip to Utah to see Elizabeth."

"He told me that Elizabeth didn't even hug him when she first saw him," Abbie began. "Actually, she shook his hand. Isn't that great? And they hardly had any time to talk. And when she did talk, she just talked about her mission. Nothing about them. He's pretty sure it's all over between them."

"That must be a big relief to you," I said.

"Yeah, it is. The one good thing was he had a chance to talk to her dad. He's in the Utah legislature. He told Eldon he thought he should go into politics some day. Maybe even run for governor. So, anyway, Eldon's seriously thinking about that now."

"That sounds interesting. I'd like to talk to him about that," I said. "See if he can come by and join us."

She called but it went straight to voicemail.

"What's he doing?" I asked. "He can't be going door-to-door this late."

"Sometimes they're out of town and don't get back here until ten or eleven. That's probably what's happening tonight."

"Call him and ask him where he's at."

She punched in the numbers and waited, but Eldon didn't answer. "He's probably talking to his district manager. He has to report their numbers at the end of every day. He'll be off in a few minutes."

I realized I'd ignored Megan. "How you doing, Megan?" I asked.

"Good, real good. What's going on in your life?"

"Not much. How about you?"

"Not much for me, either," Megan said, then after pausing, said, "Can I ask you guys a question?"

"Of course," I said.

"If you were going to have a fireplace in your house, would you rather have it in the family room or in the master bedroom?"

"Would you tell that idiot to quit bothering you?" I complained.

Abbie stared at me. "Am I missing something here?"

I told her about Sterling.

"I would go for a fireplace in the master bedroom," Abbie said. "It could be very romantic . . . hot chocolate, the lights down, a big throw rug on the floor next to the fireplace."

I glared at Abbie. "Don't encourage this! The guy hasn't ever even dated Megan. He has no right to talk to her about a fireplace."

"Let's see, Dave, my guess is you'd want the fireplace in your shop located about a hundred yards away from the house. I can picture it now. A cold snowy night. Dave's alone in his workshop doing magical things with his new router while his wife paces the floor wondering when he'll be done. By the way, Dave, what the heck is a router? And don't go denying you've ever talked to me about routers because I distinctly remember you explaining routers to me on the night of our senior prom."

Megan burst out laughing. "Are you serious?"

"Oh, yeah, I'm serious. Mr. Romance here whispering sweet words in my ear . . . about routers!"

"That is hilarious!" Megan said, then got all serious on us again. "I thought about the fireplace being in the master bedroom, but in the end I chose the family room. It would be great for family home evening."

Abbie then filled Megan in on other ridiculous things she remembered about going with me in high school. After a while I quit paying any attention to them and started thinking I really needed to spend more time with guys. I needed a friend who was a guy. We could work on his car or learn to surf or play golf together.

Guys are great to be with. You don't need to worry about hurting their feelings. They never tell others every stupid thing you ever did or said.

We ordered some drinks and more sweet potato fries and ate them as we talked. The next time I looked at my watch, thirty minutes had passed. "So, you want to call Eldon again?"

She called again, but he still didn't pick up.

"Those must be some big orders that Eldon is calling into his district manager, huh?"

After I'd said it, I knew it was a mistake. Abbie looked away and brought her hand to her lips, something she only did when she was having a hard time.

"Hey, he's probably just having problems getting through," I said. "What with all the others trying to phone in their sales too."

"That's probably it."

After that she called every few minutes. But he never picked up.

Twenty minutes later, she said, "He's probably talking to his folks. He calls them every week."

"I bet that's it," I said. "Well, it's getting late. Let's go."

We paid our bill and went out to the parking lot. Three people, three vehicles, right? No wonder there's an energy crisis.

"I'll try one more time," she said.

Still no answer.

Abbie looked as though she might cry. Megan and I didn't want to leave her, so we all sat in Abbie's car and talked. By that time it was mostly Megan doing the talking.

At eleven-thirty when Abbie called, Eldon finally picked up.

"I've been calling since about ten, but you never picked up," Abbie said. "Were you talking to Elizabeth?"

I could tell by her reaction what the answer was. She put her hand to her mouth and closed her eyes. "Really? I thought you were done with her."

Abbie climbed out of the car and motioned me and Megan to follow her and come closer so we could hear Eldon. Our heads were practically touching.

"She was the one who called me," Eldon said over the phone.

"And she made you talk to her for an hour and a half?" Abbie asked. "What's going on?"

He didn't answer for a long time. "I didn't think there was any harm in me talking to her."

"Is this the first time you've talked to her since you got back?"

"No. We talked this morning."

"I do not appreciate you keeping this a secret from me."

"I was going to tell you. Sorry."

"When you said good-bye to her tonight, did you tell her you loved her?"

After a long pause, he said, "Yes, but that's only because she said the same thing to me."

"When were you going to tell me all this? Never?"

"What was I supposed to do? Not take her call? That wouldn't have been very polite."

"Maybe you should call her back now! You can tell her how unreasonable I am!" She turned off her cell phone and started pacing back and forth.

She bummed a tissue from Megan and wiped her eyes and blew her nose and looked over at us and said, "What does a girl have to do around here to get a hug?"

We did a group hug.

After another hour talking in her car, Abbie said it was late and she needed to go, so the three of us got in our vehicles and went our separate ways.

* * *

The next afternoon Abbie came into the hardware store. "You got a minute?"

"What's up?" I asked.

"Eldon came this morning with flowers and apologized. He promised he wasn't going to talk to Elizabeth anymore, even if she does call. He says it will never happen again."

"And you believe him?"

"Yeah, I do."

"Great."

"He wants to come with us to Manhattan on the Fourth of July. You'll come too, won't you? I want you to ask him about Elizabeth if you get a chance. Megan's going to come, and I'll talk to Hannah and Antonio, so we can find out what's going on with them."

"We're going as a group, right?"

"That's right. Please come, Dave. I want it to be a good day for you, too. We'll go there in the morning. We'll take the train in and then about five we'll head out to President Alexander's house and stay there for the fireworks show they have at the beach near his house, and then we'll go home."

I thought about it. What else did I have to do? Maybe it would even be fun. "Okay, I'll go."

"Good." She reached for my hand. "I'm excited to show you the sights of New York City!"

Murray was coming. She squeezed my hand, winked, and asked, "Where's Hannah?"

"I don't know. Probably helping a customer. Just wander around. You'll find her."

"How are things between you and her?"

"All she talks about is Antonio."

"It's probably just because he's the first single LDS guy from New York she's met. The charm will wear off after a while."

"Maybe not. They're both proud of their Italian heritage, and they both love boating. I don't have that much going for me."

"That's not true and you know it. You're an amazing guy. Well, I've got to go. I'm so excited that we're all going to spend the Fourth of July together in the City! You're such a small-town Idaho boy. You have no idea what you're about to experience, Dave! No idea at all! You're going to love New York City!"

* * *

On Sunday in sacrament meeting, Antonio and Hannah sat on the same row with Abbie and Eldon. Megan and I sat together in the back row.

My mind wandered, and I began to think that life is a lot like baseball. Things tend to shake out with time. The two best players on your team get traded to another team. And a young player you brought up from the minor leagues starts to show promise.

So once again the batting order had changed. Megan was now hitting first, with Hannah batting second. And Abbie had now moved to the bottom of the order.

Megan really was a looker, and during a viola solo in sacrament meeting she caught me looking at her. "What are you thinking about?" she whispered.

I smiled. "You."

She cuddled closer. "I was thinking about you, too."

I could totally marry this girl, I thought. *Not right away of course. Not right after she's graduated from high school. I needed to give this some time. Like maybe in December, after fall semester. Then she'd just be another college student. And who could blame me for marrying a college girl?*

I liked the idea. There was still a possibility I could get married before my folks left on their mission. I knew that would make my mom happy.

So even though I was in a bit of a slump, I was still in the game.

CHAPTER TEN

At ten-thirty in the morning on the Fourth of July we were all standing at the train station in Port Jefferson, waiting to catch the train to New York City.

Port Jefferson is the town where President Alexander and his family lived. We'd each driven to his home separately and then gotten a ride from him in his SUV to the station.

Besides Abbie, Megan, Hannah, Antonio, and me, we also had a new nanny from Utah named Nicole. She was a frail-looking blonde with a soft voice. She didn't seem to know much about makeup and hair. I felt a little sorry for her.

As we waited for the train, I was standing next to Hannah, but I might as well have been miles away for all the attention she gave me. Antonio was telling her about his sailing adventure to North Carolina. As he talked, it seemed to me he looked better than usual, but I couldn't tell why. Eldon still hadn't shown up.

Abbie motioned for me, and I walked over to where she was standing on the station platform. "What's with Antonio?" she asked.

"What do you mean?"

"Did you notice his new Bela Lugosi look?"

"Who's Bela Lugosi?"

"He played Dracula in the old vampire movies. Antonio looks

just like him. He's got his hair combed straight back, and he's put mousse on it."

"I knew he'd done something different. Is that a good look for him?"

"I actually think it is. Sorry, I know that's not the answer you wanted."

I shrugged. "I have my charms, too, right?"

She cuffed me on the chin with her fist. "Absolutely. Also, most girls aren't in the market for vampires, so that gives you an edge."

"Where's Eldon? Is he coming or not?"

"I don't know. They were working in New Jersey last night, and he probably got in late. So maybe you're going to be stuck with me being your personal tour guide all day."

"How personal?" I teased.

She ignored me. "Have you thought about seating arrangements on the train?"

"No."

"It's not going to work for you to be sitting with Hannah and Antonio. You'll only make yourself miserable. Sit with us, okay?"

Nicole came over to talk to us. "My mom told me never to go to New York City. She said if I did, I'd get robbed."

"That's not true," Abbie said. "Tens of thousands of tourists go to New York City every day and very few of them actually get robbed," she teased.

Apparently teasing was not a part of Nicole's life. "It's just my luck I'll be the one who does. Jimmy warned me not to go today."

"Who's Jimmy?"

"Jimmy is the reason I came out here."

"How's that?" Abbie asked.

"I had to get away from him. He wouldn't leave me alone. He says I have to marry him."

"Why?"

"He says I have no future, so what else am I going to do?"

"Oh."

"So I came out here, but he still keeps calling. Sometimes ten times a day."

"And you pick up every time he calls?" Abbie asked.

She nodded. "If I don't, he gets mad."

"What do you care as long as you're not talking to him?" Abbie asked.

She thought about it. "Oh."

Her cell had an annoying tune. She looked at the number. "That's him."

"Don't pick up," Abbie said.

She thought about it. "You sure?"

"I'm sure."

"He'll keep calling."

Abbie shrugged. "Keep ignoring him then."

"He'll ask if I was with another guy today."

"Really? And what if you were?" Abbie asked.

"He'd get real mad. He's got a bad temper."

"What would he do? Get on a plane and fly out here?"

"No. Jimmy says he's never going to fly."

"So he'd get in his car and drive out here?"

"Well, actually, the car he drives would never make it out here."

"So he'd get on a bus or a train and spend a week coming out here?"

"No. He works for his dad. This is their busiest time of year."

"So he'd stay in Utah and be mad?"

"Yeah, but he'd call and yell at me over the phone," Nicole said.

"Only if you picked up."

She thought about it. "That's right."

"Interesting. Excuse me." Abbie went over to talk with Megan. A minute later she returned.

"Does Jimmy have a cell phone?" she asked Nicole.

"Uh-huh."

"Let's send him pictures of you and Dave in New York City."

"Why?"

"To show him you can get along without him just fine. To show him he'd better start treating you better or you'll find someone else. Can I use your phone to take the picture?" Abbie asked.

"I guess so."

Abbie took Nicole's phone and handed it to Megan. "I'll be the director and Megan here will be the photographer. Dave, put your arm around Nicole."

"No."

"C'mon, Dave," Megan said. "It will teach this guy a lesson."

I reluctantly put my arm around Nicole.

"Nicole, you lean into him. Rest your head on his shoulder," Abbie said.

"Kiss her, Dave," Antonio said.

"I don't even know her."

"When has that ever stopped you before!" Antonio called out. He had such a booming voice I'm sure they heard him in Jersey. "Nicole, Dave here holds the record in the branch for kissing the most girls in one week."

I rolled my eyes.

"Turn toward her like you're about to kiss her," Abbie suggested.

I did as I was told. Megan took the picture on Nicole's phone and then passed it around.

"Nicole, send that to Jimmy," Abbie said. "It will give him something to think about."

"He'll get really mad."

Abbie laughed. "I know. Isn't that great!"

Nicole looked worried but then finally started laughing, too.

I looked down the track and saw the train coming. It would be at the station in thirty seconds. Suddenly I felt very happy. I was going to be with Abbie without Eldon all day and maybe even for the fireworks show that night.

But then I spotted a familiar car racing into the parking lot. Eldon parked his car and ran toward the platform. I figured he wouldn't make it because it takes time to get tickets at the machine and the train would be gone by then.

Apparently he had a pass because he ran up the stairs and over to Abbie just before the train stopped.

Antonio and Hannah boarded first and then Abbie and Eldon. That left Megan, Nicole, and me to ride together.

Our New York City adventure began. As the train rolled along, in front of us, Antonio and Hannah had their heads together, looking at some photos of his old sailboat. Eldon and Abbie were talking and laughing together. Nicole, Megan, and I were excited just looking out the window of the train at the passing scenes.

We started far enough out on the island that homes had lawns and stores had parking lots. As we came to them, the names of each town—Stony Brook, St. James, Smithtown, and Kings Park—were announced by an automated system.

By the time we reached Jamaica in Queens, there were no more lawns, and the parking lots were replaced by parking garages. There was lots of construction going on—buildings being torn down, buildings being put up.

And then for a brief moment we could see the Empire State Building in the distance. And then the train dropped down and entered a tunnel.

Abbie turned around in her seat. "Guys, we're in a tunnel that goes underneath the East River," she announced.

"Does it ever leak?" Nicole, wide-eyed, asked.

"No, never." Abbie glanced up and put her finger on a spot on the side of the train. "Oh, my gosh! It's wet! We're doomed!"

Nicole looked scared.

I leaned over and said, "Relax. There's no water. That's just Abbie."

Nicole smiled weakly.

"I got you, didn't I, Dave? You totally believed me," Abbie boasted.

"I never believe you."

"I know. That's starting to get to me."

Eldon looked a little jealous of me with Abbie. He didn't have that kind of relationship with her. She never teased him. I was glad about that. How can you marry somebody you can't tease?

When the train reached Penn Station, everyone else hurried to the exits before the train stopped, but not us. We were rookies.

A minute later we were in the central corridor of Penn Station. It runs for blocks and is full of shops on either side.

Abbie led us to where we could take a subway. We took the Number 1 train uptown to Times Square. A few minutes later we climbed some stairs to go outside.

And there we were, in New York City!

Nicole and I just stood there and gawked. So many people, so much traffic, so many pedestrians. Street vendors selling everything from hot dogs to jewelry to watches to hand bags.

"Close your mouths, you guys," Abbie said. "You look like tourists. Let's go. Follow me."

We started walking.

"Where are we going?" I asked.

"To the top of the Empire State Building."

"Are you sure we're not going to get mugged?" Nicole asked.

"Look around you. This is the Fourth of July. All you've got here today is other tourists, mostly families."

I didn't say much as we walked. It was hard enough just trying to dodge other pedestrians. But I did listen to Eldon and Abbie. He was like a car salesman who keeps talking about the merits of the car even after you've decided to buy it.

He had big plans. After he finished at BYU, he wanted to go to law school and then into politics, maybe working on the staff of a congressman in Washington, D.C., and then positioning himself for a run for governor some day.

He seemed different to me than when I first met him. I wondered if it was because Elizabeth's dad had given him the idea that he could be governor of Utah some day.

I was a little surprised Abbie didn't tease him like she would have me if I'd said I want to be the governor of Idaho. She listened to him carefully and was very respectful of his goals.

Suddenly I understood why Eldon wasn't jumping at the chance to marry Abbie. Now he needed a trophy wife who would fit in as Utah's First Lady.

Megan also heard Eldon talking about what he hoped to achieve. I think she felt sorry for me because she knew I'd never be able to match up to Eldon's vision of what his life would be. At one point she looked over at me and said, "I'm glad you don't want to be governor."

I reached for her hand and squeezed it.

That seemed to cheer us both up.

We entered the Empire State Building, took the elevator to the floor where you buy tickets, and got in line.

At first it didn't seem like a long line. Although I had to use the restroom, I didn't see one around. I thought we'd only be in line maybe ten more minutes and then we'd be at the observation area for the building, where I was sure they would have a restroom.

But they fooled us. The line on that floor did only take twenty minutes, and then we ended up in a very long hallway and another line. And then we took an elevator up a few floors and there was another line.

I was getting desperate.

Abbie noticed something was wrong. "What's up, Dave?"

"Nothing."

"No, there is. Tell me."

I whispered in her ear. "I have to go to the bathroom, but I don't see one anywhere."

"Let me see if I can find out where they are," she said.

Abbie found a bored attendant about fifteen feet in front of us. "We've got a little guy with us who really needs to use a restroom. Can you tell me where I can take him?"

Abbie came back and gave me directions. "Davey, do you need me to stay outside until you're done?" she asked in her super-sweet nanny voice.

I scowled at her and hurried off.

"You're welcome," she called out after me.

By the time I'd finished, Abbie and company were way ahead of me. So I moved up through the line to catch up to them.

Some people glared at me for walking past them. So to put their mind at ease, every few feet I would say, "I was in line but I had to go to the bathroom. I'm just getting back to where I was in line. With my friends."

And then I hit a wall, or rather a man who filled the entire hallway. A man who at night could be mistaken for a bus.

"Excuse me."

He couldn't actually turn around, but he did turn his cow-size neck a little.

"What do you want, Punk?"

I gave him my prepared message.

"People like you make me sick. Stand in line like everybody else."

I didn't have much choice. I couldn't go around him, and I couldn't go through him.

Finally, after another twenty minutes, as we were approaching the place where they take group photos with a backdrop of the Empire State Building, I could hear Abbie and Eldon arguing. They couldn't see me because of the giant in front of me, but I could hear them.

"Let's just go," Eldon said. "He can catch up with us on the observation deck."

"No, we have to wait for him so we can all be in the picture," Abbie said.

"How do you know he's even coming? Maybe he got sick and went home. Why do you waste time with him anyway?"

"Because he's my friend. And I'll tell you something else. He would wait for me if the situation were reversed."

"That's because he thinks he's still got a chance with you," Eldon said.

"No, it's because Dave never abandons a friend. Unlike you, of course. You'd cut off your mom if she didn't make quota."

"I don't think we should be arguing in front of others," Eldon said.

"We're waiting for Dave and that's it," Abbie said. "I don't abandon my friends. If you don't like it, Eldon, then go on by yourself and we'll catch up with you."

"He's no friend of mine. How about the rest of you? Antonio? Hannah? Megan? And you?"

"Her name is Nicole," Abbie said.

"I'm staying, too," Hannah said. "Dave is one of my best friends."

"What am I?" Antonio asked.

"You're a newcomer."

"I'm in, too," Antonio said. "Dave made it possible for me to meet Hannah, so I owe him big time."

"I'm staying, too," Megan said.

"Me, too," Nicole added. "He's helping make Jimmy really mad today, and I like that."

I saw my opening and darted around the moving human wall.

"Hey, Punk, come back here!" the giant called out.

Abbie saw me coming. "What took you so long?" Abbie asked.

"That guy," I said. "He didn't want me to go around him."

"Oh, my gosh," Abbie said under her breath when she spotted the man.

"We're wasting time. Let's just get the picture taken so we can get going," Eldon said.

"Stand by me for the picture," Abbie said to me.

"You sure?"

"Yeah. Eldon's being a jerk today. He doesn't handle a day off well. He's too much of a workaholic."

"Sorry."

"It's okay. That's just the way he is."

Eldon was furious at me. "I don't even want to be in the picture!"

"Whatever," Abbie said.

The rest of us came together for the photo, then the attendants sent us on our way.

As soon as we made it to the observation tower, Eldon grumpily left us to take pictures. What can you say about a guy who takes pictures of buildings? Is he a people person? Not likely.

Standing on the observation deck was a real experience. As far as you could see in any direction were skyscrapers with bridges and shining waterways in the distance. "This is quite a view, isn't it?" I said to Abbie.

"Yeah, it's great. I've been here before," she said.

"When?" I asked.

"The first Saturday I had off right after coming east. I came by myself and did my own personal tour. That's when I fell in love with the City."

"I can see why." I paused. "You want to talk about Eldon?"

"I love the guy, okay? Sometimes though I'm not sure I like him."

"Ouch."

"But what can you do? You know what I'm saying?" She was mimicking someone from New York.

"Fuhgetabout it," I added.

"We always have fun together, don't we?" she said.

"Yeah, we do. Always."

I put some quarters in a viewing telescope. "My treat," I said.

She peered through the telescope. "This is great. Thanks. You want a look?"

"No, you look at the buildings. I'll look at you."

She squinted into the eyepiece. "I have no doubt that Eldon will accomplish every goal he sets in his life. He'll go to law school, and some day he'll actually be governor of Utah. Oh, yes, he's got success written all over him."

While she was looking through the telescope, Eldon showed up. He was standing next to me as Abbie looked through the telescope.

She kept talking. "I'm just not sure if he'll ever take the time to fix one of our kids' bicycles when it gets a flat, or if he'll go out and shoot baskets with our boy, or if he'll take our kids out on Saturdays for grand adventures like going to a museum or going fishing."

"I will," Eldon said.

Abbie turned to face him. She was obviously embarrassed. "Sorry, I didn't know you were around."

"In the future, if you have issues, I'd prefer you talk to me about them."

That was the wrong way to go at Abbie. "Don't take that high-toned attitude with me. I'll talk to anyone I want to about you. Let me take a wild guess here. You talk to Elizabeth about my failings, don't you?"

"No."

"Then what do you two talk about for hours at a time?"

"We have gospel discussions."

"Oh, sure, that's because she's a returned missionary, right? You think I wouldn't be able to understand deep doctrine, is that it?"

"Okay, look, I'm sorry you got your feelings hurt," he said.

"So now everything is my fault, is it?"

"I was only trying to speed things up. We have so little time to be here if we're going to get out to Port Jefferson for the fireworks tonight."

Abbie shook her head in disgust.

"What's wrong now?" Eldon asked.

"Go away, Eldon. Dave put his hard-earned money in this telescope for me to see the sights, and I don't want to miss a precious second of it."

Eldon glared at me and stormed off.

"What's wrong?" I asked.

She mimicked Eldon. "'I'm sorry you got your feelings hurt.' That's no apology. It puts all the blame on me. And then he goes, 'I was only trying to . . .' When you apologize to someone, you've got to accept responsibility for your bad behavior."

"I didn't pick up on that when he said it," I said.

"You will now, though, right?"

"Yeah, I hope so."

"That's the difference between you and Eldon. You learn from your mistakes."

Ten minutes later Eldon came back and said he wanted to talk to Abbie.

"Yeah, sure, I'll go," I said, starting to leave. Then I couldn't resist. "With all due respect," I said, "what is taking you so long to decide between Abbie and Elizabeth?"

"I'm making it a matter of prayer."

"Really?" I said. "So, I suppose you pray about it every day, is that right?"

"Of course I pray every day."

"Yeah, but I'm not talking about praying to sell more security systems. Do you ask to know if you should marry Abbie or Elizabeth?"

"I don't see that's any of your business."

"Look, Eldon, I'm going to help you out here. We're about, what, ten minutes from the temple. And even though it's a holiday, they're open. So how about we drop you off, you go to a session or whatever. While you're in there, say a silent prayer if you should marry Abbie. I think that's all it will take 'cause let me tell you something, Heavenly Father loves this girl. And who wouldn't, right? So you do your prayer thing and then this will all be settled today and we can all get on with our lives. How does that sound?"

He looked at me and then said, "It must be so nice to have an outlook where nothing is complicated. The thing you don't understand is that, unlike you, I have a real future."

I was about to throw a punch at his noble face.

"Guys, c'mon," Abbie said. "Let's just drop the subject and join the others, okay?"

I looked at Abbie. I could tell she was worried what I'd do. I cared about her too much to ruin her Fourth of July.

"Yeah, sure. Sorry, Eldon," I said. And then added, for Abbie's benefit, "My fault."

"No offense taken." He reached for Abbie's hand. "Let's join the others."

She pulled away from him. "I'll go with you, but I won't hold your hand."

"Why not?"

"Because you're being too much of a jerk today."

They left.

I went the opposite direction.

A few minutes later I found Megan and Nicole.

"Dave, we were just looking for you. We want to take a picture with you and Nicole to send to Jimmy."

"Sure."

"I just turned on my phone," Nicole said. "Jimmy's left four voice mails."

"Have you listened to any of them?" I asked.

"Yeah, I did. The first one he said we're through."

"Good."

"The second one said he's going to come out here and beat you to a pulp."

"Good for him. Five days on a bus will mellow him out."

"His third message says if I don't call him right away he's never going to call me again."

"I like the way this is going."

"The fourth one says I've ruined his Fourth of July."

"Oh sure, it's all your fault, right? It always is with guys like that. Let's send him another picture."

I put my arm around Nicole.

Megan was in charge. "Dave, do something different on this one."

"You want me to kiss her?"

Megan had a hurt expression on her face. "No."

"Let's try this," I said, kneeling down like I was about to propose.

"Say it, Dave. I'll put it on video."

"Nicole, will you marry me?"

"Yeah, sure, why not?" she said. "You want to do it today?"

People around us clapped and congratulated us. And one guy gave us a snow globe of NYC. I gave it to Nicole. She seemed so grateful. I wondered if it was the first time a guy had ever given her anything.

We sent the video to Jimmy.

Eldon, still angry at me, came and told us we were leaving and that we needed to hurry if we were going to visit all the sites he'd designated before we got back on the train and headed back to President Alexander's house.

I didn't much care for his take-charge attitude. "Things to do and places to go, right, Eldon?" I said.

"That's right. Please try to keep up. If you need to go to the bathroom again, this would be a good time to do it. I won't have you slowing us down."

From that point on Eldon became the official tour guide,

pointing out in advance how long we could stay at every place we went. My heart wasn't in that kind of a trip so I stayed behind with Megan and Nicole, all the time watching Antonio and Hannah become better friends.

On our train ride back to President Alexander's home, Eldon and Abbie had a *define the relationship* talk. Hannah and Antonio were enjoying each other. That left me with Megan and Nicole.

I sat in the middle seat with Megan on my right and Nicole on my left by the window.

"Looks like you're back to your number three choice," she said. "That's me, right?"

"Yeah, numbers one and two are out." Even though that's the way I had begun to think, it sounded stupid to say it.

"You know, I'm pretty sure I like you more than Abbie or Hannah do," Megan said.

"I'm a lucky guy then."

"I know it will take you some time to get over Abbie, but I just want you to know I'll be waiting for you."

"Thanks."

"Would you mind if I put my head on your shoulder and took a nap?" she asked.

"No, go ahead. I might do that, too."

The next thing I remember is Antonio saying, "That is so sweet!" he said it quietly but with a mocking tone.

I opened my eyes and looked around. Megan and Nicole were both asleep, each of them resting her head on my shoulder. And Abbie, Eldon, Hannah and Antonio were standing over us with big grins on their faces.

"We're almost at our stop," Abbie said softly to me.

I sat up. My movement caused Nicole and Megan to wake up.

The rest of the day we were involved in group activities, mostly volleyball and swimming at a neighbor's pool.

Megan and I spent about an hour helping Sister Alexander prepare food.

She was a gracious hostess to all of us, always cheerful, totally unruffled by so many people coming through her house for drinks and bathroom breaks and endless snacks.

After that I helped President Alexander grill hamburgers on the barbecue in his backyard. And then we had a family home evening where he talked about the price of freedom and reminded us how lucky we were to live in America.

Just before dark we walked down to the beach for the Port Jefferson fireworks show.

As I walked with Megan, I reached for her hand.

"Dave, I need to tell you something."

"Okay."

"I don't want you to kiss me anymore until we can both see this is getting serious. You keep going back and forth between Abbie and Hannah and me. That's not what I'm looking for in a guy."

"You're right. I need to figure out what I want."

Some holiday, right? Eldon and Abbie were still together. Any hopes I had for Hannah and me were disappearing. And now Megan was starting to have second thoughts about me.

Even though I'd seen New York City, all in all, it was a pretty depressing day.

CHAPTER ELEVEN

At work on Thursday, Hannah cornered me in plumbing as I was checking inventory. She handed me a ticket. "That's for you."

"What is it?"

"A ticket to a Yankees game Saturday. We'll have to leave about five."

"We work Saturdays."

"I talked to Murray. It's okay with him if we leave a little early."

"What about Antonio?"

"He's coming, too. This whole thing was his idea. He paid for the tickets."

"Why?"

"How should I know? Ask him yourself. You coming or not? Make up your mind. Oh, and don't be a schmuck about it either. I need a decision in the next five seconds. If you say no, I'm going to kick your backside down the aisle from plumbing to electrical."

I looked down the aisle. "You'd never do that."

"Oh, really? C'mon, Dave. I'm sure you've heard of the Yankees, even in Iowa. What's the problem?"

"It might be awkward with the three of us."

"He's my friend, you're my friend. And you two are, or could be, friends. What's there to be awkward about?"

"Yeah, I suppose."

"Please let us do this for you. We both owe you big time."

I sighed. "Okay."

"Good, I'll call and tell him."

At five o'clock on Saturday, Antonio entered the store wearing a Yankees jersey and baseball cap. He tossed a shopping bag to Hannah and me.

"Put these on and let's go."

He'd gotten each of us each a jersey and a baseball cap. Mine was a Derek Jeter jersey, Antonio had a Jason Giambi jersey, and Hannah's was an Alex Rodriguez.

"Let's go, team!" Antonio called out.

"Wait a minute," I said. "These must have cost a lot. Let me pay for mine."

"Fuhgetabout it," Antonio said. "My dad used to get me a new one every year. Yours was one I'd outgrown. I got Hannah's on sale. I know a guy."

Antonio was in charge of getting us there. We took the train to Penn Station, grabbed the A-train to 125th Street, then transferred to the D-train.

By the time we were on the D-train, most everyone on the train was also going to the game.

Antonio started talking to a dad and his son. The boy and Antonio had the same Giambi jersey. "Hey, we're the same, you and me! You a big Giambi fan, too, huh?"

The boy smiled.

Antonio pointed to Hannah and me. "This is my friend Derek Jeter and my other friend Alex Rodriguez! We'd better hurry or we'll miss the game."

The boy laughed.

I'd never been much of a sports fan growing up. I played football my sophomore year, but that didn't turn me into a fan. But this was different. It wasn't so much about baseball as it was sharing an experience with people you didn't know and would never see again, but that was all right because for a brief moment of time it was like we were all part of this very large family.

We got out at 161st Street, just a short distance from Yankee Stadium. After going through a security check we found our seats in the nosebleed section. There was no problem about getting hit with a foul ball. We were too far away from home plate.

When I got my first glimpse of the inside of Yankee Stadium, it kind of took my breath away. Even though it wasn't dark yet, the stadium lights were already on, and the grass on the field was a bright green. The infield dirt had been sprayed to keep the dust down, and with the white bases and the huge scoreboard, the field was quite a sight. As the home team, the Yankees were wearing their famous white pinstriped uniforms, and even from where we were sitting, I could hear the pop of the ball in the players' gloves as the pre-game warm-ups concluded. I didn't think I was going to be that excited, but I couldn't help myself.

I turned to Antonio. "Hey, Antonio. This is great! Thanks for bringing me."

"You know what?" Hannah said. "I'm going to sit between you two guys because if I don't, you'll talk baseball all night and totally ignore me."

"I'd never ignore you," Antonio said.

I was glad to be sitting next to Hannah. Even if I only got the left side of her.

The scoreboard had a huge TV screen on it, and a roving camera was zeroing in on couples in the stands. If a couple came up on the screen, they were supposed to kiss each other. At least, that's what was happening.

We were amazed when we were singled out and our three faces were displayed. Antonio quickly leaned around Hannah and looked at me and said, "Let's do it, Dave. On her cheeks on three. One, two, three."

Antonio and I each kissed her on the cheek, and the crowd roared its approval.

During the fourth inning, Hannah said she was going to get us some hot dogs. "What do you want on yours?" she asked me.

"Ketchup."

"Fuhgetabout it! You're having mustard and relish."

"Why?"

"Because that's what we do here," she said.

"Why'd you ask, then?"

"I was testing you. You failed."

"You need any help carrying everything back?" Antonio asked.

"No, I got it. You guys watch the game."

She left.

"While she's gone, there's something I want to say," Antonio said.

"Okay."

"About a month ago, I told my mom I wasn't going to go the singles branch anymore. She asked why. I told her it was because all the girls are from out west."

"You don't like girls from the West?"

"What's the last thing their folks tell 'em before they leave to come out here? 'Don't marry a guy from the East because if you do, you'll live out there and we'll never see you.'"

"That's probably true."

"And I don't want to move west. I like it here."

Derek Jeter lined a ball into center field for a base hit, and Antonio and I and the entire crowd cheered.

After the hit, Antonio continued. "So my mom goes, 'Someone from here might show up at the branch.'

"I go, 'Fugetabout it. It's not going to happen.'

"She goes, 'Pray about it.'

"So I prayed about it, and a week later Hannah shows up at family home evening. Coincidence, right?"

"Maybe not."

"Yeah. So that's where we are now. I consider Hannah an answer to prayer. And you made it happen. So I owe you big time." He paused. "Look, I'm not asking your permission because you don't have any claim to her, right?"

"That's right. We're just friends."

"Oh, one other thing, my folks really love her."

"My folks would have loved her, too."

"You mean after you and she got married and moved back to Idaho? Idaho doesn't need another member of the Church. We do, though."

"That's probably true."

"You like her, too, don't you? That's what Abbie said when I talked to her."

"Well, you went to the right source. Abbie knows everything about me."

"Yeah, she seems to. Look, I just wanted to say thanks for being such a good friend to Hannah and bringing the gospel to her."

"Thanks. It's been an amazing experience for me," I said.

"I hope we can still team up again and give Security Boy a hard time."

"I look forward to that."

The Yankees scored two more runs before Hannah returned with the food.

"When you go back home, you can tell all your friends you ate an official hot dog at Yankee Stadium!" Hannah said, handing me a cardboard container with my hot dog. You'd have thought she'd just given me a bar of gold.

The hot dog was okay. I mean it's not like we don't have hot dogs in Idaho, you know what I mean?

In the eighth inning it started to rain. For some reason Antonio had only brought two plastic rain ponchos. He and Hannah shared one, which meant they had to cuddle together.

At first I sat ramrod straight and wished Abbie was with me.

We'd have had fun sitting together in the rain. Of course, she'd have accused me of hogging the poncho. I'd have told her it was only because I was a manly man and took up a lot of room. She'd have laughed about that and punched me in the side and come back with something. I'm just not sure what it would have been. That's why it's better to have her with me than having to make things up in my mind.

Because I felt alone in that crowd of fifty thousand people, I covered it by standing up and yelling about every little thing that happened, like it was the play of the century.

Antonio and Hannah were impressed that I was so into the game. So I fooled them. That was good. It was better not to let anyone know how alone I felt.

Then it really started raining. It was a cloudburst, and after the umpire called a halt in play, the groundskeepers hurried to unroll a huge tarp that covered the infield. The players went into the dugouts, but all we could do was sit there and watch it come down. We sat there for a long time. Finally, an announcement was made that play would not be resumed. The crowd started to boo. Antonio explained to me that because the teams had played over five and a half innings, the game was official and with the Yankees behind, they were the losers. It didn't go over well with the fans, who were not only soaked but also on the short end of the score.

On our train from Penn Station, Antonio and Hannah started talking about sailing.

I fell asleep.

They woke me up at our stop.

"Dave, we have a question for you," Hannah said.

"Okay."

"Antonio and I are planning a ten-day sailing trip to North Carolina. Do you think it would be a problem for us to be alone on a boat for ten days?"

"I'm not sure what you mean."

"You know, in terms of us not being married and all."

"Well, I don't know about you two, but it would be a problem for me to be alone with a girl I liked for ten days . . . and nights."

"That's what we were thinking, too," Hannah said.

"Also, you have to consider what other people would think. You come back and tell people you two were together for a ten-day trip, they'll think the worst."

"True."

"So, we were thinking, maybe we should get married," Hannah said.

I was getting mad. "What? You don't run off and get married just so you can have a better vacation!"

"We feel like we've known each other all our lives."

"You know what? Abbie and I actually *have* known each other all our lives! But do you see us getting married? No, you do not."

"Maybe you're right," Hannah said. "Maybe we should just drop the idea of sailing to North Carolina this summer. Thanks."

* * *

On Sunday after church, Megan invited me to the house where she was a nanny. We sat on the patio in the backyard and filled out my application to BYU—Idaho. She would be attending fall semester, but my plan was to work for my dad and help my folks get ready to serve a mission. So I wouldn't be a full-time student until winter semester.

"I'll be glad to have you all to myself in Idaho," she said after we'd submitted my application.

"You have me all to yourself now."

"Not really. You're still too wrapped up in Abbie and Hannah. You never just come over and see me. I wish you'd do that more often."

"I will. I promise. From now on."

Sometimes life puts you on autopilot and it just goes by and you can't remember much of what happened. That was the way the next few days went.

Hannah and Antonio spent all their free time together. Abbie and Eldon kept to themselves. Megan wanted me to spend more time with her, but I kept putting her off.

On Thursday, after the store closed, Murray and I worked on completing an order.

When I returned to my place, I fixed something to eat and watched the last of a Yankees game on TV.

Yeah, I know. I used to hate the Yankees, but the thing is, once you've been to a game and have a Yankees cap and a Derek Jeter jersey, you're going to be a fan.

At ten-thirty, Abbie called. "I need to talk to you." She sounded desperate.

"What about?"

"Can you meet me at the diner in fifteen minutes?"

"Yeah, sure."

I arrived first and ordered sweet potato fries and drinks for us.

When she came in and sat down at the table with me, she didn't look good. Her eyes were puffy. I could tell she'd been crying.

"What's up?" I asked.

"Eldon just told me he's flying out tomorrow to Utah for Elizabeth's birthday on Saturday."

"That'll cost a lot of money."

"Her dad is paying for it."

"Well, then, I wouldn't worry about Eldon."

"You never worry about Eldon."

"That's true."

"He says it doesn't change anything between us."

"And you think it does?" I asked.

"Of course it does!"

She talked while I ate my sweet potato fries. And then, after she told me she wasn't hungry, I started on hers.

I kept telling her how unfair Eldon was being to her.

"Eldon's changed," she said. "And it's not just because of Elizabeth—it's her dad. All Eldon talks about now is preparing himself to run for governor. If he marries Elizabeth, it will be because he needs her dad to help him."

"What a stupid reason to marry someone."

"It's not just Eldon, either," she said. "The past year has been a nightmare dealing with one guy after another. That's why I didn't write much. We'd see each other a few times and then either he or I would pull the plug. Each time I'd start out hopeful, and then before long it was over. I'm just so tired of the stupid games you have to play when you're single. Sometimes I just wish it were all over and I was married and didn't have to deal with this garbage anymore."

"That's the way I feel, too."

"Maybe we should just get married. We don't have anything else going for us, do we?" she said.

"Well, I don't know about you, but I sure don't."

"We could just jump in the car now and drive to Niagara Falls and get married by a justice of the peace and then call our folks and tell them what we've done. No planning, no explaining, no arranging a time when all our family can come to it. Just get it over with."

"That sounds good."

"We should just do it. I'm sick and tired of all this."

I shrugged my shoulders. "Hey, I'd do it. In a New York minute."

She looked at me. "Would you really? I mean, like tonight?"

"Tonight?"

"Yeah, sure, why not?" she said.

"It's nice to think about, that's for sure."

"I'm serious," she said. "I don't want to be single anymore."

"Abbie, the truth is I'd marry you any day, any time, any place."

"You're the only guy I've ever been able to count on."

I was about to take another handful of sweet potato fries when she moved the plate away.

"What?" I asked.

"Forget the fries. Let's drive to Niagara Falls right now." She stood up. "Let's go get married."

"Would you actually go through with it?" I asked. "Don't talk about it unless you're serious, okay? I'm messed up enough as it is."

She slapped my hand away from the fries. "Dave, quit eating my sweet potato fries and propose to me right now!" she ordered.

I used a napkin to wipe my face and hands. "Abbie, will you marry me?"

"Yes, I will."

"You will?"

"Yes. Now that we're engaged, let's go get married." She grabbed my hand and pulled me out of my seat.

"Are you serious? We're actually going to get married?" I asked as we walked toward the cashier.

"Yeah, we are. Tonight."

"Where are we going to get married?" I asked.

"Pay attention, okay? Niagara Falls."

"Don't mess with my mind, Abbie."

"I'm not. I want to marry you tonight."

"You're sure?"

"I'm positive. Who else can I marry tonight? I don't even know the busboy."

"Okay, let's do it!"

I hurried to pay the bill.

"I'll need to pack something," she said.

"No, we can't pack. That will take the adventure out of it."

"But we'll be in the same clothes for two or three days," she said.

"We'll wash 'em out at night and let them dry. C'mon."

"We're going to get married tonight!" I said to the manager as I laid ten dollars and the bill on the counter. "Oh, keep the change."

He glanced at the bill to make sure I'd given him enough, then looked up at us and smiled. "Here, take a couple of eclairs as a gift from me!" he said.

He gave me the eclairs, and we hurried out to the parking lot.

I steered her toward my pickup. "Get in. We'll take my pickup," I said.

"I can't leave my car here in the parking lot."

"Why not? It will be okay."

"No, it'll get towed. Besides, it's not my car. Follow me, and I'll drop it off. It will only take a few minutes."

"All right, but hurry."

Twenty minutes later she pulled into the driveway of the home where she worked and lived as a nanny, while I parked at the curb.

"Let me just run in and pack a bag and tell them what we're doing. It will only take a minute."

I got out of the pickup and paced back and forth. I was worried that Abbie would change her mind. After a few minutes, I could hear a woman yelling inside.

Then Abbie hurried out of the house, carrying a small suitcase. We threw it into the back of my pickup and drove off.

"Duane and Addison are pretty mad at me. When I asked them to pay me, that's when Addison started yelling."

"I could hear her. She's got some voice."

"Do you want to pick up some clothes at your place?" Abbie asked.

"No."

"I really think you should. It isn't out of the way."

"I just want to get on the road. That's all."

In the end she convinced me to stop and pack up some things. I grabbed what I could in five minutes and then we took off again.

"How long do you think it will take to get to Niagara Falls?" I asked.

"I don't know. Maybe six or seven hours."

"What if we can't find someone to marry us when we get there?"

"We'll sleep in the car until a justice of the peace opens up," she said.

"And then we'll get married in the morning," I said.

"Right."

We rode in silence for a few moments, then Abbie said, "When will we call our folks?"

"After we're married."

"That makes it seem like we don't care about them. Why not before?"

"Because they'd try to talk us out of eloping."

She thought about that. "Yeah, they would. That's for sure."

She unfastened her seat belt and slid over next to me and put her head on my shoulder. "This is just like old times, isn't it? You and me on a big adventure."

"Yeah, like the time we broke into the school and put Saran Wrap on the toilet seats in the teacher's lounge." The memory made me smile.

"Life was so simple then," Abbie said dreamily.

"It can be simple now. People fill their lives with things that don't count, until they don't know if they're coming or going."

"Things that count," she said, then paused, and added softly, "You mean like a temple marriage?"

I really didn't know how to answer her.

"Did you hear what I said?" she asked.

"Yes. We're worthy of a temple marriage," I said.

"You mean you are. You can't really speak for me, can you?"

That was a depressing thought. "Are you worthy?"

She thought about it. "Yeah, pretty much."

"Good."

"Yeah, good for us." She paused, then asked, "So if people ask us why we got married in a wedding chapel in Niagara Falls by a man who makes a living impersonating Elvis Presley, what do we tell them? That we were worthy of a temple wedding, but we decided against it because we were in too much of a hurry. Is that what we're going to say to everyone who asks us for the rest of our lives?"

"We'll tell them it's none of their business how we got married."

"And if I'm ever a Laurel adviser, what do I tell my girls? That a temple marriage isn't that important?"

Abbie's cell phone rang. "Hello." Pause. "Oh, hi, Megan." Pause. "Oh, not much, what are you doing?" Pause. "No, I don't know why Dave hasn't called you lately." Pause. "Well, I think he likes you, but he's been real busy. Look, Megan, I've got to get off the phone now, but I'll call you in the morning, okay?"

She closed her phone and said, "That was Megan."

"I know. I heard you talking."

"She's worried you don't like her."

"Why didn't you just tell her the truth?"

"And what would that be? Gosh, Megan, I really do think Dave likes you, but right now he and I are running off to get married by a justice of the peace in Niagara Falls. Why Niagara Falls, and why tonight? Good question. It's because we're so sick and tired of the games you have to play when you're single. We just want to have it over with. We're tired of everyone telling us to get married. We're tired of cycling through one person after another when nothing works out. Dave and I have known each other all our lives so at least we know what we're getting. That's better than most couples who get married. It may not be perfect, but it'll be better than most. At least there will be no surprises."

"Abbie, maybe you should just try and get some sleep. I'll wake you when we get to Niagara Falls."

She closed her eyes and put her head back on my shoulder. "I wish I could just fall asleep and wake up tomorrow morning married to you."

"I think that's why they make the bride say 'I do.' To make sure she's awake."

She laughed. "We always have a good time together, don't we?"

"Yeah. We do."

"You don't like the way my hair is now, do you? Do you want me to change it before we get married?"

"No."

"Because I can. It'd only take maybe an hour," she said.

"No, it's okay. I'm used to it now."

"Have I ever told you how much I respect your dad?"

"No."

"Well, I do. I always figured you'd turn out a lot like him. And you have. That makes me feel very comfortable doing this." She sighed. "Except I know he'll be disappointed we weren't married in the temple."

"I suppose."

"Your mom, too. And of course my folks. And Courtney. I won't be setting a very good example for her, will I?"

"Abbie, the reason I need you to sleep now is so when I get tired, you can drive."

"You don't want me awake, do you? I keep asking so many questions."

"It's going to be okay, Abbie. I promise you it will. I love you. I've loved you since kindergarten."

"Since kindergarten? How come I didn't know that?"

I smiled. "Social pressure from other boys."

"You caved in to peer pressure?"

"I did. But I never stopped loving you. All through grade school I always watched you. In eighth grade, sometimes in class when I sharpened my pencil, it didn't really need to be sharpened. I just wanted to get a good look at you."

"So what you're telling me is you became a stalker at an early age?"

"Yeah, pretty much."

"Actually, I always knew when you were watching me. Sometimes in eighth grade I'd ask you to buy me a candy bar at the student store just because I knew you'd do it. It was like I had secret powers over you. I liked that."

She had another call. She looked at her cell phone. "It's Eldon."

"Don't talk to him." I glanced at her. "Please."

"Okay."

She turned off her phone. "Can you drive with one hand?" she asked.

I took the hint and held her hand.

"I wish we were married now so this would all be over," she said.

"I'm not sure that's how you're supposed to be thinking."

A short time later, a few tears silently rolled down her cheeks.

"You okay?"

She wiped her face. "Yeah, I'm fine. Just a few regrets, that's all. But I guess that's natural, right?"

"What's your biggest regret?"

"All my life I've dreamed of getting married in the temple. I guess that's not going to happen, though, is it? Oh, well, life is like that sometimes. Don't worry though. I said I'd marry you and I will. Tomorrow morning when some dumb chapel of love opens up for business, we'll be there. You think they'll give me a bouquet of plastic roses?"

"Sure, why not?"

"Dave, can you pull off somewhere?"

"Yeah, sure. Are you hungry? Do you need to use the bathroom?"

"No, I just want you to hold me."

We ended up standing in a Dunkin' Donuts parking lot.

"Just hold me," she said.

I held her in my arms, and that was okay, but when I tried to kiss her, she put her hand between our lips. "No, not that, not now, just hold me."

So I did.

"I'm trying to remember when I first knew I loved you," she said.

"Was it the summer before our sophomore year when I used to mow the lawn with my shirt off when I knew you were home?"

She laughed. "Oh, please, give me a break! You were the skinniest boy in our class. I could count your ribs."

"But see, the thing is, if you did count my ribs, that means you were totally interested in my body."

"You think your ribs were a big turn-on? Fuhgetabout it. I'll tell you the exact moment when it happened. It was when we'd just turned seventeen. It was on a Sunday during the sacrament when you were handing out the trays to the deacons, I remember thinking, *He's the same on Saturday night with me as he is on Sunday blessing the sacrament.* I was impressed by that. Not every guy is the same all the time. Some guys forget what they've been taught when they're out with a girl. But you never did."

"Thanks for telling me."

I held her in my arms as tight as I could. But, even so, I could still feel her slipping away. "I love you, Abbie. You're the only girl I've ever loved. The only girl I will ever love."

She was crying.

"Abbie?"

"Yes?"

"It's not going to happen, is it?"

She let out a big sigh. "No. I'm so sorry. I just can't do it this way."

"I know. Me, either. But look on the bright side. If Niagara Falls had been ten minutes away, we'd have made it. So it was more a matter of geography than anything else."

She pulled away. "Stupid geography."

I took her hand. "We could do it the right way, you know. I mean, we could get married in the temple with our family there and with a reception afterwards."

"Yeah, we could." She sounded even more depressed than before. "Let's just get in the car."

I opened the door for her and then went around to the driver's side and got in. "You're not sure you want to marry me in the temple, are you?" I said.

She didn't answer.

"You know I love you, don't you?" I asked.

"Yeah, I know that. I've always known that."

I was almost too afraid to ask, but I finally said, "Do you love me?"

"I do. I really do, Dave."

"Then why shouldn't we get married in the temple?"

She shook her head.

"It's okay. You can tell me. I'm a big boy. I can take it."

"You're the nicest guy I've ever known. And you're always good to me. And we can talk about anything."

I waited, but she didn't go on, so I asked, "But what?"

"The tricky thing is imagining planning a temple wedding. All the announcements. Me telling my friends that you're going to take over your dad's store and we're going to stay in Ririe. That's where it gets complicated." She stopped.

"Because?"

She shook her head again. "I don't know how to say it."

"It's okay. Just tell me."

"I can't. Please, don't ask me to tell you, Dave."

"Look, I'm a guy, okay? You can't really hurt a guy's feelings. Just tell me, and then I can quit hoping you'll change your mind and move on with my life."

She took a deep breath and looked out the side window as if she couldn't say it facing me. "I want . . . more."

I've heard people talk about having their heart broken. I always dismissed it as just something song writers said, and that it wasn't real. But when she said that to me—that she wanted more—I thought, *So this is what it means to have your heart broken.*

I didn't want her to know how bad I felt. I needed something to do. I turned the ignition key and then hit my lights and backed out of our parking place.

I drove while she sobbed. She must have told me a hundred times how sorry she was.

In a way I wished she'd never told me. But I wasn't going to let her see how much she'd hurt me. I had too much pride for that.

I forced myself to smile. "Look, it's okay. Really, what you said makes perfect sense. Someone like you should have more than a hardware guy. What was I thinking? Well, thanks, that really clears it up for me. I'll take you home now."

I turned on 1010 WINS for weather and traffic.

The only other thing I said on our way back was, "You ever notice that it doesn't matter what time of day or night it is, there's always at least a twenty minute delay on the GW Bridge? Same with the BQE. What's with that anyway?"

When we got back to where she lived, I walked her to the door.

"I am *so* sorry, Dave."

"Don't be. Look on the bright side. We were within hours of getting married. That's closer than we've ever been. I'll always have that to remember."

I started down the stairs and then stopped. "Oh, one thing? What about the eclairs? You want yours?"

"No, you can have it."

"Okay, thanks." I waved and got in my car and drove off.

As soon as I turned the corner, I tossed the stupid eclairs out the window.

CHAPTER TWELVE

The next morning at work, I wanted to be by myself. I asked Murray if I could clean out the back room. It was slow up front so he said to go ahead.

About ten-thirty Hannah came back to see me. She looked around at what I'd done. "I just want to say, you're duen a heck of a job 'ere," she said sarcastically.

"Thanks."

"You okay?"

"Just a little tired. I stayed up all night watching European soccer," I lied.

"I didn't know you liked soccer."

"I don't. Even less after last night."

"So why'd you stay up all night watching it?"

"Look, I don't want to talk about it, okay?"

"It's because of Abbie, isn't it? She called me late last night and told me what happened. Sorry she got cold feet at the last minute. Do you want to talk about it?"

I glared at her. "What do you think?"

"Probably not, huh? Well, I'll leave you alone then."

"Thanks."

Abbie's "I want more" was now a hammer in my head to be used to make myself even more miserable. More? More of what? I thought. Just tell me what you want, Abbie, and I'll change. I'll become whatever you want me to be. You want me to be taller? I'll find a way to do it. You want me to be more like Eldon? No problem, I can do it. I'll get a job selling security systems. I'll change the way I talk. I'll lose the Idaho twang. I'll tell everyone I'm planning on going to law school after I graduate from BYU. If you want, I'll tell the world I plan on being governor of Idaho some day. And when I give a talk in church, I'll do the pregnant pause to make my points more effectively. I'll do anything, Abbie, just give me another chance.

Abbie wants more.

More than me, that's for sure.

I didn't make the cut.

Abbie wants more.

There's no one who will ever love her as much as I do. But that's not enough. Abbie wants more.

An hour later Hannah returned. "Murray says he needs you up front. We have actual customers now."

"Okay, thanks. I'll be there in a minute."

"You want to go sailing with me and Antonio after work?"

"Not really."

"Hey, don't do me any favors, okay?"

"Sorry. I'm having a bad day."

"When I have a bad day, I go sailing. That might work for you."

"You also go sailing when you're having a good day, so I don't see it as a cure-all."

"Yeah, so? What's it going to be, Buddy Boy, sailing with me and Antonio, or arranging all the screws in the bins so they face the same direction? It's up to you."

"With Antonio there, I'd just be in the way."

"That's not true and you know it. We like having you with us. I'm serious."

I nodded. "Okay, I'll think about it."

"Great. Now pretend to be a happy guy and go help someone with their septic tank problems. I'll be up front working as opposed to hiding back here like you've been doing all morning."

As I put on my Ace Hardware vest. I looked at my reflection in the mirror. It was probably not a good time to do that because looking at myself in the mirror I could hear in my mind what Abbie had said. *I want more.* I couldn't blame her. The trouble with me is that I looked like a guy who'd work in a hardware store.

Hannah snuck her head in the back room as I was doing a self-appraisal in the mirror. "I just want you to know that a very special customer just came in, and he won't talk to anyone but you. Apparently none of us can match the excellent service you have given this customer in the past. Let me just say how honored we are to have you a part of the Ace Hardware family."

"Yeah, yeah."

She walked with me out to the front. The customer who'd requested me was Mr. Denuchy, the old guy with cell phone problems.

"So you're still here," he said. "They haven't fired you yet. Go figure."

"Can I help you?"

"See this phone. I want you to call someone on it."

"Who do you want me to call?"

"I don't care who you call. Just do it. Anyone."

"Why?"

"Because after you hang up, the phone will call you back and tell you the number you've dialed is not in service at this time. Try it, you'll see."

I glanced at Hannah and Murray. They were enjoying this.

"I'll call the store," I said.

Hannah, knowing it was me, answered. "Hello, Ace Hardware. How may I direct your call? If you wish to speak to our plumbing associate, press 1; if you wish to speak to someone about your screen doors, press 2; if you wish to speak with the associate who wasted the whole morning in the store room, press 3; If you want to—"

I hung up on her.

After a few seconds, Mr. Denuchy's phone rang. When I answered it, a recorded voice said, "The number you have dialed is not in service at this time . . ."

"What'd I tell you?" the old man said.

I sighed. "Okay, let's get to the bottom of this. Do you have a company phone number I can call?"

He pulled a scrap of paper out of his pocket. "I called them once. They put me on hold. When I described the problem, the guy says, 'Our phones don't do that.' I tried to give him a piece of my mind, but he hung up on me."

"Let me try it."

I found the number and called and was put on hold.

"What did I tell you?"

"Let's go in back. I've got some work I can do while we wait."

"Good luck, fellas! We're rooting for you!" Hannah called out, suppressing a grin.

We were put on hold for fifteen minutes and then a "service associate" came on the line. Mr. Denuchy explained the problem.

A minute later, he turned to me. "It's the same thing," Mr. Denuchy said. "He says their phones don't do that."

"Let me talk to him."

I tried to sound like a lawyer. "Hello, this is David J. Beckstrom from the Ace, Hard, and Ware Group in New York City. Did you just tell my client that you and your company have no idea what is wrong with his phone?"

"Our phones don't do that."

"This one does. May I speak with your supervisor?"

"What?"

"Your supervisor. I want to speak to him."

"He's not here."

"Give me his home phone, and I'll call him there."

"We don't give out that information."

"Well, give me the phone number of the company CEO."

"Why?"

"So we can begin proceedings. Look, I'll cut you some slack. You either give my client a new phone that works, or we will be all over you people in ways that you cannot even imagine at this time. You got that?"

There was a long pause. "Let me give you another number you can call."

"Is it the number for your supervisor?" I asked.

"No."

"That's what I want. Either that or the number of your CEO."

Another long pause.

"I don't have the authority to authorize a new phone."

"Well, you obviously can't help me then. I want to talk to someone who can. Give me the number of that person."

He gave me another number. I called the new number and was once again put on hold. When the next person answered, I asked, "Do you have any idea why I'm calling?"

"No."

"So I have got to start all over again explaining my problem? What kind of an operation are you people running?"

"What is the nature of your problem?"

'"I want a new phone. This one is a piece of junk."

"Could you be more specific?"

After I explained the problem to him, he asked, "Have you called the service number?"

"Yes, I did. They're clueless. They sent me here. My client wants a new phone."

"Sir, if you will send us your phone, we'll service it for free."

"Fuhgetabout it! I want a *new* phone! But I want you to have this one for your own personal use. I don't have time to wait around for you to fix this pile of junk. I can't go a day without a phone."

"I see."

"Who is your supervisor? I want to talk to him."

Half an hour later I found a supervisor with authority.

I turned to Mr. Denuchy, "You'll get a new phone tomorrow about noon. They're Fed-Exing you one here to the store."

"And what if I don't get it?" he asked.

"We'll do this all over again tomorrow."

As he made his way out of the store, Mr. Denuchy made a public announcement. "This young man should get Employee of the Month!"

He stopped to talk with Murray. "This boy is a gem! A real find! Don't ever let him leave! I'm telling all my friends to shop here. Even Lennie, the cheapskate, the crook, the pen thief. You'll see. Your business will double."

After he left, Hannah came up to me and patted me on the back. "This boy is such a gem!" And then she burst out laughing.

"When it comes to hardware, I am a gem," I said.

"Let's see, it's about noon. How many customers have you helped so far today? Gosh, only one? Yeah, sure, you're definitely Employee of the Month."

After her lunch break Hannah approached me. "Come show me what you did in the store room."

I followed her back there.

"You okay?" she asked.

"Yeah, sure."

"I was serious about wanting you to come sailing with Antonio and me."

"Not tonight. Give me a day or two, and then I'll go out with you two."

Megan called me at four and invited me to have dinner with her on the beach in front of the home where she worked.

"No, thanks."

"Please, Dave. It'll be fun. We'll have a fire on the beach. I'll make up some hobo dinners, and we'll have s'mores and even go swimming if you want. Abbie told me you're going through a hard time now. Let me be with you. Maybe I can help."

Against my better judgment, I finally accepted her invitation.

I got to her place about seven-thirty. Megan tried her best to cheer me up, but I wasn't very good company. I glumly ate my way through my hobo dinner and then the s'mores she'd worked so hard to make perfect for me.

"Abbie called and told me what happened last night. You want to talk about it?" she asked.

"Not really."

"Why not?"

"Because you'll tell her everything I say, and I don't want to give her the satisfaction of knowing I can't seem to let go of her."

"What if I don't tell her?"

"You know you will. Look, Megan, don't you think I know how pathetic I am? How many times does Abbie have to break up with me? She wants more than I can give her. That's it. Plain and simple. Why do I keep hoping that will change?"

"Sometimes it's hard to face the truth, isn't it?"

"Do you want to know what I hate the most about this conversation? That an eighteen-year-old girl is giving me advice on how to live my life."

"I'm almost nineteen."

"And we're all proud of you for reaching that milestone. I know it's been a lot of work."

That made her mad. She stood up and began lecturing. "You've never had any interest in actually knowing who I am or what I've been through, have you? I know a lot more than you think I do."

I had been staring at the embers of the fire, but suddenly I looked at her.

She continued, "All you've ever said about me is that I have a beautiful face. I'm more than that. Much more. But you'll never know that, will you?"

"You're right." I sat up. "Tell me something about yourself I don't know."

She paused. "Well, for one thing, I play the clarinet."

"No kidding?" I asked, pretending to be interested.

"I played all the way through high school. I went to State three years in a row. I've got it in my room. You want me to play for you?"

"Yeah, sure."

She ran and got her clarinet and brought it back. She played what she could remember of a solo for state competition. It sounded out of place on the beach.

After she finished, she said, "I got a superior rating from the judges."

"I can see why."

"I wrote a song for Sterling just before he left on his mission. You remember me talking about Sterling, right? He and his dad have been our home teachers for as long as I can remember."

"The guy who's building a house for you, with his dad, right?"

"Yeah, that's him."

She played her song. It sounded like what someone would write when they were in their early teens.

"Very nice," I said.

"I wrote words to it, too. Would you like me to sing it for you?"

"Yeah, sure, that'd be great."

Basically the lyrics were, Thanks for being such a good home teacher. You're going on a mission but we'll still be here when you come back and then you can home teach us again. Blah . . . blah . . . blah.

"That was real good," I said, trying to be as enthusiastic as I could.

"What else can you tell me about yourself?" I was beginning to feel like a long-lost uncle who'd just come back from a long trip.

"Starting my sophomore year, I was a cheerleader."

"A cheerleader? Wow! Isn't that something? Do you remember any of the cheers you used to do?"

"Let me think. Oh, yeah, here's one."

Watching her do a high school cheer was probably the lowest part of my summer. *What am I doing here?* I thought. *I'm reliving her high school years with her. Is she going to take me back to when she was in junior high, too? This is pathetic.*

"Go, go, go!" she shouted as she ended her cheer.

Even though I should have told her it was late and I needed to get some sleep, I let her go on. Not actually with more cheers because I was afraid the neighbors would complain and also because if Megan told Abbie that I kept asking for more cheers, Abbie would accuse me of being sick and twisted.

Megan told me about her experience being a co-chairman for a stake youth conference. The meetings, the assignments, the deadlines—you can imagine how riveting that was.

I'm not sure why I let her keep talking. Maybe because you can't be unkind when someone starts to open herself to you.

I cut her some slack. Being as young as she was, her greatest interest was herself. Not that I'm much different, of course. It's one of those things you can so easily recognize in others and find it so hard to admit to yourself.

By eleven that night she'd told me a great many things about herself. I'd tried my best to be enthusiastic.

"I've probably really bored you tonight, haven't I?" she said as we walked back to the house.

"No, are you kidding? It was great to learn more about you. You're a wonderful and talented girl, Megan. I wish we'd known each other in high school."

"You mean, like you knew Abbie in high school?"

"Exactly."

"I didn't tell you everything, though," she said, then sighed. "I didn't tell you anything about Sterling."

"Why not?"

"Because I knew it would make you mad."

"Go ahead, tell me."

"Well, he emails me every night and tells me all about his day. And I tell him about mine."

"So he's still being a good home teacher, isn't he?"

"It makes you mad when I talk about him, doesn't it?"

"Yeah, it does."

"How come?"

"I worry you're going to confuse him being a home teacher with him trying to convince you to marry him. Those are two different things."

"I know that. He's not my home teacher now. The thing with Sterling is I've always known he cares about me as a person." She paused then added, "He's not someone who would kiss me only because he's trying to get over someone else."

Ouch. That hurt. "You mean, like I did?"

"Yeah, but it's okay. You talk about me getting confused. I think you were the one who was confused. Did you think I was Abbie when you kissed me the first time?"

"I knew who you were."

"You know what? I'm not sure you'll ever know who I am."

"I will. From now on, Megan, I'm going to do better by you. I promise."

I gave her a quick hug and left.

That night I called my folks. I told them Abbie was definitely out of the picture.

"Didn't we already know that?" my mom asked.

"Well, last night, we almost eloped to Niagara Falls."

"Oh, good grief," my mom said.

"But don't worry. She changed her mind well before we even got off Long Island."

"What about that other girl? Hannah? Is that her name?" my dad asked.

"Uh, well, she's actually seeing another guy now, so I would definitely say she's out of contention. But don't worry. There's still . . . uh . . . Megan. She's almost nineteen, so that's a little young, but she is from Utah, so that's good, right?"

"You do understand that you don't *have* to get married before we go on our mission, don't you?" my dad asked.

"I know."

My mom added, "But if you are going to get married, it would be better to do it before we leave because otherwise I'm not sure we'd be able to get permission to leave the mission field to attend the wedding."

"I don't know what to tell you. Megan and I are just friends now. But she plans on going to BYU—Idaho this fall, so we'll be seeing each other. Maybe we'd be ready to get married by the end of December."

"This is not a race," my dad said. "Oh, by the way, we were thinking of setting our availability date for our mission for January 30."

"Good. That will give me time to help you guys get ready and also whatever legal arrangements need to be made for me to take over while you're gone."

"What can you tell us about this new girl, this Megan?" my dad asked.

"Well, she plays the clarinet and she was a co-chairman for a youth conference her senior year."

"Anything else?"

"She goes to church. She's a nanny. She's good looking. Oh, and she likes sweet potato fries."

"What are sweet potato fries?" my mom asked.

"Well, they're like french fries, but they're made from sweet potatoes."

"What?" my mom said. "The farmers out here don't have enough problems, now people are making fries from sweet potatoes?"

In order to escape confessing my sweet potato fry addiction, I jumped into another topic, "Oh, guess what? I just thought of something else about Megan. She was a cheerleader in high school and she can jump real high and kick her legs out sideways and touch her toes just before she lands."

There was an awkward silence on the phone. "Well, I would hope she's not showing you those kind of moves," my mom said.

"Oh, no, of course not. But she has played her clarinet for me."

After talking to my folks, I felt even more depressed.

On Monday of the next week, Murray called in and said his wife wasn't feeling well. He asked if Hannah and I could manage by ourselves. We told him that would be no problem.

Antonio dropped by to take Hannah to lunch.

"Ow ya duen?" he asked.

"Good. Real good."

"Have you asked anyone to run off to Niagara Falls with you today?" he asked with a big grin.

That's when I realized that everyone in the singles branch knew what had happened.

"Not yet."

"Well, don't be discouraged. Something will turn up." And then he laughed.

They left for lunch. A two-hour lunch. Leaving me alone to take care of all the customers.

Isn't love grand?

* * *

On my mission I always prayed that I could be a blessing to the people we met each day. I continued to pray for that after my mission. By the first week in August I could see that my prayers were being answered.

Because I got on Eldon's case and told him to go to the temple and pray about Abbie, he actually did it and said that he was now sure about Abbie. Isn't that great I could be so helpful to him?

Hannah and Antonio had one successful sailing expedition after another. It meant that she began to take Saturdays off, which meant I had to work all day.

They were so excited about taking their planned sailing adventure to North Carolina that they decided to get married. Just civilly, of course, since she hadn't been a member a year.

In retrospect I guess I should have put in an addendum to the prayer. "Help me to bless others, but not in such a way as to totally mess up my life." Who knew?

To continue my baseball analogy, two of my original three top players were off the team. But at least Megan was still in the lineup.

My mom used to tell me that my philosophy of life was: "If a little is good, then a lot is better." I guess in a way that explained my drive to get married before my folks left on a mission. I'd set a goal to get married before February and was doing everything in my power to make it happen, if not with Abbie or Hannah, then with Megan.

I began spending every possible moment with Megan. Things seemed to be going well. So on Monday, August 8, after home evening, I asked if we could spend some time on the beach in front of the house where she worked.

After handing her a marshmallow I'd browned in the bonfire, I said, "What would you think if we got married?" She'd already rejected the first three I had done because they were on fire and black when I handed them to her.

"You did a good job on this one," she said.

"Did you hear my question?" I asked.

"I did. I'm not sure what to say."

"You know I love you."

"Actually, Dave, I don't know that. Are you asking me only because Abbie and Hannah are out of the picture?"

"No. I'm asking because my folks are going on a mission and my mom really would like it if I got married before they leave."

You know what? Never give a girl an honest answer. She laughed so hard that I knew she'd tell Abbie.

She stood up. "Things have changed. I have something I need to show you. I'll be right back."

She was gone almost an hour. By then I'd eaten so many marshmallows, my stomach felt like a pillow.

Finally she returned. "Sorry I took so long. I had a phone call."

"From Sterling, the Magic Carpenter?"

"Uh-huh."

She'd brought her laptop with her. We sat down on a log and watched a DVD Sterling had sent her. In it he gave her a tour of the house that he and his dad were building for her if she married Sterling. The house wasn't completely finished yet but enough so he could show her each room.

Sterling was tall, thin, and painfully awkward. He had a habit of pushing his glasses up on the bridge of his nose when he talked. He didn't make eye contact with the camera but kept his eyes on the floor most of the time.

"You said you wanted an island in the kitchen for food preparation," Sterling said on the DVD. "Well, this is it. We got a real good deal on these marble counters." He pointed to an open space. "This is where the dishwasher will go."

Someone off-camera said, "Tell her about the grill."

"You tell her, Dad."

They traded places. His dad was like a chunkier version of Sterling. "Hi, Megan. We're sure looking forward to you coming back. And we hope you'll come be a part of our family. I've never seen anyone work harder than Sterling has on this house. He might not be flowery with words, but I know he has real feelings for you, and his mom and I love you, too. We always have, for that matter. We can't think of anything that would mean more to us than having you be in our family."

By then Megan had tears running down her face.

When it was over, we were both silent.

"What a great gimmick to try to get you to marry the poor schmuck," I said.

Megan didn't want to hear that. "It's more than a gimmick, Dave. And he's not a schmuck, whatever that is. This is . . . love in action."

"Well, I'm not sure I'd go that far. I mean for a guy with limited social skills like Sterling, I suppose it's about the only way he'll get a girl to marry him."

"I feel really bad," she said.

"Hey, don't. He'll find some girl who will take him up on his offer of a new house. Some girls are immature enough to go for something like that."

She blew her nose. "No. What I feel bad about is hurting your feelings. You've had such a hard time lately with girls, haven't you?"

"Huh?"

"The reason I took so long is that he called me while I was in my room. I told him I'd love to live with him in his new house."

"You're not going to just live with him, right? Because that'd be wrong."

"I actually think Sterling and I are engaged now. That is, if you can do something like that on the phone. He was so cute. He said he was on his knees when he asked me, but, of course, I have no way of knowing that." She smiled, apparently impressed by the weird proposal.

"You're going to take some stupid house over me?"

"It's not just a house. It's a symbol of the love Sterling and his family have for me."

I didn't know what to say and just sat there.

"I'm sorry. I feel really bad for you."

"When are you leaving?"

"I called Abbie just before I came back and arranged to ride with her and Eldon on their way back home. We'll be leaving on the twenty-fourth, the day after Hannah and Antonio get married. Did you know the company is giving Eldon the car he drove all summer? Isn't that great?"

I stood up and started pacing back and forth. I threw my hands in the air. "Of course it's great! Everyone I know is doing so well! Abbie's leaving with Eldon and you in his new car! Hannah is getting married to Antonio and going on a ten-day cruise! You're leaving to go marry Sterling and move into a brand new house! Abbie and Eldon will certainly be married within a very short time. It's all such great news! Imagine how happy I am for every stupid one of you!"

She said cheerfully, "Look on the bright side."

My mouth dropped open. "The *bright* side?"

"Yeah. Girls from the same agency in Utah will come and take both Abbie's and my place as nannies. We'll tell the new girls they're supposed to like you."

"Oh, that'd be good. Well, then, I guess my work here is done."

"Can we talk?"

"No. What good has talking ever gotten me? Make sure the fire's out before you leave, okay? Just my luck, the sand will catch on fire."

I walked quickly to the pickup and drove off.

* * *

As bad as they were, my problems didn't compare to those Murray was experiencing. His wife continued having health problems. Sometimes he wouldn't come into the store until eleven, and he'd usually only stay a few hours and then have to leave again. Two days later he asked if I could stay on until after Christmas.

Even though my folks had wanted me home soon so I could

help them get ready for their mission, after talking to my dad, he was okay with me staying.

So I told Murray I'd stay.

On August 23, Antonio and Hannah were married by President Alexander in his home. Abbie and I were there for the wedding. Eldon was working, of course.

The next day Hannah and Antonio left on *Blue Skies* for a honeymoon sailing adventure. Also on that day, Eldon, Abbie, and Megan left to go back west.

So, what does a guy do when every girl he's approached dumps him? He buys himself a used car that needs a lot of work. And then he works on it every chance he gets.

At least that's what I did.

CHAPTER THIRTEEN

Murray's wife had an operation the first Wednesday in September. Murray told me it went well, but he never told me what was wrong with her, so I had to take his word for it.

I was the only one working at the store for the next two weeks and then, little by little, once his wife was able to get along at home without him, he began coming to work again.

On Sunday, September 18, Abbie called me from Idaho and told me Eldon had just broken up with her.

"Why?"

"He says we're too different to ever make it together. But I think it's his political ambitions. Eldon keeps talking about what Elizabeth's dad said, about him running for governor some day. He's decided that's what he wants to do, and it looks to me like he's willing to marry her to get her dad's help."

"You can't be serious. Nobody would do that."

"Eldon would."

"What about Elizabeth? How does she feel to just be a signing bonus for Eldon?"

We talked until three in the morning. Well, it was three for me, only one for her.

"Look, give me a couple of weeks and I'll quit my job and come out and be with you," I said.

"I'm not ready for much of anything now except a friend. I would guess you'd be the same way, too, what with getting dropped by me and Hannah and then Megan."

"Well, yeah, it has been a little rocky, but the thing is, you're my default."

"What?"

"It's like when you're working on your laptop and you really mess things up, so you turn it off but don't save what you've done. When you reboot, everything comes back just the way it was before. That's how my love for you is. It's what happens when I wake up every day. You're my default."

She laughed. "I can't decide if that was actually romantic or the most pathetic declaration of love ever expressed."

"It was actually romantic."

"I still care about you, Dave. You make me laugh. You're the one I always turn to when I'm having a bad day." She paused. "Or even when I'm having a good day."

"That means I'm your default, too. You know what? I'll call up Murray and quit my job and come out to be with you. With Eldon out of the picture, maybe I'll have a chance."

"That's sounds great, except I'm not sure where I'll end up living. I've got a couple of job possibilities. One in Provo, another in Idaho Falls, and one in Boise. Your mom says you're planning on coming back the first part of January. Maybe that's what you should do because by that time I'll know what I'm going to do."

"And then we'll start seeing each other again? Okay?"

"Yeah, I'd like that."

Abbie ended up taking a job working as a legal secretary in a law office in Idaho Falls. She also decided to take night classes at BYU—Idaho. We traded emails every day.

About a week later, she mentioned a guy named Thomas, who

was working as an intern at the law firm. His name started creeping into her emails, at first just because she was helping him on a project.

September is a great time for people to do home improvement, so the store was very busy. I was working about seventy hours a week. Abbie and I watched conference together on Sunday. She on her TV in Idaho, me on my laptop in New York.

In mid-October she told me that Thomas had taken her to a concert on campus.

"Was there some kind of lawsuit involved with the concert?" I asked.

"No, I told him I wanted to go, and he offered to take me."

"Oh, sure."

Near the end of October, Abbie told me about a business trip she had taken to California with two people from the law firm—one of them being Thomas. She told me how exciting it was to be in the inner circle in the law office and how much she admired and respected the men she worked with.

That was the last she told me about her job. After that, nothing. In fact, her emails also dropped off. And it was harder to get her on the phone.

On December 20, I received a four-page letter from her. It had been sent overnight Fed Ex.

It started with an apology. "I never intended for this to happen. You have every right to be angry at me. You know I've talked about Thomas a few times. Well, we've been seeing more of each other lately. I like him very much."

And then the kicker. "He's asked me to marry him and, although it's too soon, I really think that it's something I'd like to consider. I've tentatively agreed to his offer."

You can tell she'd been working in a law office, right? I mean, who ever sends a "Dear John" letter with the phrase "tentatively agreed to his offer"?

In her letter she kept saying, "I'm so sorry."

But on a good note, her letter ended with "Love, Abbie."

At least she still loves me, I thought.

* * *

Two days after I received that letter, my folks got their mission call. They were called to the South Dakota Rapid City Mission for twenty-three months and would be reporting to Fargo, North Dakota. They would be entering the MTC on March 15.

"Twenty-three months?" I asked on the phone.

"That's as long as they let senior missionaries serve," my dad said.

With Abbie out of the picture, and with Hannah married, and with Megan married, and the car I'd fixed up now actually able to make long trips, I had no reason to stay in New York. But, on the other hand, I had no reason to go back west either. Except for running my dad's store.

The reason I didn't move back home is because I didn't want to be reminded every day of what I'd lost with Abbie. Also, I'd gotten used to the excitement of living close to New York City. I was now as bad as Abbie had been. I loved to go into the City. I loved wearing my Yankees baseball cap. I loved the feeling of being part of something very big and very important.

I might have mentioned once to my dad that I wasn't sure I even wanted to go back to Idaho, but that I'd do it to support them on their mission.

Murray had me over to his home for dinner on Christmas. He and his wife told me how much they appreciated me staying on during the time she was sick. They gave me a Derek Jeter autographed baseball. Murray told me they'd never been able to have kids, so if it was all right, they'd like to think of me as their son. I told them I was honored to be thought of in that way. Murray shook my hand

and gave me a hug. His wife gave me a hug and told me she thought God had sent me to them.

So even though I had dreaded spending Christmas all alone, it turned out all right after all.

Two days after Christmas, my dad called. He never did that.

"Hi, Dad, is anything wrong?"

"No, not really. How are you doing?"

"Real good."

"Something just happened I thought I'd better run by you. A fella just walked in the store and offered to buy it."

"Why would he want to do that?"

"He's had four daughters come to BYU—Idaho for school, and all four got married and stayed in the area. So he's got eight grandchildren within a hundred miles of here, but he and his wife never see them because he works in a hardware store in Michigan. When some folks told him we were going on a mission, he stopped by to ask if I'd consider selling to him."

"Is he offering a good price?"

"Yeah, pretty good."

"But what would you do when you and mom come home from your mission?"

"Well, we were thinking we'd like to serve as ordinance workers in the temple for a year or two and then maybe go on another mission. Oh, there is one other thing."

"What's that?"

"He'll be looking for a house to live in. So he gave me an offer on that, too."

"Oh."

"So my only question is, what would you think if we did that?"

"I'd say it's up to you."

"You don't think you'll want to take over the store some day and run it for your career?"

"Not anymore. I guess I've changed."

"Well, then, maybe we'll go ahead with it."

"Yeah, sure, whatever."

So that's what they did.

* * *

On Friday, March 10, I flew out to be with my folks before they left on their mission. The next day my mom asked me to go through some things in my room and decide what I wanted to do with them. Otherwise, the house was empty.

So there I was, in my room, sitting on the floor, surrounded with photos, certificates of achievement, and a trophy or two—the sum total of all the things I'd hung onto to remind me what I'd done in high school and who I was.

I had a lot of photos of Abbie and me, some of them going back to junior high. I'd also kept my report cards where a teacher had actually said something good about me, but of course there weren't many of those.

My mom told me the storage unit was nearly full so I could have only a couple of boxes to store it all. At first I thought it wouldn't be enough. The trophies alone took up most of the room in one box and that didn't even take into account my clothes from high school.

I forced myself to go through every photo of Abbie and me. For most of them I could remember where we were and what we were doing when the picture was taken: Church outings, holidays, hay rides, school dances, and just hanging out with friends at the drive-in. For as long as I could remember, it had always been "Abbie and Dave." It was tough, recalling all those times and remembering how I had always felt about her. And to think of her being someone else's wife was almost too much. I had a hard time and was glad no one walked in on me.

Remember in "Back to the Future," where Marty McFly looks at a photo of his family, and he starts to fade out, like he'd never even existed? That's the way I felt. I felt like I was being deconstructed.

I ended up stuffing most of my things into plastic bags and putting them in the trash.

Because my mom would get crazy if she knew I'd thrown everything away, I found some old copies of *The New Era* in my room, put them in the box, taped it shut, and told her I was done.

"Just this one box?" she asked.

"Yep," I said.

She seemed pleased. So that was good.

I could hardly wait to get back to New York. I had nothing to keep me in Idaho anymore.

My mom and dad gave good talks in sacrament meeting. The bishop said what good people they were and how lucky the people in Fargo, North Dakota, were to have them going there. And I was proud of them for being willing to serve a mission.

After the meeting, I got to meet Abbie's Thomas. He looked polished and formal and highly educated and he spoke with a certain crispness unheard of in Idaho. He also had lots of hair, dark brown, and a very deep voice. He sounded a lot like James Earl Jones. I figured he'd win every case just on his voice.

Abbie looked good. She seemed happy, and her hair no longer was the color of a school bus. It was her natural color, and she was growing it out—the way I'd always hoped it would be for me when she and I got married.

They told me they would be getting married in June, and I wished them well.

The next day, I left to go back to New York.

* * *

For about a week after I got back to Long Island, I stayed away from people. I didn't go to family home evening or sports night or institute. Instead I watched European soccer. I learned to say "Idiot!" in five languages.

But two Sundays later President Alexander called me into his office after sacrament meeting and called me to be a Sunday School teacher.

I know that doesn't sound like much, but it was a big deal to me. Suddenly I had a responsibility to be a good example. There would be no more violations of the Nathan Rule for me.

My duty, as I saw it, was to be a nice guy and just be a part of the group. Go to branch activities but not date anyone. If you do that, every girl in the branch is your friend. But the moment you start dating someone, you've only got one friend who's a girl. And when you break up with her, you're down to zero friends for weeks.

To be a friend to every girl in the branch became my new goal—just one of the guys they could hang out with. That way nobody ever breaks up with you, and you don't become the topic of every discussion among the females in the branch.

I became like the poster child for a singles ward. I went to every activity but never dated anyone. I had friends but never got too friendly.

You know what? It's actually a good life.

CHAPTER FOURTEEN

In June 2006, my one-year anniversary of coming to New York state, I was doing pretty well. I didn't know exactly where I was going in life, but I was in a routine. I was still working at the hardware store and that plus the branch activities kept me busy. Teaching Sunday School each week and going to the temple as often as I could were also a big help in keeping me on track. I had a few casual friends, and I was even getting over thinking about Abbie as much.

My parents were serving in Fargo, North Dakota. Once a week we'd send emails. They were involved in activation and seemed to be enjoying it.

I was one of the most dependable guys in the singles branch—someone who could always be counted on to be at every activity. Even service projects, if they didn't interfere with work.

But once in a while, in our singles branch, there was a disturbing event. It always happened on Sunday. It was called the high council speaker.

If you're in a singles ward or branch, sooner or later some member of a high council will decide that what the young single adults really need to do is to get married. So he'll give a talk, which if titled would be called, "Why Don't You Pathetic People Just Get Married?"

I found a way of handling The Talk. I'd start coughing until I had to leave the chapel. Nobody can blame you if you have to leave the meeting because you're coughing. But if you just walk out without the coughing, that will prompt the high councilor to lean over to President Alexander and whisper, "Who's that young man who walked out while I was talking? Does he have issues?"

I guess a few people in the branch might have noticed this pattern because one time when we were getting The Talk, another guy coughed a couple of times and went out into the hall before I could.

What's this clown doing? I thought. *The Cough is mine! He's got no right to use it!*

I was left there, desperate to escape but not knowing how. That was when I came up with The Good Samaritan Ploy. I looked at the door the first guy had gone out of, tried to look concerned, and then got up and hurried out as if I were going to check on him.

It worked.

In the hall I told the imposter that he had no right use The Cough.

"Are you serious? I perfected The Cough in my home ward," he complained.

"No way, The Cough is mine."

We decided to compromise. One of us would be the cougher, the other the concerned friend going to the rescue.

So we worked it all out.

Once in a while, though, usually in my apartment late at night, I would crash and burn. I'd start telling myself what a loser I was and how I was never going to get married. I'd look in the mirror and think I should have gotten married at eighteen because I had more hair then. I was going downhill fast.

But I did find a bright side to it all. Maybe I'd only have to wait until the beginning of the Millennium and then meet some recently-resurrected young woman and talk her into marrying me. Now there's an untapped resource, right?

I realized it might be a little tricky telling people her age. Like if she died in 1700 at the age of twenty, and people would ask how old she is, what would I say? "I'd like you to meet my bride. She's over three hundred years old."

I decided you got to go with how old she was when she died. So, at twenty, maybe she'd still be too young for me.

I didn't always think about things like that. Just once in a while. Most of the time I was the perfect guy for any singles branch. I was polite, interested in girls, but incapable of forming any deeper friendship than a "Hi, how's it going?" in the hall.

For me, the idea of once again putting myself out to try to develop a serious relationship with any girl in the branch was about as inviting as having open heart surgery without anesthetic.

Nobody could fault me for the way I was living. I was totally active in my branch, and except for having a bad cough during a few high council talks, I was in excellent health. I worked out every day, too, and eventually got rid of the paunch I'd picked up on my mission. I'd sent for the free DVD about hair restoration and was saving up for the operation. So far I'd saved one hundred dollars. Only three thousand, nine hundred more dollars to go.

My life was a little boring, but very predictable. But sometimes predictable is all a person needs.

After a while I got some clarity about Abbie and me. You know how if you're in an accident the insurance company makes you get two or three estimates on how much it will cost to get it fixed? Some people have already decided what auto body shop they want to do the work, but they go through the motions to get the estimates anyway.

With Abbie, she just needed another estimate, even though she wasn't going to act on it. And that was me. I was her other estimate.

That helped me quit beating up on myself about losing her.

But all the trauma associated with her resurfaced briefly the second week in June when I got a phone call from a guy with a deep bass voice. "This is Thomas."

I couldn't remember a Thomas being in the singles branch. "You must have the wrong number."

"Abbie and I are getting married tomorrow."

My pent-up anger gave way. "Oh, I see, and you wanted to call to rub it in? Great! Hey, Tom Boy, where are you going on your honeymoon? I want to know all the details!"

"Dave?" It was Abbie's voice. "Don't blame Thomas. I told him I wanted to talk to you one last time before I get married. Out of the goodness of his heart, he agreed to let me call. I wanted him to listen in so he'd know everything we say. He's on our other phone."

I realized she'd heard everything I'd said. Once again, with Abbie, I felt off balance.

"Why are we even talking?" I complained to Abbie.

"I talked to Nicole a few days ago."

"Oh, sure, Nicole. She's in my Sunday School class."

"I asked about you. She said it's like you're drifting."

"That's not true. I don't know why she'd say that."

"Are you going to college?" she asked.

"No."

"Are you dating anyone?"

"No."

"What are you doing, then?" she asked.

"I'm getting by, like everybody else."

"How long are you going to stay out there?"

"I don't know. I haven't thought about it. I'm in no hurry to make any changes right now. I like my life."

"You're like Peter Pan, you never grow up. There will always be a new batch of nannies to admire you, right? Casual friends, of course, but that's all you want, isn't it?"

"You taught me everything I know, Abbie."

"If that's true, I apologize."

"Abbie, we need to go," Thomas said.

"You guys have a great time on your honeymoon, okay?" I said. "I'll be thinking about you two tomorrow night about this time."

That made Thomas angry. "Our honeymoon is none of your business. Goodbye."

I hated the guy, and I'm sure he felt the same way about me.

That was my last contact with Abbie.

So that was it. The next day Abbie and Thomas got married. Hannah and Antonio were already married. They'd moved up-state where he was going to school. Megan was, of course, married to Sterling, living in her new home in St. George, Utah. And someone told me she was expecting. Nathan had finished med school and was working in Rochester, New York. I heard talk that he'd met someone and that they were engaged.

I found out that there's some good fly-fishing places on the eastern end of Long Island, especially Shinnecock Bay. Some days after work I'd drive out and try my luck. It was good to get out by myself. It gave me peace of mind.

I was thinking about maybe taking a class or two at a community college but as yet hadn't done much except look at some of the classes they offered.

That was pretty much my life.

* * *

In August I was called to be the branch clerk to President Alexander in the branch presidency. That made me try even harder to live the gospel.

On the third Sunday in August, when someone didn't show up for their sacrament talk, President Alexander asked me to speak about "Building Zion."

This is how I began my talk. "Okay, everybody, we're going to have a service project on Saturday to build Zion. Everyone show up at eight and bring hammers and rakes. We'll be driving to Missouri."

And then I looked back at President Alexander, as though he

was correcting me, then turned to the congregation again. "Oh, sorry, we won't be going to Missouri. Zion is also North and South America. So pack a bag. Those with passports are especially invited."

One more turn to President Alexander, who I noticed wasn't smiling.

"Oh, sorry. President Alexander just reminded me that Zion is also the pure in heart. So we'll be working to make your hearts pure. I'm not sure what to tell you to bring for that. We'll leave that up to President Alexander."

Eventually I said something serious, about the importance of living good lives so that we could establish Zion wherever we are.

When I sat down, President Alexander didn't say anything, but I could tell he wasn't impressed. Neither was I. I realized I shouldn't have made light of the subject, and I felt awful for disappointing him. I'd made a mockery of what to him was a serious topic. It was worse because, being a clerk, people thought of me as being in the branch presidency. I had misused that position of trust to make myself look good.

The thing is I had great respect for President Alexander. Everyone did. He always had time for us. Anytime of day or night. And he told us what we needed to know. And he got after us if we didn't live up to his expectations for us.

From this experience I learned that you don't make light of sacred things. Even if you don't understand them.

From that time on I approached every assignment from President Alexander with great seriousness.

He asked me to give a talk the Sunday before October general conference. The topic was "Getting the Most out of General Conference."

I spent all week preparing the talk. I think I did a good job, too. I quoted several General Authorities about how we should prepare spiritually for conference, how we should pray for answers we wanted to receive, and how we should take notes, not of every word that was said but about the impressions we received.

I'm not sure what the talk did for anyone else, but it changed the way I approached general conference.

After work, the next Saturday, I was in the chapel with my notepad and scriptures, watching the priesthood session of conference.

It seemed to me there was a theme to the priesthood meeting that night. Beginning with Elder D. Todd Christofferson's talk entitled, "Let Us Be Men" and ending with President Hinckley's talk entitled, "Rise up, O Men of God."

I felt these messages were personally directed to me and that it was time for me to rise up and be a man.

What that means is not easy to define, but in my case I felt I needed to go back to Idaho and attend BYU—Idaho and get a degree. I needed to follow President Hinckley's counsel and get as much education as I could as fast as I could.

I'd never been someone who received a great deal of inspiration. Even on my mission, I worked based on plans we'd worked out, not much on promptings of the Spirit.

So this was a first for me. I felt strongly that I needed to get on with my life, get an education, and begin a serious search for someone to marry.

On Monday at work I gave my two-weeks notice, but since I had some vacation time coming, I only worked to the end of the week and then boxed up my few belongings and started driving home.

On my last day, just before closing, Murray's wife came into the store. She told me once again how much she appreciated me staying when she was sick. Murray shook my hand and gave me a wrapped present. It was a heavy-duty cordless drill that retails for nearly three hundred dollars. I realized how much I had come to love these people and struggled not to cry as I hugged them both and we promised to keep in touch.

And then I left.

* * *

As usual, my timing on going to Idaho was bad. October put me in the middle of fall semester, but I thought I'd use the time to find a place to live and get a job and apply for student aid.

The first place I went to apply for a job was my dad's old store in Ririe, Idaho. It was crazy to walk into the place where I'd grown up. For the most part everything was the same. I think I half expected my dad to be there.

But he wasn't.

"Can I help you?" the new owner asked me.

"I'm looking for a job."

"We don't have any openings."

"Oh." I paused. "My dad used to own this store."

"Oh, yes! Of course. I see the resemblance now. Your dad has told me a lot about you. You're always welcome here. Look around the place, if you'd like. And if you need any help, let me know. I'll be in the back."

I wandered around, but to be honest, it depressed me because for such a long time the store had been a big part of my dad's life. I wondered if I had been wrong to let go what could have been a family tradition.

Brother Anderson entered the store. I'd known him all my life. He'd shown it was possible to make money farming and, even in his mid-seventies, continued to farm. He had lived a few houses away from us when I was growing up.

He saw me and smiled. I'm not sure he realized things had changed.

"Dave, it's good to see you. How's school?"

I wondered if he thought I was still in high school. "Real good."

"How're your folks? I don't see them much anymore since they changed the ward boundaries."

"Yeah, that's true. What can I help you find?"

"Nuts and bolts."

"Sure. Just follow me."

I went to the place they used to be, but they weren't there. Things had been rearranged, and it was a shock to me. I felt as though I was a stranger and that I didn't belong there anymore.

The new owner came and helped Brother Anderson, and I left.

I drove past our old house. It looked about the same, as did the home where Abbie had grown up.

It was weird. I felt like my entire life had been erased. The home I'd grown up in, the store where my dad and I had worked, the girl I'd loved, the place I'd had in the community—everything was gone.

I don't know how long I would have stayed there, but I saw a movement of a curtain in Abbie's folks' house. I didn't want her mom seeing me and telling Abbie she'd seen me parked outside the house. I mean, how pathetic would that be? Like I hadn't moved on. Like I couldn't face my loss. That I still thought about her. That I'd gone over in my head a hundred times what I should have done, even though it was too late for that now.

I did not want anyone to know I was living in the past, so I drove away.

I didn't know where to go, though, because I had no place to call home anymore. I felt like I'd hit bottom. And when that happens, you play the "I should have . . ." game. I should have moved out here earlier, taken over my dad's store, lived in their house while they were on their mission, and taken night classes until they came back and then I could enroll as a full time student.

When Abbie left New York to come home, I should have gone with her, even if she did think she was going to marry Eldon. I should have seen her every day. I should have made it clear that she was my number-one priority in life.

I felt as if I'd thrown away the life I should have had. And that I'd disappointed my dad for not taking over the store he'd spent his life building, and my mom for not doing what she wanted me to do.

At least in New York I had an identity and a purpose. Here, I had nothing.

No, it was worse than nothing. Here I was reminded of "roads not taken."

I spent the night in my car at the park in Ririe. I guess I could have asked someone from the ward to take me in, but the thing I feared the most from these people was for them to ask why my dad had sold his store and why Abbie and I hadn't got married and what year in college I was. That's why I slept in my car.

It took me about a week to put my life back together. I got a job working at BYU—Idaho, in what they call Stores and Receiving. It was like when I used to go in the back room of the hardware store and open up boxes of things we'd ordered. Except now that was the entire job.

I got an apartment. Not campus housing because I wasn't a student and, even if I had been, I wasn't ready for roommates. The place I got was far enough from campus that I could almost forget school was there.

I picked some classes for winter semester, even though I didn't really know what I was going to major in. I felt like I was taking the first steps toward finally putting my life together.

Once when I was on campus, I saw Courtney, Abbie's younger sister, but I made no effort to talk with her. That afternoon I went to the Idaho Falls temple.

I arrived in time for the five o'clock session. It helped me get over my depression at feeling like such a loser. Because nobody is a loser in the temple. Heavenly Father is like the Eternal Optimist about us, no matter how much of a disappointment we've been to ourselves in the past.

I stayed in the celestial room after the session and in my mind prayed for help. Somewhere in that prayer I might have mentioned I wanted to get married in the temple but that I had no prospects and wasn't sure I would ever find anyone who would want to put up with me.

After maybe half an hour, I was done praying. I stood up, walked out of the celestial room and into the hall. I saw some ordinance workers getting ready to help with the next endowment session. Most of them were old, but there was one who wasn't.

She looked to be about my age. She was tall but not taller than me. She had excellent posture and looked like an angel dressed in white. Okay, the older ordinance workers looked like angels, too. Just really old angels.

I'm not sure what it was, but the thought came to me, except it didn't seem to be from me, and the thought was "What about her?"

I go on a mission for two years and receive precious little revelation and then I look at this random girl in the temple and get, "What about her?"

Okay, it could have been "How about her?" I can't remember, but it definitely wasn't from me because she wasn't that outstanding. I mean, she was okay, but you know, not something to write to your folks about.

If the thought had come from me, it would have been worded differently. The question, if I'd asked it of myself, would have been, "What's wrong with her?"

"What's wrong with her?" is always an easy question to answer. In just ten minutes, I can come up with ten things I don't like about any girl. The way she parts her hair. Or maybe her laugh is too loud. Or maybe she walks with her shoulders rounded. Or else she has no opinions about anything. Or her nose. I'm very particular about a girl's nose.

Oh, yes, I was very good at dealing with the question, "What's wrong with her?"

But that wasn't the question I thought, so I was pretty sure it wasn't from me.

Was this from God? Not very likely, right? Why would He care about me and this girl?

The trouble is I never know if I'm receiving actual inspiration or if it's just my imagination.

I decided to stick around long enough to at least talk to this girl. But, of course, first I would need to find out if she was indeed single.

I went back into the celestial room where a sister ordinance worker was directing people.

"Uh, excuse me," I said softly, "could you step outside and look at the line of sisters. I need to know if the fourth one in line is single."

She gave me a funny look, but nodded, stepped out, and came back. "Yes, she's single."

"Good. I'm interested in meeting her."

"Really? She's at least seventy years old."

I paused. "Let me just take another peek, okay?"

I went out and looked again and came back. "Sorry, she's fifth in line now. One of the older women must have cut in line. That's kind of pushy for a temple worker, wouldn't you say?"

She looked again and came back. "Yes, she's single. Do you want to know her name?"

"No, that's okay. Thanks."

I went to the hallway and found a seat and waited.

About half an hour later, the ordinance workers came out of the terrestrial room.

And then, there she was, coming toward me. In the half hour I had been waiting, you'd think I'd have come up with what I was going to say, but I hadn't.

But in the next two seconds, unless I did something, she'd be past me. I stood up to block her way. "Do you come here often?"

She looked startled. "What?"

"Do you come here often?" At that point I might have been just a tiny bit wild-eyed.

"Well, actually, I'm a temple ordinance worker, so, you know, I come here . . . every week."

"Oh, sure." I glanced down to read her name tag. "Camille Colbin? Is that your name?"

"That's right. Do you need meds? If you're diabetic, we have orange juice right over there in that cabinet."

"They said you were single. I'm single, too."

She sighed. "How old are you?"

"Twenty-two."

"I'm twenty-six."

My mouth dropped open. "You're twenty-six?"

"Excuse me, I have another assignment."

I had to sit down to get my bearings. *She's twenty-six years old?* I thought. *That's four years older than me. When I was in seventh grade and she was a junior in high school, would I have wanted to date her then? So why would I consider it now? What is going on here? Does Father in Heaven really have that morbid a sense of humor?*

I felt like an idiot. I'd certainly acted like one. Could I have been more clumsy? Talking to her had been embarrassing to me, and I'm sure to her also.

I wondered why she told me her age right away. Had she ever started to become friends with a guy but when he found out how old she was, he dropped her completely, like it was unacceptable for them even to be friends?

I'd seen some sadness in her eyes, too. She might have seen the same in mine. It was the sadness of not having your dreams come true, of seeing someone you care about get married to someone else when you knew that if you'd somehow been "more," it could have been you.

I wanted to get away—from her and from the embarrassment of how badly I'd handled meeting her.

I go twenty-two years, and in some odd quirk of fate I get a "How about her?" prompting from Father in Heaven.

Well, I had a question for Him. *Why did you put four years difference in age between us? What's that all about?*

Although I wanted to forget about it, I felt as though I had to give it another shot.

I needed to speak with her again when she wasn't busy.

I waited on a couch outside the cafeteria. When I saw her, I hurried over to talk to her. "Are you on your way to the cafeteria?" I asked.

"Yes."

"Can I eat with you?"

"Why do you want to eat with me?"

"Is it going to kill you if I eat with you? I won't be a problem. Just for you I'll chew with my mouth closed."

She smiled faintly. "Well, that's an offer that's hard to pass up."

We went through the cafeteria line. She got a bowl of soup and a salad. I just got a sandwich.

Just after sitting down, I asked, "Do people actually call you Camille?"

"Yes, they do."

"Oh. People call me Dave."

"Is that your name?"

"Yes. So it all works out, right?"

She looked at her watch. "I don't have much time before my next assignment."

"You eat, I'll talk."

"All right."

"You have nice eyes. What color are they?" I asked.

"I don't feel comfortable with the direction this conversation is going."

"I like your smile, too."

"I'm not aware that I've smiled since meeting you."

"I've seen you smile."

"How many Fridays have you been here watching me?"

"Just today. Believe me, It's not like I come here every week."

"So you don't come to the temple much?" she asked. "I'm sorry. Your personal life is none of my business."

I took a big drink of water and wiped the sweat from my forehead.

"This is like waiting for the other shoe to drop, isn't it?" she asked.

"How do you mean?"

"I'm wondering what bit of information about myself will cause you to take your sandwich and leave," she said.

"Why do you say that?"

"Because that's what always happens. I'm either too smart, too tall, or too old. What will it be this time? Your choice."

"We've already covered you being older than me."

"I guess we have," she said.

"Also, I'm a little taller than you so that's no problem for me. So that just leaves smart. Are you smart?"

"Yes, I am."

"How smart?"

"I teach calculus and differential equations at BYU—Idaho."

I sighed. "Oh."

She reached to shake my hand. "Look, it's been real good meeting you. Please come to the temple often. If you're worried about seeing me again, let me point out there are four days a week when I'm not even here."

"You want to know why I'm not threatened by the fact you teach calculus and different equations at BYU—Idaho? It's because I have no idea what you're talking about. With me, ignorance *is* power."

"Actually, it's not *different* equations, it's *differential* equations."

"Whatever. I can overhaul the engine of a car. Can you do that?"

"No."

"I can do a lot of things. When I was growing up, my dad owned a hardware store. I worked there starting when I was in ninth grade.

I know everything about what to buy when you want to fix something."

"Are you going to take over the store some day?"

I sighed. "No. That's what should have happened, but it didn't."

"Why's that?"

"My dad sold the store before he and my mom left on their mission."

"I see."

"And the girl I went with all through high school married someone else. So I'm at rock bottom. That's why I came to the temple."

She nodded. "You seemed a little desperate when I first saw you. Like you were hoping to marry the first single girl you saw in the temple. Oh, wait, that was me, right?" She actually did smile.

"Sorry for freaking you out."

"Don't worry about it." She looked at her watch. "I really need to go now. I have another assignment."

"How long will it take?"

"I'll be busy until the temple closes."

"I can wait."

"Why would you want to do that?" she asked.

"When I first saw you, Heavenly Father put this thought in my mind. It was *What about her?*"

"Heavenly Father said 'What about her?'"

"I think so but I'm not exactly sure. It could have been me, but I don't think so. You're not someone I would ordinarily be attracted to. So that pretty much leaves Father in Heaven."

She smiled.

"What?"

"I'm now certain you don't make a habit of walking up to girls in the temple and saying what you just told me. Because if you did, you'd be a lot better at it."

"That's true. You're my first attempt at this. If you want, I can give you an evaluation sheet for you to fill out."

She stood up. "I have to go."

"Can I walk you to where you're going?" I asked.

"Partway, I guess."

"Okay, look, it was more than just a 'What about her?' The feeling was like, 'Why don't you find out what is wonderful about her instead of looking for an excuse to write her off like you usually do?'"

"Heavenly Father actually used the term 'write her off'?"

"Okay, it wasn't exactly like a revelation, okay? Maybe it was just me seeing things from His point of view for just a second. So that's when I decided I had to talk to you."

"Well, I'm so happy to have helped Father in Heaven provide you with a teaching moment about the worth of souls. Now, if you'll excuse me . . ."

"Let me wait for you until you're done, and then we'll go out for something to eat, and then, if you want, that will be it and I won't ever bother you again."

"I don't think so."

"Look, what's the worst that could happen? Are you worried we'll find out we have nothing in common? We already know that."

"That's true, so why put ourselves through what can only be an agonizing experience for both of us?"

"Look, I don't get much from Father in Heaven in terms of help. I'd like to pursue this as much as I can, just in case this actually was from Him."

She sighed, hesitated, then said, "Okay, I should be done by ten o'clock."

"I'll meet you in front of the recommend desk."

At ten o'clock some senior temple couples who'd heard about Camille and me smiled at me as they left. "She's a keeper," one of the men said to me as he and his wife passed me.

I hoped he was right, but, personally, I had my doubts.

CHAPTER FIFTEEN

When Camille showed up, she was wearing a plaid business suit that made her look like an officer in the Scottish army.

"I'll follow you in my car," she said as we made our way to the temple parking lot.

"Actually, I think we should go in my car."

"You'd just have to drive me back here when we're done."

"It'd be more like a date if you're in my car."

She thought about it. "I'll follow you in my car."

I led her to a truck-stop café in Idaho Falls.

"Order anything you want," I said as we slid into our booth.

"I desperately need an aspirin."

"Sure, no problem. Money is no object. Get two aspirin if you want."

I noticed she had a dimple that appeared when she smiled. For me it was like a signing bonus.

The waitress came to take our order. Camille ordered some fresh fruit along with her aspirin.

"Do you have sweet potato fries?" I asked the waitress.

"No."

"They're very good."

"This is Idaho."

"Right. I'll have regular fries, then."

Then we were left on our own.

Camille noticed a mustard smudge on the table, dipped a napkin into her water glass, and began rubbing it.

Oh, good grief, she's a clean freak, I thought.

"How'd you ever get a job teaching college math?" I asked. "That's kind of hard, isn't it?"

She gave me a blank stare. "I graduated from BYU summa cum laude, I have a master's degree, and I'm working toward my Ph.D."

I nodded. "That's real good. Math is very important. I don't think a day goes by I don't use math."

"What do you use it for?"

"Oh, you know, balancing my checkbook." My voice dropped off as I said it.

"I see."

"Oh, and before my mission, when I worked at my dad's hardware store, I could estimate how much paint a customer needed to paint a room. What do you use math for?"

"In my graduate research I'm trying to find a generalized way to define inflection points for curves in a multi-dimensional, non-orthogonal space."

I cleared my throat. "Oh, sure. I can see where that would come in handy."

"You can?"

"Absolutely. I mean, where would we be without inflection points to spread a little cheer on a dreary day?"

She stared at me.

"It was a joke," I said.

She leaned forward and spoke confidentially, "Look, we can still leave and pretend this never happened."

I panicked a little bit. "Okay, I'll admit, this isn't as clear to me as it was in the temple, but I'm not ready to give up."

"I don't want to be unkind, but to be totally honest, I really can't see any reason for us to continue. We have nothing in common."

The waitress brought our food, and I waited until she left to say, "I'll be getting more education if that's your hang-up. In fact, I'll be continuing my college education next semester."

"What year will you be?"

I sighed. "It'll be my first year actually . . . actually my first semester."

"So you haven't taken any college level classes?"

"No, not yet. But I'll be full-time winter semester."

"Well, it's nice that you're starting."

"But I'm not dumb, okay? I'll go online and find out what an inflection point is, so don't give up on me just because I don't happen to know this one little thing in math."

"An inflection point is where the second derivative of the function changes sign."

I nodded. "I thought it was something like that." I felt like I was about to have a panic attack. There had to be *something* we could talk about.

"Are you Scottish?" I said.

"No, why do you ask?"

"I figured there had to be some reason why you were wearing that dress, you know, like maybe it's the family plaid or something."

She gave me a funny look. "No, I just liked it."

"Really?"

She started to eat faster. "Let me just finish this and then we can go."

Without thinking I picked up the napkin she'd used to wipe up the mustard off the table. I used it to wipe my perspiring forehead.

She stopped eating. She stared at my forehead.

"Do I have mustard on me now?" I asked.

"Yes."

I grabbed a clean napkin, dipped it in her water glass, and rubbed it with a clean napkin. "How's that?"

"Better, but why did you use my water glass?"

"Well, you used it."

"That's because it was my water glass. You have a water glass, too, you know."

"Oh, yeah, you're right. I should have used mine. Sorry."

"It's all right. I'm not very thirsty."

I knew that things were not going real well up to that point. It had been a mistake to ask her about mathematics. It had been a disaster to admit how little education I had compared to her.

I needed to talk about something that all members of the Church have in common, and that is a love of the family. I wanted her to know I whole heartedly supported the Proclamation on the Family.

"Do you like kids?" I asked. "Because I sure do. I've always wanted to have a large family. What about you? How many kids do you want?"

She only had one piece of fruit left, a large piece of pineapple. She used both hands to cram it into her mouth and then stood up. "Imdun," she mumbled as she struggled to chew the pineapple. "I mean, I'm done. I'll pay for mine."

After we each paid, I tried to keep up with her as she hurried toward her car. It had not gone well, and I felt so stupid. But I couldn't stop babbling. "I'm sorry for putting you through this. I mean, I've never been this awkward around a girl before. I apologize. Please forgive me. Look, if it will help any, I'll stay away from the temple on a Friday nights, so with any luck we'll never see each other again."

"Can I depend on that?"

"I'm not usually this bad around girls. This was worse because this was, like, important, especially if the feeling I had actually was a revelation."

"What are you thinking now?" she asked. She was going through her purse, searching for her keys.

"I'm beginning to doubt that it really was from God."

She found them and looked at me. "Yeah, me, too. But you know what? We gave it a shot."

"For a second or two in the temple, it was like I was seeing you from Heavenly Father's eyes. And in that second, I could feel how much He loves you. He really does love you, you know."

She had unlocked her car but hadn't gotten in yet. After a long pause, she said, "I know."

"So if He loves you, why couldn't I? You know what I'm saying?"

"One of the many differences between Him and you is that He knows what inflection points are."

"Maybe if you and I got together, like one more time, just in case . . ." I said, lamely.

We were standing about five feet apart. I started to walk toward her.

"What are you doing?" she asked, holding up her hand as if to ward me off.

"Coming closer."

"I'd rather you didn't."

"No problem." I stepped back.

We stared at each other.

"What are you thinking?" she asked.

"Well, I'm not thinking about kissing you, that's for sure."

Her eyebrows shot up. "What I meant was, what are you thinking about what we'd do the next time we saw each other? If that happens."

"Oh, sorry. Can I come to one of your classes sometime and listen to you teach?"

She thought about it. "That sounds like a possibility."

"All right. Give me a time and I'll be there."

* * *

On Monday I attended her ten o'clock class. The best thing about Camille was she wasn't wearing plaid. But it was almost as bad. She was wearing a skirt and an oversized, creamy white dress shirt with puffy sleeves, hoop ear rings, and a jaunty scarf around her neck. She looked like a pirate queen. *Where does she get her fashion advice, Disney Studios?* I thought.

But then I felt bad for being so critical of her. I tried to call myself to repentance. *She's a daughter of Father in Heaven, who loves her,* I said to myself. This was followed by, *Look for the good in her.*

I didn't care much for the other students in her class. Camille had told me this was a class for math majors. To me they looked like they all were in serious need of counseling.

"Do you have any problems you need help with?" she asked at the beginning of the class.

Several hands went up.

Now we're getting somewhere! I thought. I could hardly wait for them to spill their guts about their emotional and social issues.

One student raised her hand. "Number three," she said.

"Oh, yes. Let's look at it."

Camille patiently went through each step in solving one of their homework problems. Because I could actually understand some of what she said, I decided she must be a good teacher.

I was impressed that people were taking notes. I couldn't remember anyone ever taking notes on anything I'd ever said. Except a cop once, after I hit a cow in the road my senior year. But that wasn't my fault.

Through all this she was cheerful and seemed to have a real desire for the students to understand what she was saying.

I tried to look for good qualities, but somewhere during the lecture I crashed. *What am I doing here?* I thought. *There must be a hundred other girls on this campus I could be seeing, so why pick a math professor who thinks about differential equations in her spare time?*

I spent the next few minutes making a mental list of girls I could date. Girls from my high school class who I hadn't seen since my mission. Girls I'd known. Not someone I had to go through a lot of changes in my life before I'd be acceptable to her.

Girls who wouldn't expect me to know what a differential equation was. Girls who still remembered I'd scored the winning touchdown in one unimportant game my sophomore year. Girls who didn't want to move from Ririe but would be content to stay there in a home next to my folks' place. A girl I could marry who wouldn't mind if I stayed the way I'd been in high school.

That sounded so good. To stay the same and never change. A girl who wouldn't mind if I took a couple days off to go hunting in the fall and was okay with me having a big boat to go fishing whenever I wanted to.

I text-messaged one of my friends from high school. He hadn't gone on a mission, so I thought he could tell me what had happened to the girls from our graduating class. Ten minutes later he sent me an abbreviated message. Of the eight girls I'd listed, three were married, two were still single but away at college, one was divorced with a kid, and two had left town and never come back.

He suggested I talk to Abbie's sister. Or someone even younger. I text-messaged him that I wasn't that desperate yet.

Okay, then, so much for local girls.

I glanced over at the girl sitting next to me. She looked at me. I smiled. She scowled and looked away. So what? I didn't care. She was wearing a green shirt that made her look like a leprechaun. What is it with math majors, anyway?

There was a girl directly behind me. It was hard to get a good look at her without turning around and staring, but I could hear her as she carried on a whispered conversation with her boyfriend over her cell phone. "No, Johnny. I don't think so, okay?"

I didn't mind that she didn't agree with Johnny about something, but she had a whiny voice, like she believed she didn't have any power, like she was asking permission not to agree.

"Johnny, the last time we went to a monster truck rally you totally ignored me, okay?"

Five minutes later she was still asking permission to disagree with Johnny.

I turned around, took her cell phone out of her hand, and turned it off. "We're in class now and you're annoying me. Talk to Johnny after class."

"Why did you do that? Johnny will be mad."

"Good. Look, I want you to repeat a phrase I learned in New York. Fuh-get-about-it! Say it to Johnny as often as you can."

She decided to give it a try. "Forget about it, okay?"

"Don't say *okay* all the time. It makes you sound like you're asking permission. Bite into the word. Fuh . . . get . . . a . . . bout it."

"Fuh-get-about-it!"

"Good job. Now let's listen to the lecture."

As I turned back around, I realized Camille had stopped lecturing and was glaring at me.

"Oh, sorry, you can go ahead now," I said.

"As I was saying . . ."

A few minutes later I had considered every girl in the class and found each of them lacking in one area or another.

And having discarded all of them, I focused my attention once again on Camille.

She seemed self-conscious and a little awkward in her motions as she lectured. And she had a strange way of holding her mouth when she was waiting for a reply to one of her questions. And when she turned to point out what she'd written on the blackboard, and I could see her profile, her nose wasn't perfectly straight and seemed a tiny bit too long. It wasn't noticeable straight on, just from the side. There was no doubt about it. She didn't have an ideal nose.

That's it, I thought. *I'll find someone with a better nose. She's history.*

I'll talk to her for a few minutes after class and then get out of here. And that'll be it. I'll make sure I never go to the temple when she's working there, and I'll never see her again.

I turned around to look at Johnny's girl. She had a good nose. I gave her a big smile.

"Fuhgetabout it," she said.

"Good job."

"Actually, I meant it for you."

"Oh."

I turned back around. *What's that all about?* I thought. *Maybe she can see I'm losing my hair in back. If she'd been in front of me, this wouldn't have happened. I need a hair transplant.*

At first I felt bad because of my hair situation, but then a little later I felt bad because I'd gone through all the girls in Camille's class and found them all unacceptable. Of course, they were math majors, so who could blame me? But, on the other hand, I realized it was the same mental state I'd had in the singles branch in New York.

Everyone is unacceptable, right? And if I wasn't careful, everyone would be unacceptable until finally I became so unacceptable that nobody would take a second look at me, either.

As I watched Camille teach, I could easily imagine her as the girl who grew up being obedient. When she was taught that beer and cigarettes were bad for her, she promised herself to live the Word of Wisdom. When she was told it would be good to keep a journal, she began keeping a journal. When she was encouraged to pray every night and morning, she began praying. When she was asked to read the Book of Mormon, she read the Book of Mormon.

I was fairly sure that, growing up, she was the girl who prayed, the girl who obeyed, the girl who received a patriarchal blessing and read it often. The girl who went to girl's camp and did her best to be a good camper.

A lifetime of obedience, and when there was need for repentance, she repented and went on with her life. A girl who grew up loving the Savior and Father in Heaven.

She was a girl who, even though she didn't need to, decided to serve a mission. And on her mission she gave it her best shot.

And so you take this girl, who now serves as an ordinance worker in the temple, a woman of virtue and reverence for what is holy, loved by Father in Heaven and the Savior, and you put her in my path, and in a few minutes I end up trashing her and discarding her and moving on to somebody better, somebody I thought would be more my caliber.

Why? Because I wanted . . . more.

Yeah, I know. It did make me feel guilty for thinking the same thing Abbie had thought about me, but honestly, it's what I felt.

Then it hit me. Maybe the problem wasn't the girl who dressed like a pirate, or the girl who looked like a leprechaun. Maybe the problem was me.

Like with Camille. Because she kept having to turn to face the blackboard, I'd seen her from every angle. And she was good looking from every angle except one. So what did I do? Focused all my attention on that one less than flattering feature. Why? So I'd have an excuse to drop her.

I was pretty sure that if I stood in the hall during a class change, I could find a reason to reject every girl who passed by.

Maybe it's not what's wrong with them. Maybe it's what's wrong with me.

I asked myself, *How can every girl be unacceptable?* Every girl except Abbie. Now that Abbie was married, she had become to me the girl with no faults. But only because she was safely out of consideration.

I can find fault with every girl except Abbie because she's married, except Hannah because she's married, and except Megan because she's married.

So everyone is unacceptable except the ones who are going with someone or engaged or married.

I felt disappointed in myself. For someone who taught on a mission that we are all children of a loving Father in Heaven, I certainly had an easy time trashing other people.

So with all that running through my mind, I thought a prayer. *Father in Heaven, please help me. I'm back to being overly critical of every girl I meet. I'm back to just wanting to hang out in groups and never date and never work toward getting married. I'm so critical of girls and yet I'm going downhill so fast. If Thou could either slow down the hair loss or increase my chances of meeting someone I can actually marry, I would be very grateful.*

Father in Heaven, in the temple I looked at Camille, and it was as though I was seeing her through Thy eyes, and for like a second I could see her the way Thou looks upon her. It was as though I could feel how much love Thou has for her. To tell the truth, I've never looked at any girl that way before. They're all special to Thee, aren't they? That is so amazing.

Father in Heaven, please help me. It's going to be hard for me to want to spend any more time with Camille because all I can see are her flaws, just like every other girl I've known, except for Abbie.

Please help me. I don't need much. Just give me one or two things that I can actually like about Camille.

I opened my eyes and noticed Camille staring at me. She probably thought I'd been sleeping. I smiled and began writing on a piece of paper like I was treasuring her every word.

"Good question, Christopher. Let's see, how can I explain this? It's like when you go fly-fishing."

I sat up. *Wait a minute! Did she just say fly-fishing? Could it be she knows how to fly-fish? That's Impossible. Girls don't fly-fish.*

"Do any of you fly-fish?" she asked.

I raised my hand and stood up. "Yes! I do! I fly-fish!"

She smiled. "Anyone else?"

Nobody else raised their hand.

"You can sit down now, Dave."

I sat down.

"Well," Camille continued, "those who are good at it know that it's more like hunting than ordinary fishing. You spot the places where the fish are surfacing to feed, and you cast so your fly lands just above that and floats down to the fish. But you have to make sure the line doesn't precede the fly or the fish won't strike. It's like this problem. You can't just throw equations around. You have to do some reasoning first about what it is you actually want the equations to give you."

"Oh, yes! Yes! That is so true!" I shouted.

What a beautiful girl, I thought. Followed by *I'm so grateful, Father in Heaven. She fly-fishes!*

Watching her now suddenly became a different experience. She was skillful, she was effective, she was clever and funny, and beautiful. There she was, all alone, facing thirty grumpy students, poking them, prodding them, lecturing to them, joking with them, and all to one end, to teach them mathematics.

After class was over, I waited for her as students gathered around her and asked her more questions.

"Thank you, Sister Colbin. I got a lot out of class today," a girl said.

"Good. See you tomorrow."

After they had all left, I stood up and walked down the steps to her.

"You still awake?" she asked.

"I had a great time here today."

"What did you learn?"

"That you fly-fish. I've never known a girl who fly-fished before."

"My dad taught me."

"Good for him. Let's go sometime in the summer. I know some great places around here."

"I'd love that. Of course, I haven't done it for a while, so it might take me a while to have it all come back."

"Just being with you will make it worthwhile."

"Until I get my line hung up in a tree and make you go get it."

"That's just part of the fun of fly-fishing."

She hesitated a moment, then asked, "Would you like to come to my office? I've got a fridge in there with orange juice, and I've got a few granola bars too."

"Can I carry your books for you?"

"Yes, please." She handed me her books, and we walked down the hall together. A minute later, she unlocked the door to her office, and we went in.

"Why don't you close the door?" she said. "Sit down. I'll get you some juice. And would you like a granola bar?"

"Yeah, that'd be great."

"So this is my office," she said. "Kind of small, but it's okay. Actually, sometimes I come here when there's nobody else in the building, and I just look around and think, *This is my office! These are my books! I am so lucky to be able to teach here.*"

She poured the juice into some paper cups and handed me one, along with a granola bar. Instead of sitting behind the desk, she sat next to me in one of the two chairs reserved for students with problems. Math problems, that is.

I opened the granola bar and took a bite and looked around at all her books. "You understand everything in these books?" I asked.

"No, not really. Some of them I've studied in great detail though."

I stood up, picked a book at random, and thumbed through it. "I could never understand this. It's like a foreign language."

"It's not that hard."

"Teach me something."

"What?"

"I don't know. How about calculus? People in high school were always talking about how hard calculus is."

"I can teach you everything you need to know about calculus in ten minutes. Ready?"

"Should I take notes?"

"You won't need to. This will make total sense to you. When things make sense, you don't even need to try to remember them. They just stick in your head."

She went to the board in her office and drew two slanted lines. One she labeled A, the other B.

"Which is steeper, A or B?"

"B," I said.

She threw the chalk on the tray, came over, and shook my hand. "That's it! You've got it! Good job! Calculus has only two concepts. That's the first one, and you've mastered it."

"What's the second concept in calculus?"

"You can always undo what you've done."

"That's all there is to it?"

"Yeah, pretty much."

"It's got to be harder than that."

She took a very small bite of her granola bar. I figured at the rate she was going it would take weeks to finish it.

"Nope. That's it."

"Teach me some more."

"Really?"

"Yeah, please."

She returned to the board. "How did you know that line B is steeper?"

"You can just tell."

"How?" she asked.

"Well, it's like with a road. A six percent grade would be steeper than a three percent grade."

"What does it mean that a road has a six percent grade?"

"Well . . . it means . . . like, if you go one hundred feet horizontally, the road would have a vertical climb of six feet."

"That's right. Good job."

She started in again but this time with more detail. I could follow most of it, but to tell the truth I was a little distracted. No matter what way she turned to write on the board, I couldn't find her one unflattering side. Suddenly she was attractive at all angles.

Somehow her bad side had disappeared.

So, it had never been about her. It had always been about me.

That's what I learned about calculus in Camille's office that morning.

CHAPTER SIXTEEN

On Saturday Camille and I did some hiking on the Idaho side of the Tetons. Even though it was late October, it had been a mild fall and the trails were snow-free. I wanted to go all the way to Table Rock, but halfway up it clouded over and looked as though it might snow, so we started back. We were on the trail about three hours.

We had a good time. No, that's not it. *Good* doesn't capture it. *Exciting* doesn't either. What we had was a *comfortable* time. It's like when you've been to church all day and you come home and put on an old pair of jeans and your favorite sweatshirt. That kind of comfortable.

Our time together was pretty much stress-free. I'm not sure why. We just relaxed and enjoyed being with each other.

We talked the entire time. I told her about Abbie. She told me about Darren, a guy she'd met before her mission who got married when she was four months out. By the time she returned, he and his wife already had a child. Camille said that losing him had been painful at the time but that she was over him now.

A bit of good news came from all this chatter. When we compared our actual birthdates, we discovered she was only a little over three years older than me. That made us both feel better.

We talked about our missions but not in a competitive way.

I'd been trying to impress girls since second grade, and yet I didn't feel a need to impress Camille. What was that all about?

I told her about my New York experience, had her practice with me all the New York slang expressions I'd picked up, and even confessed my passion for sweet potato fries. I told her how amazing President Alexander was and what I'd learned serving with him.

We got back to her apartment about nine that night. We were both physically tired, but we were happy.

Or at least I was. "Can I tell you something amazing?" I asked.

"Okay."

"I had such a good time today that I haven't even thought about what it would be like to kiss you."

She smiled. "I think you just did."

"Well, yeah, that's true, I guess. But that doesn't count."

"And this is different than with most girls you've been with?"

"Are you kidding? Usually that's all I think about."

"But not me?"

"Right."

She smiled. "And that's a compliment?"

"Actually it is. I was having so much fun talking to you that it slipped my mind about the fact that sometimes, you know, people like us, well, kiss."

Her eyebrows rose. "On the first date?"

"No, of course not. What do you take me for?" I bluffed.

She smiled. "A guy."

"Okay, well I am that."

"I didn't think about it either." After a brief pause, with an embarrassed grin, she said, "Well, maybe once . . . or twice . . . three times at most."

"If you don't mind me asking, when did you think about it?"

"Why do you need to know?" she asked.

"Research. I'm always trying to improve the product."

She snickered. "The product?"

"You know, if you think of me like a commodity that needs to be marketed."

"When you were in Primary did they ever teach you a song called 'I Am a Commodity of God'? I don't think so."

I took a step backwards. "I'm going now. And I'm still not thinking about kissing you."

She started laughing. "You are such a romantic."

I took two more backward steps and then stopped. "One more thing."

She started to laugh. "I'm almost afraid to ask."

"Right then, when you were teasing me. I like that too sometimes. Abbie teased me all the time."

"Thanks for telling me."

Two more steps and then she called me. "Dave?"

"Yeah?"

"You know what I like about you? That you feel comfortable learning from me. Like when you asked me to teach you about calculus." She paused. "Do you know why I like it?"

"No, why?"

"Because Darren always felt threatened that I was so good at math."

"His loss. My gain."

"Maybe so."

"You be good at what you're good at, and I'll do the same," I said.

"Sounds like a good arrangement."

"I'm going now," I said.

"Call me?" she asked.

"Do you want me to?"

"Uh-huh."

"That's a good sign, isn't it? That we want to see each other again."

She smiled. "I think it is a good sign."

"I'm going to my old ward tomorrow in Ririe. Want to come along?"

"I would but I have to teach Sunday School. And then at four there's a leadership meeting. I'll be free anytime after seven. Oh, wait, my home teachers are coming at seven. They'll probably stay half an hour. So anytime after seven-thirty."

"I'll come at seven-thirty then."

"Good."

We were standing there facing each other, but we didn't want it to be over.

I could now see her the way she actually is and not in the distorted way my mind presented her to me when I was trying to find a reason to reject her and move on. She is about one inch shorter than me. She has smoky-blue eyes and shoulder-length sandy brown hair, almost the same color as Abbie's. She has a few freckles that make you think she's some down-home farm girl. Her smile is usually quite reserved but when you really make her laugh, a dimple magically appears. She has long fingers that make you think she'd be a good piano player. Which later I found out she is. Oh, and she wears contacts.

I suddenly realized I'd been just standing there staring at her. "Did I say I had a good time?" I asked.

"I think you did. Did I say that, too?"

"I believe you did."

"I know you're not thinking about us kissing," she said. "But would you consider a hug?"

"I think that would probably be totally acceptable."

"Come ahead, then." She opened her arms out wide and then as if she were guiding a truck driver into a tight space "Keep coming, a little to the left, that's it. Keep coming." Only when we were in each other's arms did she say, "That's good. Hold it right there. You can turn off your engine now."

"Actually, I'm not sure that's going to be possible," I said.

We both started laughing.

I think we'd have both broken away after the mandatory five seconds, but there was a comfort factor that had to be dealt with.

The hug lasted a long time.

Oh, my gosh, I've come home, I thought.

After about a minute, we separated.

"Well, how about that?" she said, sounding pleasantly surprised.

"Yeah, I know. Can I ask you a question?"

"What?"

"Do math teachers, such as yourself, those working toward a Ph.D. and teaching university level calculus classes, have . . . well . . . hormones?"

Talk about a romantic mood destroyer. She couldn't stop laughing. She threatened to tell all the other math teachers. I made her promise not to.

"I'll see you tomorrow," I said.

"Right. Seven-thirty."

* * *

On Sunday I drove to Ririe for church. Why? Because the people in my home ward were like family to me. And I wanted that even if for only a few hours.

It was great to be surrounded by people who had been important in my life growing up: the teachers who'd taught me, and the man who'd been my bishop all the way through my high school years and who had interviewed me for my mission.

Abbie's mom invited me to have lunch with them after church. I said yes because in high school I knew she liked me spending time with her daughter. I think she was a little disappointed that things didn't work out for us.

I was glad Abbie's younger sister Courtney wasn't there. She looked so much like Abbie I would have been distracted.

I had a good talk with Abbie's mom and dad, though. They had a lot of questions about my plans. Actually, they had more questions than I had answers. But one thing I could tell them was that in January I'd be a full-time student. I owed that to Megan who had gotten me to apply. Even though it was a year later than I thought it would be, I was still in the system.

I didn't ask about Abbie very much because I didn't want to come across as one of those pathetic losers who can't move on with their life after a breakup. But after a while they told me about Abbie's new married life. And then her mom added, "Oh, Abbie's pregnant."

"So married life must really agree with her, right?" Right after I said it I realized it was a totally stupid thing to say, especially to her mom and dad.

"What I mean is . . ." There was no good way to end that sentence. "Never mind. Tell her hello for me the next time you talk to her."

They told me about Abbie's new life. She was taking classes at a university while Thomas worked as an attorney. "He wants to get an MBA now," her mom said.

"Good for him. Education is very important." This said by a twenty-two-year-old about to take his first post high school class. That class would be a four-week community education class called "Beginning Spanish." Yes, I'm sure the world was interested in my perspective about education.

I stayed and talked for another hour and then thanked them and said good-bye.

I felt better about things after I left. It was like closing the book on Abbie and me. She and I were now in the category of old high school friends who would trade Christmas cards and letters every year for the rest of our lives.

On my drive back to Rexburg, I realized I hadn't told them about Camille. Maybe because I didn't know what to say. "I have a friend who teaches calculus and differential equations on campus. She has a master's degree but is working on her Ph.D. She's a returned missionary. She's also a temple ordinance worker once a week. Her name is Camille. She's a little over three years older than me. We're not in love yet but we are very comfortable with each other."

The whole thing seemed so improbable to me. Do people actually fall in love with university calculus teachers? When I was sixteen, did I ever fantasize that some day I'd marry a math teacher? What would I say to my high school buddies if I met up with one of them. "She's so hot! I love it when she does research on inflection points in a multi-dimensional space! Oh, yeah, that's what I'm talking about!"

What am I thinking? Why am I seeing a girl who has ideas running through her mind that I'll never understand? What would people think if we got married?

That little doubt was magnified when I thought about her math-geek friends who would probably tell her she could do a lot better than me.

On Sunday night we took a walk and told each other about our day. And then she invited me into her apartment and we had some homemade cookies and milk. We talked until eleven and then gave each other another long hug.

"Do you know why I like hugging you?" I asked.

"No, why?"

"We're about the same height, so there's a good fit, wouldn't you say?"

"Excuse me?" she asked, pulling away, her eyebrows raised like red flags.

"See, the thing is, neither one of us has to bend down to hug. I think it's much healthier for our necks and backs."

She laughed so hard she had to sit down.

I stayed another half hour. I felt so comfortable with her I didn't want to leave. Ever.

On Monday we were both busy with work. But Monday night at seven I rang her bell for family home evening.

When she opened the door, she had a big smile on her face. "I have a big surprise for you! Guess what it is?" She said it the way Primary teachers talk to the children. Like everything in life was a song. A happy song.

She led me into her kitchen, and there on a the stove was a frying pan full of sweet potato fries covered in oil, very close to being done.

"Oh, my gosh! That is so awesome!"

She speared one out of the pan and let it drip, then handed me the fork. "Try it."

I blew on it to cool it, then took a bite. I closed my eyes as I savored the taste. It was like being in a Long Island diner once again.

Once again, with Camille's help, I'd come home.

I thought about kissing her. But there was no way I was going to kiss her at that moment. For two reasons, really. One, she might get mad at me and throw me out before I'd eaten the sweet potato fries. And, second, Camille is not a girl you just happen to kiss. No, first you bring up the subject, and together you discuss the ramifications. You define what the significance of a kiss might be in terms of commitment. And then when all parties are in agreement, you sign a document permitting limited kissing rights on certain, specified occasions.

So we weren't going to kiss any time soon. But look on the bright side. I was in Idaho and yet I had my own personal source for sweet potato fries!

You see the lesson here? There are definite rewards for self-discipline.

* * *

A few days later, about eight at night, I was in her office while she was grading some exams.

I'd just finished reading a copy of *Popular Mechanics.* So I'd done my academic reading for the day and I was bored. "Can I do anything to help you?" I asked.

She thought about it. "You could add up the scores on the exams I've finished grading."

"Sure. No problem."

"Do you need a calculator?" she asked.

I was a little offended. "No."

"Okay, then, here you go."

She handed me a big stack of tests.

Fifteen minutes later I was done with that.

"What else can I do?"

She looked through the exam. "Well, maybe you could actually grade this question. Let me explain it to you first, though."

Ten minutes later I understood it well enough to start grading. If I had questions on the grading, I asked.

Forty-five minutes later we were done.

"That went a lot faster with your help. Thank you so much."

As we left campus, I felt good. I had helped with the grading of a college level calculus exam. If I could do that, I could probably do anything.

"What do you want to do this weekend?" I asked.

"Whatever you'd like to do."

"I know some people in Ririe who have horses. You want to go horseback riding?"

"That sounds fun."

"Have you ever ridden a horse before?"

"No, you'll have to teach me."

"I like the idea of me teaching you something," I said.

"There's a lot you could teach me."

When she looked at her calendar so we could set a time, she scowled. "Oh, darn! I can't believe I completely forgot. This weekend won't work. I've got to go to a math conference in Oregon with some other faculty members. We're actually presenting a paper."

I was pretty sure that "presenting a paper" meant more than what it did when I had a paper route. You know, like, "Here's your paper." I didn't want to show my ignorance by asking about it, though.

So there went my weekend.

She left Friday morning. Just before she left she asked me what I was going to do that night, and I told her I would probably go to the temple. She seemed happy about that.

But later that day I saw a sign about a campus dance that night, billed as a mixer, which means lots of girls there without dates.

At first I wasn't going to go. I guess I wanted to be, well, "faithful" to Camille. But then I decided that was dumb because we had not even admitted we were more than just friends.

When I got to the dance, it was too much for me, and I snapped. All those girls just waiting to be asked to dance.

A lot of guys were just standing around. What's with that? The way I see it, you're either in the game or you're not.

By the time the dance ended I'd danced with eight different girls. I asked five of them their names and phone numbers, and four gave me the information I needed. I told those four I'd give them a call and said maybe we could do something some time. They seemed agreeable to the idea.

I felt awesome on the way home. I couldn't decide which girl to call first.

And the thing is, they have dances like this almost every week. So let's do the math. Four call-backs a week. I could easily go out Thursday, Saturday and Sunday nights. Leaving Friday nights for more dances.

Suddenly that's what I wanted. I wanted this to go on and on and never quit. I wasn't ready to settle down and couldn't see that I ever would be.

By prior arrangement, I picked Camille up at the Idaho Falls airport about ten-thirty Saturday night.

She told me about the conference and even said how much she missed me. She asked me if I'd gone to the temple.

I told her something had come up and I didn't get a chance to go. I didn't tell her about going to the dance, though.

On Monday morning as I was walking Camille to her office after one of her classes, one of the girls I'd met at the dance Friday night walked by us. "Dave? Is that you?"

"Uh . . ."

"I'm Sabrina. We met at the dance Friday night?"

"Oh, yeah, sure."

"You *are* going to call me, right?" She gave me a big smile.

"Uh, right."

Sabrina looked at Camille with a puzzled expression, as if to ask, "Who's she?"

"Sabrina, uh, this is uh . . . uh . . . my . . . math teacher, Sister . . ."

Can you believe it? I blocked on Camille's last name and just stood there feeling stupid.

Camille gave me a quick glance but recovered nicely by politely saying, "Colbin. Camille Colbin," then adding, "Excuse me. I need to get ready for my next class."

When she's mad, Camille walks faster than any girl I've ever known.

After talking to Sabrina briefly, I ran to Camille's office. The door was shut.

When I knocked she opened it and glared at me. "What do you want?"

"Can I come in and explain?"

"No." She closed the door again.

I knocked again.

She opened it again and said, "Your 'math teacher'? Is that what you think I am?"

"Okay, I know, it was dumb. I wasn't thinking. At least let me explain. Okay, I admit. I did go to the dance. And I did meet Sabrina. We danced a few times, but that's all."

"Did you tell Sabrina you'd call her?"

"Well, yeah, I guess I did. But it really didn't mean a thing."

"Yes, I can see that. I can also see I mean nothing to you either. Have a nice life." She started to close the door.

"No, wait! Please give me another chance."

A group of students walked by in the hall, and Camille waited until they'd passed before she continued.

"How can you ask for that when I've just found out I can't trust you?"

"You can trust me."

"If you'd told me you had gone to a dance, that would have been okay, but you didn't say anything about it. That means you're deceitful. I have no use for someone like that."

She shut the door in my face.

So, once again, I was back to square one.

CHAPTER SEVENTEEN

A week passed. Camille wouldn't answer my calls. When I went to her office, if students were around, she'd say she had to prepare for a class. But if we were alone, she'd brush me off, telling me she never wanted to see me again.

The only reason I'd talked to Camille in the temple was because of some random thought. What exactly does "What about her?" mean, anyway? Heavenly Father loves all his children, right? So maybe it was just a general feeling that I interpreted as being specifically for Camille.

Like if you say, "How about them Mets?" It doesn't mean you have to throw away your Yankees cap and Derek Jeter jersey, right?

I kept going back and forth in my mind about what I should do. I did have the phone numbers of four other girls. Maybe one of them would work out for a while, at least until one of us got tired of the other.

Finally I decided to go to the temple to try to get some perspective about the direction my life was going.

As it turned out, the session was too full. I was told that they could use me as a witness at the sealing of husbands and wives. So I agreed to do that.

A husband and wife had some family names. They acted as proxies for each deceased couple as the officiator married them.

They did twenty sealings. Which meant I witnessed the temple marriage ceremony twenty times.

I'd never been to a temple sealing, and I was blown away by the language and the promises made to the individual couples. Then, when they sealed the children to their parents, I began to see things in a different light. Once again I decided I needed to grow up and be a man.

But how? Later in my apartment I sat at my desk and thought about what it might mean to help build Zion and specifically about my own responsibility. The topic had been bugging me ever since I'd disappointed President Alexander in that sacrament meeting talk he'd asked me to give.

Building Zion must mean helping the work of God go forward. But that gets tricky for guys my age. Here's the problem. You can be in a singles ward or branch and be called, for example, to teach Sunday School. And because you were called by the bishop or a branch president, you can think that's God's will for you. And you can stay there for years doing the same thing.

But bishops are only in charge of a ward, right? I mean, they aren't in charge of your life. So you've got to think about your life and not just rely on a priesthood leader to get revelation for you.

As I thought about my life, I was at least able to figure out what building Zion probably doesn't mean. It doesn't mean I spend the next ten years being content to interact with one girl after another on a superficial level. It doesn't mean giving some lame excuse that I'm looking for the right person when I make absolutely no effort to become the right person for someone else.

The thing is, guys have it easy. They can say they're looking for the right girl, but when things start to get serious they can always back out by saying, "This just isn't happening for me." And then they can dump the girl and start in with someone else. So a guy can put the burden of responsibility on the girl.

It's simple, really. Make her do all the work to try to win you over. And then after a month tell her it's just not working and go on to some other girl. Depending on your degree of compassion, you can either imply it's her fault, or you can say, "It's not you. It's me."

I'd known guys who do that, although personally I'd been the dumpee and not the dumper three times in a row. But maybe I could learn to do it.

But is that building Zion?

I finally decided that for me building Zion has got to include doing what I can to move in the direction that would lead to marriage.

That night about seven-thirty I knocked on Camille's door. I didn't know why, but my heart was beating really fast and I was nervous. I'd tried to plan what to say, but I didn't even know what that should be.

Before, when I'd tried to see her in her office, she'd just always shut the door in my face, but this time she hesitated, as if she couldn't decide what to do.

"I brought you some sweet potatoes to pay you back," I offered lamely.

She took the sack from me. "You really didn't need to do that. Do you want to come in?" She opened the door wider and stepped back.

I walked in but didn't sit down. "I went to the temple today and was a witness for sealings. It made me think about, you know, the direction I need to go in my life." I sighed. "I've decided that it's very possible that I might want to marry you some day."

Her eyebrows shot up. "Excuse me?"

"It's called courtship. Elder Oaks explained what it is when he gave a CES fireside. I have a copy of it here if you want to read it."

"I'm familiar with his talk, but I'm not sure what you're saying."

"I would like to be in a courtship relationship with you, rather than us just seeing each other. Or me shopping around."

"Why me?" she asked. It sounded a little like a complaint.

"Well, first of all, I admire you very much. Also, on our hike we got along so well and it seemed so natural to be with you, like I could just relax and be myself. When I'm with you, I want to be a better person. Also, when we hug it feels, well, comfortable."

"What about Sabrina?"

I had decided to be honest no matter how embarrassing it might be. "It wasn't just Sabrina. There were actually four girls who gave me their numbers at the dance."

"Why are you telling me this?"

"I want you to know about all of them in case we run into one of them on campus sometime."

"You got four girls' numbers at one dance? You must have been busy."

"The trick is don't stand around. You've got to keep moving. It also helps if you keep going to a different area of the dance floor each time. So it's like plowing new ground each time."

"Have you taken any of them out?"

"No, and I won't."

"Do you have their phone numbers with you?"

I was a little reluctant to admit it. "Yeah, I do, actually. They're in my wallet."

"Come here." She walked into the kitchen and handed me her cell phone.

"Call them and tell them about me. I'll listen in while I make you some sweet potato fries."

"You're going to make me some sweet potato fries?" I asked, suddenly cheering up.

"But you only get to eat them after you've talked to every girl on your list."

On the first call I made, the girl wasn't picking up, so I left a voice mail: "Hi, Dana, this is Dave. Remember me? I met you at the dance a week ago. Say, uh, I know I told you I'd call, but something came up, and, well, the thing is, I'm almost engaged this week, so it looks like I won't be calling you anymore. Have a nice day."

I ended the message feeling pretty good about myself.

"That doesn't count," she said.

"What do you mean it doesn't count?"

"You can't leave a message. You have to actually talk to each girl."

"This could take all night."

"Too bad for you. Looks like I'm going to eat all the sweet potato fries."

"You are a hard woman."

"Call Sabrina next. I want to hear you clear up the math teacher comment."

I thought about leaving but I didn't. Not because of some general conference address. Not because of wanting to "rise up and be a man." Not because of a desire to build Zion. Not because of a prompting I'd received about Camille when I first met her. Not even because of the possibility of sweet potato fries.

No, it was first of all a realization that the more time I spent with Camille the better person I would become. She would help me become the kind of person Heavenly Father wants me to be.

Okay, on a less religious note, also because her hair is a natural light brown almost the same color as Abbie's hair and because she wears makeup, even though she's a math teacher. And because she has a dimple. And because the few freckles on her face make her seem like a down-home farm girl. I don't know why farm girls are such a turn-on for me, but they are. Go figure.

And also because she gives good hugs.

I was reasonably sure I could fall in love with Camille. *Fall* probably isn't the right word. For me it would probably be more like stumbling into love, or backing into it. But, hey, at least it's something.

So I made the phone calls. I did my best to be brutally honest, accept full responsibility, and then apologize.

It took me two hours before I'd finished running them all down.

Then, and only then, did Camille let me have a single sweet potato fry.

"How did I do?" I asked.

"Good. I'm sure that wasn't easy."

"It was one of the hardest things I've ever done."

"Well, you did it. I wasn't sure you would. Go wash your hands and let's eat."

The sweet potato fries tasted so good! I had to pace myself so I didn't eat them all right away. I forced myself to take only one fry at a time.

"Since this is the night for being brutally honest with each other, there's something I need to tell you," Camille said.

"Okay."

"I have Abbie's sister, Courtney, in one of my classes."

I figured this couldn't be good. I started to eat the fries faster, in case she threw me out of her apartment.

"A few days ago, on her way to class, she saw you knocking on my door. After class she asked how I knew you. I told her we had been seeing each other but that I'd found out I couldn't trust you. She seemed surprised at that, and said I might want to talk to Abbie about you. So this morning I called her. We had a good talk. Oh, she says to tell you hi."

I couldn't believe it! "So . . . how's she doing?"

"Good. She's pregnant."

"I know. Her folks told me."

"I asked her about you. She told me that you're a good guy, someone I can trust. She told me you're a lot like your dad. To her that's the highest recommendation she can make. She suggested I give you another chance."

I was stunned that once again Abbie was affecting my life.

Camille paused. "So, actually, I'm glad you came. I've been trying to decide if I should call you."

"So I have the Abbie Seal of Approval?" I asked.

"Yes, you do. Does that make you mad?"

"I would just like to get her out of my life, that's all."

"She is out of your life, but she still respects you. I'm sorry if you're mad I called her, but I was curious about you and if I could trust you or not. She couldn't say enough good about you." She paused. "Are you mad at Abbie for telling me what a great guy you are?"

I sighed. "No, not really. What happens now?"

"You're suggesting we be in a courtship kind of relationship? What exactly would that entail?"

"Well, I guess we'd see each other exclusively and try to decide if we might want to get married some day . . . to each other, I mean."

"I see."

"Look, the thing is, I need to be moving toward something and not just drifting like I've been doing."

She thought about it. "Okay, I'll agree to that."

"You will?" I was feeling pretty good.

"One question, though. Did you ever find that book you checked out from your high school library? Abbie told me about it." She had a big grin on her face.

"No, but I paid for it a few weeks ago."

"Good for you."

After a few minutes she let me hold her hand and then we hugged and then without any formal discussion about the topic, we kissed for the first time.

I was surprised she didn't want a contract or anything and that she didn't need to call her folks for permission, and that she didn't extract any promises from me.

The thought came to me that I owed Abbie big time for this. She must have said a lot of good things about me. For that I guess I was grateful. But even so it was difficult for me to have Abbie and Camille somehow connected.

As I held her in my arms, I noticed that Camille, because of cooking them, had a sweet potato fry smell to her.

You know what? It doesn't get any better than that.

* * *

One thing I missed at first with Camille is that she never made fun of me like Abbie always had. She treated me with respect. She always wanted to know what I thought.

That seems good, right? But it comes with a price. It meant to me I needed to work hard to maintain the respect she had for me.

"Have you decided what you're going to major in?" she asked a few days later.

"Not yet."

"It's a difficult choice to make, isn't it?"

You see what I'm talking about? That's way too respectful. Not at all how Abbie would have handled it.

After a couple of weeks of looking at various possibilities, I finally decided to major in construction management. It fit my interests and abilities and I was hoping there would be plenty of jobs available after graduation.

I liked many things about being in a courtship relationship. I liked that when we saw each other after being apart for a few hours that we talked about everything that had happened to us. I liked that hugging and kissing became a natural part of our time together—within the constraints of chastity of course.

I know that when Abbie and I were together she wasn't trying to train me for the next girl I might date, but that is actually what had happened.

One time because of a conflict at work I came an hour late for a dinner she'd prepared for me. Camille was mad that I hadn't called to tell her I'd be late.

I was about to say, "I'm sorry you feel bad I didn't call." But then I stopped.

Abbie had once warned me that when a guy apologizes he should avoid implying that the whole problem is that the girl is too emotional.

Next I thought of saying, "I was only trying to earn some extra money so—" I stopped again. Abbie had warned me about that, too.

Abbie had told me in general what to say, so I tried to apply it in this situation. "I'm so sorry, Camille. That was wrong of me not to call. That must have been frustrating waiting for me when the food was ready to eat."

And then I let her talk about how frustrating it had been.

And finally I promised her I would never do that again.

It seemed to work.

Thank you, Abbie.

* * *

Camille and I met in October 2006. By April of the following year we were still in the courtship phase. The whole thing was taking way longer than I'd ever imagined it would. I'd always liked the idea of getting married maybe a month after you meet a girl. But that's not what was happening with us. This was a major process.

About once every two weeks she'd tell me, "We need to talk."

That's the worst news you can get from a girl. It means you've messed up. There's nothing to do but listen to what she says, tell her you're sorry, and start over. But then you have to try really hard not to mess up again.

One time she told me, "I don't think we should be kissing so much."

"Why not?"

"We need to be careful or things are going to get out of control."

"C'mon, Camillle, you're a math teacher. What could happen?"

She cleared her throat nervously. "I have a hard time staying focused after we've been kissing for a while."

"You don't say?" I asked with a big grin on my face. In a way, this was good news. So she was human after all, even if she was a math teacher.

"Let me think about it, okay?" I said.

This was a difficult decision for me. But I could see she was probably right. There were times when we kissed when I wouldn't have been able to tell you the Yankees starting lineup.

So we put limits on ourselves.

But that's not all we had to deal with. There were a hundred other issues you never think about when you're a guy. Like the time we went to the cheaper, on-campus apartment I'd recently moved into, and she said, "I can't stand the smell here. How often do you guys empty the garbage?"

"We're supposed to do it when it gets full, but it's not my job this week."

"How can you stand to be in here when it smells like that?"

I was about to say, "You get used to it," but I could tell that would have not gone over well. So instead I said, "You're right. I'll go empty it right now."

And then there was the time I told her, "Do I have to call you Camille all the time?"

"That is my name."

"How about if I call you Cami?"

"I don't like to be called Cami."

"Camille sounds so formal."

"Well, I don't know what to say. That's my name."

I sighed. "Okay, I'll call you that then."

"Do you ever wonder how your life would be different if you had insisted people call you David?" she asked me.

What kind of a question is that? I thought. Sometimes women make no sense at all. This was definitely one of those times. But I did start to wonder if I'd get more respect if I insisted people call me David.

One time I started thinking how Abbie had told me, "I want

more." At that time I was planning on never going to college, never leaving my hometown, and never doing anything for a living other than what I'd been doing all my life, working at a hardware store.

And now with Camille's help and encouragement, I was in college and making plans to start my own construction company after I graduated.

Abbie *wanted* more, but Camille was helping me *become* more. I took that as a good sign about us being together.

Men and women are so different. So when you start seeing someone every day, it's way harder than you ever thought it would be. In high school my idea about getting married was you find a girl who accepts everything about you, and you accept her the same way, so after you're married neither of you has to change.

But as Camille and I continued to get more serious about each other, I began to realize we both would be making changes for the rest of our lives.

So what I'm trying to say is, courtship for us was full of bumps in the road. Sometimes more bumps than road.

There were times when I felt I was only in the courtship thing out of a sense of duty, but then a day or two later, Camille would dump some snow down my back on one of our walks and I'd chase her and she'd run and we'd start laughing and I would remember again why I loved being with her so much. In many ways, I was incomplete without her, and when we occasionally couldn't see each other for a day or two because of our schedules, I missed her like crazy and found myself thinking about her all the time.

One time her dishwasher broke down and I spent all Saturday morning fixing it.

At first she was at the kitchen table grading papers while I worked, and then she left to do some grocery shopping.

When she came back, there were parts spread all over the floor.

"I found the problem and I've fixed it, so now I just need to put everything back," I explained.

She sat down on the floor, about five feet away, with her back up against the wall and her knees pulled up. That was the nearest she could get because of all the parts and tools scattered about on the floor. When I looked over at her, I was surprised to see tears running down her cheeks.

"Don't worry, okay?" I said. "I know it looks bad now, but I promise I'll get it all back together again."

She wiped her cheeks with the palms of her hands and shook her head. "That's not it."

"What's wrong then?"

"How did I ever get lucky enough to have you in my life?" she asked.

I was stunned.

She continued. "I've never known a guy willing to spend so much time just to help me."

"That's probably because most other guys could have done it faster."

"Dave, I want you to know how much I love and appreciate you. You're such a great guy."

I shrugged. "I'm nothing, Camille. Guys like me are a dime a dozen."

"That's not true. Guys like you are so rare."

I didn't understand why she'd say that, but it made me feel good. Having a girl like Camille think that about me in a positive way made me want to be better.

She loves me, I thought. *How did that ever happen?*

* * *

One time, after I'd sat in on one of her classes, I walked her back to her office. She closed the door and turned to face me. "The last ten minutes of class all I could think about is how much I wanted you to kiss me."

I shrugged. "Welcome to the club. That's how my whole day

goes, from the moment I get up until I go to bed at night. I can't get enough of you."

That only seemed to make her mad. "Look, I am not looking for some philosophical discussion here, okay? No thesis statements! No expositions! No conclusions! Don't explain anything!"

I was confused. "So what do you want me to do?"

"I want you to kiss me! Is that asking too much? Right now!"

"Here in your office? What if a student knocks on your door?"

"We'll call out and say, 'Nobody's here.'"

I smirked. "Even a math major would figure that one out."

She held up her hand. "Careful what you say! I was a math major."

"Oh, sorry. I take it all back."

"Why are we still talking? Will you please just kiss me?" she asked.

We kissed a couple of times and then a student did knock on her door. I tried to impersonate her, "I'm not here," I said in a high falsetto.

She punched me and we both started giggling.

"We need to be quiet," she whispered.

But we couldn't. We kept laughing.

Finally I hid under the desk and she opened the door.

"Yes?" she asked.

"Is this a good time?"

"Oh, yeah! It's a great time!" She started laughing and then I, still behind the desk, joined her.

"Give me a minute, okay?" Camille said.

She closed the door and booted me out of her office. Every time I thought about it that day, I couldn't help smiling.

It was a great day.

What a surprise it was to me that my life now was full of amazing experiences like that. When I'd first decided to adopt the *Building Zion through Courtship* theme, I didn't know it would have such great perks.

* * *

Almost from the beginning of our courtship, Camille seemed to have a great interest in my mom. At first it was easy to say, "She and my dad are on a mission, so you won't be able to meet her."

They began to send emails to each other and in time became close.

It doesn't seem fair that the girl you want to marry always instinctively looks for a connection to your mom.

Camille caught me once being slightly critical of my mom. "Don't you get along with her?" she asked.

It was a fair question. "Not always growing up, but we get along real good now," I said.

"I would like to talk to her sometime. Can you arrange that?"

"Oh, yeah, sure."

I felt like I needed to talk to my mom before Camille did. So I called my folks on their mission. My mom answered my call. She was alarmed and asked if I was having some kind of problem.

After I assured her there was nothing wrong, I said to her, "I just want to apologize for all the times I gave you a hard time when you were only trying to help me be a better person. That was wrong of me to do. I'm sorry."

"Who is this again?" she asked.

"Dave . . . your son."

"Really?"

"Yeah. I've got more I need to say." Five minutes later I'd finished my apology. I thought she'd tell me what a rotten son I'd been, but she didn't.

Her response overwhelmed me. "You've always been good. There were just a few things you did that I felt I needed to talk to you about. Have I told you lately how much I love you and how proud I am of you?"

"You are? Thanks, Mom. Oh, one thing, Camille wants to call

and talk to you and Dad sometime. Is that okay, even if you're on a mission?"

"Yes, of course. We'd love to speak with her. Tell her to call us any night about this time."

"It's getting kind of serious between me and Camille."

"Are you being careful?"

"Yeah, we are. We're being good."

"I'm glad to hear that. Do you think this might lead to marriage?"

"Yeah, I really do."

"When are you thinking you might get married?"

"Well, I'm not sure. I'd like to wait until you and Dad are home."

I made that call in early May. They would not be released from their mission until February. That's a long time when you're almost engaged.

"That would be wonderful. Will you be able to wait that long?" she asked.

"I don't know, Mom. It's getting really difficult. Not that we've done anything wrong, but sometimes I get really, well, frustrated, I guess you could say."

"Your father and I were like that, too."

I really wished she hadn't said that. It was too big of a leap to think of my mom and dad as ever having those kinds of feelings for each other.

On Memorial Day weekend, Camille and I went to visit her folks in Brigham City, Utah. It wasn't the first time I'd been there to be with her family. But this time I had a purpose.

On Saturday morning I went out into the garage, where her dad was working on getting his lawn mower ready for the summer.

"Need any help?" I asked.

"Maybe so. I can't get it started."

We worked on it together. I actually knew more than he did about lawn mowers, and that made me happy.

Twenty minutes later, after we had gotten the mower started, I said over the sound of the engine, "Sir, I would like your permission to ask Camille to marry me!"

He nodded. "It works great now! Thanks!" he shouted.

I worried we were running an engine in a closed garage, so I opened the garage door.

He turned the mower off.

"Good as new," he said.

"Did you hear my question?"

"Yes, I did. I'm still thinking about it. If you don't mind me asking, how are you going to support my daughter?"

I cleared my throat. "Well, sir, that's a real good question. I have about three and a half more years of college ahead of me. I'm majoring in construction management, so I should be able to get good jobs in the summer. And I am working part time at BYU—Idaho. With Camille's salary, we should be able to get along fine."

"It's possible you two might have kids within those three years."

"Yes, sir, I would assume that very well might happen."

"So what will you do when she has a baby? Will you insist she get a baby sitter so she can continue working?"

"No, sir. We'll do student loans. And I'll work as much as I can and still keep up my grades."

"That's not going to be easy."

"I realize that."

"We won't be able to help you out much," he said.

"I wouldn't want you to do that. I'd rather we get through this ourselves."

"Are you temple worthy?"

"Yes, sir, I am."

"And you're going to stay that way when you're engaged?"

"Yes, sir. We're real careful about that."

He nodded. "Well, then, I'd say go ahead. You have my permission."

I couldn't help grinning, and I said to him, "I would like to wait until next Monday to actually propose, so if you could keep this a secret between us, I would appreciate it."

"I'll do that."

"Thank you, sir." I turned to leave the garage, then stopped. "Sir, one more thing?"

"Yes?"

"You do know it's dangerous to run an engine in an enclosed space, don't you?"

"Yes, I was just going to run the engine for ten seconds and then open the garage door."

"Good. Thanks."

I planned to propose to Camille in her calculus class on Monday of the next week. I had been sitting in on the class since the semester started, so she wouldn't think it was odd for me to be there.

The day finally came. Near the end of the class, she asked if there were any questions.

"I have a question," I said.

"Really? Okay."

"I need to go to the board so you'll see what my question is."

"All right."

I went to the front of the class and knelt down in front of her.

"What are you doing?" she asked.

I took out a ring box, and she suddenly became a strange mixture of giggling and tears. "Camille, will you marry me?" I asked.

She turned to the class. "You see what some people will do for extra credit?" They all laughed.

She took my hand and brought me to a standing position. "I would be very happy to marry you."

We hugged and kissed as the entire class stood and applauded.

Even the math majors were delighted. Those who had figured out what had just happened, that is.

* * *

Once we were engaged, we found it difficult to keep our hands off each other. We were like two racers at the starting line waiting for the gun to go off.

We started spending most of our time together in public places and avoided sitting together in a parked car.

After he found out Camille and I were engaged, my campus bishop asked if he could meet with us once a week—to keep us on target for a temple wedding.

This is how it worked. We'd go into his office. We'd chat for a while, then he'd lean forward and ask, "Have you two been good this past week?"

We knew what the question meant. We'd say yes. And then he'd give us some advice about marriage and then we'd reschedule for the next week.

It worked well.

Except for one Saturday night in August.

We'd rented a Disney movie, thinking that it'd be all right to watch that in her living room. What can happen watching Disney, you know what I mean?

Well, after a few minutes we totally forgot about the movie. We started kissing and we couldn't seem to stop. We started the movie sitting up but were fast approaching a position where we would soon be lying next to each other on her couch.

Suddenly Camille stood up. "This has got to stop! I am not going to go to your bishop tomorrow and explain to him how we lost control!"

I sat up. "We haven't lost control yet."

"We are losing control, Dave, and you know it!"

"But we haven't done anything wrong yet."

"We're not going to, either! Get out! Go home! I can't be with you anymore."

On my way out, she said, "I shouldn't be the one in charge of saying when it's too much. You have a responsibility, too."

So I went home and called on the phone and apologized for breaking the rules we'd made to keep ourselves in check.

On Sunday we had a long talk with my bishop. He gave us some good advice. He suggested we go to the temple once a week. We asked him if we were still worthy. After a few more questions, he said we were. Then Bishop Carlisle gave us a challenge that really helped me.

"You know," he said, "when you get married you'll likely receive some nice gifts as wedding presents. Why don't the two of you plan to each give each other a gift as well—not jewelry or anything like that, but rather the gift of your virtue? Dave, imagine the joy you'll feel on your wedding night when you're able to say to Camille, 'I've saved myself for you and for this night, and I've loved you enough to wait until now to fully express my love.' And, Camille, imagine how it will feel for you to be able to say the same thing."

It was great advice, and it gave us something to think about and look forward to.

Going to the temple also helped us stay worthy. If we went to the temple Wednesday night, then of course Wednesday after having been to the temple was never a problem. Tuesday wasn't a problem either because we were about to go to the temple. Thursday we were careful because we'd just been to the temple. On Friday she was an ordinance worker at the temple, and Saturday nights we were careful because we knew we were going to see our bishop on Sunday night. So Sundays were good, too. And on Mondays we had family home evening with some others in her ward, so we weren't alone, and that was good.

* * *

Camille and my mom began to talk to each other once a week. My mom loved her from the very beginning. That didn't surprise me. But what did surprise me was how much better Mom and I got along as well. It was like the pressure was off my mom. All my life she had worried about me, and I realized that when she corrected me or gave me advice while I was growing up, it was her way of protecting me. Now, she could anticipate a time when I would be safe from some of the things she always worried about. I think she was grateful to Camille for her good influence. Of course, my dad loved her, too. Who wouldn't love someone like Camille?

Sometimes I would look at her and try to remember what it was I hadn't liked about her when I watched her teach the first time. I couldn't see anything but beauty, every time I looked at her.

* * *

Planning a wedding is a big deal. It takes time and coordination. After a while that began to take up most of our time and effort. In a way it was a relief to have so much to do.

We decided to get married in the Idaho Falls Temple. Once when we were in the temple Camille asked one of the workers if we could look at the room where we would be married.

We entered the empty sealing room and sat down next to each other. She took my hand and rested her head on my shoulder. "Dave, can I ask you a question?"

"Yeah, sure."

"Why do you want to marry me?"

I panicked. I'd learned that when a girl asks you a question, you have to be careful and not necessarily give her the first answer that comes to your mind.

For example, if a girl says, "Are you going to wear that tie?" what's the right answer? If a guy asked the question, you'd say, "Yeah, sure, why do you think I got it out of the closet?" But if it's a woman, or more particularly if it's Camille, you say, "Is this the wrong tie for the suit?" And then she suggests another tie.

So you've got to be careful. Think before you answer.

But on the other hand, you don't want to think too long—like I was doing now with her question about why I wanted to marry her.

"Dave?" she asked. Her voice had a little tremor to it.

"Many reasons, really," I said, stalling for time.

"Can you give me some of them?"

My mind was racing. First of all, why was she asking the question? She knew that I'd had a prompting in the temple about her. But if I told her that, she'd might conclude I was only marrying her out of obedience. So I couldn't say that.

She also knew I was looking forward to the physical intimacies of married life, but if I answered that, she'd be disappointed, thinking that's all she meant to me. So I couldn't give that answer either.

Think, man! Give her a reason she won't be disappointed in.

It took me longer than it should have, but I finally came up with an answer.

"I want to marry you because I love you with all my heart and I want you at my side forever. You're my best friend, my closest adviser, and the love of my life. I'm a better person when I'm with you. You inspire me, you light up my life, and we always have a good time when we're together."

She sighed contentedly and snuggled closer. It was a close call.

My mom and dad returned from their mission on February 8. They hugged Camille a lot longer than they hugged me when they first returned to Rexburg.

We were married in the Idaho Falls Temple Friday, February 16. Camille already had Monday off because of President's Day, and she had arranged with someone in her department to cover her classes that Friday and on Tuesday, so we could have a short honeymoon.

The bad news on that glorious day was that it was freezing cold, and it had snowed eight inches the night before.

We wanted to have photos taken outside the temple. So I picked Camille up and trudged through the snow to stand on the little circular rise they'd created for such pictures.

The photographer was wearing a parka, so he didn't mind the cold as much. He took one picture after another, while Camille and I shivered and tried to look as though it was as balmy as summer.

"I need to change film," he called out. "I'll be right back."

"Hurry up, we're freezing," I called as he ran off to the warmth of the foyer of the temple.

"You cold?" she asked me.

"Yeah, how about you?"

"A little. Mostly, though, I'm very happy."

"Me, too."

She leaned into me and said softly. "Can I tell you a little secret?"

"Sure."

"I'm looking forward to exchanging our special gifts," she said. And I couldn't have agreed more.

We had a wonderful time on our honeymoon. We spent those few days in a hotel in Salt Lake City. Funny thing, we didn't even visit Temple Square.

On the following Tuesday afternoon we returned to Rexburg and as husband and wife officially took up residence in our new apartment.

On Wednesday Camille had a ten o'clock class to teach. I would be working from seven to noon in Stores and Receiving, and I had three classes in the afternoon.

While she was still sleeping, I got up to get ready and made lunches for both of us and put them in the fridge. We would be eating lunch together in her office, but it would be five hours before I'd see her again, so I left a note on the table.

Dear Camille,

I love you so much. Thank you for bringing so much happiness into my life!

With all my love.

As always,

David